EMILY ENGLISH

UNITING THE HEAVENS

BOOK ONE

Uniting the Heavens is a work of fiction. Names, characters, places, and incidents are the products of the author's imagination or are used fictitiously. Any resemblance to actual events, locales, or persons, living or dead, is entirely coincidental.

Printed in the United States of America

First Printing, 2016; second print, 2018

ISBN 978-0-9979300-0-9

English Scribbles (Publisher)
8116 Arlington Blvd., #318
Falls Church, VA 22042

www.englishscribbles.com

Edited by Scott Alexander Jones, www.scottalexanderjones.com
Cover design by Terri Edillon
Cover illustration by Marisa Erven, www.marisaerven.com

For Mark. That's what you get for believing in me: my undying love and a silly book dedication.

For Teresa and Sofia. Because I write at night, in secret, so I don't have to miss the waking moments with you. Also, I'm a ninja, and that's just when we do things.

For Mom and Dad. It's about time, right? Thanks for getting me here. Your patience over the years may actually qualify you for sainthood.

For Ruby and Ryan. Because sibs. And a pony called Apashoopia.

Messages

ONE

$\mathcal{A}$ ren had a talent for attracting chaos. It's not the kind of talent you want when you're a man of twenty years old—give or take a year—but you learn to live with it, just like you learn to live with voices screaming in your head at inconvenient times. So, when the two flailing figures came hurtling along the riverbank towards him, Aren only sighed as he set down his book and willow fishing pole. Swatting a bug that had landed on his tan skin, he addressed the black swan that had been preening itself in the river shallows a few feet away. "This is not how I wanted to start my holiday."

The swan paid Aren no mind as he checked for the blade he usually kept strapped to the outside of his right boot. When his hand brushed against nothing but leather, he cursed under his breath in several dead languages as he reached for his pack. Rifling through it, he found blankets, water, a whistle flute, and the little girl's beat-up shoes—but where was his knife?

He glanced up at the men, who were closing the distance. They were yelling, waving, stumbling like drunkards kicked out of a tavern. Aren pushed the longer strands of his chestnut-brown hair away from his green eyes. One of the men looked to be carrying a large stick. It was a fishing pole—no, a broken oar. Aren squinted against the late-summer sun sparkling in the river like a shower of broken glass.

"That's a staff!" Aren said, dropping his pack and scrambling into the tall grasses to find his blade. The swan honked, startled by his sudden movement and the approaching disturbance. It spread its wings, black feathers drifting in its wake as it took off towards Tiede Wood. Aren watched it for a moment, his mind racing. Even the bird knew better than to stick around and take its chances against a mage wielding a staff. Aren had never seen a real mage in action before, but he'd read enough about the magic-wielders to know how deadly they could be. According to the histories, a single mage with a staff could destroy an entire army with a simple spell. "Damn it!" Aren said, trying to quiet the voices fighting for attention in his head. "Why'd it have to be magic?"

TWO

Aren pinched the bridge of his nose with his left hand, determined to get a handle on the situation. If he could stifle the voices in his head just a little, maybe he could be the calm, rational House Apprentice he pretended to be on a daily basis. He took a deep breath and let it go, focusing on the approaching men, allowing his mind to take in and map out all the variables.

Two strangers with no gear, aside from a single staff, heading deeper into Tiede territory with only hours left before nightfall—they were either stupid or dangerous or both. The River Taethe was no good as an escape route. The water moved too quickly this close to the falls, and crossing the bridge to head south would take him out of Tiede territory, where the land would be unfamiliar. Heading west, away from the strangers and towards the falls, was not an option either unless he preferred to face a thousand-foot drop into the sea. To his north was Tiede Wood—that ominous, massive collection of dark, knotted trees that served as the defensive border southeast of the city. There was no way in hell he was going in there.

Aren stood up, his shadow lengthening, slipping onto the glittering water. There was nothing to do but face whatever was coming. He knew he could hold his own in a fight—but against magic?

A gleam in the water lapping against the fishing pole caught his eye, and Aren let out a guffaw before he could catch himself. He had forgotten that he had buried his blade there in anticipation of gutting a fish for dinner. He pulled it out of the soft, wet soil, welcoming the familiar fit of the hilt in his hand.

"Now, we have a chance," Aren said. "A slug's chance in the middle of a beach come high tide, but a chance just the same." He waited for the men to approach, one beginning to drop further behind the other.

Aren could hear the ragged breathing now, the clumsy crashing of boots flattening the tall grasses and snapping the rigid river flora. Strange smells began to pierce the familiar scent of water, soil, and tree: the thick scent of sweat, the sharp tang of fear, the metallic punch of blood. To stay focused, Aren counted in the Ancient language, slow and rhythmic, the timing like a form of self-hypnosis. He shifted into a defensive stance, his blade held out in warning.

The first stranger cried out while coming to a halt a few feet away, his hands gripping the staff, pointing it as if to attack. His waxy, gray face was bruised to a deep purple. Strings of black hair snaked across his triangle nose, and blood filled the gaps between his teeth. He breathed through his mouth, gasping and choking.

Aren didn't move, keeping his eye on the staff. "I'm just fishing. I don't want to fight you. I'm no god-worshipper." Even though it was true, part of him felt a little guilty for saying it with such conviction. "Regardless," he added, "it's a silly reason to want to kill someone."

The stranger blinked the sweat away from his eyes as he indicated Aren's knife with his chin. The man's lips moved a little, but no words came out. He swallowed, then erupted into a coughing fit that turned into dry heaves. When the man regained control of himself, he managed to rasp, "Are you mage?"

Aren almost laughed. "You're the one with the staff."

Ignoring Aren's comment, the waxy man spit out a gob of blood. "Then what are you doing here on Tiede lands? You don't look Tiedan." He studied Aren for a moment, taking inventory of the dark trousers rolled up just below the knees, the linen shirt, and the thin, goose-down vest.

"I'm adopted," Aren said with all the hostility he could muster. Nothing irritated him more than when people pointed out how different he was. Compared to a true Tiede-born, he was way too tall, his eyes too light, and his skin too golden. He looked like he came from a House of Light as opposed to one of Night. "You're not Tiedan either, though I couldn't even begin to guess where a stick man of your smoke-like coloring is from."

The second intruder finally arrived, stumbling and collapsing between them. Aren sheathed his knife, the threat of being attacked by a mage forgotten. He rushed to the crumpled body, straining to turn him over and lift his head so he could breathe. Aren knew this man; he was a fisherman from Tiede, but his leathery skin was torn to shreds from head to torso, blood pouring out from his wounds.

Shards of a red, glasslike substance littered the fisherman's face, and veins of black spread from each nick like a disease. Aren could just make out the sign of the water goddess—waves and a crescent moon—tattooed below an exposed and broken collarbone.

Aren glared at the waxy gray man. "What have you done to Henrik?" Aren asked, indicating the fisherman.

The stranger let out a relieved cry as tears fell from his eyes. "Thank the gods! You're really not a mage!" The gray man fell to his knees, weeping. "Henrik said he thought you might be fishing here—that you'd help."

Aren reached for the canteen near his pack, then dribbled water onto the fisherman's lips. The liquid ran pink, and Henrik winced as it ate through his open flesh. Aren felt the panic of helplessness fill his chest, failing to think of any way to save his life. "Henrik, who did this?"

The fisherman's expression didn't change, but Aren could see where muscles would have contorted the face into a theater of pain had they been able to. Henrik's voice was thin, making his words sound like a mere suggestion. "Tiede is going to fall."

THREE

Tiede is going to fall. The words made Aren's chest tighten, and they burned through his lungs.

"Tiede will only fall if I don't warn the House," the gray man explained, as if Henrik's statement were a child's exaggeration. Aren glared at the man, waiting for an explanation. Crumpling under Aren's gaze, the stranger said, "I'm a messenger for the House of Rose. Everyone's frightened because news has come of mages rising in the east. I was on my way to Tiede when I ran into Henrik. I lost my horse because—"

"Horses bred outside of these lands don't care for Tiede's *atmosphere*," Aren finished for him. "Everyone in Cordelacht knows about the Old Magic that leaks from Tiede Wood."

"I made the rest of the way on foot," the gray man pushed on, "and met Henrik as the Laithe Inlet came into view. I just had to catch the next ferry into Tiede Harbor, but he told me the Harbor was closed, that he was turned away and was going to wait in one of the nearby towns until it opened again." Aren frowned at the news, but before he could ask about it, the man explained, "The Harbor's been closed off because of a string of grisly murders in the city. No one's allowed into or out of Tiede, except through the southern gates."

Aren squeezed his eyes shut to contend with his headache. Then, opening his eyes, he said, "Are you even aware of how far that is?"

"Through those trees—"

"Those aren't just trees. That's *Tiede Wood*," Aren said. He would have stood up and walked away if he weren't cradling a dying head. "No one gets to Tiede by going through the Wood."

The stranger patted at his chest, and Aren heard the crinkle of parchment. "But I need to get this message to the House. If we stay here any longer, the mage will find us. He knows about the message, and he doesn't want it to reach Tiede. Henrik saved me when the mage attacked us. We fought, managed to take away his staff, and ran." His gray face lengthened and looked as if it might melt. "Henrik knows. We have to get this message to the House. Tiede needs to know about the mages."

"Henrik is going to die, and you're in no condition to make a run for the House," Aren argued, pointing his chin at the man's bloodied face. "You'll only make it as far as the cliff's edge before night falls. There's no cover on the road. On one side, you have a thousand-foot drop into the Parthe Sea; on the other, you have the cursed Wood. You only take that road if you're not traveling alone and you know what you're doing. It takes *days* to get to Tiede's southern gates."

Aren was disturbed by the determination in Henrik's voice when he managed to speak again. "Don't let..." Aren and the messenger both opened their mouths to argue, but Henrik continued. "Magic..." Henrik's eyes lifted towards the messenger's gray face. "Run..."

"I can't leave you here," Aren said.

"He won't make it, but we can throw the mage off your trail," the messenger said, glancing over his shoulder to make sure they were still alone. "I'll head south. If I make it to the House of Kaishar, I can ask them to send assistance to Tiede." He coughed, choking on blood, then said, "Or maybe the mage will follow my trail and—"

"No," Henrik wheezed.

Aren pursed his lips as he contemplated Tiede Wood. Standing sentinel at random points along the perimeter, the white-barked ghostwood moaned and creaked as the northern winds rushed past. The dead, crunchy leaves on the forest floor were rustling as something trampled them, running through the Wood's liquid darkness and approaching its edge. A small shadow was barely visible, scurrying just inside the tree line, and a little girl's laughter shimmered like chimes in their ears.

"What was that?" the messenger asked, getting to his feet, ready to run. A violent shiver passed through him.

"Faeries, gnomes, walking mushrooms—any of those," Aren replied. "Phoenix, *chima-kun*, and those gelatinous blobby things— you know what I'm talking about."

The look on the messenger's face said that he had no idea what Aren was talking about. Aren ignored him, then took one last look at Henrik's bleeding eyes. Aren sniffled, holding down a cry of frustration, then set the fisherman's head on the river's edge. "I'd say the prayer for your water goddess, friend, but I don't remember it." Aren's words felt rough in his throat, and he turned away to mash his belongings into his pack. He couldn't look at Henrik anymore. The guilt of having to leave him was too heavy a burden.

The messenger pulled the parchment from his inner pocket and handed it to Aren, who shoved it inside his vest, causing the man to wince. "The seal of Rose..." the man whined. Aren grabbed the staff from the man's other hand. "Hey, wait—"

"I don't need this to get back in the mage's hands," Aren said through clenched teeth, gripping the gnarled wood, challenging the messenger to argue. "Pray to whatever gods you worship that I make it because if the House of Tiede really is in trouble, all of Cordelacht is doomed."

There was a disturbance from the east, in the direction Henrik and the messenger had come from. Aren could see the tall grasses shaking as something disrupted their peaceful swaying along the river. Aren and the messenger exchanged a look, and Aren knew that the messenger wasn't going anywhere. The gray man's bottom lip quivered, and Aren turned away, taking off towards the Wood before he could change his mind.

FOUR

As Aren traveled quick and low through the grasses, he heard the struggles and the screams of the two men. By the time he reached the protective shadows of Tiede Wood, they had died. He would be next if he didn't keep running. It was a long way to Tiede's southern gates, and the bloody piece of parchment in his pocket was feeling heavier with each step.

Aren ran alongside the tree line, waiting for the little girl to show herself. She exploded out of the haunted Wood's depths and tackled Aren, causing him to drop the staff. When the stars in his vision began to fade and the partial curses stopped trying to slip through his clenched teeth, Aren scooped the girl up by the waist, snatched the staff with his left hand, and continued to run. She was a doll, hanging from his arm without resistance, giggling a little when he tripped over a hidden root that almost sent them crashing to the ground again.

Once he was certain they were clear of the river's sight, Aren slowed down. Now that they were safe, he set the child down on her feet and put his weight on the staff, taking a moment to catch his breath. The girl clasped her hands behind her back and shifted from one bare foot to the other, her violet eyes wide and full of questions. Aren's arms prickled with goosebumps, which he blamed on the wind.

"Well, Selina?" he asked, poking at her shoulder and receiving a giggle in response. "Where have you been? Do you know I had to convince someone that you were a faerie playing in the Wood?"

The little girl looked up at him. She was petite, even for a child her age—which Aren had estimated at about five or six years. The top of her head came just to his hips, and she was thin without looking bony. Her face was round and serene, framed by soft black hair. Her creamy skin flushed pink with exertion, and her violet eyes danced with happiness and mischief, the latter of which made Aren raise an eyebrow as he waited for an answer.

"It was the gnomes." She laughed. "They were tricking with me again! I promise I wasn't making trouble! We were just having fun and making jokes."

Aren put a hand over her mouth as he glanced over his shoulder. "Not so loud."

"Why are you covered in blood?" Selina asked once she had pushed Aren's hand away from her face. "Are you okay? It's not your headaches again, is it?"

Aren held a finger to his mouth to quiet her, then whispered, "There's a mage after me. A fisherman and a messenger from Rose died trying to deliver a letter for Lord Tiede, and now I have it." Selina's eyes, already too large for her face, widened. "We need to go before he picks up my trail."

"You're going to go into the Wood?" she asked.

"Not if I can help it." Aren grimaced. "I've passed the age of reason, remember? We'll start following the tree line around towards the west. If the mage finds us...well, we'll do whatever we have to do."

Crisp, dead leaves shuffled in the gloom of the Wood, and Aren's body shivered. He pulled Selina close to him and held the stolen staff out with one hand. A red beak with a white stripe across the tip emerged from the darkness as a black swan waddled towards them making high, gurgling whistle noises. Aren cursed the bird under his breath, but Selina looked to where the bird's attention was focused, to where a shadow folded into a glare of light moved towards them.

"Aren..." she breathed.

The tattered, grimy man trudged up the slope. Aren held his breath, wondering if it was the messenger, hoping against all reason that it was Henrik. But the man's bare arms were covered in burns old and new, and Aren glimpsed the strange, silver markings of the magic wielder on his shoulders, glistening with sweat and blood. The mage looked tired, beaten, and furious.

"Run, Selina." Aren pushed at the little girl's back. She stood rooted to the spot, horrified by the sight of so much blood and by the drifting smell of burning flesh cutting through the fresh, highland air. "Run!" Aren growled, grabbing her small hand and half dragging her away to follow the sun.

FIVE

Kaila had no business making contact with mortals in Tiede Wood. First of all, the Wood was her sister Sabana's domain. Second, the mortals were off limits. Still, it wasn't as if Kaila had set off that day looking to break whatever rules she could; she had intended to stay in the river to begin the seasonal trout rush. She hadn't planned to stumble upon the handsome young man who was doing a terrible job of fishing. She hadn't planned to be so amused by the way he talked to himself, to the fish and frogs, and even to her. How was she to know how enjoyable his company would be?

It was when those other mortals showed up that everything changed. Even as a bird she could smell the danger approaching; she could taste the after-burn of magic in the air—something she hadn't sensed in decades. Magic meant the return of the mages—the heretics. Magic signaled the beginnings of another holy war.

Kaila had decided then that her chance encounter with the young man was an omen, and that she needed to find out what sort of trouble was heading for Tiede. Tiede was the most powerful House in all of Cordelacht, and it belonged to the Night Realm, to her god Alaric. Alaric would be so proud of her if she not only warned him of the mage threat, but also took care of it herself. She would need a strategy, though. In the presence of mortals, she would be unable to use her powers. Perhaps, she thought, this young man could be of some use.

Kaila waddled into the cool dark of the Wood, where she would be safe from the sun's wicked rays, and transformed into a heavy mist that blanketed the rocks, shrubs, and layer of dead things littering the forest floor. She watched as the young man and the little girl ran away, watched as the mage struggled up the hill, beat upon by the heat of the waning sun, and whipped by the northern winds. She could see in the mage's pale eyes that he was determined to retrieve his staff, and the glowing birthmarks on his shoulders indicated that he was not yet ready to die, despite the angry burns on his arms and the torn flesh on his face and torso. He was not going to be easy to kill, and Kaila had no idea what her young mortals were capable of.

At some point, they would have to reenter the Wood to try to lose the mage. That would be Kaila's opportunity. If she was going to use them, she would need to learn as much about them as she could. Kaila drifted along the forest floor, working out the details of her plan. The little girl would be the best way, since she hadn't yet reached the age of reason. All Kaila had to do was separate the two mortals.

SIX

The early-evening sun stretched out her lithe fingers to brush Aren's sweat-coated skin as he ran along the Wood's western edge. He had picked up Selina in a clumsy scoop, cradling her against his chest after pushing the staff into her small hands. "Stop!" an angry roar commanded. Aren took a deep breath and plunged into the Wood. The mage was getting too close, and he wasn't loaded down the way Aren was. He and Selina could hear a few of the mage's threats: "I'll pull out your eyeballs and burst them in my fist!" "I'll blast you so full of magic that your bits won't be big enough to feed the worms!"

Once the darkness of the Wood surrounded them, Aren had to stop. He was temporarily blinded, his eyes working to take in any possible light. He used the precious time to readjust his load, moving his pack so that it was at his chest while Selina held tight to his back, the gnarled wooden staff pinning the pack against his chest by the fierce grip of her small hands and arms. Once everything was situated and he could at least make out the outline of objects — a tree, a shrub, another tree, a rock — Aren resumed his run.

"I hear him a little bit, but far away now," Selina said after a while. Aren's breathing was getting more labored, his pace slowing.

"It's hard to tell. The Wood can get you turned around. I want to get to the point where we don't hear him at all." Aren continued to move through the Wood, failing to identify any markers. He didn't dare tell Selina that he had lost sight of the tree line marking the way out. He just had to keep going, keep imagining the light beyond the trees, but he was tired and his legs would give out soon. He felt for a tree trunk or boulder to steady himself as his eyes constantly readjusted. Fuzzy cobalt moss covered everything, and the sensation of spiders crawling over his skin made him hesitate. He breathed, letting the smell of soil and water and tree ground him.

Selina slid off his back, landing with a soft thud. "I don't hear him," she whispered. "I think we lost him."

A sharp whistle cut through the darkness and Aren cringed, taking the staff from Selina. He looked down at her, ready to pick her up and keep running, but he was thrown off by the big smile on her face. She was giddy and began to pull him towards the source of the whistle.

"Wait!" Aren pulled back. "Where do you think you're going? We'll get lost!"

"It's Pretraun! He'll help us!"

Yes, Aren thought. *He'll help us. We need help.* Confused, Aren found himself allowing Selina to take him further into the Wood. She was so determined, so happy and confident, that he didn't think twice about it. *This is the Wood's magic*, he thought. It was drawing them in and turning them around.

Stars, what was he thinking?

Aren was about to tell Selina that they were going to take their chances with the mage when a deep rumbling voice barreled towards him. "*Ri lei*, Aren!"

Before Aren could puzzle together the images of silver whiskers, flannel plaid, and a blur of dirty toes, the thing that cried out slammed into Aren's chest and held onto his midsection, knocking the air out of his lungs. Aren stumbled backwards, caught himself, then yelled in horror when he managed to breathe again. He pulled his face up and away from the thing whose feet were almost wrapped around the small of his back. Aren pushed against its shoulders.

A gnome. Stars, help me.

"It's okay." Selina giggled, her hands clasped in front of her as if her prayers had just been answered. "It's Pretraun!"

The gnome slid down Aren's legs, waddled about two feet away, twirled, then dropped onto its ass. It proceeded to pull cream-colored mushrooms out of the sack slung across its belly-chest. It stopped to look up at Aren, patted the ground, then grouped the mushrooms into little piles.

"He wants us to eat with him," Selina said, sitting down. "I'm really hungry. Could we please? Just for a bit?"

Aren squeezed his eyes shut and pinched the bridge of his nose. "Selina, we have a mage on our heels hell-bent on killing us, and you want to eat?"

A barrage of strange, tangled words fell out of the gnome's mouth as it gestured towards the food and then in the direction from which they had come.

Selina nodded. "I think he says we'll be fine. You know. You understand all the strange languages."

"We are not fine," Aren said through gritted teeth. "We're in the most feared and haunted Wood in the world with a gnome and a mage. Should we find out if the hermit witches or blood hunters would like to join too?"

The gnome chuckled, then patted the ground again. "*Gaw'so.*"

"No, you're a myth," Aren replied. He was about to argue further, but his throat burned. He wondered how it was that he was still standing because he wasn't sure if his legs were even attached anymore. He sighed, shrugged off the pack, and lowered himself to the soft, mossy dirt, wary and watching for any trickery. He laid the staff across his lap just to have a weapon handy. "I must have gone mad."

The gnome handed Selina some yellow flowers, then rummaged in his sack and pulled out a small, round tin. His stubby fingers pulled off the top to reveal coarse chunks of sea salt, which he sprinkled over the mushrooms. Then he handed Aren a half loaf of bread. Without thinking, Aren bowed towards the gnome then cracked the bread in half, and then in half again.

Selina was busy pulling the stems off the yellow flowers, and then pinching the outer petals and pulling them off as well, squeezing the base of the bloom. When only a few petals were left, she handed what remained of the bloom to Aren. He felt as if he were the little girl's doll, as if something else were controlling his actions at this enchanted meal. He took a piece of bread in one hand and the bloom in the other, then pinched at the flower's base until it secreted a fragrant oil from its center. He drizzled the oil over each piece of bread, laying them down beside the salted mushrooms.

Selina giggled and picked up a piece of bread, crunching down on it. The gnome grunted before displaying his full set of perfect white teeth in a wide smile. He helped himself to two mushrooms and motioned for Aren to eat. Aren picked up a chunk of bread and took a bite. A dab of the flower oil moistened his lips, and he licked it, the faint taste of almond and salt and butter on his tongue. He took another ravenous bite, ignoring the pain of the bread crust slicing up his parched throat.

"Do you remember him at all?" Selina asked, patting the gnome's shoulder.

"How could I remember something I've not met?" Aren grabbed a mushroom and shoved it in his mouth. He was hungrier than he thought. Selina looked offended on behalf of the gnome, who seemed not to care whether Aren remembered him or not. "Don't look at me like that," Aren mumbled. "I don't mean to be rude, but I think I would remember a gnome."

Selina's brows furrowed. "He told me he watched over you in the Wood when you were little—that you played with him and his brothers and the hatchlings and even a baby gree."

"Gnomes," Aren said, trying to find the best way to explain to her, "like to play games. They say things and don't always know what it is they're saying." He added in a mock whisper, "They're not people." Selina looked at Pretraun, who was munching on his bread, looking pleased with the entire conversation. "The gnome has been filling your head with his stories. I work in the greatest Library in all of Cordelacht. If the mage doesn't kill us, and we manage to get out of this cursed place, I will tell you any story you want."

"Tell me now. Tell me about the gods! Where do they come from?"

Aren sighed. They were lost in the Wood, being chased by a mage, eating with a gnome, and she wanted to hear a story. There was no way this day was going to get any stranger. Exhausted and defeated, Aren said, "There are a few stories about how the gods came into being, but I'll tell you how Tiede was created according to legend." Selina nodded, folding her hands in her lap the way he had taught her so that he would know she was ready to listen without interrupting. Aren looked to the gnome again. "You're certain we're safe here? Will you lead us back out? I can't entertain you all day, though we're thankful for the food and rest." He added in the Ancient tongue, "*Yst ilja'i'ko?*"

The gnome just waved at him to continue.

Aren shot another wary look at the gnome, then opened his hand, palm up, to catch a thin stream of light that had managed to slip through the dense tree canopy. "In times untold," he began, "the lands were washed in a sad, gray light. The earth was rocky and barren, the air was still, and the seas trapped beneath layers of dust and bone. In the beginning, there was only Fire, pulsing and glowing, waiting.

"When the god of Night finally descended upon these mighty cliffs, he recognized in it a great and sacred House, and in his perfect vision of that which would be, he called forth the mighty Fire that dwelled here. The Fire god had been waiting for this moment, and he erupted from his secret caverns and crevices, reshaping this holy ground as he traversed the veins that lay deep beneath the soil, filling those veins with the life-blood necessary to awaken the land.

"'All-powerful god of Night, I have slept, waiting for your arrival as my dreams have foretold. I am called Tanghi, and I am yours to command.' The Fire god bowed and placed his fist over his heart. This pleased the Night god.

"'I am Alaric, son of Mahl. My darkness gives you strength,' said the Night god. He darkened the skies, causing Tanghi's power to glow with greater ferocity. The Night god Alaric captured the sparks of light that sprang from the Fire god and tossed them into the skies, where once the Fire could not reach. The stars blazed brilliant and hot across the heavens.

"'On this cliff, I shall raise a House, and you shall be its Guardian. It shall be a monument to our alliance, and it shall rule over every other House. Its people will be strong and honorable, and nothing shall destroy it,' said Alaric. 'I would seek another ally, another power to complement your own.'

"Tanghi stepped forward. 'A magnificent goddess lies beneath the broken bones of this world. She has been restrained for so long that she has given up any hope of freedom. Release her, and I swear your rule will never be questioned.' And so Alaric released the Water goddess. Her joy at being freed was so overwhelming, she covered almost all of the world's surface in water, and the Night and Fire gods had not the heart to contain her.

"'Protect this House, Kaila, goddess of Water,' Alaric said to her, 'and its people will worship you for the rest of time.' The Water goddess Kaila smiled and placed her heart within the cliffs of Tiede." Aren shrugged, then said, "That's the legend of how the House of Tiede was born, and why it is eternally devoted to the Night and the elements of Fire and Water."

Selina's eyes were full of wonder, and Aren waited for the usual stream of questions that she had after every story he told her, but before she could say anything, a humming noise began to fill Aren's ears, and he looked around. Other than Pretraun putting things into his bag, the Wood was still. True to the gnome's word, the mage they were trying to lose hadn't made a peep. Aren closed his eyes, and the hum grew louder. He opened his eyes, but still the humming intensified.

"How do you know how to believe in the gods? I never see them," Selina said. "How come they don't visit anymore the way they used to do in the stories?"

"I can't teach you faith. In fact, I'm the last person you want to learn faith from."

Selina asked Aren another question, but the sound was garbled, difficult to piece together. The noise was making him dizzy, and he squeezed his eyes shut again. Pretraun grunted before uttering a series of words that Aren couldn't comprehend. Then, the gnome put a gentle hand on Aren's chest, forcing him to relax against the fallen tree behind them.

"Is it the headaches again?" Selina asked, making her way to his side.

When he had matched the sound to words, he replied, "I don't know what it is—" A cry of pain escaped him, and he gripped the staff that lay across his lap.

Selina addressed the gnome, panic in her voice, "He's been sick in the head all day, and I don't know how to help him."

Pretraun put a hand that smelled like dirt on Aren's forehead, then over his heart. He muttered a few words accompanied by gestures to help translate. Aren caught the Ancient words for "water" and "flower" and "healing."

"I think he's talking about a stream and some kind of plant," Selina said, excitement replacing her worry.

"Flower," Aren corrected, his head buzzing with voices now. "'Bring the flower to the stream, and she will give you healing waters.'"

"I know just the flower he means!" Selina exclaimed. "I'll go get it! Stay here with Pretraun; he'll take care of you. I won't be long!"

Aren sat up, then crumpled onto his side, writhing at the sounds filling his head. What in the stars had possessed her? This damned Wood. Aren pushed the end of the staff into the soft dirt and pulled himself up, trying to keep his balance. He drew in his breath, then said, "I should've known better than to trust a gnome," before stumbling after Selina.

SEVEN

Aren wasn't sure how it was possible for black to get blacker.

He slowed down to keep from tripping over roots and branches, but his chest thumped hard with panic. He stopped to catch his breath in a small clearing where trickles of fading light had managed to sneak through the canopy of trees and fell upon him like a rain shower. His eyes filled with dots of shadow and light, mingling with the noise in his head, making him feel nauseous.

He leaned on the staff and risked calling out, "Selina! It'll be dark soon, and we need to get out of here!" Perhaps yelling was not inconspicuous, but the hairs on the back of his neck were sending prickle signals down his arms. His damned headaches had caused a lapse in judgment. What was he thinking letting a child lead him into the Wood to meet up with a gnome? "Tell me where you are, sweetheart! I'm fine! I don't need any magic water; we just need to get home!" He could be talking to himself for all he knew. She could be another half click away towards the south—though he couldn't pick out south from any other direction at this point. "What if I told you the stupid gnome wants you to come back?" He blathered at a charcoal burrow squirrel that had peeked out of its tree. "I take that back; he's not stupid. He's great, hilarious actually. We're best friends. Stars, Selina, where are you?"

He needed a plan. There were two—maybe three—hours of sunlight left outside of the Wood, which meant less than one hour of quasi-visibility where he stood now. He could try to go back the way he had come and hope that Selina would do the same after she realized there was no such thing as healing water. Or he could stay where he was and hope that Selina would come this way, if she had passed through here at all.

He hated how familiar the whole ordeal felt, how his bones woke up and burned with life. Something in the air heated the blood that raced through his veins, and he felt like he could destroy something. The magic of the Wood was driving him to madness while the voices in his head cooed and seduced him. They had to get out of here.

Something pulled at Aren's bootstrap.

"What the stars?" He looked down and lifted his leg, ready to kick, when he recognized the gnome with whom he had broken bread. Its dirt-laden hands tugged at the worn leather bootstrap, nearly unbuckling it. "Quit it! Stop pulling on me." Aren nudged at the gnome with his toe, trying to push it away, but it kept pulling back.

"*Ka'bu a'ali gy-id.*" The gnome was tugging on Aren's trousers now, and Aren grabbed at the waist to keep them up.

"Stop it!" He lowered himself to the gnome's height and gripped its round, meaty shoulders. "Pretraun, was it? Whatever language you speak sounds bastardized with Old Magic, and my Old Magic knowledge is that of an infant's. You need to speak slower." Pretraun stared up at Aren with droopy, watery eyes. Aren wasn't sure if he had made it cry, but when it broke out in a huge grin, Aren was ready to shake the mites out of it.

Taking no notice of his frustration, Pretraun moved Aren's hands away with the patience of a parent teaching a child. It pointed at a golden brown mushroom. Aren's eyes followed as the gnome's stubby finger pointed at another mushroom next to it. Next to that was another with a fringe and then another and another in a radius that encompassed the whole of the clearing.

"*Ka'bu a'ali gy-id,*" Pretraun said again.

Aren's eyes widened. He didn't have to follow the full sweep of the gnome's arm before he realized what he had stepped into. "F-f-f..." the air escaped between Aren's teeth and lips. "Faerie ring!"

Pretraun clapped as if Aren had just won a contest, and Aren leaped out of the circle of mushrooms, then jerked his chin up to look at the sky—or what he could imagine of it. The shower of light had thinned. It couldn't be dusk already; this was the summer season, and the sun would remain high well into the evening. Aren looked back into the ring, which seemed darker and more mysterious now. The good news was he didn't hear anything other than what was already in his head—no laughter or chimes or singing. And it wasn't so dark that anything could properly luminesce, which was, as all the scrolls and books would tell you, one of the main reasons the faeries came out at night: to luminesce.

Pretraun watched Aren with a silly grin peeking through its beard. "*A'alin*," it grunted.

Aren faced the gnome, furrowing his brows. "I don't have time to decipher your words. If you want to help, then find Selina." He wiped at his brow with the rolled sleeve of his shirt. "Why is it so hot in here?"

Pretraun squatted to expose the ridged underside of a mushroom. It had begun to take on a fiery-orange glow in the center. Aren's eyes widened with horror. Tiede Wood was about to awaken, and he and Selina were lost.

EIGHT

Selina always had the same dreams: rain and trees and light and shadow, all in shades of gray. But on the night before she was to accompany Aren on his fishing trip, she dreamt of a small silver stream cutting through the darkness of Tiede Wood like a glowing liquid glass. Strange purple flowers floated along the surface, tiny dancers twirling in the eddies, beckoning her to join them. Selina watched herself step into the water and slip into a vast nothingness. The water swirled around her, smooth and thick like the rich silk and velvet drapes in the Library where Aren worked. Then, she was falling through the night sky, stars streaming alongside her, falling forever through the velvet black.

When she woke that morning, Selina wondered what had caused her to dream such a thing. She had no idea what any of it meant, but she liked not dreaming of rain and trees for once. She toyed with the images in her head, puzzling them out, making sense of it all only after Pretraun had spoken his funny words. *Bring the flower to the stream, and she will give you healing waters.* Her dream had been a message. It all made sense now.

Selina examined a thick patch of deep purple leindra flowers, listening to Aren calling to her from far away. He was yelling something about Pretraun being his friend. She wished he would calm down; he was going to make his headache worse. Still, she was glad that he and Pretraun were getting along. She turned her attention back to the leindra flowers, making sure not to inhale them. She had learned about the flower from Aren once, when he was forced to study a book about plants. He had said something about how it could make a person sick if you breathed too much of it. Even at a distance, she could distinguish its clean, dizzying scent.

Selina felt the air warming around her, and the flowers rustled, preparing for night. She had to hurry so she could protect Aren from the faeries. They might want to keep him if they found him, and with all the noise he was making, he would be easy to find. She plucked one bloom from the leindra shrub. Now that she had the flower, it would lead her to the stream. She walked towards the sounds of rustling leaves and gossiping dragonflies, careful not to crush any of the glowing mushrooms.

After seemingly circling around the same group of mossy boulders several times, she reached a clearing. She couldn't hear Aren calling anymore; her ears were filled with the calming sound of water, and her eyes widened at the sight of the small, gurgling spring opening up into a thin stream. The clearing was lit with a warm, soft-orange glow; the trees sparkled as millions of peppermint fireflies flittered through the leaves, little flames rising and falling all around her.

"Did you bring me a gift, little one?"

The gentle voice caught her off guard, and Selina's mouth opened to form an O when the lady to whom the voice belonged stepped into the clearing. The lady's skin took on the warmth of the firefly light, and her long black hair hung like silk past her waist. A thin gown the color of wispy clouds wrapped loosely around her slender figure, the fabric trailing on the moss and dirt and leaves, following her like water flowing down her back. Her bare feet stepped into the creek, and Selina could not make out where the lady ended and the water began.

The lady beckoned and Selina stepped forward and held up the leindra flower, finding it difficult to look away from those blue eyes, which looked like the Laithe at sunrise, when the water seemed as if it were covered in a layer of diamond dust. The lady brought the flower to her lips and took a deep breath, her eyes closing as she did so. Then she tucked the purple flower into her hair and bent at the waist to cup Selina's face and place a kiss on her forehead, whispering words that Selina didn't understand. The world seemed to melt and disappear around her, and Selina felt as though she had tumbled over Tiede Falls.

"I need the water for Aren. He's sick and I need to bring him the water." Selina's eyes closed as a question escaped her. Her head reeled with images that made her feel suffocated and uneasy. Images of rain and trees and shadows seemed to cloud everything. "Am I dreaming again?"

"It's all just a dream, little one," the lady cooed, stroking Selina's hair. "I've put you through so much, made you try to remember so many things." How long had it been? Selina felt weightless and heavy all at once. It was like floating on water, being carried along so effortlessly with the possibility of drowning looming over you. The lady's voice cut into Selina's thoughts with urgency. "Selina, when you open your eyes, find Aren and run. The Wood is about to wake up, and I can't help you here."

NINE

Aren found Selina lying in a small clearing surrounded by a ring of mushrooms. Actually, Pretraun was the one who found her, but it was Aren who braved stepping into the faerie ring to pull her out. Pretraun was too busy dropping to his knees and touching the ground with his forehead. Aren rolled his eyes; he had no idea why this odd creature insisted on accompanying them.

"Sacred," Selina breathed as Aren carried her away from the glowing mushrooms. He set her down, then crouched beside her to check her face, hands, and arms for any scratches or wounds. He couldn't see much in the eerie glow of the Wood, but she seemed all right. "I'm sorry, Aren. I don't have the water; I think it was just a dream. I'm not sure anymore."

Aren kissed her forehead, satisfied that she hadn't been hurt. "Don't ever run away from me like that again. I'm running around a cursed forest, and you're napping in a faerie ring. Stars, you're going to send me to an early grave!" She looked up at him with big, sorrowful eyes. "Selina, I appreciate what you're trying to do for me, but I'll be fine as long as we get out of here. My headaches are being drowned out by the fear of being trapped in this Wood forever, and then there's your gnome friend, who said he'd help us, but I'm not sure he could find his own toes. We're lost, but we have to keep moving. The Wood is about to wake up." Selina gasped, then tried to run off. Aren grabbed her skinny arms. She seemed somewhere between excitement and panic. "What's gotten into you, Selina? Didn't you hear a word I just said? We need to stay together," he said, squeezing her.

"But I met a lady." Selina's eyes were wide, crazed. Aren was confused. The Wood's magic shouldn't work on her; she was still a child. "The lady was in the stream, and I gave her a flower. She said we had to run..."

Aren stood up, keeping a firm hold on Selina's hand. Pretraun had rejoined them and was pointing one way then another while mumbling something incomprehensible. "You can tell me about the lady in your dream later," Aren said, wondering if the gnome was trying to give them directions. "Now's not time for ghost stories—"

"It's no story!" Selina protested.

Aren cut her off with a raised hand and glanced at Pretraun, who must have also sensed something odd because he had stopped talking as well. There was a rustling nearby, and Pretraun crouched as if facing a horned gree: feet planted, knees bent, arms out to deflect if necessary. When the creature's head broke through the shrubbery, Pretraun stood up at once, and pushed at his companions, making frantic gestures and crying out orders. It was not a horned gree.

Aren deciphered all he needed to know: *Run*.

TEN

Aren stared in shock as the creature stepped into view. It wasn't the large wildcat that Pretraun had prepared to ward off. This beast was as tall as a carriage, its muscled flanks a brilliant white contrasted against the Wood's darkness. A mane of a million silken threads draped its neck and hung tangled over silver eyes. Vapor escaped its nostrils like a freed spirit, twisting up and dancing around the ivory horn. The word barely escaped Aren's lips: "Unicorn."

"*D'naragon!*" Pretraun pushed harder at their legs.

Finally, Aren grabbed Selina's wrist and took off, half dragging her with no route. They were lost, but that wasn't as bad as being skewered by a unicorn. A mist was gathering, rolling over the ground like the tide around their ankles. Aren feared they might drown in it, and he paused to scoop up Selina, slinging her over his back, where she clung without question to his neck. Every once in a while he could feel her head turn, and he knew she was looking for the gnome.

Aren considered dropping the staff, since they'd already lost the pack, but he held onto it anyway; the weapon could be helpful.

The unicorn hadn't moved yet. It was squealing and stomping as if it had been just as surprised as Aren and Selina were. Aren was thankful for the head start; they would need every second they could get. It was difficult to see where he was going, but the mist seemed to move to create a path for them to follow. Aren dodged trees and rocks, and leapt into and out of faerie rings, hoping that he would be fast enough to jump out of each one. He spared a second to chuckle at the thought of daring to stampede through the magical rings, which, it was rumored, could trap you in the Wood forever.

The unicorn was moving now, and Aren could feel the vibrations race over the ground. Selina was crying; he could feel her sobbing against his neck. He would get her out of here. This was just a forest. There was an end to this Wood if you just kept going. If he chose to believe in anything at all, he had to believe that.

Aren couldn't remember ever pushing himself this hard in such a small span of time. Even when he was sent to the Fighters Guild to earn his mark, he had spent years training and conditioning. Today, he'd had to run miles over obstacles and in darkness while carrying a child, a pack, and a staff. His head was pounding, and he felt as though his legs might give out. Twice he had stumbled—on a rock and a raised tree root—almost falling to the ground, but he caught himself, inspired by the angry thudding of hooves behind them. He wondered which would be the preferred way to die: being stomped or skewered. It sounded bloody either way.

Then Aren spotted it: the break in the tree line and the light of the setting sun bleeding beyond it. He squeezed Selina's calves and gave her a shove to boost her further up on his back. He was going to put everything he had into this final sprint and hope that he didn't trip over his own feet. The sound of the unicorn tearing up the brush was just behind them, but there were too many trees for the beast to navigate, and the mist seemed to close behind them to provide cover. The voices in Aren's head had silenced themselves.

The Wood's edge was so close now, teasing, laughing. If this were some optical trickery or hallucination, so be it. Aren would run for the edge until his lungs dried out. He mustered every ounce of adrenaline he had left and pushed harder, but when the shadow stepped in front of him, Selina screamed. Aren's instincts took over, and he brought the staff up two-handed and horizontal, holding it away from his chest to drive through the obstacle. He rammed the staff into the shadow, but the force wasn't enough to push them out of the Wood, and the shadow leaned in to take the impact, grabbing the staff so that he and Aren were both holding it, trying to wrestle it from each other.

Aren was surprised to see that the mage was young, somewhere around his own age, maybe his early twenties. A blade had recently licked the mage's grizzled, ashen face and neck. Long gashes peeled the skin back, bone showing in places, and Aren realized how hard Henrik had fought for his life and to gain control of the staff to protect Tiede. Aren and the mage were pushing and pulling on the staff, kicking up dirt and dead leaves. Aren's heart was hammering, and he kept forcing them towards the Wood's edge. They could continue fighting out there, away from this Wood, so that he could breathe. The sound of hooves disturbing the forest floor was getting closer.

"Let go of my staff, Tiede, or I'll burn you like I did your friend," the mage growled, his breath close and hot and smelling like rotting meat.

"Hold tight, Selina!" Aren said through gritted teeth, ignoring the man's threats.

The symbols on the staff were beginning to glow red, and Aren could feel the power the mage was summoning. In less than a minute, magic would explode between them, killing them all in the blast. Aren grunted, then put all of his weight into turning them around so that he and Selina were closer to the tree line, facing into the Wood. Selina cried out as Aren lost his balance. Aren stumbled backwards, using the fall's momentum to pull away from the mage and clear the Wood. Aren managed to retain hold of the staff as they separated, and Selina let go of his neck before they fell, landing on her feet before stumbling and hitting the ground. The magic in the staff dissipated, returning to wherever it had come from.

In the space where they had been standing only seconds before, a spiraled horn, stained and dripping red, tore through the white mist in a large upward sweep, displaying the mage's body impaled upon it. His arms dangled lifelessly, and Aren caught a glimpse of a strange leaf tattooed onto his skin. Selina screamed, and scrambled over to where Aren lay. He got to his knees, kept Selina behind him, and hoped that the stories were true: that the creature couldn't cross. The unicorn snorted, tossing the dead mage aside before stamping its hooves in a tantrum. After a final shake of its ivory mane, it turned back in the direction from which it had come, disappearing into the fog and trees. Aren collapsed onto his back and stared up at the darkening sky, trying to get air back into his burning lungs.

Selina wiped the tears from her face with the palms of her hands. "Pretraun," she sniffled.

Aren sighed and sat up, putting a hand on her shoulder. "He's a tough little guy." He wasn't quite sure what else to say to make her feel better. "Sweetheart, we're safer now, but we have no supplies, and night is falling. We've got to move away from here and find a safer spot to rest." She crawled onto Aren's lap and cried into his chest. He stroked her hair, feeling guilty and helpless. "I'm sorry," he whispered.

When Aren had regained enough energy, he carried Selina away, following the road north. Emotional exhaustion overtook her along the way, and when he felt they were far enough from the carnage the unicorn had left behind, he chose a spot by the side of the road where they could sleep. The night had been swift in its arrival. He laid Selina down on the soft grass and placed the staff next to himself. Then he covered her with his vest after emptying the pockets. He had coins, a tin of fire magic, a piece of graphite, his small notebook, and the message. The parchment was crumpled and smeared with dirt and sweat. He ran a thumb over the wax imprint and found that it was no longer sealed.

He looked to see if Selina was still asleep, then glanced around to see if anyone was nearby, though he knew they were alone. In the Wood, strange lights bobbled through the darkness; discordant songs mingled with the laughter drifting through the trees. He hesitated, then slipped his finger under the broken seal, unfolding the message. The words seemed to rearrange themselves, and he closed his eyes to will his headache away.

Aren took a deep breath, opened his eyes, then read the entire message under the glowing light of the rising moon. When he had finished, he tucked the parchment away and lay back in the grass, wondering if he'd be able to fall asleep. He had escaped a mage, a unicorn, and Tiede Wood, yet his bones felt something waiting, something looming just beyond reach, biding its time, waiting for just the right moment to take him back into the darkness. What did they want from him? He might give it if they asked nicely—after he delivered the message.

Out of habit, Aren traced the Guardian constellation with a finger, then closed his eyes and hoped his dreams would be free of the Wood's visions. He could feel the Wood-folk watching, and goosebumps broke out over his arms. He felt for the staff and gripped the gnarled wood until his hand pulsed from the pressure of it.

Come and get me, he dared them.

ELEVEN

Not bad for a couple of mortals, Kaila thought. She watched the young man from behind one of the scarred ghostwood trees. She had seen everything: the unicorn, the mage, the way the young man had held the crying girl. Kaila watched him care for Selina with the tenderness of a father, and she studied his green eyes as he read over a piece of beat-up parchment.

His name was Aren. Kaila had learned that from sifting through Selina's memories. She had also learned that he was everything to the little girl. He wasn't her father—though Kaila had already assumed he wasn't, since he seemed so young himself—so perhaps he was her brother?

Kaila had been able to glean very little else from Selina's memories. There was no birthmark, so the girl's family hadn't cared to present her to a Priestess before the end of her first year. This wasn't completely uncommon; many, like the mages, had lost faith, while others had become orphaned from the faith. What had surprised Kaila was that all of Selina's memories were disjointed. Never, since the beginning of Alaric's rule on this planet, had Kaila encountered a mortal with such memories. Mortals were supposed to be coded with a fate line that recorded their life story from beginning to end so that it could be read like a book with moving pictures during the final judgment. This little girl was broken. There was no record of her birth, no beginning. In fact, the oldest images Kaila could find were incomplete and in eerie shades of gray: torrents of rain, streaks of lightning, darkness. There were pictures of a very small girl running, stumbling, and crying; a woman pleading on her hands and knees, her face shadowed by trees; a great beast; a magnificent sword; cobblestone streets and a skinny, stray cat. So much rain.

The most powerful picture Kaila found was of Aren rushing towards Selina, his green eyes the only color in all the visions, concern etched all over his boyish face. Kaila had been so heartbroken by it all that on impulse she placed a blessing on Selina. Alaric would be angry about it, but Kaila would deal with him later; besides, what he didn't know couldn't upset him.

Right now, there was Aren to deal with. She had to learn more about Aren so she could use him to find out what trouble was heading for Tiede and try to stop it. She also hoped that his memories would provide more insight into what had happened to Selina.

Aren had finally fallen asleep, but Kaila waited a while longer. He had surpassed the age of reason, so she couldn't reveal herself to him the way she had with Selina. Kaila closed her eyes and took a deep breath. Alaric would be furious if he ever discovered that she had approached a mortal. He would question her judgment, tuck her away, and remind her of all the other times she had done something reckless.

Kaila shook off her doubt. She wasn't some weak little spirit who was going to swim home to tell her lord that the scary mages might rise again so that he could send Tanghi and his armies to take care of it. She didn't need Alaric to keep her safe, to coddle and baby her like he always did. She was going to keep this uprising contained, to eliminate the threat on her own because she was an Elemental Knight, just as powerful as Tanghi and the others. She would prove it to them.

Kaila looked up to the stars and spotted Tanghi's Guardian, the twisting Isle of Night, Sabana's Harvest, and the bright tip of Geir's scythe, the weapon marking the point where the skies were rent to delineate Night and Light. The constellations glittered as bands of thin clouds swept past.

When her thoughts returned to earth, Kaila shuddered, causing silky black feathers to drift from her body as she transformed back into a swan. It would be the safest way to approach the mortals. She shook out her webbed feet and stretched her long neck. She had nothing to worry about; everything she had seen so far showed that Aren was a kind person. Kaila had also watched him trace the Guardian constellation in the sky; only those who worshipped Fire or Night did that. It was a good omen.

Kaila watched for the rhythmic rise and fall of Aren's chest and listened for the steady breathing. The moon was high now, distant and pale, a silver nick in the dark, pinpricked sky. She craned her neck as if to touch it, closing her eyes and inhaling the sweet air. Then, steeling her resolve, she waddled towards her mortals, thankful for the soft grasses that made no sound beneath her webbed feet.

Selina lay on her back with her arms and legs splayed out in all directions. Aren slept on his side, facing the Wood with his back to the road. Kaila moved in closer so she could study the soft yet defined angles of his face. His dark-brown hair was unkempt and fell past his eyes, and she resisted the urge to brush it away from his face, rough from not having shaven. He was tall and lean-muscled; his skin was tawny, and hints of long faded scars crisscrossed here and there. She examined his long fingers and strong arms.

From his actions and because he lived in Tiede, Kaila had taken him for a Night worshipper, but now that she saw him up close, he looked like he had been blessed by one in the Light Realm—perhaps her sister Sabana or her brother Geir. She blushed as it occurred to her that he was so handsome, maybe the goddess of Light had blessed him herself. Kaila brought her head close to his chest to hear and feel the steady life flow there. She kept very still, waiting to connect with his circadian rhythm, waiting to fall into the story recorded on his fate line.

She found no birthmark or blessing on him either. It saddened her that he was Unblessed, just as Selina was, and she lowered herself to the ground beside him. She closed her eyes, wondering if the images he carried with him were just as broken as Selina's. When his story played into Kaila's mind, she was relieved to see that his memories were mostly intact, his fate line a little stronger.

Aren's memories hadn't begun at birth. The imagery was there, but it was clouded and unreadable. Kaila pressed on, knowing that she had little time. His infancy wasn't important anyway. She scanned past his childhood, learned that he read a lot of books and earned the mark of the Fighter Initiate. He had been chosen a few years ago to live and serve in the House of Tiede as an Apprentice to the Elder in the House Library. He kept the company of the legendary Blacksmiths of Tiede, abundantly blessed by her brother Tanghi. That would explain why he had traced the Guardian constellation.

Kaila gasped, and her eyes opened wide when she felt the hand wrapped around her slender neck. She fought the urge to struggle as she cursed her stupidity. She hadn't felt or heard him move. He was still lying on his side, and she dared to meet his gaze.

"Either you're fae or you're the strangest swan I have ever had the pleasure of meeting," he said, his quiet voice laden with sleep. "Or you're a very silly dream. We've met before, haven't we? We had a lovely afternoon together, and later you warned us of the mage." Aside from the knife at his boot and the staff—which would be too clumsy to use in the position he was in—he didn't have a weapon in hand. Of course, he didn't need a weapon to break her neck. Kaila waited, her heart racing. "From my recent experience"—he stifled a yawn—"the fae can't break the outer tree line." She watched a sleepy smile light up his face as he loosened his hold on her. She forced herself to be still, but remained alert, realizing now that he was trickier than he looked. She let out a soft honk, and he chuckled. "I'm not going to hurt you. I just wanted to make sure you weren't going to hurt us. You must be used to having people about." He let go, and she took a few steps back. His laughter was soft. "If you were looking for company, you're more than welcome to stay."

They stared at each other—he with his disheveled hair; she with her black, ruffled feathers—and Kaila couldn't force herself to run or fly away. Never had a mortal made her feel this confused. He broke the silence. "Stay out of trouble, all right?" He gave her one last smile, then closed his eyes, rolling onto his back before returning to sleep. She remained frozen, wondering what had just happened, catching the familiar rise and fall of his chest as he returned to Alaric's Dream Realm.

When the spell lifted, Kaila stretched out her wings, testing the northern winds. She stumbled a few steps, then took flight, circling once before heading southwest towards Tiede Falls. She could work with this. Aren would help her save Tiede, and she would keep him a secret. He had spared her life, after all.

TWELVE

He was the *Catar* and wore the guise of an Apprentice: black robes over black linen trousers and a plain, collared top; a drawing compass and thin sticks of smooth metal as long as his middle finger peeked out of his breast pocket. He kept his hood drawn and obscured his eyes with the goggles common to alchemists. No one looked twice at him as he walked through Tiede, his arms laden with books and scrolls, his hand stuffed with graphite and a chunk of obsidian.

Tiede was swarming with apprentices, fools who prattled on about the city's great guilds and advances in technology, each of them thinking that they were going to change the world. *Self-absorbed idiots*, he thought, wishing he could snap their necks. They knew nothing of the world outside of the so-called Blessed Houses, and they knew nothing of change. Real change, the change he was a part of, required years of planning and making sacrifices that weaker persons would regret for the rest of their lives. These fools were limited by the possibilities fated by their gods.

The streetlamps that lined the main roads were beginning to glow now that the sun had set, but Tiede was busier now than it was in the mornings. The vendor stands that lined the north end of the Harbor District began to light their lamps as they pushed their wares.

"Last catch of the day! Saltwater trout!"

"Pies! Fish pies! Meat pies! Vegetable pies! Fruit pies!"

"Scented soaps! Smell like a summer garden with scented soaps!"

Why were people so loud here? He couldn't hear himself think, and twice he got bumped hard enough to drop one of his books. Stopping to pick it up only resulted in getting jostled some more, and it was all he could do to keep his temper in check.

Then, there were all the conflicting scents: fire-roasted meats, rotting sweet fruits, and the summer salt air. He couldn't wait to be done with Tiede so he could return to the peacefulness of the woods and the slow-paced town that was his home, with only the scent of wood and dirt and the after-burn of magic.

A horn sounded, long, low, and lazy, announcing the closing of the docks some thousand feet below the Harbor District. Why did they even bother blowing the horn? The harbor had been closed off to travel for several days. Regardless, it was the signal he had been waiting for. He paused at a vegetable stand, pretending to be interested in artichokes, when he spotted his quarry: an old man he nicknamed Goat for his gray, straggly hair and knobby knees that seemed steady yet unsure.

Catar had been trailing Goat for five days now, and every day was the same. Goat left his house in the western district in the late morning. He took his own special route to the north, cutting through forgotten alleyways and cursing the worn steps that wound their way throughout Tiede, always heading towards the great House that overlooked the city. Goat carried a rosewood cane, his old fingers tight around the middle, never once using it to assist in his walking. He just pumped it up and down as if he were marching a great army through the streets.

Goat would stop to pray in the western worship chapel, its imposing black marble walls an eyesore in the dark district, with its cobblestone streets and mismatched buildings built too close together. Then, he would linger around the ridiculous myriad of fountains that littered the ostentatious town center, raking the bottom of his cane over the water here and there as he melted into the pattern of moving people until he finally reached the Mermaid's Song, the most popular tavern in all of Tiede. There, he would order some charred lump of meat and a stout as black as tar, then sit in a corner to read whatever daily papers were left behind. Later, it was off to the Harbor District markets to check the prices on goods and see if any new vendors had come in. By midafternoon, the old man would make his way down to the docks, stumbling in that lopsided nimble way of his down the precipitous stairs that hugged the sheer cliffs of Tiede.

Catar had only followed him down to the Harbor once, and once had been enough. The heights were dizzying, and several times he thought he might throw up. Seasoned Tiedans passed him going up and down, a few laughing and pointing out the green apprentice who was obviously new to the city. He should've taken the lift, a strange metal contraption comprised of gears, levers, magnets, and other feats of physics and force, but he trusted it less than he did the stairs. At the docks, all Catar had learned was that the Goat checked for shipments and simply enjoyed being close to the water for the remainder of the afternoon. Catar found the strong smell of salt and fish and rust nauseating, and he cursed Tiede all the more, telling himself how glorious it would be once the mighty House on the cliff was destroyed.

From almost any point in the city, one could see the magnificent House of Tiede sitting in all its moon-bathed majesty, brilliant white stone and marble façade, on the highest point of the cliff. Tonight, as he had done on nights previous, Catar spat in its direction, lowered his head, and continued walking, following the Goat away from the House's condescending eyes, away from the crowded eastern sector, where Tiede's people and visitors flocked to the lively markets of the Harbor District and the night life of the town center and Guild Row.

The Goat proceeded south towards the Wedge with a hop-step in his gait that made it seem like he would trip into the pile of gree droppings no one had bothered to clean up. Instead, he managed to navigate his way around the fly-infested pile of caramel-colored mess as if it had been there since the dawn of time. The area known as the Wedge verged on neglected, and Regulators rarely bothered patrolling it. The unending sounds of dogs howling and whimpering echoed off the broken buildings, while feral cats screeched and hissed in return. The scuttling of bone-thin rats and the stale stench of decay rounded out the place. It was where desperate apprentices sought out substances to keep themselves alert, and where clandestine affairs could find cover from judging eyes.

For the Goat, it was just part of his daily circuit.

Catar didn't follow him too closely here; there weren't enough people to make his pursuit look natural. It was easier to watch, slip into an alley, and head in the same general direction. The Goat was still a good way from home, making the Wedge perfect for what

Catar had to do, and he had to make his move tonight. If blood wasn't spilled soon, the spell wouldn't work, and it would be his head.

As Catar turned down a wide alley, he reached into his robes, feeling for the knife he had strapped to his belt. The Goat would cross at the end of the alley, and Catar just had to pick up his pace to beat him there. He dropped his fake parcels onto a heap of fermenting trash as his heart hammered, beating in his throat and echoing in his ears. He kept the few books he had, pressing them close against his chest to still his nerves.

The Goat's cane came into view, and Catar hurried forward to close the remaining few feet, his hand reaching again for the knife, ready to draw it this time. Sweat coated his skin, and he took a deep breath. It was time for the sacrifice. He could smell the blood filling his nostrils as the Goat came into full view.

"Halt!" The sound was a word, and it seemed to swim at him. Catar's body froze as the voice began to break through his focus.

The Goat paused for a brief moment, his brows furrowed as he spared a moment to look down the alley before continuing on his way. Catar felt time catch up to him and he watched slack-jawed as his quarry moved out of reach.

"Talking to you, apprentice! Turn around!" another voice said. Catar cursed himself as he complied. Two Regulators stood behind him. Engrossed in his task, he hadn't heard them approach. "You're a little far from Guild Row," the taller Regulator with the wide shoulders said. She looked like she could wrestle a bull and win.

The Goat was getting away. Catar cleared his throat and clutched his books tighter against his chest, wondering if he should just kill them. Instead, he lowered his head, thankful for the hood that shadowed his features and the goggles that concealed his eyes. He spoke in a low voice, almost whispering. "I'm not, n-not from here— from Tiede, I mean. Some apprentices said, they said there was a girl could m-maybe help me get through my ana-anatomy class."

The shorter Regulator burst out laughing, and even his female counterpart broke out in a grin. She elbowed her partner in the chest, then said, "Your friends were having a go at you. Get out of here. You don't want to learn about anatomy from anyone in the Wedge."

Catar wanted to break their necks, but instead he bowed his head, making sure to add some nervous jitters to the movement. The man smirked, tapped Catar's arm with his baton, and then the pair left him.

Catar seethed, then spun around, running back the way he had come, past the parcels he had dropped, and through a different maze of alleyways to put him back on track. He headed towards the rotted red door of a building that looked like it had been licked by fire at one point in its miserable life. He had explored most of the abandoned buildings during his volunteered imprisonment in the city and found he could use them like shortcuts through the Wedge. This particular space was empty, save for a dust-coated glass bottle that had rolled up against a wall. The air was dry and stale, and it stirred to life as his presence disturbed it. He threw his books aside, trying to control his breathing.

He navigated through the small rooms, intent on coming out through what would have been the main entrance, which opened up onto the street that the Goat was on. There were cracks in the small window, and through the film of dust and dirt he made out the shadow of the Goat down the road hobbling along, pumping his cane.

There was no time to waste. He slipped out the door and closed it behind him with a small click before making his way towards the closest alley. The evening breeze chilled the sweat on his skin, and he took several deep breaths to get a handle on the situation. The Goat would be making his next winding pass one block up, and once he finished that, he'd be in Lower Western. Too many eyes.

Catar looked up and down the desolate street. The lights were dim, wavering like a dying firefly, many of them no longer lit. He broke out into a run across the street and around a corner into a thin alley. He unsheathed his knife. If he didn't do it now, the opportunity would be gone forever. The plan was already in motion, and all that remained before the key was in place was the sacrifice. He reached the end of the alley, and bent over slightly, trying to catch his breath. He peeked around the corner of the building and saw the Goat coming up the walk towards him.

Just a few steps more, Catar thought as he straightened up. *Hurry up, old fool.*

The Goat kept his pace, up and down with the cane. Catar could reach out and pull the cane right out of his hands, but he would wait until the Goat passed so he could grab him from behind.

A wailing of agony and pain filled the alley around Catar, and his muscles contracted as the noise paralyzed him. The Goat's eyes turned and met his, and they stared at each other for what felt like an entire season. The blood rushed through Catar's veins, reanimating him as he tried to decipher the look that shadowed the Goat's face. Confusion? Surprise? Annoyance?

Certainly not fear.

A thin, condescending—*Tiedan*—smile widened on the Goat's wrinkled face, and his random whiskers twitched. "Don't be frightened, apprentice," the Goat chuckled, pointing at a skeletal feline whose shiny black fur contrasted its malnourished frame. "She sounds like she's in heat. Our dear Calamity will likely be crying all night."

Catar nodded, coming to his senses. He took a step towards the Goat, muttered a spell, then jabbed his knife into the old man's side.

THIRTEEN

Aren let out a sigh of relief when they crossed the roaring columns of fire, four each flanking the loose-pebbled road into Tiede Proper. Selina walked a little behind him, her feet sweeping the ground, leaving snaking trails in their wake. She had been gloomy since they had woken that morning, and Aren let her be. He hadn't slept that well, and he was in no mood to make her disposition worse than it was. Besides, she had lost her gnome friend and had watched a man get impaled on a unicorn's horn. He couldn't fault her for being out of sorts.

They had been camped only two hours away from Tiede's entrance last night, but waiting until morning had reenergized Aren, and he knew they still had a long way to get to the House so he could get rid of the message. They passed the military training grounds first, and Aren nodded at the captain of the guard, who held up a shaking hand to greet them. Selina took a fistful of Aren's shirttail and attached herself to his side. The captain headed up a line of soldiers, dressed in black and armed with heavy swords and shields, standing sentry along the front of the high, black iron gates of the compound.

"You look rough, Apprentice." A smile stretched across the captain's face, and he made to put a fist at his chest. When he realized Aren wasn't wearing the House crest, his hand paused midway. He motioned for water instead and a soldier rushed over with two flasks. "Rougher than usual. Fight with a wildcat?"

"Is it that obvious?" Aren laughed. He considered the message tucked into the inner pocket of his vest, thought of the secrets scribbled on it, then put it out of his mind. He handed Selina one of the flasks, and she began to drink. "Thank you. It's been a long trip, and we lost our supplies."

"Why didn't you take the ferry to the Harbor?" the captain asked. "Nothing to attack you on a ferry."

Aren almost spit out his drink and ended up choking on it, coughing to breathe. "I was told the Harbor's closed—something about grisly murders in the city? All the fishermen are camped out on the river or in one of the small towns wondering when they can return home. If I had known someone would've let me on a boat, I wouldn't have gone all the way around."

"You could've tried," Finroy said. "No one ever comes this way except the Tinkerer. That's Tiede Wood, you cursed fool! What were you thinking?"

Aren swept the back of his hand across his mouth. "You have double the bowmen on the wall, your first line is in ready formation, and you have what looks like an escort unit preparing by the gate." Aren's eyes met the captain's. "We've known each other since we were pups, Finroy. If no one ever comes this way, what are you geared up for?"

The captain's face turned a shade of pink, and he adjusted the cap over his head of limp black hair. "Tiede is locked down. We have orders to detain anyone who tries to enter or leave through these gates."

"So you're going to arrest us?" Aren laughed. "Fin, I'm a House Apprentice—"

"You brought this on yourself," Finroy cut him off. "When our sentinel spotted you coming down the road, we thought you were a mage, so I got on the lark to let the House know. Now everyone's in a panic." He removed his cap, placed it over his face, and let out a frustrated breath. He replaced the cap, attempted to control the quiver in his left eye, then said, "My orders are to escort you and the girl to the House at once. Maybe if I can explain what happened, I won't get in too much trouble."

Aren finished off the water and returned the empty flask. "I'm flattered. All this metal is for me and the vicious Selina?" When the corner of Finroy's right eye twitched, Aren said, "Let me use your lark. I'll call the House and tell them what happened." The long-range communicator, commonly referred to as the lark, was a technological wonder invented in Tiede and used in about half of the Blessed Houses. Aren pretended to hold a receiver to his ear and speak into a mouthpiece. "Lord Vir? Good day, it's just Aren—yes, the strange boy who works in your Library, that one. I'm calling to let you know that all is fine at the southern gates. You see, I'd heard rumors that the Harbor was closed, and I was looking forward to returning to my beloved books, so my little charge and I took the long way back." Aren nodded as if he were listening to the other end of the conversation. "Yes, I know the Wood is meant to deter anyone from coming in this way, but you know us Unblessed types; we just don't think straight. I had to fight off a few dozen wild gree with a staff I found. This made me look like a crazed, bloody mess, so when I approached the gates with a staff in one hand and my darling little sister in tow, I must have looked a terror. I'm sorry to have raised such a fuss, but really, all is well here. Carry on with your…well, whatever it is you do, my lord."

Finroy's face was mottled red. "I dare not disturb the House more than I already have because of you. The mounts are almost ready."

Aren glared at the captain. Here he was, risking his life and Selina's trying to save Tiede from the mages—though the stupid message he read made little sense—and he was being treated like a threat. Why? Because he happened to use the less popular entrance into the city?

Finroy proceeded to get the escort ready to move, and before long they were on their way, saddled atop charcoal-colored gree with faint white markings. Each large cat wore what looked like a black doublet with the Tiede crest emblazoned in silver across its broad chest. At least, Aren thought, they didn't have to walk the rest of the way. The ride would only take a few hours, as opposed to the entire day.

They ate from a pack of fruits and cheeses as the gree trotted on soft-padded paws. Selina's mount remained close to Aren's, and every now and then Aren would reach over to scratch the beasts behind their ears and whisper soothing words. The gree's purring sent rumbles through the group, causing Selina to giggle a little. They passed the industrial sector, where all the smiths had set up shop, and Aren wished they had been permitted to stop so that he could visit home. Finroy looked at Aren as if he had asked to rule his own House, and Aren decided to stop wasting his breath.

To the west lay the heavy residential area, and to the east, the bustling Harbor District, where merchants displayed their wares and farmers and fishermen sold their harvest. The white buildings of the Harbor District were blinding in the late morning sun, and the bright-blue banners atop several of the buildings were whipped to attention by the sea winds, looking like birds eager to fly free. Aren took a deep breath, savoring the smell of sea salt in the air, feeling it permeate his skin and fill his lungs. More people were going about their business, and on several occasions, he noticed that some of the townsfolk would stop what they were doing to stare at them as they rode by. Feeling self-conscious, he exchanged a glance with Selina, who seemed to have noticed the same thing. They were no strangers to the curses and wards and the evil eye, but this was different.

Aren was well recognized, if not well known, in Tiede. It was no secret that he was an abandoned infant who had not been blessed, but when he was adopted into the Gerrit family, the legendary Blacksmiths of Tiede, he had secured a special place of honor and bewilderment in the eyes of the townsfolk. Why did such a noble line risk having such ill luck in their lives? Why would they let something so unclean carry their name? Aren's life only became more complicated when he was selected by the most revered Tiede Elder to serve as an apprentice in the House. Typically, one had to be born in Tiede and blessed by the Night gods to serve in the House, yet Aren was given the honor and distinction of the position. The people didn't know whether to admire him or hate him.

Finroy must have noticed the extra attention because he ordered the escort to keep close to the towering, textured white slate walls that were the distinct architecture in Tiede. The walls created several tiered levels throughout the city, which varied drastically in elevation depending on what part of the city you were in. The highest elevation in Tiede was also the northernmost point, upon which sat the House, over two thousand five hundred feet above the sea. The Harbor District was over twelve hundred feet below that, and the harbor docks over a thousand feet below that. The engineers had designed the city using a gradual tiered approach with a lot of curving stairs and winding slopes that gave the impression of a gentle elevation change.

When they reached the second highest tier, the gree meandered towards the Mermaid's Song, the popular tavern and inn located between the Guilds and the city center that served as a sort of welcoming station. Finroy ordered everyone to dismount so that the animals could be stabled and watered after the long trip under the high sun. They would walk the rest of the way to the House.

The tavern's lunch crowd was just picking up, and as they passed the front window, a young man with red-tinted, jet-black hair and an unshaven face careened out from the tavern entrance and stopped them in the middle of the road. "Aren! You're back! I've been waiting since they put out the word; I wanted to be the first to tell you! Father refused to let me go out to the river to get you, but I said you weren't coming back for at least another two days, and I even went to Elder and told him I'd volunteer to go get you. Everyone said it could wait, but really? All of life was being put on hold because you're out fishing? Even when you aren't around you're causing trouble. And what in the gods' names happened to you? You're a bloody disaster!" The man's eyebrows shot up as he noticed the escort. "Good day, Fin! What brings you up from the gates?"

Finroy and his small army were thrown off guard by the sudden interruption, and before the captain could get a word in, Aren said, "Fin, you remember my brother Dane." Aren placed a hand on his brother's shoulder. "It's good to see you too. I know I look like I just went toe to toe with a River Guardian, but what in the stars are you talking about?"

Dane gripped Aren by the shoulders. "The Priestesses of Syrn are here! That's why I've been waiting for you!" Dane ruffled the top of Selina's head. "I see you took good care of him, Selina. Next time, though, remind him to comb his hair."

"And what does Syrn have to do with Selina and me?"

"I've heard different things, but I'll tell you the more believable reasons." Dane tried to slow down, but his words continued to gush out like a fountain. Finroy tried to interject, but Dane had returned to ignoring him. "One story is that the Priestesses want you as a slave." He added under his breath, "You know, *that* kind of slave." Aren rolled his eyes and was ready to push him out of the way, but Dane continued. "Another story is that Elder volunteered you to their library, to translate their old scrolls."

"Only a hair more plausible than your first explanation," Aren said, feeling uneasy about the number of people gathering around them. "Syrn keeps all of their literature a secret, and to have a *male* come in to read their writings is laughable. If these are your more believable reasons, then I hate to think what other rumors have been floating around."

"The other thing I've heard," Dane said, "is that Selina's been chosen! Mother and Lana have been at the House every day, worrying and waiting for an explanation."

Aren looked down at Selina—scratched up, dirty, and scared— and wondered what in the stars she had been chosen for. She was only five—six at most. They wouldn't have chosen her, an Unblessed, to become the next Priestess. Still, it would explain all the looks they got as they traveled through town. Aren could feel the crowd growing, and he lowered himself to look her in the eyes. "Don't worry, sweetheart. We're going to find out what this is all about."

Aren straightened up, herded Dane to his side opposite Selina, and Finroy ordered his unit to keep the crowd back. There were more people now, wanting to catch a glimpse of Selina as if the news had transformed her somehow. Aren was about to lead them down the alley towards the quieter Guild Row when someone pulled at his shoulder, forcing him to turn around.

"Apprentice, I've been ordered to escort you and the girl to the House. Captain Ohpan Finroy, you're dismissed. We'll take it from here." A wiry young man dressed in the House's midnight blue stood before Aren, flanked by three of the House Guard. An official House Messenger. This was a bigger deal than Aren had thought.

FOURTEEN

Through the black, imposing front doors of the magnificent House of Tiede was the renowned Tiede courtyard. The enormous courtyard was open to the skies, and at each corner stood a massive statue of the Fire god, carved from rough, black stone. Each statue acted as a column with one hand supporting the courtyard structure and the other hand holding a burning torch twice the size of a man. The torchlight tossed shadows against the fierce faces, making them terrifying to look upon.

In the middle of the courtyard was a large, circular fountain consisting of two tiers linked by a serpentine, fire-breathing sea dragon coiled around the middle. On the topmost, smaller basin lounged a mermaid, pouring water from a conch shell with one hand while resting the other on the dragon's triangular head. The mermaid, whose beauty sharply contrasted the fire sentinels, had long, wavy hair and a gentle face from which blank eyes stared into the water. Each scale on her fishlike tail was carved into the creamy marble with amazing precision and detail, and flecked with bits of gold and crushed turquoise.

This afternoon, the light-filled courtyard was full of servants, buzzing with the added chores of catering to the esteemed guests from Syrn and eager to catch a glimpse of Selina. When the House Messenger and Guards led Dane, Aren, and Selina through the doors, the Priestess Minor Nianni and Lyte Tanda, Tiede's most senior Elder, descended upon the group. Nianni's nut-brown skin was radiant in the light, and her cheeks were flush with heat and anger.

She didn't bother gathering up her airy white chiffon skirts as she strode towards Selina, her face a mask of purpose. She took Selina's hand, but Selina pulled away and wrapped herself around Aren's leg.

"You are a complete mess, and I need to get you cleaned up; the Head Priestess and our guests have been made to wait long enough," Nianni scolded, tugging at Selina's skinny arm.

Aren put a protective hand on Selina's head. "No need to be so scary, Priestess. She might cooperate if you asked nicely."

Nianni, more than two heads shorter than Aren, wrapped her arms around Selina's midsection and tore her from his leg, carrying the kicking girl away. She stopped to shoot Aren an angry look. "You are a lazy toad with little respect, considering the situation."

"And you, Priestess, are a fly-bug in my first ale of the summer season," Aren retorted as she stomped off, her silver bracelets and anklets jingling. He pointed the gnarled mage's staff at her. "If you hurt one hair on her head, I will personally…"

Elder Tanda, using his walking staff, jabbed Aren and Dane hard in their abdomens, causing them to double over. "Leave us," Elder said to the Messenger and Guards before casting angry eyes at the servants milling about. They started and returned to their chores at once. Elder smacked the side of Dane's arm hard with his staff. "Young blacksmith, go home before I tell your father to collect you from the dungeons." Dane rubbed at his arm and gave Aren a lopsided grin. He signed that they should meet at the tavern later, then left before Elder could follow through on his threat. Elder's fluffy white brows furrowed, adding more wrinkles to his high forehead. He glared at Aren with sharp, raven-black eyes.

"I've done nothing wrong," Aren said, folding his arms across his chest. "The Priestess Minor has always hated me; you know that. I don't even know what this *situation* is she's talking about."

"If you can't act with respect in the courtyard—in the heart of this House—what good are you to me?" Elder's thin, pale arm struck out from the flowing midnight-blue House robe that swallowed him, and he poked a bony finger at Aren's chest. "Was that any way for a House Apprentice to behave? Especially one of your standing?"

"But Selina was scared, and—"

"Even she must learn that there is a time and a place, and now she will have that opportunity. I'm afraid it's too late for you to learn anything."

Aren sighed, dropping his arms to his sides, one hand rolling the staff. "I'm sorry, Elder. It was a rough trip home."

Elder snorted, but Aren heard a softening of his tone. "Excuses. The only good here is that you've returned earlier than I expected; I thought you had planned on a longer trip."

Aren perked up. "Elder, remember that time I calculated how long it takes to travel from the River Taethe to Tiede as the crow flies? My best estimate was three days. Well, forget that theory; I now know from experience that it takes as long as the Wood wants it to take. We went from river to Tiede Proper in hours." Elder's face was expressionless. "*Hours,*" Aren repeated, drawing out the word.

"Where did you get that awful stick?" Elder asked, as if Aren hadn't spoken, "and why did you bring it in here?"

Aren looked at the staff. He was so accustomed to carrying it, he had almost forgotten. "It's a long story, but the impetus for why I'm back early is this message for Lord Vir. A messenger found me at the river." He pulled the parchment out of his vest, tried to straighten it a little, then presented it to Elder.

"Do I look like Lord Vir?" Elder snapped. "Request an audience, but before you do, try to look and smell somewhat presentable."

Aren clutched at the parchment. "Yes, Elder."

Elder turned to walk away, his majestic robes giving the impression of floating. "It's good you're back. There's a lot of work to catch up on." He added, "And the girl will be fine."

So one of Dane's rumors was actually right: Selina had been chosen. Aren was the guardian of Cordelacht's newest Priestess— well, legally his sister Lana was Selina's guardian. In any case, he thought his brain might explode.

He was so lost in thought and lulled into a state of relaxation by the splashing fountain that he didn't hear the footsteps until they were a few feet away. He turned to see who it was and found himself standing before Lord Tiede Vir. Aren dropped to one knee and bowed his head, bringing his fist to his chest.

Tiede Vir was an imposing figure with his jet-black hair and deep-set, dark-blue eyes against his fair skin. He was almost as tall as Aren—which was not a Tiede trait—but his physique was bigger, more bulky. Aren could almost imagine the statues that would be made in this man's image.

"Up." Vir watched as Aren stood up. "The girl?"

"Selina is with the Priestess Minor, my Lord."

Vir looked tired and a little irritated. "One less thing to be concerned with."

"I'm actually back earlier than I had planned; I've a message for you," Aren started, almost dropping the parchment and the staff, but recovering. "I was going to request an audience, but here you are—though, if you prefer, I can still go through the proper channels." Vir opened a hand to accept the message, then studied the dusky, rose-colored wax seal. "It was a very long and dangerous journey," Aren explained, realizing that the message was not in the best of conditions. "I lost my pack, gained this staff, and the message took the same beating I did." He wondered if he was babbling, but continued anyway. "A messenger from the House of Rose spotted me at the River Taethe, and he asked me to deliver it."

Vir unfolded the parchment. "Why didn't he deliver it himself?"

Aren bit his lip hard. Was this the right time to tell Lord Vir that a mage had attacked him? It might come across as some crazy story to get attention or a sad excuse for his disheveled state. The last time the mages had risen was decades ago, and according to the histories, they were scattered and killed off. Let Vir read the message. He might think it more credible than his Apprentice did. Aren spit out the words he knew Vir wanted to hear. "Tiede Wood, my Lord. He was scared."

A hint of a smile lifted the corner of Vir's mouth. "Good."

Aren watched as Vir read over the message. Nothing on Vir's face betrayed what was written, but Aren heard something like a growl crawl up from his throat. Vir folded the parchment, keeping the edges aligned, his mind focused on the task, but otherwise elsewhere.

"This message doesn't exist. If I hear one word of a message that you delivered, I will toss you into Tiede Wood myself." Vir's voice was calm and even, but there was a note of tension beneath it.

"Yes, my Lord."

"Did you read it?"

Lord Vir, husband to Rose's most beloved daughter, it is with great distress and anxiety that I write you this letter.

Aren didn't flinch, looking straight into Vir's eyes. "No, my Lord."

FIFTEEN

Selina stood before the Priestesses in Alaric's worship room, which encompassed the west wing of the House. It was situated on the first level, but rose to the second in a manner similar to the Library. Most worshipping was done in this room, the most elaborate in the House. Thick, silk drapes in midnight blue flanked the large windows, and candles adorned the smaller open window casings. Urns of various sizes made of tortoise shell, turquoise, and jade were full of water and gathered at one corner while in another section of the room flames jumped on candelabras. It smelled of the sea and moonflower and leindra incense.

Selina had learned long ago that Alaric was the Night god, the one that all of Tiede worshipped above all other gods, and she could see now how serious the House was about paying their respects to him. She felt smaller than usual, insignificant and lost in this space.

Nianni stood behind her, as if to make sure she wouldn't run away. To Selina's left was Min. The raven-haired House Priestess was soft-spoken and hadn't said much to Selina aside from welcoming her to the House, but she watched Selina with curiosity, her amber eyes seeming to record her every movement.

To Selina's right was Tiede's Head Priestess Crina. She had sparkling gray eyes and silver hair pulled back from her sharp face. She looked ageless, yet Selina could see the years in those strange eyes and hear the wisdom in her calm voice. Crina explained that the Priestesses of Syrn would need to confirm that she was the chosen, and that she didn't have to do anything but stand still.

There were three Priestesses from Syrn: Syrn's Head Priestess Estelline, Priestess Teyna, and the Seer. Selina would have sworn they were goddesses or some kind of faerie because of their regal elegance and ethereal beauty. Like Tiede's Priestesses, they seemed ageless, and she wondered if youth was a gift they had received from the gods.

Estelline was tall, the white hair piled atop her head, making her look even taller. She stood with her hands clasped in front of her, a solid silver bracelet on each wrist catching the firelight in the room. She examined Selina without betraying her emotions.

"Your chosen," Crina said. "The House of Tiede offers her to Syrn."

No one spoke, but the Seer, standing to Estelline's right, began to hum low in her throat. Her emerald-green eyes glazed over, and her long red hair stirred in the breeze that had slipped unnoticed into the room. "This is the girl from the visions," the Seer confirmed, the mist lifting from her eyes. "But she's not been blessed."

Teyna smiled, and her dark features and singsong accent reminded Selina of Nianni. "Where are you from, child?" Teyna asked.

Selina looked to Crina, and when the Head Priestess nodded in approval, she said, "Aren found me here in Tiede."

"The Historian's Apprentice," Crina explained. "He's regarded as the child's guardian, though not in any official capacity. We're told that he found her three years ago, and that she has no recollection of home or family."

"This is fascinating, but it does present a problem," Estelline said, a sigh weighing down her words. "Never has an Unblessed been chosen."

"And yet," Teyna said, "the Seer has confirmed."

"We will have to pray on this. With the gods' guidance, we will find an answer. In the meantime, we place a blessing on you, Selina, and welcome you into the sacred worship of the gods," Estelline intoned, and all the women placed their hands over Selina's head.

Dozens of images, broken and colorless, new and happy, overwhelmed her senses until at last her mind settled on the sensation of the Lady in the Wood kissing her forehead.

SIXTEEN

When their father Mahl left them on this once-wasted planet, what seemed like an eternity ago, back when there were still eight cursed continents, he had woven certain rules into the condition of their being. There was no way to ignore or defy those rules; like puppets, they were compelled to obey, dangling about on strings with an invisible handler. The idea of it felt so real that Alaric often stared up into his evening skies, imagining and tracing the thin, unbreakable strings that led to his father's hands.

Alaric and his twin sister Aalae had discovered their father's rules over the course of their lives, recording them, and in Aalae's case, trying to find ways to break them. Their list of rules, while short, limited them in various ways. They couldn't kill each other, for one, and they were tied in such a way that they could summon each other as long as there was no intended malice. It was a tortured existence, and they were stranded, unable to leave the planet or call on any other gods.

It was the Summons that was annoying Alaric now, and he fastened his cape as he walked towards the borders of his Realm, waiting for his Elemental Knights to fall in behind him. He had no fear of his sister, but he knew that her Knights would be at her side. He wasn't so vain that he would face them alone.

They also hadn't yet discovered whether any of the Knights could kill a god.

A piercing cry cut through the air, and he glanced up at the phoenix that circled overhead, its tail and wings a trail of fire blazing bright against the dark sky. He watched as it tucked its wings back before diving towards him, its features blurring, the whole of it vanishing into black smoke as it neared, until the core of it smashed into the ground beside him.

The fireball sparked and erupted, and the large Fire spirit emerged from the ashes, dressed in full black regalia.

"Tanghi," Alaric acknowledged the other. "Where's Kaila?"

The Fire spirit looked down at Alaric, his brows furrowed. "I thought she would be here by now; I haven't seen her since morning."

How was it going to look when he showed up with one Knight to Aalae's two? She'd probably make some joke about how he had no control over his Realm, and right now he was beginning to think that it wouldn't be far from the truth. He resumed his trek, taking the shell-littered path away from the Keep, with Tanghi in step behind him.

"Do you know what the Summons is about?" Tanghi asked.

"The Priestesses. She claims we're unbalanced."

They walked in silence from that point, Alaric aware of Tanghi doing the calculations in his head: eight Houses, three Priestesses each, another one from each House in Syrn for training. He would find that the number belonging to Light and Night across the Houses was even and that the selection of a new Priestess, rumored to be from Tiede, would tilt the balance towards Night.

The darkness was receding, indicating that they were nearing the Realm's borders, and Alaric squinted as his eyes adjusted to the additional light. The long, inky shadows began to give way to a hazy landscape of endless fields covered in tall white grass and littered with large, charcoal boulders, broken pieces of the pink and lavender sky sprinkled about as if they had let go of the heavens.

Aalae was leaning against a towering rock, her Knights in full white regalia on either side of her. She was long and willowy with skin the color of honey, eyes of jade, and hair like silver snow in this light. She was everything Alaric was not, and he questioned how on Mytanth they were related, never mind being twins.

"I would have preferred to meet at Dawn over this lifeless place," he said, referring to the borderland where the sun was fixed low and bright on the horizon. "Sabana, Geir, I trust my sister is treating you well."

The two Knights bowed their heads low, and Tanghi followed suit, paying the proper respects to Aalae. Sabana's rich, dark skin contrasted the white she wore, and with her head covered by the helm, her earthy-green eyes seemed to dance all the more. She was lord over all the dry land and flora and vegetation. She was as beautiful and cunning as her mistress; she was Aalae's most valuable asset.

Geir, on the other hand, was to Aalae as Kaila was to Alaric. Geir questioned Aalae's motives and methods and often disappeared for long periods of time. He was tall with unkempt, sandy-blond hair and attractive, angular facial features. The oddest thing about him was that he wore a linen cloth over his eyes, though he wasn't blind. He'd been wearing it for so long that no one questioned it anymore.

"You would prefer Dawn just as much as I would have preferred Dusk," Aalae said, her voice as sweet as a child's song. "Let's please try to be more honest with each other."

"You first," Alaric said, folding his arms across his chest. "What's the real reason for this Summons?"

She waved a hand at him, as if dismissing his question. "Tanghi, it's wonderful to see you, and so handsome in the full black." Tanghi bowed his head again to acknowledge her compliment. "But where is your beautiful sister-in-arms?"

"I have Kaila on a task at the moment," Alaric said. "Now what do you want of me?"

A knowing look stole across her face. "The new Priestess is from Tiede; this throws off the balance."

"Just because she's from Tiede doesn't mean she was blessed by my Realm," he countered. "Yes, the chances are greater, but it's still unknown. We can argue this once we know for sure. Next time, just send a message through Taia," he said, referring to his mate.

"What of the Priestesses at Syrn? Have you counted them?"

"Syrn is neutral, regardless of where the Priestesses are from. The Seer's gifts to select the next Priestess come from father, and to date the selection has been balanced, so what are you worried about? Your worshippers are providing you with the power you require, as are mine. We are at our second equinox. You've nothing to worry about."

"I don't care for equinox," she said, pushing herself away from the boulder and taking a step towards him. "Father didn't leave us here to keep order; he wants one of us to rule—that's when he'll return, and one of us will receive the full powers of godhood and finally get off this forsaken planet."

"And that's why you're concerned about the Priestesses," Alaric said flatly. "You're looking to increase your power, your hold over the god-life."

"The books say," she said in a singsong voice, "the mortals are the key."

"There's more to it than that, and if you don't pull back the reins on your reckless ambition, you will bring about another holy war, and it won't matter how many Priestesses there are to lead the mortals to you because they'll all be dead. We've managed to annihilate seven continents full of god-life thanks to our bickering."

"I'll not be like you, satisfied with being stuck here for eternity. I will get off this rock, even if it means I have to destroy you first."

"You know nothing of what I want of this life, and you are the naïve one if you think I'll stand idly by while you wreak havoc on what we've finally achieved: this tenuous balance," Alaric seethed. "This isn't a competition, and father's not coming back to crown a victor. We protect the god-life or we die; it's as simple as that. Father left us here because we were a threat to his godhood."

"Balance does not create power," she said.

"Your opinion has been noted." He turned his back to her and began to walk away, with Tanghi a step behind him.

Aalae called out, "Sabana and Geir tell me that Kaila was in Tiede Wood, then ventured into Tiede. I didn't think you ever let her out of your sight, never mind allowing her to walk among the mortals."

Alaric gritted his teeth and tried to tell himself that she was baiting him. He felt Tanghi's presence, and the heat emanating from the fire that encircled his body pushed at Alaric, telling him to keep moving. Alaric took a breath, then continued walking.

Kaila needed to be found and disciplined.

SEVENTEEN

After a much-needed bath, Aren sought out his desk in the House Library, eager to surround himself with something familiar and comfortable. Tiede's Library was renowned throughout Cordelacht as the most beautiful and bountiful archive. It encompassed two floors on the front, eastern side of the House, its vaulted ceiling depicting the story of Alaric calling forth Fire and Water to bring life to Tiede.

The Library was warm and extravagant. Heavy silk curtains in midnight blue framed the large windows. Stone and marble floors on the first level made the room seem more spacious than it already was, and the plush midnight carpeting on the staircase and upper level created a comfortable, cocoon-like counter-effect. The second floor had a large oil painting of one of the earlier Tiede ancestors hanging on the wall between the two balconies that overlooked the front of the House; the rest of the walls were lined with shelves stuffed with books and scrolls. There were tables for quiet study, little tucked-away corners with deep velvet chairs for relaxed reading (and napping, when Elder wasn't around), and an impressive vault of Tiede's most historic and treasured writings. The Library was also one of the few places in the House that used electricity.

Elder and Aren had grand desks made of satin spiraled nightwood, a rare lumber harvested from Tiede Wood generations ago, before everyone was convinced that anything that came out of the Wood was damned. They worked in close proximity on the first floor in view of the main entrance and grand staircase. Aren had managed—with the help of Dane—to move his desk in such a way that the bookcases nearby allowed him some privacy so he could work in relative peace.

Aren pulled out his pen, ink, and a few sheets of parchment from a drawer and began writing up his report on the death of Fisherman Begles Henrik. He recalled the scene in his head, replayed the conversations. A mage, the last of a dying cult, was determined to stop a message from getting to Tiede—a message Aren didn't find particularly noteworthy. Did it matter anymore? If Aren wrote the truth, Elder would ask why he had kept the whole thing a secret in the first place.

Tiede-born Begles Henrik, promised at birth to the goddess Kaila, died on the banks of the River Taethe from what appeared to be an altercation. His lifeless body was found by [Gerrit] Aren, House Apprentice, while on holiday. It was difficult to determine whether Fisherman Henrik died from blood loss due to blade wounds or from a wild animal attack.

Aren crumpled up the parchment, tossed it aside, laid out a new sheet, then began to scribble a picture of a swan as he considered the lie. Henrik was a good man who had died because he had delusions of grandeur—because he thought he was going to save Tiede. Looking back on the incident, Aren wondered if he had overreacted as well. He had risked his and Selina's lives—for what? Was one mage going to destroy Tiede because of a silly message?

Tiede-born Fisherman Begles Henrik, promised at birth to the goddess Kaila, died on the banks of the River Taethe under the impression that he was protecting the House of Tiede from an unconfirmed threat.

Aren let his forehead rest against the parchment as he suffered over his words. Perhaps his subconscious was too focused on Selina. He hadn't been allowed anywhere near her, and the servants kept whispering about secret ceremonies. Some of them thought Selina had been selected as a sign from the gods, showing how merciful and forgiving the gods were towards the Unblessed. Others saw it as outright blasphemy and began to spread rumors that it was a sign of the end times—that the gods could no longer be relied upon to protect them. A handful of servants wondered if Selina would be offered as a sacrifice to get the gods' attention.

Selecting Selina to be a Priestess had to have been a mistake, and Aren needed to find a way to get the situation straightened out. He had to come up with a way to gain an audience with the Head Priestess. It wouldn't be easy; he was pretty sure the Head Priestess hated him too. At least he was in his element now. He could think here, and some of his best plans had been designed in this very room. He breathed in the scent of old books, curling papers, and fresh ink.

"What have you done this time?" Elder Tanda asked in his usual exasperated tone.

"I haven't done a thing. I was just theorizing on why Lord Vir wants to keep the message a secret," Aren said, lifting his head off the desk. He wondered what information he could get from his old master.

"Are you talking about the message that doesn't exist?" Elder said as he looked over some recently acquired scrolls. "The message Lord Vir asked you to make sure wasn't spoken of ever again?"

"Yes."

Elder lifted his eyes as if it took great effort, then stared at Aren. "I thought I asked you years ago to acquire some common sense."

"I'm just curious. There's been rumor of a shift of power in Cordelacht towards the Light Houses, and everyone knows that Rose arranged the marriage with Tiede for protection. The messenger from Rose also talked about the mages rising in the east."

"You would do well to keep those rumors to yourself and not allow them into the House, of all places." Elder returned his attention to the scroll he was working on. "I will not have Lord Vir's wrath in this Library because you couldn't keep your mouth shut. I don't want to hear another word of an arranged marriage either; Lord Vir fell in love with Lady Geyle, and that is the end of that." Aren opened his mouth to say something, but Elder cut him off. "Before you start asking about Selina and the Priestesses, I need you to pick up some oil. The mess at the docks has left the entire House short, and I know you were planning on meeting Dane anyway." Elder added, "And try to be careful; there's a killer out there. Some people have gone missing and others have been brutally murdered. If I lose you, I'll have to find and train a new apprentice, and I don't have time for that."

Aren rolled his eyes but smiled, leaving the stacks and scrolls behind. Though he knew he'd never make Elder proud, never impress him, Aren loved the old man. Elder would never admit it, but Aren sensed that the Master Historian and Librarian saw a potential in Aren that Aren didn't even see in himself. Why else would he bring an Unblessed into the House? Aren sometimes told himself that the old man was going senile.

Aren closed the heavy black doors to the Library and crossed the hallway towards the courtyard, nodding at the maids with their linens as they passed. Two of them giggled and blushed, while the third traced a star of warding on her palm and hurried the others along. Aren ignored the gesture, as he always did, then stretched out his arms as he walked through the courtyard. Twilight filled the expansive space with a soft, lavender glow, and the first of the peppermint fireflies were descending and alighting upon the fountain. He stopped for a moment, entranced by the beauty of the marble mermaid. Her eyes were as blank and cold as the stone she was carved of, but her lips curved into a generous, gentle smile. The firefly glow lit her cheeks, and he could almost imagine that the waves of hair that framed her face were billowing in the cool, dusky breeze.

A shadow lengthened across the courtyard as the sun sought its rest. Curious, Aren walked around the fountain to find out who it was. At this time, most of the House was gathering in Alaric's worship room to welcome the night. A petite woman was sitting on the fountain's outer rim, her legs curled up under her, staring up at the mermaid as if begging in prayer. She wore a light, simple evening gown of yellow and orange silks that cascaded like molten gold over the edge of the fountain's rim, pooling onto the floor. Her hair, the color of ripened wheat, fell in long, loose curls around her shoulders. She was a small, solitary light in Tiede's darkness.

The lady's voice was small as she asked, "Did the gods send you?"

EIGHTEEN

Lady Tiede Geyle noticed Aren from the corner of her eye and turned to look at him. For a moment, they just stared at each other, lost in the rhythmic splash of water. She was fair and pleasant to look at. Her eyes were cornflower blue and distant. Her mouth was small, and her nose was small. All of her facial features seemed petite, right down to the abbreviated smattering of golden freckles across her nose and the tops of her cheeks.

All at once, Aren remembered his manners and bowed from the waist, bringing a fist to his chest.

"My Lady," Aren rushed, "I apologize. I wasn't expecting you—I mean, I didn't think you were here. Although, this is your House, so I suppose of course you would be here, I just mean that—"

"Apprentice, be still," she said, cutting him off with an upraised hand and moving to lower her bare feet to the floor. The sound of water filled the space between them again. She seemed to consider him, then spared a quick glance at the mermaid before saying, "Your timing couldn't be better. Sit with me."

He obeyed without hesitation, seating himself to her left, an appropriate distance away. He felt the water that had puddled on the wide bench soak through his pants, and he had to stop himself from bolting and cursing his dull mind.

She must have sensed what he was thinking because she laughed and said, "Your room isn't far, and I'm sure no one will notice in the meantime. The sun is setting, and the shadows will hide you well. Besides, rumor has it there's not much you can do to stop women from swooning over you, wet pants or not."

Aren felt his cheeks grow hot, and he cast his eyes downward, rubbing the nails of one hand against the nails of the other. "That's a strange rumor, my Lady."

"I first heard your name during the festivals that celebrated my marriage to Vir," she said, ignoring his words. Her eyes seemed further away now, as if looking into the past. "Do you remember the celebrations?"

"Of course. It was a joyous event for Tiede, and we were happy to welcome you."

"That's very kind of you to say." Geyle blushed. "I remember your name because it's unusual."

"I suppose, but how would you have heard my name then? I had only just been summoned to the House around that time."

"In Tiede, you have the custom of maidens bringing the bride a slip of paper with a young man's name."

"A wish with the bride's blessing."

Geyle lifted an eyebrow, her eyes sparkling in the courtyard's firelight. "Apprentice, over half the slips of paper had your name written on them! I had to show Vir after the seventh or eighth one; I was so tickled!"

Aren felt the flush of heat on his face. He opened his mouth to speak, but closed it, trying to think through the ringing and burning in his ears. Geyle began to laugh, high-pitched and lyrical like a songbird. He kept his face down, concentrating on the water rippling in the fountain, and chuckled a little. "Those girls had no idea what they were writing, probably daring each other to write down the name of some awkward boy just for the fun of it. More likely it was a way of cursing each other."

"Stop being so modest." She poked his upper arm. He didn't say anything, a little taken aback by the direction of the conversation and the fact that she had touched him. She sighed. "This is nice, talking and laughing with someone and remembering happy times. It feels…normal."

A silence slipped over them again, and he watched as her smile faded like the setting sun. She was looking up at the sky, past the mist of water and flickering fireflies. Aren wondered if he should leave.

"Do you know anything of Rose?" she asked at last.

The Rose is a symbol of the ideal. The Rose is trampled in battles and wars.

Aren felt a lump in his throat. What did she know of the message he delivered? Should he feign ignorance? Was it a trap designed by Vir to test him? Before he could say anything, she continued, "It's nothing like Tiede, with its oceans and history and...dominance."

Aren felt a wave of relief wash over his conscience. She wasn't asking about the message; she just wanted to talk about her home. "I've never been, but I've read that it's all meadows and grasslands."

Geyle's face lit up. "Yes! And the flowers in the spring cover every inch of the hills; it's warm, and beautiful. Tiede is more regal, and everything about it is structured and defiant. Cold." She stopped herself as if only just realizing where she was and with whom she was speaking.

"Are you homesick?" he asked. "Maybe a trip back would do you some good."

"I wish I could, but it's so far away and Vir is not likely to let me leave. We're expecting many guests over the coming weeks for this reason and that; it would be inappropriate for me to be away. It's always like this in Tiede; no one ever stops or slows down."

"It's good the House is busy. It means that it's respected; its counsel has weight enough to dictate the future of Cordelacht as a whole."

"Do you know much about the history of Tiede? The curse?" she asked as if he hadn't spoken. "All of Cordelacht knows of the curse of Tiede, especially the strange stories about the Wood."

Aren tightened his lips, furrowed his brows. His fingers began to scratch at the stubble on his chin, which he hadn't bothered shaving after his bath. "I'm familiar with the stories of Tiede Wood"—and the reality, he added internally—"but as far as a curse is concerned, I can't say that I've encountered any text that mentions a specific curse. There are countless records in the Library, though. I'll be as Elder before I come close to knowing them all."

"I'm surprised you don't know. Tiede blood is cursed, and they say the House is dying. Have you read anything of previous generations? Lady Cath disappeared. Assassins murdered Lady Kaye. Tiede Ril died as an infant from unknown causes. There was that fire that killed those two Tiede children. The list goes on and on and on."

He shrugged. "Even if it were all true, what does it matter now?"

She looked at him as if he were dim. "The most recent of all the Tiede histories: Vir's father killed his wife. There was madness in her from being so close to the Wood, and the darkness in his blood is now in Vir. How can I not be concerned? Things have changed over these past few years."

Aren almost laughed, but remembered his manners. "The death of Lady Elleina was nothing violent or supernatural. There is nothing I've read that said Lord Ren killed her, and Lord Vir is a fair and reasonable man. The only darkness that flows through them is that of the natural night, if you believe in that sort of thing."

"You're so naïve." She gave him a weak smile. "But your idealistic attitude warms me." Aren wanted to ask what she was getting at, but she held up a hand. "Don't tell," she said as she brought her palms together.

Her eyes fluttered closed. Aren watched as her shoulders began to glow with a soft light, and he leaned away from her, his eyes wide. He knew the Lady bore the marks of a magic wielder—everyone knew—but he didn't realize that she could summon magic. It wasn't uncommon to see people who bore the marks upon their shoulders; this didn't mean that they were mages, just that the magic had been in the bloodline, and for some reason or another, it chose to manifest itself in certain individuals. It didn't mean they could actually use magic.

When Geyle opened her eyes, the light from her shoulders dimmed until it vanished. She made no explanations, only asked, "Will you do me a favor, Aren?"

This time, it was her familiarity with him that caught him off guard. "My Lady?"

"Can I trust you?" Aren felt his throat dry up, and no words came out. "I worship the Light goddess Aalae, but I was praying to Kaila when you arrived," she explained, indicating the mermaid. "Do you...Are you her worshipper? I saw you with the Priestess Initiate earlier, and she looks like she was blessed by Night. You don't look related, though. Yet, you're of Tiede. You must worship the Night god Alaric, then?"

Aren chose his words carefully, wanting to be precise without offending her. "Considering how quickly rumors spread, I'm surprised you've not heard. I was an orphan, as was the new Priestess, Selina. We're not related by blood, but we are family. There's no record of a blessing for either of us. I pay my respects to the gods as is required by the House, nothing more, but if it pleases you, I have always found the likenesses of the Water goddess beautiful."

In a soft voice, Geyle said, "Kaila is said to be soft-hearted and easy to flatter. Perhaps she has sent you to me." Aren felt uncomfortable and was about to change the subject or find a polite way to excuse himself when she leaned towards him. He had to strain to hear her words over the incessant splish-splash. "In the Weavers Guild, there is an apprentice named Caley," Geyle said. "She has hair the color of winter plums. Do you know of whom I speak?" He nodded. "Tell her I wish to know if the fabric for my dress is ready. She will present you with a box." Geyle opened her hand to reveal a small iron key. She took his hand and pressed the key into his palm hard, closing his fingers around it.

Aren slipped it into his vest pocket without looking at it, glancing around to make sure they weren't being watched. He wasn't sure what was going on, but if Vir or one of the servants noticed, he would probably be questioned about why he was in such close proximity to the Lady. Then, he'd be thrown into the dungeons.

"I've placed wards around the courtyard, but they won't last long," she said, noticing his watchful eyes. "Open the box Caley gives you, and bring me the contents."

"Any of your servants could do this for you. The apprentice from the Weavers Guild could find a way to bring you what you need. I don't understand the need for secrecy."

She moved closer, and he could smell the rosewater on her skin, feel the heat of her breath against his cheek. "Please, Aren. Everyone else is too terrified of Vir. You aren't from Rose; no one would suspect you."

Aren wanted to voice how terrified he was of Vir too, but he couldn't find the words. He locked his eyes onto hers and saw the desperation there. She was so close to him, trying to persuade him with whatever magic still lingered around her. He almost thought she would kiss him, but she moved away and stared at the mermaid again.

"The wards will be fading," she said, her voice sad again. "One needs a staff to work any proper magic."

Aren stood up, sweat dotting his forehead and neck. "I need to change my clothes, and I probably shouldn't leave the House without my robes."

She nodded, her shoulders slumped as she turned her attention to the myriad of blue diamonds embedded into the bottom of the clear pool. Her dress slipped off her shoulder and before she could move it back, he caught the silver markings of the magic wielder.

"I will reward you for this."

"I serve the House, my Lady," he replied with a slight bow, then walked away.

NINETEEN

It only took a few minutes for Aren to run to his room and change into a dry pair of pants. Then, he picked his robes up off his bed, threw them on, and secured the silver clasp that held the heavy, black velvet over his shoulders and across his collarbones. He pulled the hood over his head, emphasizing the shadows that had darkened his eyes since last night, and smoothed out the House crest that was embroidered in fine silver threads on the upper left arm.

He felt the Lady's key hot against his chest as he walked the cobblestone streets. It was a constant reminder of the clandestine task he had accepted, and he decided that her errand would be the last one he completed before returning to the House. A key was nothing on its own. If for some reason he was robbed or searched, it wouldn't signify anything.

The street outside of the Mermaid's Song glowed with the soft bioluminescence from the lamps that stood at regular intervals down the road. Music spilled out into the night, chunky guitar chords and dancing piano arpeggios, intermingling with laughter and the off-key singing of drunkards sloshing their beers. The people made way for Aren to enter the tavern without fuss or hassle, and Aren spotted Dane seated at their usual spot, a pitcher of amber beer on the table and a guitar against his chest. He was singing along with the musicians on the stage, strumming with such energy that his hair whipped forward and backward, throwing sweat into the air.

With his good looks and outgoing personality, Gerrit Dane was a natural showman. As far as looks went, he—and the whole Gerrit family, for that matter—was the epitome of the ideal Tiede citizen. The strong, compact build was indicative of a dedicated working class. Jet-black hair, dark obsidian eyes, and pale skin symbolized their connection to the Night god, whom Tiede worshipped. On top of that, Gerrit hair was layered with strands of a deep, blood red, and their pupils showed motes of crimson and amber in the light. The traits branded them as belonging to the Fire god, the family's patron god.

Aren watched Dane and felt that pang of jealousy that struck him every once in a while. He loved his family, especially his brother, but he would never look as they did, ingrained as the Gerrits were in Tiede's very soul. Aren forced his demons away, hating himself for being so childish, and tuned back in to the laughter and music and Dane's rich, gravelly baritone. When the song ended, the crowd erupted into cheers and Dane handed the guitar back to the lead musician, raising his hands to the crowd in modesty, which only caused them to cheer even louder. Aren shook his head before making his way over to his brother.

The musicians picked up another tune, slower this time, and the crowd took it as their cue to get more drinks and find a spot to sit and chat, or head home for the evening. Aren took a seat at the table, just as the waitress put down fresh glasses; Dane poured.

"*Tse frie*," the brothers said the traditional Tiede toast in unison, clinking their glasses before taking a drink.

"Starved for attention tonight?" Aren asked, tapping the tips of his fingers against the frosted glass. He noticed a bump accompanied by the telltale purpling of a blossoming bruise on Dane's chin.

"I was getting bored waiting for you. Had a rough day after I left you at the House."

"*You* had a rough day? You and I have different definitions of 'rough.'" Aren took a long pull on his beer, welcoming the cool and frothy liquid down his throat. He slid down the chair just a little so he could lean back.

"Lana designed a new set of daggers, and Kel Bret spent the last week making the prototype, so Father wanted Gryf and me to fight with them, figure out if there were any flaws." Dane leaned back in his chair, mirroring Aren. "First, I showed up late, and Father yelled at me. Then, Rieka comes over, hot as the gods, yelling at me because I forgot we had made plans. Gryf starts laughing his ass off—"

"Gryf doesn't laugh." Aren smirked, thinking of their older brother's fierce, stone-like demeanor.

"You know what I mean. He gets that look like he might…" Dane took a gulp of his drink. "So after I punched Gryf, mother started lecturing me about my lack of sensitivity—"

"So that welt on your chin is where Gryf hit you back."

"It's been a bad afternoon." Dane rubbed at his face. "I guess it can't be as bad as yours was, considering what a mess you looked earlier. I was right about the rumors, though! Selina is going to be a Priestess!"

Aren drank down more of his beer. "Initially, you said I was chosen to be a sex slave."

"I said there were three popular rumors. Don't try to pin the wrong ones on me. You should be glad the House finally put out the official word about Selina. People were coming up with weird stories about you."

"Should I be glad that Selina's been chosen at random to serve gods she doesn't understand? Glad that she'll be joining a group of holier-than-my-shoes women who take care only of the blessed?" Aren grumbled, taking another swig of beer.

"What'll you do?"

"What can I do? They won't even let me near her—probably for fear that I'd corrupt her. I thought that I'd at least be able to be there so she won't feel alone and terrified."

"Together and terrified. You're right, that's much more comforting."

He nodded at Dane's chin. "I hope that hurts."

Dane grinned. "It does, if it makes you feel better." He took a drink. "You worry too much. You're overprotective. You need to take a step back and think about Selina's future."

"Since when did you become familiar with the word 'future'?" Aren chuckled, refilling their glasses. "Last I recall, father was lecturing you on selecting an apprenticeship."

Dane raised his glass, and Aren clinked his against it. "This isn't about me," Dane said. "This is about your narrow-minded way of thinking. Selina will never have a future because there's no record of a blessing."

"I have no blessing, but I've managed to do something with my life."

"You're my brother, blood or not, but the rest of the world sees you as Unblessed. With Selina, that'll be erased forever."

Aren took a drink, then put his glass down harder than he had intended, splashing some beer. "The world puts too much value on sacred, flowery words and not enough on what a person truly is."

Dane signaled the waitress for another pitcher of beer, then looked Aren in the eye. "You can't change the world, but like you said, you managed to change your life. You're apprenticed to the most powerful House in Cordelacht. Why not give Selina the same chance?"

"She's being forced to be a Priestess," Aren argued. "She didn't ask for it."

"Stop being so negative," Dane said, his tone conciliatory. "You're the only one she listens to. At least teach her to face a challenge head on. This won't be the hardest thing she does."

Aren stared into his glass, watched as little bubbles played on the surface. They were silent for a moment, and he was frustrated because his brother was probably right. The waitress came over, poured fresh glasses and left the new pitcher. Dane must have seen it as an opportunity to change the subject because he asked, "So what trouble did you get into that made you smell like rotting fish?"

Aren laughed, thankful for his brother's ability to read him. He took another swig and sobered up. "I watched Fisherman Henrik die out on the Taethe." Dane cocked his head as if he hadn't heard right, but Aren held up a hand. "Then, this mage, the one that killed Henrik, chased us into the Wood, and we got lost."

Dane nearly spit up his beer. He dragged an arm across his mouth. "What in the gods' names were you doing in the Wood? Have you gone mad?" A few patrons at the bar looked over at them. Dane cleared his throat and leaned into the table. "I'm sorry to hear about Henrik. I know he was a friend, but you're lucky you aren't dead too! Remember all the times Gryf and I had to drag your unconscious ass—"

"There's more," Aren interrupted him, feeling a little lighter now that he was able to get it all off his chest. "There was a gnome, mushrooms were lighting up, the headaches—stars, the headaches." Aren was rambling now, his memories flashing before him. "Then the unicorn, but that was kind of a good thing because it killed the mage—"

"The headaches are back?" Dane interrupted.

"Yes," Aren confirmed, leaning forward. "Did you hear me say 'unicorn'?"

Dane placed the flats of his palms on the table. "Unicorns were all killed off hundreds of years ago. You imagined a unicorn because of the headaches, and the headaches made you go into the Wood."

"This time was different. We ran into the Wood to get away from the mage. I wasn't called into the Wood like the other times, so I remember everything. There was a gnome; he claimed to know me."

Dane shook his head. "This is always how it starts. You get a headache, then it gets worse, then we're having to restrain you from going to the Wood—"

"And I manage to go anyway," Aren finished for him. "I remember that much."

"Well, the rest of us remember how we find you unconscious, sometimes beaten. You're ill for days afterward." Dane softened his tone. "I know you don't want to go through these episodes again, but the rest of us are just as gutted about it when we see what happens to you."

"I know."

"Gods, the number of times you've wandered into the Wood like a ghost and come out unable to remember a thing."

"I know."

"Stop agreeing with me," Dane demanded in a harsh whisper. "You were found beside the Wood. What if that's where you're from, and the creatures want you back? Why would a gnome claim to know you?"

"Mother said the Tinkerer found me by the road."

"By the road beside the *Wood*," Dane stressed. "Why were you even there?"

Aren jabbed at the table with a forefinger to emphasize each of his points. "First of all, I was just a child. How am I supposed to know? Second, it makes much more sense that I was dropped off or abandoned—or what have you—by travelers on the road, not travelers going through the Wood."

"Unless you're the spawn of lunatics," Dane offered. "Which, knowing you, is a real possibility."

"It doesn't help that I can't find a hint of who these lunatics were." Aren slumped in his chair. "The greatest Library in Cordelacht, and I can't find the two simple folks responsible for my birth."

"Maybe it's best we don't know what happened to you," Dane said. "It was a long time ago, and you have a family now. Finding out who your biological parents are isn't going to change you or where you belong. You've been obsessing about it for years; maybe it's just time for you to let it go." Dane thumped a finger against the table, then said, "It seems strange that these things are happening. I really thought you were done with this."

The musicians were playing more upbeat songs now, and people were getting up to dance. Aren and Dane watched for a while, letting the silence between them sweep away any tension. After a few measures, Dane took a big swallow of his drink, then poured again. Aren raised his glass in thanks, then said, "I can't stay much longer; I'm on an errand for Elder." He took down a gulp. "I might have had too much as it is."

"You just got back. Relax."

"Relaxing was the purpose of my trip, and look how successful that was. Everything was normal when I left, but since I've been back it feels like the world's tilted."

"Where've you been? The world's been tilting for a while now," Dane said, catching the condensation running down his glass. "People say the gods have been too silent. They say the Houses are going to go to war."

"You sure do listen to a lot of rumors," Aren chuckled.

"Father says we need to step up production," Dane continued, ignoring him. "He's had me working with Kel Bret while you were gone. Gryf's also been coming by the forge. We could use your help. The work went faster when you were still living at home."

Aren smiled at the memory. "I'll try to find time tomorrow. Right now, I'm on a quest for certain scrolls." He wanted to tell Dane about his conversation with Lady Geyle, but decided against it.

"What topic are you obsessed with now?" Dane asked.

"Curses."

"The kind you get when you wander into Tiede Wood?"

Aren dropped his voice to a whisper, ignoring Dane's comment. "Curses on the House."

Dane lowered his voice as well. "I'm guessing this isn't something Elder asked you to do. Why are you looking? The only curse I can think of is the death of Lady Elleina."

Aren looked perplexed. "The family volume says she died of an illness."

"Of course that's what it says, but people think that Lord Ren killed her or that she killed herself." Dane straightened up. "We shouldn't talk about it here. Lord Vir might lock us up."

"Well, he's going to lock me up anyway if he finds out I read that message I brought back," Aren whispered. "But you didn't hear me say anything about a message."

Dane looked like he wanted to punch Aren in the face. "I don't know about it. Gods, Aren, have you lost your mind?" He paused, then added, "What did it say?"

Aren got up, dropped enough silver on the table to cover Dane's entire evening. "Best you don't know."

Dane nodded. "You're probably right. Hey, stay a while longer. Sing harmonies with me on just one song, and we'll get enough in tips to pay for three nights of going out."

"I would but I can't, and you know I'm not big on singing in front of people the way you are. Give my love to Rieka."

"And you give Elder a swift thump on the back with your ugly new staff for me. Tomorrow, you'll tell me what that's all about."

Aren chuckled, readjusted his hood, then made his way out into the night. He was tired, but there was still so much left to do before he could return to the House. He should've grabbed something to eat. He decided to order a little something to take with him. He stood at the edge of the tavern crowd, his eyes darting, fishing for a waiter when he had the uneasy feeling that he was being watched. He looked around, his eyes concealed by the depths of his hood. No one paid him any mind, carrying on with their drinking and talking and laughing. He moved away from the lamplight and slipped a hand into his vest pocket; the key was still there. He was being paranoid. The key was making him nervous, and he had to get on with it so he could return it to Geyle. Eating would have to wait.

He was turning back towards the town center when he caught sight of a slender figure dressed in black crouched on the tavern's rooftop. He took a step forward to call out, when a shower of stars began to dance across the sky. It was so dazzling that it caught everyone's attention, and the people looked up, delighted and terrified. This was a rare omen from the Night god, and several people fell to their knees out of reverence.

Aren was enthralled by the display, but he returned his attention to the rooftop, where he watched a cloak follow its wearer away into the night.

TWENTY

Kaila cursed herself for allowing Aren to see her, but when his eyes had locked onto something in the skies, she found herself following his gaze and watching as the shower of light glittered. She shot upright, her eyes wide. "Alaric," she said under her breath, running across the tall and elaborate rooftops of Guild Row towards the Parthe Sea. When she descended from the guild house at the far eastern corner, she ran the remaining distance over the sand-littered cobblestone and hopped up onto the white slate wall. Over a thousand feet below, the Parthe Sea crashed against the sheer cliffs as if begging to be let in. She looked over her shoulder to make sure no one was around, then pushed herself off the wall, diving into the cold, churning water.

Alaric had been very clear in his message. *Come home immediately, Kaila,* the stars had relayed to her. She had been away for longer than she should have been, but she was so caught up and fascinated with her two mortals that returning home had slipped her mind. She'd made a reckless mistake.

Alaric's Keep sat overlooking the sea in the Realm of Night in a manner similar to Tiede. It was an imposing, black fortress patrolled by black-winged demons and protected by a gate of fire on one side and water on the remaining three sides.

There were thin crevices in the cliff through which the sea could enter, and Kaila allowed herself in, following the tight, underground vein that opened up into a fire-lit cave with high, smooth walls. She washed onto the course, black sand, squeezing the water from her hair and walking towards a section of mirrored wall. She straightened the silken black robes that concealed her as she stepped out of the water and examined her reflection. Then she secured the wide, turquoise, satin sash around her waist.

She took a tunnel leading from the underground cavern, passing several demons, who tucked in their wings and bowed their heads to her in respect. At the end of the tunnel, she walked up a short flight of stairs that led to a slab of marble door, where a large demon greeted her. She placed her hand on the door, and the demon followed suit, causing the door to vanish, allowing her into the Great Hall.

The Hall appeared to be a section of the vast night sky, without walls or ceilings or floor. Being in the room felt like falling through the stars, and only Alaric's people knew where to find the doors that led into and out of the Hall.

Tanghi was treading a path along the Guardian constellation. He rushed to Kaila when he saw her. "Where have you been?" he asked, concern etched on his dark face. "Alaric had a Summons, and you were supposed to be there," he said as he walked her to Alaric's study. "He was worried."

Kaila rolled her eyes. "What's to worry about? I can take care of myself."

He shortened his stride so that she could keep up. "Neither he nor I will ever forget that time when the fisherman—"

"That was a very long time ago!" she exclaimed.

He stopped her in the middle of the hallway. "Going to see Alaric in a bad mood isn't going to help. Sabana and Geir told Aalae they spotted you in Tiede among the mortals. What were you thinking?"

She wondered how they had known and why Geir would have given her up so easily. "I wasn't in any danger," she said at last.

They walked the remainder of the way in silence, but she reached for Tanghi's hand and gave it a little squeeze before letting go. If Alaric was angry then this was going to be unpleasant, and she needed a little of Tanghi's courage.

The doors to the study were wide open, and Alaric sat behind his desk, which was covered in maps and scrolls, glass vials of various sizes, and instruments used for measuring. Stardust littered the surfaces and floor like sand, glittering in the twilight.

Alaric held a long, thin dagger in his left hand, the thumb and index finger of his right sliding back and forth along the flat of the blade. When they entered, he didn't look up or acknowledge them. Tanghi took a seat by the hearth, far from Alaric's desk, and opened a book, pretending to read it.

Kaila stood before Alaric, her eyes focused on the rows of books behind him, waiting for him to speak. To her left, she could hear the sea rising and crashing. The crickets and cicadas called out to each other, chirping and singing like day birds. Thunder rumbled low in the clouds overhead, and the fire that wound itself around Tanghi crackled. Kaila waited, the noises seeming to get louder with Alaric's silence.

When he finally chose to speak, his voice was lower than a whisper, drifting in and out of the evening's rhythms. "I always expect you home by dawn, and I expect you immediately when I call, especially when I have to answer a Summons."

Kaila shifted her gaze from the books to his face and wished she could look into his eyes, which were focused on the weapon in his hand. His black-indigo hair was straight and fine as silk, falling past his shoulders to his elbows, and every so often was stirred by the winds drifting in and out of the room. His features were sharply defined: from his arched brows and strong nose to the jut of his cheekbones and the angles of his chin and jaw. His lips bordered on thin but had a softness and the slightest bit of color that made them inviting and pleasing to the eye.

You're so beautiful, she thought. *Please don't turn.*

He looked up from the blade and locked his eyes onto hers; she couldn't help but gasp, the anger evident in his gaze. "Why do you insist on disobeying me?" he asked without raising his voice. "What business did you have that kept you from coming home?"

She thought of Selina and Aren and felt it would be best not to mention them, but knew that she had to give up some truth or Alaric would see right through her. She concentrated on the shifting hues of night in his eyes, trying to find the gentleness she knew was there.

"I got caught up watching the mortals in Tiede. The Priestesses from Syrn have arrived, and the whole city is excited. I sat in the tavern, listening to their songs and watching their dances. I lost track of time. I promise no one saw me."

Alaric growled in his throat and slammed the blade onto his desk. Several vials shattered, the glass scattering. Kaila winced but held her ground. She knew her answer would upset him. She had counted on it.

He rose with the care and precision of a wild cat stalking its prey. He wore a black, fitted coat with a high collar, three wide leather straps buckling it tight against his chest. A long cape slipped from his shoulders to the heels of his boots. He leaned forward on his desk, palms pressed into the shards of glass, staining the papers beneath with a deep, inky red.

"Leave us, Tanghi," Alaric demanded.

Tanghi frowned and looked at Kaila. He opened his mouth as if to argue but closed it when Alaric's eyes bore down on him. He clenched his fists, bowed, and left the room. Alaric slammed the doors shut with a boom that caused more than a few books to tumble off the shelves.

Nothing could be as bad as the time when the fisherman had almost killed her or when Alaric had turned demon after he found out she had played cards with a mortal man. If he didn't turn, she could handle this.

Alaric dusted the glass off his hands and pulled a piece of fine linen cloth from a waist pocket, wiping off the blood as if it were water. He tossed it onto his papers and walked around to the front of the desk, his tall boots thumping against the stone floor. He stopped in front of her, leaned against the desk, and folded his arms across his chest. "We are preparing for war," he said, emphasizing each word. "The fate lines are changing so fast that my sister feels compelled to summon me over the Priestess count. Did you even know that Sabana and Geir were following you?"

"No, but I understand what you're saying, my Lord. It will not happen again."

Alaric hung his head and sighed. "Just words. You say this only to pacify me; you have no intention of changing."

She couldn't deny it, but she did feel a little bad for not making the effort. She didn't know what he had to go through to keep Aalae in check, and she understood that there was much more at stake than hurt feelings between the twins. There were mortals whose lives depended on the peace between the Night and Light Realms. It was their faith and worship that fed the gods and gave them power, so it was her duty to protect them as best she could, and she could accomplish that by listening to and obeying Alaric. She loved him, after all.

"I disobeyed you this time, but I will take care not to do it again."

He moved closer and she could feel him gauging her honesty. His lips turned up into a slight smile, and he placed his hands on her shoulders. "I worry about you," he said. "With the latest readings on the fate lines, and the concern about the new Priestess—"

"If there is anywhere on Cordelacht I am most protected, other than the Islands, it's Tiede."

He lowered his head, breathed in the scent of her, then placed a kiss on her cheek. "Watch the House and let me know what you hear of the new Priestess. She should fall under the Night's blessing, and Aalae has her sights on her. But I want you back here tomorrow morning and every morning after."

Kaila brightened and left Alaric to his papers and books and planning. She couldn't help but sigh in relief as she left the room, even though she knew he was still watching her. Tanghi waited just outside, leaning against a wall, staring at the floor. The ribbons of fire that were snaking around his forearms were dull and lifeless, but as soon as the doors to the study opened, he perked up. She grabbed his hand and led him back towards the Great Hall.

"You're pushing your luck," Tanghi pointed out. The fire surrounding him had become lively and bright again, but the tone of his voice told her he was being serious. "You're fortunate he didn't turn."

"He's so overprotective!"

Tanghi swept a large hand in the air, as if brushing aside her argument. "He's in love with you, and he has been for a very long time. If anything happened to you—"

"He is bound to Taia." She stopped and turned on him. "He can love me all he wants, but that won't break his bond, and I won't sit by his side like a lovesick mortal dreaming of the day he'll be free to be with me."

"I just want you to be more aware of why he acts as he does. Be honored that he should hold you so dear."

She nodded, but it hurt too much to talk about it. "I'm returning to Tiede with his blessing."

Tanghi stared at her for a moment longer, then said, "If you happen to come across Geir, make sure he's okay. He was at the Summons, but I sensed something off about him."

"I'll talk to him," Kaila promised. She'd find out exactly why he ratted on her too.

TWENTY-ONE

The Laithe Inlet was breathtaking. The waters were deep blue and washed up onto a creamy pebbled shore. The stark white cliffs of Tiede towered over the inlet, and remnants of a natural bridge seemed to stretch and reach to the point where it once connected the high western cliffs to the lower ones in the east. On a moonlit night, the Laithe was surreal: inky liquid, glowing rocks, and the splash of ghostly foam.

Kaila stretched out her legs and leaned back on her arms, watching the play of moonlight on the ocean surface as she tried to make sense of her actions. She had become fascinated with a pair of mortals and went so far as to place a powerful blessing on one and stalk the other. What was she thinking? No wonder Alaric was irritated; she was beginning to question her own logic.

She shook her head as if to make the doubt go away. She always had reasons for doing the things she did, and Alaric needed to learn to trust her. Kaila had blessed Selina because she wanted to protect her. It had been the right decision. The little girl had turned out to be the next chosen Priestess, and without a birth-blessing, she could have been taken in by either Realm. Kaila's blessing couldn't replace a birth-blessing, but it did bind Selina to the Night Realm. Alaric should thank her.

A breeze lifted Kaila's hair, and she turned in anticipation, joy filling her chest. The man who appeared resembled one of the angels, with his large white wings stretching then folding. Kaila jumped to her feet, leapt up onto the rock on which he was standing, and threw her arms around his neck.

"It's good to see you too," he said, returning her embrace. His breath was warm against her cheek, his voice like a lullaby.

"I've missed you, Geir."

"You would have seen me earlier had you shown up for the Summons." He let go of her. "Aalae took advantage of your absence."

Kaila remembered her anger with him. "She wouldn't have been able to take advantage if you hadn't told her I was in Tiede!"

"It wasn't me. Rafi has been tailing you."

"Rafi?" she echoed. Rafi was Aalae's mate, a master of potions, devious and oily. "Why would he be tailing me?"

"Because you are Alaric's weakness," Geir said, as if it were obvious.

She felt stupid and realized that everything Alaric had said about her being naïve was true. She didn't want to think about it, though.

Geir was with her now, and she always felt better in his presence. "What are you doing here?" she asked.

He kicked a pebble off the rock's ledge. "I have things to attend to, fate lines to untangle. I just happened to be in the area when I felt your presence."

"But you hate Tiede."

"Most days."

A silence settled between them, disturbed only by the wash of water over the rocks. Kaila wondered what she could say to make him stay longer.

"What are you doing here?" he asked, surprising her. "You're usually in the Islands when you're in a brooding mood."

"I don't brood!" she shot back. She cocked her head to the side and furrowed her brows. "I don't mean to brood."

He laughed a little, and the sound of it was heaven to her ears. Over the last several decades, Geir had changed. He used to be more carefree, always taking risks and following his heart. He never hesitated to relinquish his powers just to walk among the mortals, and it made Aalae furious. As rebellious as he was, he managed to remain obedient; so it came as a surprise when Geir disappeared one wet, spring day. He couldn't be found for weeks. He eventually showed up months later at a Council, his face shrouded, his body battered and scarred. Alaric said it was because his sister had punished him when he finally came home. The blindfold appeared not long after. Geir stopped laughing and joking, and spent most of his time with his birds.

To hear him laugh just a little was something akin to a miracle. Kaila had to keep talking, to keep him close. "The new Priestess has been chosen. I'm to watch over her until the initiation," she said.

"Everyone is waiting to find out about the blessing."

Kaila bit at her lower lip, wondering how much she should share. There were things she hadn't puzzled out, things that she had yet to tell Alaric, but she trusted Geir, and she was ready to tell him almost anything just to have him stay a while longer.

"The girl was Unblessed. I placed a blessing on her before I even knew she'd been chosen."

Geir's expression didn't change. "Now you're bonded, and you haven't told Alaric. It explains why you're brooding."

"The connection is stronger than any blessing I've bestowed before." Kaila wrung her hands. "Unless I figure out what compelled me to bless her, I can't tell Alaric, and I beg you not to mention a word of this to anyone."

He shrugged. "What does it matter? Because of what you've done, Aalae can't touch her."

"I just want him to hear it from me, and he's going to want a good reason as to why I've connected myself to a mortal. He'll want to know how I did it, what the situation was, and what risks I've created."

Geir spread his wings. "I promise I won't tell, but figure it out soon because war is coming; I can hear it on the winds. You did what you felt you had to do; let that be reason enough. Trust your instincts."

"I'll figure it out," she assured him. "I don't want Alaric to get angry because there was a man with the little girl, and—"

"Past the age of reason?" Geir's wings shuddered.

Kaila wondered why she was blushing. "Well, yes, but—"

"You know better, Kaila. Remember what happened to the card player in Kaishar? Go near this man and you endanger his life," Geir warned, spreading his wings open again. "He's in Tiede?"

"Yes; he's nothing—just the girl's guardian," she said, downplaying what she knew. "He works with the Elder in the House Library. He's harmless."

"Every mortal is something," he said, spreading his wings wider. "And I sense you're hiding something about this one."

TWENTY-TWO

Aren had to hurry. His paranoia over the key was growing, and he was imagining people stalking him. *Relax,* he told himself. *Look natural and everyone will either ignore you or curse you the way they always do.* He cut across the town center, the large House crest laid into the marble pavement in a gleaming star-metal. A ring of water protected by a shield of glass encircled the crest, the constant movement produced by an elaborate underground system that also fed into the various ornate fountains on display.

Aren reached into a pocket and pulled out a Tiede qint, a small copper piece, and flicked it into a random fountain without pausing. As he began to descend the northern steps of the market district, he recited to himself, "Wisdom to see beyond the reflection."

It was from a story he had read about a young man who explored one of the dozens of caverns tucked into the cliffs overlooking the

Laithe Inlet. Deep in the tunnels, he discovered a cave whose floor was made up of a gigantic looking glass. When he peered into the glass, his reflection showed him everything he desired: riches, women, power. He was mesmerized by how different he looked: handsome, strong, and well kept.

Then, a beautiful woman appeared, telling him that the reflection wasn't real. He didn't understand, so she asked him to throw a copper qint at the mirror. The mirror swallowed the coin, and ripples pulsed across the surface, concentric circles disturbing the once pristine reflection.

The woman turned out to be the Water goddess, and she told him that the pools were where wishes and dreams were stored, waiting to be released. To look into them was to see all that you wanted, but to look beyond the reflection, beyond your own shallow desires, was to find wisdom. The man was devastated and longed for the images he had seen. He stepped into the pool, and the moment he touched the water, a hundred hands reached out and pulled him under before the goddess could save him.

Aren wondered what he would see if he were the young man in the story. An image of whom his biological parents were, perhaps? A home where he blended in with all the other people, where he didn't look out of place? A woman who loved him for who he was and not for whatever she perceived him to be?

Wisdom to see beyond the reflection, he reminded himself. He shook away his wishes and pressed on.

Wethern's Oil & Torch Shop was nestled between a hat shop and an apothecary, both of which were closed. Aren had seen several signs along the way indicating that one shop or another was closed while the owner was away at the annual Relythaun Market. He hoped Wethern's had remained open.

Aren frowned at the darkness in the front window, then turned the door handle and found it locked. He rang the bell by giving the string by the doorframe a few tugs. At first, nothing happened, but he gave it a moment, his eyes scanning the upstairs window for any sign of movement. He was about to ring again when a man with a large head covered with thick brown hair leaned out the window.

"What is it?" The man's voice was gruff and slurred with sleep. Aren pushed back his hood to reveal his face and took a step into the pool of white light that fell from the streetlamp behind him in order for the man to see the crest embroidered on his sleeve. "House," the man mumbled. "I'll be right down."

Aren waited, then heard three locks click and grate against their will. The man pulled the door open with a grunt and gestured with meaty fingers for Aren to come inside. "Where's Mister Wethern?" Aren asked as he stepped inside, the man closing the door behind him. The shop smelled of straw, sandalwood, bitter citrus, and noxious incense. He winced, tempted to cover his nose but not wanting to offend.

"Headed to the Relythaun," the man said, walking past Aren to strike a matchstick and light a lamp sitting on the counter. The resulting light had a rose-colored tint to it, as did the oil from which the wick drank. The glass in the shop took on a strange grainy quality as the light touched it. "I'm Igmalanius Tunforq, his—as you call it here—apprentice. I go by Tun, since my name is hard for you Tiedans to pronounce. Now, who are you, and what can I help you with? I see you serve the House."

Tun had a way of leaning his upper body forward when he moved and spoke, as if his head were so heavy it caused him to tilt. The lean must have blocked something in his throat because his speech sounded like his words were being stepped on.

"Well, Apprentice Igmalanius Tunforq," Aren said the name with a clarity that informed the other that he wasn't stupid. "I'm Aren, the House Historian's Apprentice, and I need to purchase oil." Tun maneuvered himself around to the other side of the counter, where flasks and vials of all shapes and sizes winked along the wall like the liquors in a tavern. "Long-burning, smokeless. Wethern kept a special type for the House as well as an additive for use in the Library."

Tun grunted and something gurgled in his throat. He pulled a small flask down from the top row by using a long pole with a tiny horseshoe-shaped implement on the end. "This is the additive that won't cause the build-up," he mumbled, rubbing the hair on his immense head. "The House uses more oil than most. They should consider modernizing."

"It's a zealous Night House. Worship to the Fire god is important," Aren said. "I'll need a case of the House oil—better make it two."

Tun leaned the pole against a corner, and Aren pulled out his coins, counted out the right amount, then placed them on the counter.

"We're out of the fancy House oil," Tun said, scratching his head. "We're expecting a shipment from the docks tomorrow. The Harbor's been backlogged, as you can imagine."

"I'll see if someone can come by tomorrow," Aren said as Tun took note of the order in a large, leather-bound ledger. "Where are you from? It's odd that someone would apprentice here for"—Aren thought for a moment—"oil. We don't even have a guild here for this sort of thing. Rose would've been better."

"Rose might be better, but it's also further away. You won't have heard where I'm from; it's a small town on the southeastern end of the Plytain Wood."

"Pren-Holder," Aren said. "Belonged to the House of Kaishar, but something happened; nothing substantial written on it."

"The people of Pren-Holder have no allegiance to the House of Kaishar; we fought for our independence and won. Kaishar learned quickly that we're not meant to be its lapdogs."

"That's…interesting," Aren managed, pulling his hood over his head, then picking up the flask. "Maybe I'll visit Pren-Holder one day and do an exchange with their library."

Tun walked him out, his large shadow blanketing the glass and boxes as they passed through the store. "Really? I bet you've never even stepped foot out of Tiede."

"On the contrary, I just got back from the River Taethe this morning."

There was an awkward silence.

"The river," Tun said. "I misjudged you, Apprentice. It's good you made it back safely." He rolled up his sleeves as if preparing to lift more boxes. Aren caught a glimpse of the inking that seemed to cover the man's upper arm. Part of it looked like a leaf or plant, but he wasn't sure, and he didn't know what purposes they inked for in Pren-Holder. After a beat, Tun said, "I'll drop the House oil off tomorrow if our shipment comes in."

"I really appreciate it," Aren started as he stepped outside, but Tun had already closed and bolted the door.

STORIES

ONE

Aren's final stop for the evening was the Weavers Guild, but he felt a bit apprehensive about the task at hand and found himself looping around towards the residential district, taking the long way back to Guild Row from Wethern's.

His mind wandered as his feet took him down an alleyway. The shadows were at play here, and he cursed himself for not staying on the main roads. There wasn't enough light down this corridor—only enough to make his imagination create monsters out of darkness. A rough wind raced down the alley, and a chill followed in its wake, forcing him to reach for the hilt of the sword at his hip. He placed the flask of oil additive on the ground against the wall, certain that he wasn't alone. He glanced up at the rooftops, found nothing, then checked both ends of the alley, feeling trapped and stupid.

He didn't see a soul, but something felt very wrong. It had turned too cold for a summer night in Tiede, too dark for a high, clear moon and raining stars, and the wind had vanished as quickly as it had arrived.

Sensing a presence coming up behind him, he unsheathed his sword, bringing it up to block the shadow and bone that peeled itself off the wall and attacked him. The grating of Aren's sword against bone made him clench his teeth, and he pushed the thing back, preparing to defend himself against another strike.

Black smoke began to swirl, hinting at arms and legs, a shrouded head. Aren felt his mouth go dry as he wondered if this was the thing killing Tiede's people. Maybe it hadn't been caught because it wasn't a person; it was some sort of creature. The smoke vanished and he felt his heart beat faster. He forced himself to breathe, then concentrated on the air currents around him. He felt the shift of space behind him before he heard the movement of broken pebbles underfoot, and he brought his blade up again to deflect another blow. The creature was strong, and a hiss accompanied by a rank, sulfurous smell slipped out from where he imagined a face might be.

Aren pushed again, this time following up with a series of strikes. How long could the thing use its bones to defend itself? As if to answer Aren's unspoken question, the creature manifested a blade. Gleaming crimson, pulled from some invisible sheath, blocked Aren's every blow. This thing was good, and he had a feeling it was just playing with him. Then, it sniffed his hair.

"*T'jand!*"

The monster's raspy voice had a smile in it, and Aren filtered through all the languages in his head, unable to place this one. Lost language or bastard language, maybe. He committed the monster's words to memory, determined to research them if he made it out of this alive.

"*A'diekki mei,*" Aren replied in Ancient. It was the oldest language he was most proficient in, and that wasn't saying much. "I don't understand."

The creature laughed, like bone scraping against bone. Aren winced, but his eyes caught the faint glow of red pulsing just beneath the surface of the smoke. He tried to focus and piece together the disjointed symbols. The crimson sword vanished.

T'jand, you did well. I smell the blood. It spoke some of its words in Common, and Aren was even more confused than before. The creature leaned its head in closer, and Aren could make out yellow, reptilian eyes. It inhaled, and Aren took a step back, his sword at the ready. *Magic. Niaf'kur. Soon, I will be strong. Do not worry. Catar ni zri.*

Aren opened his mouth to ask what it meant, but the smoke vanished, and he was alone. What in the stars had just happened? He sheathed his sword, feeling the air around him return to normal. He blew his hair out of his eyes, then recovered the flask. Damn this errand for the Lady. He needed to get back to the Library and figure out what that creature had said to him. He had to tell the House that a thing made of smoke was on the loose. He sounded like a crazed lunatic, even to himself.

Footsteps began approaching down the alley, and Aren drew his sword again, wondering what was going to attack him next. Flashes of green caught in the unsteady light like the eyes of a wild beast, and three heads moved towards him with unified purpose. Aren considered throwing the flask of oil at it to give himself a head start.

His throat dried up and he licked his lips, torn between taking off and standing his ground.

Aren was frozen in place when the streetlamp at the end of the alley made a sizzling noise, flickered for a moment, then illuminated the area with a moon-like wash.

"Aren! I knew it was you!" the young woman squealed, running over and latching onto his arm. She wore a miniature black velvet top hat over her reddish-gold curls. Her face was touched with blush, shiny copper shadow, and rouge, and the bare tops of her breasts were heaved up by the dark corset she wore over her frilly white blouse. Her silk, jade-green skirts were bustled and long in the back, but short in the front, showing off black thigh-high boots laced snug along the shaft. Around her neck was a dainty yet stunning collar of sparkling, light-green gemstones. At twenty-two years old, Trista acted like a child and flirted like a harlot.

Cocking her head at him, she said, "Are you all right?"

Aren lowered his arms and sheathed his sword, feeling like an idiot. A drop of sweat rolled down his temple. "You should've seen that rat; I swear it was the size of a gree. I must've scared it away." He looked down at the wide, blue eyes staring up at him and forced a smile. "Good evening, Miss Trista." Then he looked to the two men who had accompanied her and inclined his head in greeting. They wore the robes of the Apprentice, but he couldn't tell their field of study. The bigger man only stared at him, but the tall, lean one nodded. So much for Aren's three-headed monster.

Trista giggled and squeezed his arm. "Stop being so formal with me. Where have you been? The whole town was looking for you."

He began to walk, letting her cling to his arm for a while longer. "I'm on House business."

"There's more to life than the House and your books and the old man." Her voice, which he had once considered bright like a golden bell, was starting to give him several small headaches behind his eyes, each stabbing pain reminding him of how idiotic he was to fall for a pretty face.

"The House, the books, and even the old man *are* my life," he said. "It might not seem like much to you, but it makes me happy. You forget that we have nothing in common." She frowned, and he could see the gloss of tears in her eyes. He could try to be gentler, but she hadn't picked a good time to bring up whatever imaginary relationship she thought they had. "I'm sorry. I didn't mean for you to get the wrong impression about us," he said, softening his tone.

He turned and walked away, done with the conversation and the sour memories that came with it.

Aren was nearing the end of the alley when she cried out, "I still love you!" She was walking towards him again. "You need to give us a chance!"

He stopped and sighed, his shoulders slumped. "Trista, please go home. It's late and your friends don't need to hear this."

As if on cue, her companions joined her, and the leaner one wrapped an arm around her shoulder and looked at Aren with amusement. "At least now we get to see what the fuss was all about," he said, a slight accent in his voice. Like Aren, his skin tone was tawny, but his eyes were hazel, his hair a lighter brown. He looked Tennari. "She's called me Aren once or twice when she's had too much to drink."

Aren raised an eyebrow; he didn't care to discover the context in which his name had been misspoken. "You know my name but I don't know yours."

The bigger man didn't say a word, but a soft glow emanated from his shoulders, indicating he was marked. Aren wasn't sure if he should take it as a threat.

"Inra Mercer of Tennar. You apprentice in the House, then?" the Tennari asked, interrupting his thoughts.

"Yes," Aren hesitated, "and I should be getting back. I don't want to make Lord Vir angry."

"Of course not," Mercer said, glancing at Trista before shooting Aren a look that made him uneasy. "Trista, I hope this has been enough to get him out of your system. Let's leave him be. He's apparently a very busy man."

TWO

If Aren had believed in bad omens, he would've returned to the House and gone straight to bed—the Lady and her key be damned. The monster in the alley was the drawing of the death card, but bumping into Trista and her weird friends had ended the game for him. Unfortunately for Aren, there was no quitting the game. He had nothing to win or lose; he could only go about his business, do what was asked of him.

Aren stopped in front of the Weavers Guild and looked up at the building. Its clean architectural design, with its tall columns and triangular pediments, was reminiscent of the neoclassical period. But this particular Guild wasn't anything magnificent, unlike some of the others. The Horticulture Guild, Aren recalled, with its steep gables and arches, was more in line with current architectural styles— breathtaking both inside and out, with its elaborate gardens and showy vine work. And the Technical Arts Guild, where his sister Lana taught, was a wonder of glass planes and lines of lacy metal within its high domes and vaulted ceilings.

Aren took a step forward and thumbed the mechanical bell, then glanced up at the rooftop and checked the streets from the depths of his hood. Nothing suspicious. He wondered if he seemed suspicious. While it wasn't uncommon for the House to send servants and apprentices about at any time, he wondered if it was strange for him to be asking about fabric this late in the evening.

When the door opened, a young girl draped in black apprentice robes stood before him, her head lowered and unhooded. "Master, how may we be of service to the House this evening?" she recited.

"Just 'Apprentice,'" he said. "I'm on an errand for Lady Geyle. She asked me to see Apprentice Caley."

She stepped aside and gestured for him to enter the foyer. The white marble floor reflected the ornate, crystal chandelier that hung from the ceiling. Just ahead was a staircase, and to the left and right, archways opened up to various rooms. When the young apprentice closed the door behind him, Aren lowered his hood. A small gasp escaped her, and she averted her eyes, the tops of her brown cheeks flush. "You may leave your things here, if you like," she said, indicating the flask he was holding. He complied, setting the flask on a rosewood console table against the wall just inside the door.

Aren had only entered the Weavers Guild a handful of times, each time on House errands or to get fitted for his robes. When they entered the parlor, Aren's eyes were drawn to the large painting hanging over the fireplace that dominated the room. It depicted a woman with rich, black skin. She sat at a loom, her long fingers working. She wore a gown of emerald green into which the most intricate patterns of knots had been stitched with golden threads. Her feet were bare, and her head bowed at her work, long braids of gold, silken hair spilling around her.

"It's our patron goddess Sabana," the girl whispered. "The Guild received the painting as a gift from Rose when Lady Geyle was married to Lord Vir."

"She's beautiful," Aren breathed, unable to look away from the striking colors and the way the goddess seemed to move within the frame. She was regal and strong, the very definition of perfection.

"Gods, yes. You are beautiful," the girl breathed. She cleared her throat. "Please, just wait here."

Aren snapped out of his reverie and furrowed his brows. His guide made her way over to a girl sitting on a plush, green velvet chaise studying fabric patterns and then whispered something in her ear. The older apprentice looked towards the doorway, then stood up to follow. The others, lounging about the room with their textbooks, whispered amongst themselves, watching. Aren smiled, telling himself to look friendly and at ease. He was here to check on the Lady's dress.

When they reached him, the younger girl bowed and took her leave. "Apprentice Denfar Caley," the older girl said, a lilt in her voice that sounded similar to Geyle's. "You asked to see me, Apprentice Aren?"

"You know who I am?" He took a small step back, his eyes narrowing a little, one eyebrow higher than the other.

Caley looked like a young boy with her plum-colored hair cropped short in the back, and whatever figure she had, concealed within the black robes. Her eyes were sharp, studying his face. "And you know who I am. Now, what is it the House needs?"

Aren cleared his throat, recalling the lines he had come up with. "The Lady of the House asked me to find out if the fabric for her dress is ready." He ran a hand through his hair. "Or see how it's progressing." Stars, he was messing this up, and he felt his face getting hot. "I know it's late, but I had to attend to other errands anyway, so she asked if she could trouble me. Of course, right? As if I would turn down Lady Tiede." He pressed his lips together. "So, how's the material? I mean, fabric?"

Caley started, her brows furrowing deep atop the bridge of her nose. "The fabric for her dress. Lady Geyle's dress." There was no question in her tone, but it was all over her face.

He raised his eyebrows, cocking his head to the side. "Is there a problem?"

"I guess her maids couldn't be trusted with such a task?"

He shrugged. "I happened to be there when she needed someone. I have no idea how she feels about her maids."

She stared at him, and he did his best not to cave under her scrutiny. He thought the tip of her nose turned up in a cute way and was sure that she would punch him in the face for thinking it, so he tried to remove the thought from his head.

"Lady Geyle must be desperate. What do you even know about fabric?" she asked.

He rubbed the stubble along his jawline and made a show of thinking. "I think it's great for making dresses"—he paused—"like the one the Lady asked me to check on. Any chance we could get on with it? I have to get back to the House."

She scowled, but after a beat said, "Follow me."

She led him past the stairs then down a hallway past a few darkened, quiet rooms he assumed were for classes. They turned at the end of the hallway, and Caley led him through another room and into an adjoining room the size of a noble's closet. Large white cabinets lined three of the walls, but on the one opposite the entrance was an old wall unit with square drawers similar to ones found in an apothecary or teahouse, only larger.

Caley walked to the bottom left corner and removed a drawer full of scrap fabric, placing it on the table in the center of the room. She stared at Aren. "Are you from Rose?" Her words were blunt and demanding.

"No, and the Lady didn't say anything about being asked such questions."

Caley's eyebrows furrowed again, and he could see a flush of pink rise to the tops of her cheeks and ears; that, combined with her plum-colored hair, made him think of festival candy, and it made him hungry.

She turned back to the empty drawer space, got down on all fours, and reached inside. There came the sound of something clicking into place. Aren heard the slide of a small door against a track, then watched as Caley stood up, a small, plain wooden box in her hands. She handed it to him and dusted off her robe.

"Are you from Rose?" he asked. "I remember seeing you in one of my sister's classes about the functional beauty of lines or something crazy like that. I was dropping off a sword she designed."

Caley took a step back, and the expression on her face was one of confusion. "I don't think this is the best time to chat, and I shouldn't leave you in here by yourself for long. It would be best if you…checked on that fabric and left."

"Right," he chuckled.

"Let me know when you're done," she said and then turned to leave, casting a wary glance at him and closing the door.

Aren turned the box over in his hands, looking for any markings or hints of what could be inside. Finding none, he pulled the key out of his pocket and slipped it into the keyhole. He took a deep breath. He was running an errand for the Lady, he told himself. She had sent him on this task, and as a loyal member of the House, he was bound to obey.

Aren turned the key until he heard a click. He lifted the top, hoping the hinges wouldn't creak, feeling that if they did, the entire Guild might hear it. The box remained silent, refusing to tell him anything. He looked inside and found a light-green silk cloth. He pulled it with a flourish, realizing only when he saw something fly into the air that the object had been wrapped inside the cloth and that he had flung it towards the heavens. He cursed, dropping the box and stretching to reach out over the table to catch the thing.

The box crashed against the floor with a loud clatter. As he stretched across the table, he bumped into the drawer containing the scraps of fabric, causing it to slide. He reached to stop it from falling, but his fingers only brushed against it, tipping it enough to send it over the edge. He winced as it clattered to the floor, scattering the fabric.

Aren slid across the table, his arm out as the object fell past the tabletop. He felt the velvet as it slid between his index and middle fingers, and he squeezed his fingers together, gripping the thing tight. His momentum sent him over the table, and his left arm went out to absorb the blow he knew was coming as he careened towards the floor.

His long legs managed to flip over his head and collide with the drawers of the wall unit, causing a few of them to bounce out of their spaces and fall onto the floor beside him. He stood up in a panic, smashing his head against the underside of the table, then collapsed onto the floor again, curled up in pain.

There was a soft knock on the door. "Apprentice, is everything all right in there?" Caley asked, her tone a mixture of accusation and suspicion.

"Everything's fine. You're not supposed to ask me questions."

There was a pause. He could feel her indignation through the door. After a moment, he got to his feet, more careful of his surroundings. He rubbed at his head as he looked down at the pale-pink velvet pouch in his hand. "This thing is going to get me killed," he mumbled.

He set it on the table and hurried to shove the fallen drawers back in place, then pushed the fabric into a pile. He guessed there might be a system similar to the one in the Library that defined which fabrics went in which drawers. That's how he would have done it, so he left them there for Caley to sort through.

He ran his hands through his hair, picked up the pouch, and loosened the drawstrings. He pulled out a clear glass vial shaped like a teardrop and held it up to the light that shone from the lamp hanging over the center of the room. The faceted glass mirrored the light, throwing it against the walls in strange rhomboid shapes like confetti.

He brought the vial closer to his face, tipping it back and forth then upside down. An iridescent, tinted liquid appeared to be inside. He tried to smell it, wondering if he could liken it to a type of liquor Dane drank, but the cork stopper that was sealed in place with white wax kept him from smelling anything.

He replaced the vial and pulled the drawstrings tight. He picked up the box that had housed the vial as well as the green silk cloth that he blamed for the multiple bruises he knew he would have in the morning. He closed and locked the box, then pocketed the key and pouch.

When he stepped outside, Caley was waiting, her arms folded across her chest, her fingers tapping against her arms. "I will tell the Lady of your progress," Aren recited with a nod, then made his way out of the Guild, hurrying back to the House.

As he made his way up the eastern stairs, he thought about the rooftops, the messages, the oil, and the curses. With the constant movement of people and gree around him, he never saw just who or what it was that slammed him hard from behind.

He fell forward, the flask of oil flying from his grip. Hearing it crash, he winced. His other hand went to cradle the vial in his breast pocket, cushioning it as he hit the stone steps, his arms taking the brunt of the impact.

People were screaming all around him, fleeing the stairs, and he shook his head, clearing his vision to look for his attacker. Then, something struck his head, spinning him around. His back hit a wall, and he crumpled to the steps again, the air rushing out of his lungs. He felt the sensation of being sniffed, and tried to move away.

The last thing he remembered was a man's quiet voice asking, "How is it you attract so much trouble? I hope you are worth it."

THREE

Kaila found herself in the clearing in Tiede Wood, the water from the creek she had summoned just the other day gurgling over her bare feet. After Geir had left her back at the Laithe, she had returned to the spot where she had blessed Selina, hoping something would enlighten her.

The Wood was alive with the reveling of faeries, nymphs, and spirits. Kaila could hear the music and laughter just outside of the clearing, could see the playful glowing orbs of colored lights pulsing among the trees. The Wood folk kept a respectful distance, but they made no effort to hide their curiosity, peeking from behind the trees and whispering to each other.

Kaila did her best to put them out of her mind and concentrate. The prevailing image in Selina's memories was rain. There was an image of Aren running towards her during a terrible rainstorm. Why had it rained? Kaila closed her eyes, trying to recall some of the worst storms in the past five years. She could think of a few, and most of those were the result of a heated argument with Alaric.

One such incident had occurred a handful of years ago, at the height of the aurorae displays. The aurorae were summoned at the start of the autumnal moon harvest and continued all through the winter, fading away around the spring rebirth. The spectacular light shows were the Night Realm's way of celebrating the lengthened night. It was like a game for Alaric and Tanghi, and they streaked the skies with ribbons of light and color, each trying to outdo the other.

Kaila had just returned from a visit to the House of Kaishar. It had been a fine evening, and it should have turned into a quiet morning, but Taia, Alaric's mate, was in a foul mood. She sat in Alaric's chair, a yawn escaping her burgundy-painted lips.

Alaric, on the other hand, had been in a good mood, laughing and playing like a child. He and Tanghi threw stardust at each other, taking their play fight into the skies, a mess of black wings and fire. Alaric was affectionate and made no effort to conceal his desire for Kaila, wrapping his arms around her, teasing. His actions had served to drive Taia over the edge, and she informed Alaric of Kaila's secret escapades in Kaishar—how she spent her evenings playing cards with a young man, how the mortal had fallen in love with her.

Alaric had gone mad, his demon marks covering his skin as his wings and horns emerged. Kaila, furious with his jealousy, had fought him, and it took all of Tanghi's power and persuasion to come between them. As punishment, Kaila had been confined to the Keep, and she and Alaric raged at each other for weeks. He had even gone so far as to kill the mortal, bringing her his lifeless body to mourn over.

Kaila opened her eyes and shook her head, as if trying to rid herself of the memory. She had to concentrate on Selina.

It would help to know when Selina's rainstorm took place. Kaila wondered if Aren could recollect the storm in Selina's head, or at least the timeframe. She would have to talk to him as a mortal and relinquish her powers, but it might be worth it. Selina was linked to him somehow, so he might have the answers. Kaila would keep her contact with him to a minimum, merely asking him to point her in the right direction. Tiede's Library was a wealth of information, and it wouldn't be anywhere near as daunting as having to visit the Chrono Keeper Wenyari.

Her mind was made up. As long as she checked in with Alaric by dawn, he would never have cause to worry. She would get her answers, provide Alaric with the explanation for why and how she had placed the blessing on the girl, and all would be well. She couldn't help but smile to herself, pleased that everything was falling into place.

"With a smile like that, I know that trouble is just around the corner."

Kaila looked up to see Sabana at the edge of the clearing, a green fae peeking from behind her hip while a few other faeries jostled for a good vantage point among the trees. Sabana stepped into the clearing, raising a hand to stop the fae-folk from following her.

Kaila splashed through the small creek and gave Sabana a hug. "Good evening, sister."

"Our sweet little girl," Sabana cooed, placing a kiss on her head. "What are you doing here? Have you forgotten this is Tiede Wood?"

"Just passing through." Kaila smiled, pointing at the creek. "I saw Geir earlier when I was out on the Laithe. Is he getting better at all?"

Sabana only shrugged. "He will never be the spirit we once knew. We've tried to get him back. I even gave him this Wood in the hopes that he would see it as a sort of peace offering."

"Tiede Wood belongs to Geir?"

"It was a very long time ago, before the blindfold, and he didn't say much beyond 'thank you' before returning to his mopey self."

"You know he hates Tiede," Kaila pointed out.

"All of the Light Realm hates Tiede," Sabana sighed, clearly done with the conversation. "Are you busy? The Wood is alive and merry. Join me and stop worrying about Geir so much."

"I would, but I told Alaric I'd return home. I would love it if the four of us could spend time together again, though. We used to hunt the stars."

Sabana turned, heading out of the clearing, her long emerald gown trailing behind her. "Times have changed. Our masters are at war, and so we must be. These little blessings, these rare times alone with each other, will soon fade."

FOUR

Aalae was sitting in her garden, bathed in sunlight, books spread out around her on the lush green grass. She bit down on a reddish-pink apple, savoring its crispness and tartness as she studied a passage from the Book of Inception. The passage told of how Mahl had brought her and her brother to this planet. She took another bite of the apple and reread the passage. Nothing on when their father would return or why he had left them here in the first place. No key to destroying Tiede, her brother's largest power source.

She slammed the book closed and tossed the half-eaten apple over her shoulder before leaning back on her hands. Patience was not a trait she displayed, desired, or admired.

"Temper, temper."

Aalae watched as her mate sat down beside her. He nuzzled her cheek, placed a kiss on her mouth. "Rafi, my love," she said, running fingers through his bronze-colored hair. "Do you bring news?"

"Yes, but not good news." He picked up the book she had been reading and flipped through the pages. "The mages are rising again. In the east this time."

"Those ignorant clowns," she huffed. "How long did it take to scatter them last time?"

"Several seasons," he said, putting down the book. "And that was with your brother's help."

"I want to take Tiede, but you're suggesting that I might have to work with Alaric instead?" She sent a thought out to her Knights.

Rafi slid his fingers through several strands of her long curls. "I'm afraid so, darling. Trum is in serious trouble, and I'm not sure how long the House can hold out. The mages have never been this organized, this brazen." Asking for Alaric's help to quell the mages was not how she had hoped to start this war. She tightened her fists, a high-pitched scream threatening to escape her clenched teeth. "I'll mix something up to help ease your nerves," Rafi said, running a finger up and down her bare arms. "Look, here's Sabana."

Aalae didn't look but she heard the woman's rich voice, full of concern, say, "My Lady, what's the matter?"

"Where is Geir?" Aalae asked. When no one answered, she shrieked, repeating, "Where is Geir?"

A shadow passed over them as a beat of wings disrupted the air. In one long, graceful dive, the spirit presented himself on one knee, his blinded eyes directed towards the ground. "My Lady," he said in his quiet voice.

"Where have you been?" Aalae asked.

"The northlands," he said, still on one knee. "The summer season is coming to a close; it's time for transition."

"And do you always take your time when you are summoned?" she asked.

"My Lady," Sabana said, "he was only the slightest bit later than me."

"Your back. Show me," Aalae demanded, ignoring Sabana.

As Geir stood up, his wings dissipated, feathers falling loose all around him before being carried off in the wind. He turned his back to the goddess and waited, the quickened rise and fall of his chest the only indication of the adrenaline coursing through his system.

Rafi helped Aalae to her feet. She stepped forward and ran a hand over the golden skin of Geir's back, catching the slightest scar here and there where his healing powers were still working to remove the blemish entirely. His skin was warm and smooth, but he had thinned since he had put on the blindfold, and she couldn't help but recall what a beautiful specimen he had once been. An involuntary chill ran up her arm, and she gasped as she pulled her hand away from him.

"Does it please you to touch me, my Lady?" Geir said, his tone defiant and reckless.

"Geir!" Sabana hissed. Her hand went out to grab his arm, but she stopped herself and clenched her fists, keeping them at her sides.

The sound of electricity filled the air as Aalae took a few steps back and gathered the light to her, shaping it into a whip. Rafi and Sabana moved behind her as she wielded her favorite weapon, flicking and snapping it, sparks of light showering around them. The whip glowed with white light, the power sizzling along the thong.

"Please reconsider," Sabana said, "he's no good to us if he's wounded."

Aalae shrieked, loosing the whip so that it cut diagonally across Geir's back. A sharp intake of breath came as the light seared him, burning him with the force of a thousand stars.

She loosed her whip again, but this time the thong wrapped around his neck, and she pulled until he was standing before her, wanting but not daring to grab at the hot cord.

"The mages are the only thing saving you from my wrath," she said, vanishing the weapon. Geir's hands flew to his neck, where a bright-red welt was forming around it. Pricks of blood began to ease through his skin. "Your arrogance and stubbornness are pushing my limits. Go with Sabana to Trum and keep the mages away from the House. Once you've fought them back, I want a report on how bad the damage is so I can determine if I truly must call on my brother for his aid."

"Yes, my Lady," Geir rasped.

"What's going on in Tiede?" Aalae asked, changing the subject. "Give me something to work with."

"The new Priestess has been confirmed and is in the process of pre-initiation," Sabana said. "She's just a child, and Kaila has been in Tiede watching her."

Aalae looked at Sabana with wide, questioning eyes. "Why would Alaric ask to have the new Priestess watched?"

"I don't know." Sabana shrugged. "I was hoping Kaila would give me some information, but she was nonchalant about the whole thing."

"But why Kaila?" Aalae asked. "Alaric isn't quick to let her near the mortals. She must be doing it behind his back."

"I spoke with her," Geir interjected hoarsely. "I ran into her before Sabana did. She's there with Alaric's permission, provided she remains in her element. He wants to keep her occupied, and Tiede is a safe place for her if she keeps to her element."

Aalae lifted a fine eyebrow at him, a smile lighting up her face. "Geir, I only wish I didn't have to hurt you to get you to cooperate." He lowered his head—in shame or concession or fury, Aalae couldn't tell and didn't care.

"What do you want to do about the new Priestess?" Rafi asked. "They haven't announced which god she belongs to."

"Nothing yet. Let's take care of Trum. The pieces might all come together before I summon my brother again."

FIVE

After waking with a throbbing headache, the bruises on his torso aching horribly, Aren swung his legs over the side of the bed. Everything came rushing back to him: the oil, the man with the big head, a monster, Trista, magic, the vial.

He opened the trunk at the foot of his bed and hid the vial and key in a sock he'd been meaning to ask his sister to darn for him just to make her mad. Then, he locked the trunk and took a deep breath. He needed to know what had happened. Elder would know. There would be some reasonable explanation for everything. Then, Aren could make his way to the baths. It was the best place, aside from the Library, to think. No one, aside from the House Lord, had used the saltwater baths in over half a century, which was another reason why it was one of Aren's favorite places in the House.

He stripped off his clothes, tossed everything into the laundry basket, then threw on a dark-blue bathrobe. His muscles protested with every move. He padded his way to the second floor of the Library and was glad to find it unlocked. It meant that Elder was somewhere inside, probably at his desk. Aren was silent as he descended the steps, his bare feet cushioned by the plush midnight-blue carpet.

Elder had his back to him, standing at his desk, studying a map. As Aren approached, the old man said, without turning, "Are you sneaking up on me in the hopes of giving me a heart attack?"

Aren chuckled as he came up to Elder's side. "I'm not trying to scare you. You have a sixth sense, so you always know when I'm around."

"Yes," Elder said, looking at him, then frowning. "I have a sixth sense for disaster. What in Aum are you doing in here in your bathrobe? Have you lost your mind?"

"I was on my way to..." Aren looked around as if someone else might be there to explain what had happened. "Do you know what happened to me last night?"

"Do you mean to ask why you look like you were in a fight with a demon and without the oil I asked you to pick up?"

"Well, I can explain the oil—"

"A creature was spotted after it attacked you," Elder cut him off, turning his attention back to the map. "It knocked you out and you dropped the flask you were carrying. According to witnesses, it sniffed you before tearing apart two people in front of you. I suppose you didn't smell appetizing. A soldier was nearby when it happened.

You were unconscious when he picked you up and brought you to the House. I had him leave you in your room, and Lord Vir ordered some of his own Guards and Hunters to find the thing."

"And did they? What was it?"

"They couldn't track it; it disappeared like smoke, and no one could say with any confidence whether it was man or gree or the Night god himself. The Hunters found another dismembered body at the east end of Guild Row, and there's a fruit merchant gone missing. You're lucky to be alive. I'd tell you to send a thank-you note from the House to the soldier, but in the commotion, no one knew who it was, and no one has stepped forward to take credit for saving you. Not that I blame them."

Aren shoved his hands into the pockets of his robe, uncomfortable with the fact that he'd had two near-death experiences in one night — three in two days, if he counted the unicorn. There was also that mage who had tried to kill him...

"Stop lounging around and get to the forge." Aren racked his brain to remember why he was supposed to be at the forge, but Elder interrupted his thoughts. "Your eldest brother called this morning to see if you could be spared for a few hours. He said Dane mentioned it to you last night." Aren's conversation with Dane came back to him, and he nodded. "I need you back before evening. I'm only allowing you to go because I have a great deal of respect for the Masters Gerrit."

"Yes, Elder," was all Aren could manage as his mind began to reshape the events of the previous evening.

"Make your beauty bath quick," Elder growled. "I don't know why you can't use your private bath like a normal person."

"Lord Vir uses the salt baths in the evening," Aren pointed out before leaving. He headed down the hall towards the baths and was almost there when he stopped and turned back in the direction of his room. There was no time. He'd wash in his room, rush to the forge to see his family and help out, then hurry back to work.

Aren slicked his hair back as he hurried through the stone corridors in the lower level of the House, passing a few servants on the way and wishing them a good day. The girl who did his laundry — her brown hair tied up in a black ribbon, his only confirmation of who she was — gasped, then hid her face in her hands as he rushed past her. He came up at the stairway by the kitchen and was stopped by one of the cooks, who pressed a warm biscuit wrapped in wax paper in his hand, ignoring his protests.

"You're late this morning!" she said. "Everyone's heard the news, and I'm just so thankful you're alive!"

He gave up on trying to argue, smiled, and thanked her as she giggled and pushed him on his way. Not realizing how hungry he was until the smell of the biscuit wafted up his nose, he tore open the paper, devouring half the biscuit in one bite.

He strode down to the other end of a long hallway and up a set of stairs that most people overlooked because it was tucked into a strange, old alcove that let out next to Lord Vir's bedchamber. He finished off the biscuit and wadded the paper as he took the worn, stone steps up two at a time. As he crossed outside of the room, he noticed that one of the large double doors was ajar, and he caught the scent of the sea on a breeze that drifted in through the room's large windows. He crept across the hall, not wanting to call attention to himself. As he passed, he heard Geyle's voice, and it sounded as if she were crying. He paused and listened while part of his brain told him to keep moving.

He really had to stop ignoring his brain.

"I'm so tired of this, Vir!" Geyle said through sobs. "I want to visit my family. I need some time for myself, away from Tiede."

"You're being overly dramatic about this," Vir said. "It's not safe to travel, and what would people think if I had my wife sent away? They'd think it wasn't safe in Tiede. You've heard what's going on out there."

"Why is it okay for Illithe to visit?"

"It's just my aunt and grandfather."

"Your grandfather is as fragile as a butterfly wing! He's the most ill-equipped to make the journey!"

"I'm not going to waste time arguing over this. My family will be here this evening." Vir's voice sounded a little more agitated, and Aren wondered if that was his cue to leave, but he didn't move. "Freshen up and go for a walk with your ladies in the garden. If it pleases you, I will even go so far as to ask Elder to release his Apprentice to you for a few hours since all your talk earlier leads me to conclude that you enjoyed his company, however brief. Maybe he can calm your nerves."

"You were in Council, and he stopped to talk when I asked him to." Her voice was quiet now, and Aren had to strain to hear her. "He was a complete gentleman."

"I only noted how happy you sounded when you brought it up, and I prefer it when you're happy. Have I not given you whatever you've asked for?"

"I don't ask for much."

"And what you do ask for, I always try to provide."

"I'm sorry, Vir." Her tone was submissive. "I'll take a walk as you suggest."

Aren bolted for the corner, slowing once he had turned it, telling himself to look natural. He walked the rest of the way to his room, then paused at his door. Stars, what had she said about him to Vir?

He thumped his head against the door to his room, winced from the pain, and looking down, noticed a slip of paper on the floor just under the door. He glanced around, and seeing no one, stooped to retrieve it. It was a small piece of parchment, folded and creased neatly in half. He opened it and was surprised to see it was written in Ancient. He frowned as he worked out the translation:

Keep your distance. I only saved your life for her happiness.

Aren looked around again, wondering if this was some sort of joke, but a shiver ran down his spine. In the House, only Elder was fluent in the old language, and this neat, precise scroll was the opposite of the old man's ragged script. Also, whoever left the note knew that he had a decent understanding of Ancient and that writing it in the old language would serve as a sort of secret code.

"*Kiakt'i'ko,*" Aren cursed under his breath.

SIX

Selina panicked when she woke up, the veil of dreams that had shrouded her during the night dissipating in the lamp-lit room. "Aren!" she cried out, gripping the covers and looking around.

She was in a generous bed in a large room with a carpeted floor and plain walls. There wasn't much to the room: another bed, two white wardrobes, a desk, a little sitting area with two chairs and a small table. She remembered that she was in the House of Tiede and that she had fallen asleep and dreamed of the goddess talking to a blind man on the Laithe.

A door opened and a girl came out, toweling her hair. "I'm glad you're awake," said Nianni as she tested her hair's dampness. "The washroom is through here. Be quick because we need to attend morning worship."

The worship room, dedicated to the goddess of Light, was located on the second floor on the eastern side of the House and was significantly smaller than Alaric's worship room. There were several windows, but one was much larger than the others, taking up a majority of the wall. The window provided a distant view of the glimmering Laithe Inlet.

Selina took her time taking everything in. The room was sparse and smelled of leindra flower and the woods. In the middle of the room was a wooden altar on top of which was a gold bell and hammer and various other golden objects she couldn't identify. Four large clay urns full of dark, rich soil sat beneath the altar.

The stark white ceiling was high, and there was an opening on the slope, large enough for a man to slip through. Selina wondered what they did about the hole when it rained. Several strings of tiny gold bells showered from the opening in the ceiling, and she imagined the glittering sound they made when the wind whispered by. Right now, the bells were silent.

The three Priestesses from Syrn knelt before the altar. Tiede's Head Priestess Crina stood behind the altar, her eyes closed, her palms facing upwards. House Priestess Min stood beside her and stirred a mixture in a clay bowl, causing tendrils of smoke to twist and rise from it.

Nianni led Selina to the white bench under the big window. Selina took a seat, her white-slippered feet dangling above the pale stone floor. Then, Nianni took her place on the other side of Crina.

As she watched the morning rituals, Selina tried not to fidget. She had seen them before when attending holy day rituals with the Gerrit family, and it had been hard to keep still then too. The Priestesses rang golden bells to announce the dawn. They sang songs with strange words and melodies that reminded Selina of summer flowers and birdsongs and the whispering of the wind. It made her heart ache and yearn for the soil between her toes, fresh-picked berries, and the embrace of trees.

Selina tried to focus, studying the unique vine markings on each Priestess as they went through the rituals of honoring the gods of Light. Selina could see the markings through the Priestesses' sheer gowns. Dark-green vines had been inked into their skin, winding up from the toes of one foot, up leg and thigh, and then wrapping around both hips before snaking up their waists, around their backs, and then draping over a shoulder, where it seemed as if a brooch of tiny flowers held the whole piece in place over a collarbone. The twirling petals of the silver-white moonflower on Crina. The yellow-orange fringed petals of the fervor flora on Min. The layered, blue-violet hued petals of the water lily on Teyna. Bursting white peonies with pale-pink centers on Estelline. An exotic, single, blood-red flower with eight distinct, long and slender petals and a dark center that Selina had never seen before on the Seer.

The Priestesses spread the mud over their gowns, on their breasts and bellies, chanting in low tones that Selina couldn't make out. She wondered what the point of the mud was, finding it odd that grown women would dirty themselves in this way for the goddess Sabana.

Nianni came forward with a pitcher of water and an arm loaded with small white towels to assist with cleaning as the rituals continued. They would honor Geir, the god of air and wind, next, but Selina couldn't recall what was involved. Tossing leaves out the window? Min took hold of one of Crina's hands and raised her arms as well; they looked as if they were ready to catch something. It took all of Selina's self-control to keep from laughing. The sound of her snorting popped into her head, and an image of Aren laughing at her accompanied it. She bit her lip hard and continued to bite even as tears rolled out of her eyes.

Spotting Selina, Nianni furrowed her brows, a look of concern and exasperation on her face. The look pushed Selina over the edge, and air escaped from her nose, causing an odd *khrnnkng* sound to come out. Laughter wanted to follow, so she clapped her hands over her mouth, turning to face the window as her body convulsed, the giggles tickling her from the inside.

"Little sister needs assistance," Teyna said.

Selina gulped and turned back to face the altar, her face red, hot, and tear-stained. She pressed her lips together, trying to conceal the smile that was fighting to take center stage on her face. Teyna didn't sound angry, but the look on Nianni's face as she walked towards Selina was one of annoyance and embarrassment.

Crina and Min lowered their arms, and all the Priestesses were staring at her. She knew she should feel guilty. She was old enough to know that these worship ceremonies were serious, but she couldn't help herself. Mud was everywhere and the Priestesses were trying to catch something that might fall from the sky. A bubble of laughter managed to escape her.

"Is something funny, child?" Crina asked. The silver was still swirling in her eyes, and the strangeness of it was enough to scare Selina's giggles away. "We are calling on the gods. I fail to see the humor."

"No one was answering," Selina blurted.

Nianni cringed and gave her a pained look that no one else could see.

"Eight lashes," Crina said, her voice low.

"Oh, come now, she's just a child," Teyna said, a wide smile on her face. "She's the youngest we've ever had, by far. She has no idea what any of it means; of course she would think it silly. She's Unblessed, remember?"

Estelline shook her head, the movement small, abbreviated. "Crina is Head Priestess of Tiede; she will do as she pleases."

Teyna cocked her head, her large, brown eyes wide and questioning. "And we are of Syrn, and our authority supersedes—"

"I hear the wisdom of Syrn," Crina said. "Four lashes, then. The other four shall be transferred to the Priestess Minor, whose responsibility it was to instruct our Initiate."

Nianni kept her chin high and showed no emotion, save for closing her eyes for a heartbeat. She turned towards the Priestesses and bowed her head, her hands over her chest. "Yes, Priestess," was all she said.

"No!" Selina cried out, slipping off the bench and standing next to Nianni. "It's my fault; please don't punish her!"

Crina came around the altar. There was a strange aura around her that reminded Selina of a dark blanket of clouds around a full moon. She took a step back, but Nianni remained still. Selina felt a chill run down her spine, and she wanted to run and find Aren. At the same time, she couldn't just leave Nianni. It was Selina's fault for not listening. That's what Nianni should have said, but she didn't. Selina's heart beat hard in her chest, and her mind raced for a way out of this mess. She wished Aren were here; he would have stopped it. He wouldn't care if they were Priestesses. Tears filled her eyes and her ears rang. Everything looked blurry, and she wanted to hold onto something to steady herself. The room was getting darker and her legs felt weak.

"What's the matter, child?" Estelline's voice.

Selina tried to turn her head but felt dizzy. Hands took hold of her, supporting her as she began to slip into the darkness. "Sabana mentioned a stone," she heard herself say. "It was that time—when the mage rebellions were starting to break out."

"What are you talking about?" Crina said, her voice muffled by cotton.

Selina's eyes closed and in her mind she saw a room filled with books. Windows opened up to deep night skies and an inky sea, and in the middle of the large room was a desk bigger than any she'd ever seen, covered in maps and papers and tiny glass jars. Something sparkly coated the surfaces and the floor like dust, but it glowed with a brilliance that lit up the otherwise dark space.

A woman sat at the desk rifling through papers, and Selina blinked several times when she realized that the woman's body seemed to flicker, and Selina could see through her as if she were a ghost. The chill of night was in the air, but an extraordinary warmth was nearby and she looked around to find the source of it. In a large chair sat the most frightening man she had ever seen. He had more muscles than Gerrit Gryf, the strongest man she knew, and this stranger was much, much taller. He had skin the color of shadowed bronze and hair the color of ink; his changing eyes were orange and red and yellow, as if a fire raged inside him. He wore black from head to toe and sat slumped in his chair, his feet spread wide in a pose that reminded her of Dane.

When the man spoke, she thought she could feel the rumble of his voice vibrate in her own chest. She was trapped somewhere between terror and curiosity. "Kaila, when did you speak to Sabana?" the scary man said.

"Earlier, before I came home," a woman's voice responded. Selina lit up and looked around when she heard the voice. She was dreaming of the Lady from the Wood! She wondered why she had fallen into this dream now, but was a little thankful for it since then maybe she wouldn't feel the lash of the whip.

"And what did she have to say about a stone?" the man said, interrupting Selina's thoughts.

The Lady, the goddess Kaila, sat on the settee across from the man, her bare legs stretched across the length of it, looking playful and at ease. A short, shimmering dress of aqua draped her petite form like water flowing over a riverbed.

"She said that you left a powerful token with the Priestesses during one of the mage uprisings a long time ago and that Aalae wanted it. Did you really leave something? That's so unlike you, Tanghi."

Tanghi's brows furrowed as he tried to remember. He adjusted himself on his seat, leaned his head back, and closed his eyes. "I don't recall."

"She said you left it with a Priestess from Syrn. It's a stone smaller than my fist, the white kinds you can find at the twin lakes of the Relythaun. Sabana said it has your symbol burned on it."

A slow smile crept onto his face as the memory resurfaced. "Ah, I remember now, and that's between me and the priestess."

Kaila's eyes widened. "Tanghi! Were you involved with—"

"By Mahl, Kaila!" His face contorted in disgust and he threw a handful of stardust at her. "How could you think such a thing? Absolutely not!" He nodded towards the woman at the desk, then put a finger to his lips. "It was the priestess who found your sash. It was a thank-you gift."

"It must be imbued with a great deal of your power if Aalae wanted it."

"It will give off heat until the day it's shattered. I've no idea what Aalae could do with it, but seeing as it belongs to the Priestesses, that's no worry of ours. They're very protective of the holy relics, and Aalae can't touch what belongs to them."

"Well, it was a nice gesture," Kaila smiled.

Tanghi lowered his voice. "Alaric would thank them too if he had known. Speaking of Alaric..."

The thump of boot heels on stone announced another presence entering the room, and Selina watched as a man came through the open doors. He was tall and regal—more so than even Lord Vir—and he wore his straight, black hair loose and long in the same style as they did in Kaishar. "Now this," the man said, his arms opening as if to encompass the room, "is what I like to see: my Knights and my mate safe at home."

Kaila swung her legs around so that her feet were on the floor. The man came over and placed a kiss on her head. "Did you know that Sabana gave Tiede Wood to Geir?" Kaila asked.

"I heard that a long time ago but didn't think much of it," Alaric said, walking to the desk and touching Taia's cheek. He took the papers she handed him. "I prefer Geir to be lord over Tiede Wood. He doesn't care for it and will leave it be. Sabana is much more clever, and having her so close to Tiede made me a little nervous."

"She still revels there on occasion," Kaila said, standing and walking over to Alaric's desk. "I was there with her before I came home. I don't think she cared much for the Wood either."

"It's infused with night magic, and she can't control it," Alaric said. "I think it's also a weak point for our kind, a sort of Netherealm; even I can't explain half the things that go on in Tiede Wood. It was there before my father brought us here, so I can only surmise that the planetary god still holds some influence over it."

Tanghi walked over to Kaila's side and folded his arms across his chest. He indicated the papers in Alaric's hands with a nod of his chin. "Is there trouble?"

"I'm not sure yet," Alaric said, his brows furrowing. "Taia noticed some disturbances in the spells she'd woven around the eastern Houses, specifically the House of Trum. We've been examining the patterns most of the evening while you two were out." He handed Tanghi the papers. "I know it's aligned to Aalae, but I need you to check on the House, find out what's going on."

"I can go with you," Kaila said.

"Not yet," Alaric said. "It's just a scouting expedition. I'll send you when I need to. In the meantime, I'm concerned that it might be a ploy to distract us from Tiede. That's where I need you, Kaila. You're only to watch. Do you understand?"

"Yes, my Lord." She bowed her head.

"War," Tanghi said, handing the papers back. "Aalae has always tried to attack Tiede directly, but it could be she's starting in the east, taking the Houses down one by one."

A chill went through Selina, and she gasped as something cold and wet was pressed against her face.

SEVEN

Selina opened her eyes and was blinded by the sunlight that seemed to stream through every window and crevice in the House. She groaned and put her hands over her face. She remembered being in Aalae's worship room, being told that she had to be punished, but now she was in the room's antechamber. She moved her hands away from her face but closed her eyes. She felt her arms for welts, wiggled a little to see if her back was sore. Nothing.

"You're awake," Nianni said from somewhere nearby. Selina opened her eyes, pretending that her eyelids were heavy and had to be pried open with a stick. Another cold, wet thing was pressed against her face. "You were delusional," Nianni said, pressing the dampened cloth to her cheeks. She sat on a wooden chair next to Selina, who was lying on the settee.

Selina relaxed, allowing the cushions she lay on to absorb her whole body. She cleared her throat, then asked, "Where is everybody?"

"They decided they needed to pray to the gods about you," Nianni answered, submerging the cloth in a wooden bowl, then wringing out the water before reapplying it. "You were talking while you were unconscious."

"What did I say? Did Head Priestess hurt us?"

"Was this some kind of trick to get out of being punished?"

"No." Selina pushed herself up on her elbows, pausing to let the dizziness pass. Nianni caught the wet cloth as it fell off her forehead. "Can I see Aren now? Please?"

"No. I would have to escort you, and I have no desire to be in his foolish, puffed-up presence."

"Aren is the only one who understands me." Selina gazed down at her fingers.

"You're probably the only one who understands him," Nianni scoffed. "He's difficult to get along with; everything is a joke to him."

The sound of rustling skirts distracted them both, and Nianni stood up, nudging Selina to do the same. The two waited as Crina and Min entered the antechamber and stood before them. Nianni lowered her head, and Selina, looking over to her, decided she should do the same. Maybe the Head Priestesses had decided that now was the time to punish them.

"I'm glad to see you're better," Crina said. "Can you tell us what happened?"

"I don't remember. I know I was thinking of Aren because I was scared you were going to hit me. Then I got dizzy. Then I was here."

"Priestess Minor," Min said, her voice soft, "were you able to find the Historian's Apprentice? Perhaps she has a condition we were not made aware of, and he could enlighten us."

"I looked," Nianni responded, "but a Messenger told me the Apprentice is on a task for Lord Vir and can't be disturbed."

"You mentioned the goddess Sabana," Crina said, her eyes never leaving Selina, "and a stone. What do you know of the mage rebellions?"

Selina frowned. "Mage what?"

Crina turned her head, and she and Min seemed to communicate without saying anything. Crina turned to face Selina again, this time taking one of her hands. Selina noticed that Crina's hands were cool and soft, but they tingled with strange power.

"Would you like to see Apprentice Aren tonight?" Min asked.

Selina's face lit up, her violet eyes widening with delight. "Really? Yes! Please, can I?"

"Then try to remember," Crina said. "Just concentrate on the stone. Tell us what you know about the stone."

Selina felt her heart pump, motivated by the thought of being able to see Aren again. She focused on the room full of books, tried to return to that strange place. There was a quiet, flickering woman, a man made of fire, a prince with long black hair, the Water goddess.

"It doesn't make sense, but I wasn't here anymore; I wasn't in Tiede. I was with the Water goddess, and she was talking to the Fire god," Selina announced.

Min frowned. "You aren't making this up just so you can see the Apprentice, are you?"

"No!" Selina was angry that they would accuse her of lying. "I know about the stone they talked about, but I don't know about the mage thing."

Crina nodded to placate her. "What did they say about the stone? Has the Apprentice ever talked to you about it?"

Selina cocked her head as she looked at Crina. "Why would Aren know about the stone?"

"He reads a lot of books," Crina said, smiling. "Your Aren is very bright and knows a great deal of things. I'm sure he shares stories with you all the time."

Selina nodded and was glad that the Priestess could admit that Aren was very smart. "He does tell me stories, but he didn't tell me this one."

"Could you tell us?" Crina asked. "Later, we can talk to Aren about it. I'm told he enjoys stories."

Selina took a deep breath. "The goddess asked the Fire god what token he left behind because Sabana told her about it. The Fire god didn't remember at first, but then he did. He said he gave it to a Priestess from Syrn because she found the sash that belonged to the Water goddess, and he wanted to give her a gift to thank her." Crina let go of Selina's hand, straightening as if it took great effort. She looked at Min. Both women's eyes were large, and they both had expressions of shock on their faces. Selina and Nianni watched, wondering what they were conveying to each other. Selina wasn't sure if this was enough to get her to see Aren, so she added, "The Fire god said the stone will give out heat until it gets broken, and it has his symbol on it. The goddess said it's a white stone that you can find at the twin lakes, but I don't know where that is." Crina and Min stared down at her, and she thought Crina might cry.

Crina took a deep breath, then said, "You've done a splendid job. Is there anything else you remember? Anything at all?"

Selina shook her head. "The rest of it is a little fuzzy. I still get to see Aren, though, right?"

"Yes, of course," Crina said, turning to Nianni. "Please make arrangements for dinner; you may speak to Elder to set it up. Illithe is arriving this evening, and the Apprentice is expected to attend." Nianni bowed her head. Crina looked down at Selina again, her expression a mixture of wonder and joy. "We have much to share with Syrn."

EIGHT

Aren was relieved to find Bontan in the House stables; the big cat read him well, and he wanted to leave the navigating to the gree. His mind was elsewhere; the note he had found under his door unnerved him. He wondered if it was a threat. It sure sounded like one.

Keep your distance. I only saved your life for her happiness.

He had been attacked twice last night. The first time, he had defended himself from the monster; the second time, some unknown soldier had saved him. What soldier in Tiede knew Ancient? Whoever it was didn't have to know the old language, he supposed; anyone with patience and a book for reference could have pieced the note together. And who was this her?

"Damn it," he muttered. He wondered again what Geyle had told Vir. He put a hand on Bontan's head, scruffing the cat's silky, black fur. Bontan nudged Aren, a guttural purr vibrating through his throat as Aren walked him towards the gates. "At least," he said to Bontan, "I can go home for a while, hide from all this chaos. If you run fast enough, maybe nothing will try to kill me today."

A Guard approached from the eastern gates, the servants' entrance. He raised a hand and Aren nodded, meeting him halfway. "Apprentice, just the man I was looking for. We received a delivery for you from Wethern's. Do you mind signing for it?" Aren squeezed Bontan's shoulder, and the big cat settled on its haunches, yawning and revealing its sharp, ivory teeth. The Guard handed Aren a few sheets of paper and a pen, and Aren skimmed over the receipts, signing the bottom of each. "The man who delivered it said you should conserve it because the docks are a mess. He's not sure how steady supplies will be."

Aren nodded and handed the Guard the papers. "Noted. Thank you. If it's that bad, just set all the oil aside for the House; no need to put any on reserve for the Library." Aren made a clicking noise, scratching the gree's ear, and Bontan stood up. They walked past the verdant gardens, a lush landscape of green and stone and sand punctuated by flora in all shades of blues and purples and hints of yellow. A fountain bubbled nearby, and Aren tried to hold onto the peacefulness, inhaling the sea air and releasing his worries. He was going home to help his family, then he was going to have a bath and return straight to the Library, where he could bury himself in his work. Most importantly, he was going to keep his distance from all women, as the mysterious note advised.

"Apprentice," a woman's voice called out to him from one of the garden tables. He and Bontan looked over, spotting the woman in the pale-blue, lace-accented dress. "Come say hello, dear. You just missed Lady Geyle."

Aren cringed but did as she asked, giving her a slight bow. "Good day, Lady Saris," he said. The woman was Counselor Novin Helmun's wife and was at least twenty years older than Aren. Her hair and eyes were light brown, her lips thin, but her mouth was wide with perfect teeth. She peeled off a white lace glove and stretched her hand out towards him. Aren obliged, wincing a little behind the long strands of hair that fell forward and concealed his eyes, as he touched the back of her hand to his lips, causing her to sigh.

"You are quite the charmer, aren't you? If more young men were as schooled in the ways of the Old World as you are, and half as handsome, I'd be in trouble." She laughed, the lines around her eyes and mouth showing. "You Tennari men are irresistible."

"I'm not Tennari…" Aren started. A servant Aren had never seen before came over to refill her glass of water, dropping a thin slice of lemon in it. He began to pull another glass for Aren, but he held up a hand to decline, and the servant bowed his head. "I'd stay and chat, but I'm already running late," Aren explained, rubbing Bontan's head.

"You're not going anywhere," Saris teased. "A Messenger is on his way to find you."

"Find me for what?"

The House Messenger came running towards him from the stable area. Saris sipped at her water, a knowing smile on her face. "Apprentice!" the Messenger called out. "Thank the gods I caught you before you left. Lord Vir canceled your trip home today."

Aren frowned. "What? Why? Elder cleared it this morning."

"Well, Lord Vir changed it a few minutes ago. You need to report to the parlor as soon as you stable your gree."

Aren followed the Messenger back towards the stables. "Did he say why?" he asked, pulling Bontan along.

"His wife needs a dance partner."

NINE

That was awkward, thought Aren as he rummaged through his wardrobe.

He had spent the better part of the afternoon in the parlor, dancing with Lady Geyle. A pianist and string musicians had been summoned to play, and Vir sat by the empty fireplace, reading through a stack of papers. Aren didn't miss the tension between the Lord and Lady, and he cursed them for involving him in their affairs.

Aren wasn't a dancer by any stretch of the imagination, though someone had once said he had the perfect form for it. He knew the footwork to half of the traditional and formal dances, but had fumbled enough that Geyle couldn't stop laughing, and her merriment only encouraged the musicians to play more complex pieces. At one point, Vir put down his papers with an audible sigh, stood up, then showed Aren the proper steps.

You dance with her then, Aren wanted to say.

When the Lady was tired, the musicians packed up. Servants came in with water, chilled white wine, and an assortment of fruits and cheeses. Geyle insisted he stay, and Vir grunted his approval. The three of them sat together, Vir with his papers in his own world, while Geyle fawned over Aren, asking him about his family and Selina and what his hopes and dreams were for the future.

Aren wanted to stab himself. He had never felt more uncomfortable in his life.

He pulled his formal evening attire out of the wardrobe and laid it out on his bed. The Messenger had just announced that the Illitheiens' ship had been spotted on the Laithe. Aren supposed that family got a pass when it came to closing off the docks. He had a few hours, but he needed every minute of it. He pulled on the midnight-blue pants and slipped the crisp white shirt over his head, buttoning up the collar. Then, he buckled up his shiny black boots. He debated bringing his favorite knife, a gift from his eldest brother, then decided to leave it on his desk. That was when he spotted the note he had found earlier:

Keep your distance. I only saved your life for her happiness.

He read the note over and over, the words becoming a mantra in his head. He tried to translate the Ancient text in different ways, hoping that his original translation was off by a word or two, but the message was clear. Flummoxed, he pushed the piece of paper into his notebook. There was a gentle rap on his door, and he jumped. He ran his hands through his hair, then answered the door. There stood Geyle, her fingers working at a ribbon on her dress.

"My Lady," Aren started. She was the last person he had expected. His body tried to bow, but he froze midway so that he looked as though he had just pulled something in his back. "May I...?"

She slipped into his room and closed the door behind her. "Quickly, while Vir is making preparations for his family. My things. You fetched it from the Guild?"

Aren snapped to his senses and straightened up. He was finally going to be rid of that cursed vial! He fished through a desk drawer and pulled out a black iron key, then made his way over to the trunk at the foot of his bed. He worked the lock, then dug past old books and papers, trinkets, and clothes to retrieve the velvet pink pouch from inside his sock.

"Thank you, Aren," she breathed when he handed it to her. "Gods, thank you."

He watched as she emptied the pouch into her hand. "What is it, my Lady?"

"Just trust me," she said. Satisfied, she placed the vial and key in the pouch and pulled the strings closed.

"Are you in some kind of trouble? If you are, I would help you but I need to know what's going on."

"I appreciate the risks you've taken for me, and I hope to explain it one day, but not now."

Aren took a seat on the trunk and rested his elbows on his knees. "You've put me in an awkward position. I shouldn't have—"

"Your eyes are always changing." She moved to stand in front of him. "Light one moment and dark the next, the way the shadows move across the top of Tiede Wood." She shook a little, as if a spirit brushed against her, and drew back. "It's a wonder I've not come to know you sooner, all these years in the House." After a pause, she said, "I should go. Vir will be wondering where I am." She put a hand to the door as if feeling for vibrations, muttered something inaudible, then proceeded to leave.

Aren stood to bid her a respectful farewell, but she was already gone. The key and vial were gone. He could move on with his life and pretend that the whole ordeal with the Lady had never happened. That would be his wisest course of action. He put on his vest, grabbed his tie and dinner jacket, as well as the ceremonial saber, then left his room, almost bumping into the Priestess Minor, who was poised to knock. They both jumped back, alarmed.

"Why are you trying to scare me?" she growled, her hand over her heart.

"You're the one stalking me," he pointed out. Her cheeks warmed and her eyes grew angry as she prepared to unleash a barrage of insults at him, but he held up a hand to stop her. "What did you need to see me about?"

"You are such a…" Nianni seethed. "*Pal'qa!*"

"I don't know that word, Priestess! I must've made you really mad. You're pretty when you're mad," he teased. "You get worked up and all your silver goes jingle-jangle."

"I hate you."

"I know." He smiled. "Now, what can I do for you?"

Nianni breathed in deep to calm herself, then said, "Head Priestess and Elder Tanda have arranged for you and Selina to have dinner in the small dining room while the Illitheiens are here."

"Is there a reason for this? I was told that she's supposed to keep contact with outsiders to a minimum. Even my sister, Selina's legal guardian, has been asked to wait until after this preparation period. So, this leads me to believe you need me for something."

Nianni frowned at him, but he only stared back at her, waiting. "Selina is acting strange," she said at last. "Sometimes, it's as if she's looking beyond us. She blacks out or falls under some sort of trance. She speaks of things that she has no way of knowing. She claims that she sees the Water goddess."

"I don't know what you're hoping I can do. She's no ordinary little girl, but she never told me she was communicating with the gods." His mind began to process through memories, and he recalled something Selina had said about a lady while they were in the Wood. What had she said? It was the lady with the healing waters, wasn't it?

"Helpful as always." Nianni made no effort to disguise her sarcasm. She cocked her head, as if seeing him for the first time. "What happened to your face?"

Aren checked the door to his room to make sure it was locked. "While I appreciate your concern, I have a lot of work to do before Illithe arrives," he said, turning to leave. "Let's continue this over dinner." He felt her frustration spilling out of her, but he grinned and continued down the hall. As he walked, he glanced at the courtyard below. He stopped for a moment, placed his hand on the stone railing, and gazed upon the mermaid. Seeing her in the waning sunlight never ceased to amaze him.

Falling in love with you doesn't count, he said to her in his head.

At his desk in the Library, he hung up his tie, jacket, and saber, then looked at the stack of books that had been left for filing. Three books were on the House of Illithe. Elder must have been doing some brushing up to prepare for their visitors. Aren took the first volume and paged to the back of the book to find the artwork depicting the family lineage. He examined lineages out of habit; it fascinated him to see how people were connected and rooted, and he yearned for a place in those interweaving lines.

The current Lord, Illithe Kente, had been in power for over fifty years. His wife, Lady Eiselyn, had died fifteen years ago. They had two sons, Helton and Iver, and two daughters, Valine and Elleina. Elleina, the youngest of the four, had been married to the House of Tiede and had died two years before her mother.

His curiosity piqued, Aren flipped back several hundred pages, scanning for the information regarding the daughter of Illithe who had found her end in Tiede. She was blessed by the goddess Aalae. She loved to travel with her father, and during a visit to the House of Lia'aji in the Kailen Islands she met Lord Tiede Ren, her future husband. He had been so taken by her charm and beauty that he spoke to her father that evening, asking for her hand in marriage. Illithe Kente would have been a fool not to accept. Tiede was a powerful House and an alliance would guarantee peace. A wedding was scheduled, preparations made, and in a season's passing Illithe Elleina became the Lady of Tiede. She bore only one child, a son they named Vir, and when the boy was ten years old, she lost her life.

Aren skimmed a few more pages. There was nothing more on Elleina, nothing about her death or any investigation into what might have happened. He slammed the book closed—a little harder than he intended. All history had gaps and some history was loosely based in truth; it all depended on who was telling the story. So either Tiede and Illithe did not find the Lady's death of any significance or they were both trying to hide something.

"Is there any book in here that contains the black-and-white truth?" he asked out loud, his voice resonating through the large space.

"I'm happy to see that you're working hard," Elder said, hobbling down the stairs, dressed in his formal evening attire.

Aren straightened up, brushing his hair away from his face and dusting off his shirt as if he had been covered in crumbs or lint or gree fur. He stopped fidgeting and watched Elder descend the remaining steps with a breathtaking young woman at his arm. She was petite with tawny skin and black, silky hair that she wore partially up, pulled back from her face. Her smile was generous, her eyes the bluest he had ever seen, emphasized by the loose-flowing, satin sapphire gown that hugged her torso. The style was more Tennari than Tiedan. When her eyes met his, his throat dried up and he feared that he would be unable to utter a single intelligible word. He cleared his throat, deciding that he should say something to test out his vocal chords. "Good evening, Elder. I was just getting through some research before you arrived"—with this gorgeous woman, he wanted to add.

Elder had a sly look on his old face, a grin attempting to surface through the whiskers and wrinkles. "Your curiosity is as obvious as a purple-horned gree in a coop of chickens," Elder said. "This is Lady Vesila Lake from Tennar. Lady Lake, this is my Apprentice, Gerrit Aren."

She held out her hand, palm down, and Aren bowed as he took it and brought it to his lips in the manner of the Old World without thinking, but she was Tennari, and their way of greeting involved moving one's hand from the heart, palm down, and extending it towards the other person as the hand was turned palm up. It was a sign of giving of oneself in that moment, a sign of trust and good faith.

Once he realized his mistake, Aren cursed himself and looked at her through the hair that fell over his eyes, expecting to see shock and outrage on her face. Instead, her smile brightened and her brows rose as she slid her hand out of his. "My Lady, I'm sorry—"

"You are so charming!" Lake said with a small laugh. "Elder, I can't think of a single man who has ever greeted me in this fashion. Even you didn't greet me as such! I know, however, that you are to be credited with teaching him the social graces of the Old World."

Elder laughed and Aren stared at him, bewildered. Elder reached up to put a hand on his shoulder. "I try, but truly it is your presence that simply begs the finest of graces. Honestly, I thought you much too young to know of the old etiquette and didn't want to offend. My Apprentice is fond of offending."

Aren furrowed his brows as he watched Elder carry on like a smitten schoolboy. He had never imagined—let alone seen—Elder beam and giggle and fawn so much. He puzzled over whom this woman was and why she was here. "Tennar is a world away," Aren said. "Do you travel often?"

"I do, and I was fortunate to arrive before the Harbor was closed off several days ago. I'm a Master of Celestial Phenomena. I know you don't have that line of study here, but it's very esteemed in Tennar."

"Again, please pardon my rudeness." Aren bowed his head. "I didn't properly address you, Master."

She touched his arm, and a shiver like lightning passed through him. "Please, just call me Lake. The titles and propriety are more formal in Tennar than they are here, so when I'm away I prefer to be casual. In any case, I do apologize for the last-minute visit. Elder mentioned that Illithe is visiting, and I don't want to intrude, but I was hoping to explore Tiede's grand Library."

"If Elder hasn't already, I would be more than happy to give you a tour," Aren said. "How long will you be in Tiede?"

"I'm leaving tomorrow morning."

"If it were up to me, I would let you stay while we welcomed our guests and attended dinner, but Lord Vir is very strict about how the Library is handled, and we will have to lock it up while we're away," Elder said. "Must you leave in the morning?"

"I must. Will the Library reopen after your dinner? Would it be possible to return then?"

"Of course!" Elder said, squeezing Aren's shoulder. "I have to attend Council, but my Apprentice will be here, and he can assist you with anything you desire."

"Anything," Aren breathed, and Elder pinched a nerve in his neck, causing him to gasp in pain.

Lake laughed. "After dinner, then."

"Hopefully, my Apprentice will have this place cleaned up a little by then." Elder pointed at the gnarled staff leaning up against the wall. "Please hide that piece of junk." Aren winced, embarrassed that he had left out the old stick that he had acquired from the dead mage.

"Apprentice, I'll see you later this evening." She smiled.

"Absolutely."

"I'll show you out, and if my Apprentice gives you any trouble, let me know at once."

"It was a pleasure meeting you," Lake said over her shoulder as Elder led her out.

Aren smiled and waved. His words stumbled over each other to express something memorable and clever, but in the end, his lips remained sealed. Only when the door closed behind them was he able to utter, "The pleasure was all mine." He sat against his desk and squeezed his eyes shut. Stars, he hoped this woman wasn't going to be trouble for him.

TEN

Aren stood in the courtyard next to Elder, who looked just a little younger in his formal wear. In the House Master's robes, he looked as if some floating ghoul, probably similar to the one waiting for the old man to die, was constantly swallowing him up.

Half the Council was in attendance, and they were gathered behind Vir, who stood several feet in front of the mermaid fountain with Geyle at his side. Geyle was fidgeting in a slim-fitting lavender gown that trailed over the floor. The gown was embellished with cream lace and pearls, and her curls were done up and woven through with red baby roses. She looked so small and vulnerable next to Vir, and her two servants standing off to the side looked ready to catch her should she faint. Also in attendance were Tiede's Priestesses and the Priestesses of Syrn, breathtaking to behold in their fine silver, layered white chiffon gowns and sashes in their respective House colors. Nianni and Selina were not present, and Aren thought they might show up in the dining room after the formalities.

"Elder," Aren whispered as they waited. When Elder's eyes shifted towards him, Aren said, "Where did you find the beautiful Master Vesila Lake?"

Elder's frown was deep and pulled at the lines on his forehead. He hissed back, "Are you really asking this right now?"

"Come on, Elder," Aren said, keeping the movement of his lips to a minimum. "I saw the way you were giggling over her."

Elder sighed and the frown lines relaxed a little. "I don't giggle."

"Don't worry about me. I promised myself that I'd put my love life on hold until Dane got married."

"I don't believe that's possible, but she's above your class anyway."

"No doubt." Aren smiled, watching the doors open. "I'm the speck of dirt on her stargazing telescopic lens."

"Less than that." The corner of Elder's mouth lifted a fraction. "Now shut up."

The party from Illithe entered, and leading the procession was a tall nobleman dressed in white and heather gray with a yellow sash across his chest. Behind him was a handsome woman wearing a canary-yellow gown. Her chestnut hair was braided and wrapped atop her head like a crown. Her fingers were adorned with plain golden rings of varying thickness. She looked stern, almost severe, and her gray eyes, though large and beautiful, showed no weakness and certainly none of Geyle's softness. Accompanying the woman was a man who looked older than Elder Tanda, if that was possible.

When the Illitheiens approached Vir, the nobleman bowed then stepped aside. The handsome lady bowed her head a fraction, brought a hand to her heart, then swept her hand from Vir to the old man. "Lord Vir," she said, her voice smoky. "I present to you the House of Illithe."

The elderly gentleman came forward and bowed with his eyes. Vir smiled and returned the gesture with a bow from his waist, shocking Aren. He didn't think a Tiede Lord could bow to anyone. "It's good to see you again, Gran Kente," Vir said, upbeat and proud. "As you see, the Priestesses of Syrn have graced us with their presence as well; a new Initiate has been chosen from Tiede. We have much to discuss."

"As you wish," the tall woman spoke for the elder.

Vir led them around the mermaid fountain and the Council and Priestesses followed.

Elder turned to face Aren and looked up to glare into his eyes. "Remember your place," he said under his breath. "You will act respectfully in the presence of the Priestess Minor."

Aren was about to respond when the line of dignitaries came to a stop. The old Illitheien gestured towards Aren and uttered a few words. At that, all heads turned to look at him, and Elder straightened up, ready to chastise his Apprentice at Vir's command. Vir said something in response to the old man's inquiry, and the group continued forward into the dining hall. The tall woman's gaze lingered for longer than the others'.

Elder whipped his head back to face Aren, his brows rising and falling in fury. "Did you do something to offend our guests?"

Aren was incredulous. "Why do you always think I've done something wrong? I've never met the Illitheiens before now, and you were next to me the whole time!"

"Were you ogling Lady Illithe?"

"No! Stars, she's old enough to be my mother and far too severe-looking for my taste."

Elder grabbed his forearm to yank him down to eye level. "I don't care what your taste is, boy. Do not look at our guests!"

"Elder, I swear I didn't do anything."

Letting him go, Elder straightened his ever-curling back. "If I find out during dinner that you did something to offend, I will have you copy 'The Seasons Poetic' from the Ancient language fifty times over, then throw you into Tiede Wood!" He left to join the dignitaries in the formal dining hall.

Aren sighed, raking a hand through his hair. He made his way to the room off to the right of the dining hall, where Selina and Nianni would meet him. The small dining room was used more often than the formal one and allowed for a more intimate experience. The floor and furniture were of dark wood; the chairs upholstered in rich, chocolate-brown leather. In contrast, the stone and brick walls and arched ceilings were neutral toned. The room glowed from the candlelight emanating from the chandelier centered over the heavy wooden table. As Aren approached, he could smell the chef's signature, herb-crusted roast beef and the earthy, buttery notes of a creamy morel sauce.

"Aren!" Selina exclaimed when he passed through the arched doorway. "You really did come! They weren't lying!"

He laughed and allowed her to jump into his arms and hug him tight. Then he held her out at arm's length to get a good look at her, wondering why the Priestesses were so concerned. Her face was paler than he remembered, but that could be because she hadn't been allowed to run outside and play all day as she usually did. Nianni had somehow been able to get Selina's usually tangled hair to shine like silk and had tied the top half of it away from her face and adorned it with little white flowers.

"Is everything okay?" Selina asked. "What happened to your face?"

"Don't worry about me. I just had a little accident last night," Aren said. When everyone was seated and Nianni had said the blessings, the dining staff proceeded to cut and serve the roast. Aren helped himself to a warm dinner roll, breaking it open to release the steam from its soft center. "Now tell me, Selina," he said after taking a bite of the bread, "how are the Priestesses treating you?"

Selina glanced at Nianni. "Fine. I don't get to play, but it's a little bit nice staying in the House."

"And no matter where you go, you'll always stay at the Lord's House. That's a good thing, even though the House always expects you to speak and behave properly," he said, looking at Nianni. "Isn't that right, Priestess?"

"Why are you talking to me?" she said before placing a tender slice of buttered carrot in her mouth.

He turned to face Selina. "You see? Priestess is still learning her manners." They ate as Aren shared some interesting facts about the House, Library, and saltwater baths.

"The House is nice but I miss you." Selina looked at him with sad, violet eyes. "I thought I would get to see you all the time, but I didn't see you all day."

"I don't know what you could possibly miss in this toad," Nianni mumbled under her breath.

Aren turned to face the Priestess, determined to get a rise out of her. "I love you too."

Nianni growled, slamming her fork on the table. "Really, Selina, I have to know what in the gods' names you see in him."

Selina shrugged. "He's really funny. One time, I was scared and all alone, and it was raining and thunder, and that's when Aren found me. Then another day, he tried to find my family."

"Anyone could have done that for you," Nianni pointed out.

"But nobody did. Only Aren."

He gave Nianni a wink. "I'm such a jerk."

Nianni indicated that the servant take her plate. "Eating with them is giving me indigestion."

"Aren is also really good at telling stories. Can you tell me a story now?" Selina folded her hands in her lap.

He swirled his glass, watching the wine leave streaks in its wake. "I can tell you the story of Alaric's Revenge."

Nianni pounded a fist on the table. "You will do no such thing in my presence! I'll not have you spreading blasphemy!"

"It's a real legend! I read it not too long ago," he countered. "You sure do like to hit this table."

"Does Alaric kill somebody?" Selina asked, her eyes wide.

"As a matter of fact, he does."

"Apprentice, that is enough!" Nianni was on her feet. "She is going to be a Priestess and will have an obligation to speak the truth. I won't allow you to cloud and confuse her innocent mind!"

"It's just a story, Priestess." He sighed, taking a drink.

"Let's hear it," the Head Priestess said as she entered the dining room. Aren and Nianni pushed their seats back to pay the proper respects. Selina was a little slower but managed to get to her feet, bring her hands together over her heart, and bow her head. "Please sit," Crina said. "I only came to check on Selina. I promised she could see you, Apprentice, and I wanted to see if she was happy."

"Yes, Priestess," Selina said, her voice soft.

A servant rushed to pull a seat out for Crina as she requested ambrosia. "Where did you read this story, Apprentice?" Crina asked him.

"It was in a tome from Illithe. The Library acquired it recently."

A dainty cordial was placed before Crina, who brought it to her lips and breathed its spicy sweetness before taking a sip. "Your story, Apprentice."

Aren cleared his throat and began. "This is the story of Kaila, goddess of Water, and how she came to trouble with Alaric. She's often portrayed as a troublemaker in Illitheien lore because they are Light worshippers and she is a goddess of the Night.

"In times untold, the goddess Kaila would play out in the sea, and all the creatures of the water would venture near the surface to frolic with her. Her laughter is an ocean song, and they say that fishermen have developed a sense for hearing this song. When they hear it, they know it's time to drop everything and cast their nets because they'll be rewarded with a large catch.

"Kaila enjoyed wandering around Cordelacht, but she tried very hard not to stray from her home on Mytanth because Alaric loved her and wanted to keep her close. Sometimes, she couldn't help but wander off. One day, Kaila was on one of her many adventures and she ended up on the shores of the Laithe Inlet, far from her home. She was playing near the tidal pools, and she laughed as the oysters teased her, snapping their shells open and shut, daring her to stick her fingers inside to grab the pearls. She was so distracted by her games that she didn't notice the fisherman who had walked up to the beach, dragging his weatherworn boat. He had heard the ocean's song and was answering her call, but she didn't hear him gasp as he spotted her long fish-fin tail and her scales glistening like sapphires and emeralds in the sun.

"You see, the fisherman's people told tales about beautiful sea dwellers who drowned ships and men. They believed that it was a bad omen to set eyes upon a mermaid, that to allow the mermaid to sing or speak or even look at you would doom you on the seas forever. The only way to rid yourself of the curse was to kill the mermaid.

"The fisherman raised his spear in terror. He took aim and threw. All Kaila could register at that moment was the pain and piercing of her flesh, and the salty tears that streamed from her eyes filled the oceans. The fisherman was frightened. He took a step towards her and saw her eyes, wet and aquamarine, and his gaze followed her tears, which burned down her face and dripped to her breast, where her hand clutched at the shaft of the spear. Her blood spilled upon the sands, stones, and shells.

"His heart beat too fast to contain, and he choked on the air he breathed, coughing up bile and watching as her fish tail disappeared and turned into long, slender human legs. He dropped to his knees and returned his eyes to her face, focusing on the paling lips, which mouthed a word he wished the wind didn't carry to his ears: "Alaric."

"The fisherman felt his soul tugging upwards and away from his body as the god Alaric claimed it. He doubled over, grasped at the sand, trying in vain to hold onto the earth. His life was at an end. By attacking the goddess, he had insulted Alaric, and at Alaric's side was the most terrifying of the elemental gods: Tanghi, god of Fire. Before the fisherman could close his eyes, he was wrapped in flames and darkness, then his life was painfully extinguished. His charred body was barely recognizable to his kinsmen, who had set out to find him after he had been missing for several days."

Selina was on the edge of her seat. "What happened to the goddess?"

"She was brought home and placed under the care of the goddess Taia, who is Alaric's mate. Taia wove healing spells and in a few days Kaila was well enough to face Alaric's anger. Kaila was prone to trouble and scolded often, but never as badly as when she had healed from the fisherman's spear. The people of Cordelacht knew heavy rains for several seasons, and the seas and rivers swelled, swallowing several shore towns. Darkness descended upon the land, and Alaric's voice shook the boulders from the mountains of Mytanth, causing liquid fire to pour forth from the depths."

"Why was Alaric so mad?" asked Selina. "Why didn't the fisherman ask the goddess her name first? Was he from Tiede?"

Aren looked to Crina and shrugged. "That's all I know of the tale. I'd never heard it before."

Nianni said, "I've never heard it before either. It's not in Kailen lore."

Crina finished the ambrosia and twirled the glass stem between her thumb and forefinger. "I heard of it from the older Priestesses at Illithe; however, no one knows who wrote it or how the story passed from one generation to the next. It's likely a story to explain the time leading up to the end of Equinox. As the Apprentice said, the story is from Illithe, which is why it seems to place the blame of the end of Equinox on the realm of Night."

"The first Equinox was a long, long time ago," Aren explained for Selina, "when night and day were balanced like it is now. At the end of that Equinox, there were many natural disasters: floods, mountains erupting fire, terrible ocean waves."

"And after the Equinox?" Crina quizzed him.

"Perpetual Twilight," he replied. "According to legend, twin moons dominate the skies and the House of Tiede is blessed with unspeakable power."

"But is it true about the goddess?" Selina asked. "She turns into a mermaid? What does she look like? Does she look like the mermaid in the courtyard?"

"The gods take any form they choose, but our history, our religious history," Crina amended for Aren's sake, "has shown that the gods only choose forms that correspond to their element or chronos. For example, the Wind god has made known to us his falcon form, but Alaric has also taken the form of a bird. One that we know of is an owl."

"Owls are nocturnal," Aren explained when Selina looked confused. "They wake and hunt at night, remember?"

"There are several stories that depict Kaila as a mermaid; however, no Priestess has witnessed her in that form. Without the recorded witness of a Priestess, it is not considered religious truth," Crina said. "As for what she looks like, the majority of the depictions resemble the mermaid in the courtyard: beautiful."

"All the gods are depicted as beautiful," Aren said, recalling the painting of Sabana in the Weavers Guild. "They're gods: perfect, unrealistic, and unattainable."

"Unrealistic is blasphemous," Crina said, her tone somewhere between patience and annoyance. "The Wind god used to visit long ago during morning rituals, always in falcon form."

"My people on the Islands depict the Water goddess as a lady, not a mermaid, who lives in the sea. Many claim to have spotted her bathing in the waterfalls of our rain forests. The holy texts say the gods wander among us from time to time," Nianni offered. "We just aren't always open to seeing them."

"With all due respect, Priestess"—Aren's grin was lopsided, teasing—"I would notice heavenly beauty if it were walking down the streets of Tiede."

Nianni was about to counter when Crina touched her wrist and said, "There are always those who do not believe. Our job is to be patient and to continue to guide them towards the ways of the gods."

"If they're out there, they want nothing to do with us," Aren explained. "You said yourself that the Wind god used to visit. Where has he been lately?"

"The Apprentice," Crina continued as if he hadn't spoken, "is lost. He lives day to day, wondering where he belongs. He rationalizes that if his parents had abandoned him, then why not the gods? This is why he and Selina are so close. The gods and society have turned their backs on them."

At that, Aren found the words burning on his tongue. "That is exactly the kind of talk that I'm tired of hearing! What makes any of you better than us? How dare *you* tell a child that she is nothing and then take her in as one of your own."

Nianni gasped and looked to Crina.

"I have seen time and again," Crina said, her voice strong, resonating, "the Unblessed, Unwanted children of Cordelacht end up lost and copper-less or dead."

"The same can be said of the so-called *blessed*," he countered. He looked over at Selina to make sure the arguing wasn't upsetting her; she hadn't made a peep for a while. Selina was marble-white, and her wide, unblinking eyes seemed to glow. Aren placed his hands on her shoulders and shook her gently, the Head Priestess no longer on his mind. "Selina?" he asked. "Are you all right?"

"That's what she looked like before she passed out this morning," Nianni said as she began to twist at one of her silver bracelets.

Aren reached for a glass of water and put it to Selina's pale lips, trying to get her to drink. The water dribbled down the side of her mouth, but she began to speak in a whisper. "The mages are coming," she murmured.

Crina was standing behind him, trying to decipher Selina's words. "What is she saying?" Crina asked.

"The mages are coming," he told her, their argument forgotten. He pushed Selina's chair away from the table so he could get a better look at her.

Crina's eyes widened and she turned to Nianni. "Quickly, sister. Ask Lord Vir to please excuse the Priestesses."

"What's happening?" Aren asked as Nianni rushed off towards the main dining room.

Crina examined Selina's glowing eyes and blank expression. "Can you wake her?"

"She doesn't look asleep."

"Stop playing at stupidity," Crina murmured, snapping her ringed fingers in front of Selina's face. "The way you switch from intelligent to ignorant and back again is tiresome."

There was a flurry of activity as a party entered the small dining room. Aren dropped to one knee at the sight of Vir in the doorway. "Up," Vir commanded, entering the room. "The Priestess Minor said the girl was having visions again."

Crina bowed her head as Vir walked over to where Selina was sitting, unblinking and unmoving. Aren remained by her side as he noted the people in Vir's wake: Elder, the tall Illitheien lady, the Illitheien nobleman, and Nianni, as well as Tiede Counselor Novin Helmun, whom Aren didn't care for. Vir positioned himself against the table in view of Selina's gaze. He crossed his arms against his chest and waited. When nothing happened, he motioned to the nobleman. "Doctor, have you seen anything like this before?"

The Illitheien, tall and thin like a stork, picked his way over to Vir's side and brought his face close to Selina's. "No, Lord Vir," the Doctor said. "That is to say, we have seen brain damage and other such complexities that would result in a blank stare like this; however, this glowing—I can't be certain where that's originating from. Does she bear the marks of a magic wielder?"

"She has no marks, Doctor," Crina said. "We cannot wake her."

Vir frowned. "She doesn't look asleep."

Before Aren's lips could curl into a smile, Crina shot him such a look that he thought he would fall over dead. The exchange wasn't missed by Elder, who followed up Crina's glare with one of his own. Aren made to explain himself but refrained for once.

"Has anyone tried holding her?" the Illitheien woman asked. "Studies have shown how touch can break through a state of hypnosis, and this is a child after all. Children need to be held."

Vir looked from Aren to Crina and back again, his brows raised questioningly. Crina motioned to Nianni, who had pressed herself against the wall by the entrance. She came at once and bowed. Crina indicated that she should hug the little girl. Nianni bit her bottom lip, then awkwardly approached Selina, who sat ramrod straight in the large leather chair. After examining the position from two angles, Nianni wrapped her arms around Selina's shoulders. Selina remained as inanimate as the marble mermaid.

"It doesn't seem to work," Nianni said, retreating back a few steps.

"For stars' sake," Aren burst out. The situation had turned into a carnival, and now that the Illitheiens had come in and made all of their pronouncements on Selina's mental state, he was really starting to worry. He placed his hands under her arms and lifted her close to his chest, the way he had held her when he first found her and the countless times afterward, when she was upset or had fallen asleep while following him around.

Selina took a deep breath, and her eyes returned to their usual soft violet. She looked around, then laid her head on Aren's shoulder, her eyes closing from exhaustion. "The mages are coming," she yawned. "The gods are preparing for war."

ELEVEN

The stone courtyard surrounding the Keep was drenched in moonlight, and Alaric leaned against a wall. Tanghi had returned, and the reports from Trum were not as he expected. The city was on fire, and the air was filled with an acrid black smoke that Tanghi assured him was not natural.

Magic.

When would they be done with the mages and their ridiculous uprisings? He had enough to worry about with his sister trying to destroy his Realm.

The click of heels against stone interrupted his thoughts, and he watched as Taia walked towards him, papers in hand. Her form flickered, and he recalled the incident that had caused her disability. It made him want to strangle his sister all the more. Taia smiled when she caught his eye, and he admired her strength and patience. Levelheaded and logical, she examined a problem from all angles before engaging. She was a powerful spell-weaver. When Mahl had allowed his offspring to take a mate to keep them company, Taia was

Alaric's first choice. With her skills and abilities at his side, his Realm would be absolute. Her bond with him made him stronger.

So why was Kaila always on his mind?

"You seem more lost in thought than usual," Taia said, standing before him. "I just spoke to Tanghi, so I can guess what's on your mind."

"If Trum falls, Thell will be next," he said without greeting or preamble. "We need to stop the mages now, but we can't engage in combat in Aalae's territory without her permission."

"Perhaps that's why she hasn't called on us. If there's no hope for Trum, she may decide to let it fall, knowing that Thell would be next." She tucked her hair behind her ear. "Then she could prepare her forces to defend Tennar or Rose, the next likely targets."

Alaric visualized the fate line that would result if she were right. Millions upon millions of factors could reroute the line, but by making some overarching what-if predictions, and without going into the analysis, he could see that the mages might get as far as Kaishar, south of Tiede. "At worst, that would be three of her Houses to our one, then a stand at Kaishar, where Tiede can easily come to aid. The odds aren't in her favor."

"Your reading of the fate lines is clearer than mine." She shrugged. "I just don't think Aalae cares as much as you think she does. Illithe is her stronghold and Tiede is her target—that's what it boils down to. It sounds insane but this is Aalae we're talking about."

He pressed his lips together. Her logic was convincing, as usual, but he didn't have to like it. "I need numbers. How many mages are we talking about?"

She was about to respond when a flash of light filled the courtyard, causing them to shield their eyes. Demons swarmed to Alaric's side, putting a defensive wall around them, and Tanghi appeared as a raging inferno, adding another line of defense. When the blinding light receded, three figures stepped forward and Alaric growled at the sight of his sister and her Knights. They looked tired and battle-worn. A strange red welt wrapped around Geir's neck.

"What business do you have here?" Taia demanded, pushing past Tanghi and the demons. "You weren't invited; you shouldn't have been able to enter this Realm."

Aalae laughed, taking in her surroundings. "I mean no harm. Rafi recently learned that the barriers woven around my brother's Realm work only if there is intended malice, and I have only come to visit said brother." She spread her arms as if to encompass all the demons standing there with their weapons drawn. "Is this necessary?"

Alaric was furious, but with a thought the winged creatures dispersed, returning to their posts. "I wasn't expecting company," Alaric said, moving to Tanghi's side.

She flashed him a wide smile. "I'm here to discuss the mages. All of their summoning will end up freeing the planetary god, and if that happens we can only pray that father will return in time to save us, because neither of us has amassed the power to deal with the likes of a planet."

"Father conquered the planetary god. We're safe from him or her or it, if not from each other."

She reached out, tugged on his jacket to straighten it, and brushed his hair away from his face with the back of her hand. Her tone was soft again. "I have always found your naïveté charming."

He pushed her hand away. "The mages are burning down Trum. What is your plan?"

Aalae's pale-green eyes were unreadable. "The mages are too embedded, too great in number, and I don't know if my Knights can hold the House even with your help. If there is no hope of pushing them back, I ask that you allow your Knights to fight with mine to evacuate the Priestesses."

"What do I get in return?"

"My Knights will fight alongside yours to defend Thell."

He narrowed his eyes at her. "Why would you do that? Why risk your Knights for my House? It was only yesterday that you threatened to destroy my Realm."

"What good is your Realm if it's been destroyed along with mine?" she shot back.

"I'll think on it."

"Think quickly. You can send word through Taia once you decide. She knows how to contact Rafi." Aalae was about to leave when she turned back to Alaric. "Where's Kaila? She wouldn't happen to be in Tiede watching over the new Priestess, would she?"

"Stay away from her and the Priestess Initiate or you'll feel my wrath." Alaric's eyes were glowing, and the darkness was beginning to gather at the edges of the courtyard.

Aalae laughed. "Calm yourself. I haven't the time to watch Kaila sitting in a glorified tub of water. I heard that the new Priestess hasn't even reached the age of reason, so she'll provide very little power to your Realm. You should ask the Seer to try again."

The darkness ebbed, and Alaric pointed towards the path leading out of the Keep. "Get out."

Aalae inclined her head, then turned and proceeded to walk away, with Sabana and Geir falling into step behind her. Alaric motioned with a nod of his head, and Tanghi escorted them out.

Alaric and Taia stood alone in the courtyard, only the sound of crickets and the occasional flutter of wings disturbing the silence. "If it were you, what would you do?" he asked, returning to their previous conversation. "There's no hope for Trum. If you were Aalae, would you ask me to help save the people left in the House? Would you help me defend Thell?"

"I would let Trum and Thell fall," Taia said, looking him in the eye. "I would put all of my effort into defending the next House. If I were Aalae, I would have no intention of helping you."

TWELVE

Aren trailed behind Lord Vir, Elder, and Counselors Helmun and Darc as they walked through the courtyard. He wasn't sure why Vir wanted him to follow, but he wasn't about to question him. They were just passing the mermaid when a rapid clicking of heels on stone caused Aren to turn. Lady Illithe strode towards them, her brows furrowed and her burgundy lips pressed tight. He managed to give a little bow as she passed.

"Lord Vir," she called to stop the rest of the procession. "A word, please."

Vir stopped and turned to face her. "Yes, Aunt Valine?" He waved for the others to continue onward, and Elder led them towards the council room. Aren made to follow, but Valine grabbed his arm. He exchanged a look with Vir, but she held on and continued to address Vir as if Aren wasn't even there.

"Are you taking that girl's warning seriously?"

"That's what I need to talk to my counselors about. Why do you ask?"

She sighed, looking at him as though he were a child who didn't grasp the situation. "Illithe sent scouts east several weeks ago because of rumors of mage unrest in Trum. I didn't think anyone west of the Relythaun, aside from Illithe, had heard, but for that girl to speak of mages—"

"Why didn't you call me?" Vir asked, irritation coloring his tone. "Is there anything else I should know about?"

"We weren't going to call you about a rumor," she said, lowering her voice. "The last thing the Houses need is something to panic about."

Aren looked from Vir to Valine as they spoke, feeling awkward and trapped and just the slightest bit foolish. He wasn't sure why she insisted on including him in their political and familial affairs.

"I'm supposed to be able to rely on you and Illithe, Aunt Valine. Rumors or not, news of mages is serious. Mage uprisings have resulted in thousands of deaths, and now I'm getting the news from a little girl."

"You're right, we should have called you, but understand that our methods of communication are no longer secure. I know you asked the Doctor to come, but our hesitation to trust the relaying of messages is the real reason Father and I came with him."

Aren's mind raced back to the river, to the messenger, and the words from Rose.

Word has reached us that the House of Trum has been infiltrated by mages.

Rose already knew, Aren thought. Illithe knew. And Selina has confirmed everything. If you believe that the gods are actually talking through her, he added to himself.

"I need to talk to my counselors. I will speak with you and Gran Kente tomorrow."

Valine inclined her head a fraction. "We have questions about your new Priestess as well." She finally let go of Aren's arm, and he had to stop himself from taking off. "This is the young man my father indicated earlier?" she asked, changing the topic.

"Yes. This is Elder's Apprentice, Gerrit Aren."

"My Lady." Aren bowed his head.

She stood next to him, too close for Aren's comfort, and he was surprised by how tall she was. She made no secret about studying his face, and he tried not to shy away from her scrutiny.

"The little girl's guardian, for the most part," Vir said, seeming to share in Aren's discomfort. "He, like the girl, is without known blood relatives. The Gerrit family discovered him as a very young child and adopted him."

"Interesting," she said, smiling for Aren. "You've never been to Illithe, then?"

"No, my Lady."

"You might want to have a talk with Doctor Pember while he's here. He specializes in genetics."

Aren was about to thank her, but Vir spoke first. "Aunt Valine, wish Gran Kente a peaceful night for me, and let the servants know if you need anything." Vir turned to continue towards the council room. Aren, torn between following him and paying his respects to the Lady, turned one way, then the other, making a hasty bow before hurrying to catch up with Vir.

A servant girl walked towards them at a quick pace, her face pink, her fingers working at the edge of her apron. Aren recognized the black ribbon that tied her brown hair into a ponytail. She bowed to Vir, then to Aren, and said, "My Lords, there's a Miss Trista at the gates to see you."

"Me?" Vir frowned.

Aren cleared his throat. "Miss, um…Please tell the Guard to send her away."

"But, my Lord," she squeaked, "she says it's a matter of your betrothal."

"It's just Apprentice." Aren exchanged a glance with Vir, who raised his brows. "There is no betrothal. Please have the Guard send her away with instruction to never bother the House again."

After the girl rushed off, Aren said, "Forgive me, my Lord."

The council room was large, dark, and comfortable. The walls and floor were made of dark, polished wood, the floor ingrained with an indecipherable scrolled pattern that had faded over centuries of wear. Paintings encased in brushed gold frames adorned the walls, all of them depicting the sea in some form or another. All the lamps and sconces had been lit, and the gentle flames seemed to dance along the walls.

Vir took a seat in the brown leather chair by the fireplace, accepting a glass of amber liquor that Elder had poured for him. Elder took up a chair near him and worried at the pommel of his saber, unaccustomed to not having his staff to fiddle with. Counselor Terpin Darc looked perfectly at home on the rich, upholstered love seat, while Counselor Novin Helmun paced along the wall, running his fingers over the shelved books. Aren found a spot next to the fireplace, where he stood with his hands clasped behind his back, waiting for someone to ask him to take notes or make drinks or shine shoes.

At last, Helmun asked, "Is there a reason for the Apprentice to be here?" Helmun was pudgy, Tiede's formal dinner attire doing little

to flatter his thick midsection. Aren wondered if it was the reason
Lady Saris was constantly inviting him to her bedroom. He
shuddered.

"He's essentially the Priestess Initiate's guardian," Darc said,
reaching for his drink. "If we're here to discuss the commotion
surrounding the little girl's supposed visions, what better person to
question than the one she is closest to?"

Vir nodded. "I've been informed that the girl and the Apprentice
are like siblings. They're both orphans, Unblessed. As you know, the
Apprentice ended up with the Master Blacksmiths. The Apprentice,
in turn, found the girl." He swirled his glass, then drank down a
mouthful of the liquor.

Helmun said, "I still don't understand—"

"Two days ago," Vir interrupted, "Syrn came looking for their
latest Initiate. Two days ago, the Apprentice and girl were out fishing
on the Taethe. Yesterday the girl was presented to Syrn, and
yesterday the Apprentice approached me with a message from
Rose." Vir paused to let his words sink in.

"But that's impossible," Helmun said, walking towards the love
seat. "Unless they managed to get a boat, in which case the Harbor
Masters need to be punished for letting them in."

"You came through the Wood, didn't you?" Darc asked,
addressing Aren. Aren nodded as the counselor's dark, upswept eyes
scrutinized him. "You seem to have your wits about you," he said,
his tone questioning and curious.

"But that's impossible," Helmun repeated.

"Regardless," Elder said, "the message Lord Vir mentioned is the
reason my Apprentice returned from his holiday. It turns out that
Rose fears a mage uprising, and to have the little Priestess tell of
mages—"

"Is there any basis for this fear?" Darc interrupted.

"Valine just informed me that Illithe has been investigating
rumors of an uprising in Trum." Vir looked to Elder.

"Well," Elder said with a sigh that pushed him into the cushion of
his chair. "That changes things, doesn't it?"

"What do we know of this message or the truth of it?" Helmun
asked, scratching at his trim beard. "And how do we know that Illithe
isn't trying to scare us? Besides, we've had thousands upon
thousands of travelers and messengers before. How do we know this
message and the messenger are authentic?"

"The seal was authentic, and we know Rose doesn't use or trust
the lark. On top of all that, our Harbor is closed. Apprentice, do you

vouch for the messenger?" Vir squeezed his eyes shut for a moment, as if warding off a headache.

"Yes, my Lord," Aren replied. Now was probably a good time to bring up the fact that a mage had attacked him. It seemed so contrived, though, as if he were jumping on the mage bandwagon. "The ferry wasn't taking passengers, his horse abandoned him, and he had no desire to step anywhere near the Wood. He thrust the message upon me and ran off."

"The mages are a dying cult," Elder spoke up. "Their kind has not been active since decades before my time. They've been stopped before, though at great cost."

"And yet," Darc said calmly, "Illithe is concerned or curious enough to send scouts out across the Relythaun Wood. That's a long journey to follow up on a rumor."

"A valid point," Elder said. "Should we consider that mages could be in Tiede?"

Darc lifted an eyebrow. "Would that be easier to believe than a killer we can't catch? How many deaths now? Five? Six?" Silence ensued as everyone considered his words. Then Darc sighed, took a drink, and said, "Are we chasing a man or a monster? Both, perhaps?"

Vir and Elder looked at Aren, who cleared his throat. "That thing I fought in the alley, and whatever it was on the steps that knocked me unconscious—that was no man."

"The message, then," Helmun said, taking a seat next to Darc. "If it's authentic, what does Rose want of us? Even if Trum were under attack, what does Rose have to fear? It's on the other side of the great Relythaun Wood."

Aren recalled a map of Cordelacht, saw the massive expanse of the eastern woods, the twin lakes embedded within them. He moved west from there, imagined the annual market now underway on the western borders of the Relythaun. A little further west, nestled in the rolling hills, was the simple House of Rose: beautiful but unremarkable, and completely defenseless.

Once weakened, we will eventually be overrun by the ambitious Illithe from the north and the barbarous Kaishar on the western end of the Rail.

"The concern I have is about Rose's reaction," Vir said, interrupting Aren's thoughts. "I've not shared this piece of news with anyone, not even my wife, and considering it pertains to her House, you will take to heart the gravity of the situation. I trust you to keep it a secret."

"Yes, my Lord," they responded in unison.

Vir swallowed the last of his drink and rolled the glass in his hands. "The rumors from the east are that the mages were embedded in the towns, maybe even in the House, so Rose has begun locking up everyone who bears the marks of the magic wielder. They would like Tiede to send soldiers to assist. Their people are rebelling against the detainment."

Elder shook his head and Darc leaned forward, resting his elbows on his knees and placing his face in his hands. Aren could tell Helmun wanted to say something, but all he could do was open and close his mouth like a beached fish. Aren had been puzzling over this portion of the message since he had read it. Rose had always been a peaceful House, satisfied with its hold on the quiet green hills. Rose also had a history of having a very strong and persevering line of magic in its people. That would be a lot of people to detain.

"Does Illithe know?" Darc asked, lifting his head to look at Vir. "Rather, did you get the impression from Lady Valine that Illithe knows what Rose is up to?"

"Part of the problem is that I no longer know what Illithe is thinking," Vir frowned. "They have never seen eye to eye with Rose, that much is certain."

Helmun found his voice at last and added, "If we come to Rose's aid and assist in the detainment, Illithe wouldn't stand for it. We can't risk angering Illithe."

"And yet, would we leave Rose in chaos?" Elder asked.

"This isn't something we can resolve right now. Think on it. I want courses of action and scenarios for a response to Rose's dilemma," Vir commanded.

"Yes, my Lord," they said.

Vir turned his attention to Aren. "And it all comes back to the little girl. I want you to keep an eye on her. She warns of magic and war, and I will not take that warning lightly. I'll have the Head Priestess give you as much access as possible without interfering with their rituals. If the girl has any more information, I want it."

THIRTEEN

The first to be dismissed from Vir's meeting, Aren took a moment to sit at the mermaid fountain and look up at the stars. It had been a long day, and he was trying to muster the energy to make it up to his room, get out of his clothes, and collapse into bed. He still had some work to do before he could call it a night, and there was still Master Lake, to whom he promised access to the Library. That, he didn't mind so much.

A flurry of wind danced through the courtyard and fretted the fire in the torches before spinning back up and away into the night sky. It mussed his hair, which he didn't bother trying to push away from his eyes. He contemplated lying down where he was, but he knew that Elder would beat him with his staff if he was caught.

"Aren!"

He looked up to see Rieka, Counselor Darc's daughter and Dane's lover, walking towards him, lifting the hem of her dark-blue, satin and chiffon gown so she could move faster. Her long braid of hair was coiled atop her head, and her smile widened as she approached.

"What are you all dressed up for?" he asked, standing up to greet her. "If you were hoping for dinner, you're late, and your father's in a meeting with Lord Vir."

"My father sent me to see a show that he couldn't attend. Do you know how long their meeting will be? I need the keys to my parents' house." She frowned. "What happened to your face?"

Aren touched the sensitive area around his eye. "Just a run-in with a monster. You can try checking with the Guard about the keys. If your father was anticipating you, he might have left the keys with them."

She brightened. "You're a clever boy. I'm going to assume you don't want to talk about what happened to you, but you can't stop me from worrying."

"No reason to worry. You know me, always making poor decisions." Images of Selina and the incident at dinner tugged at him, and his thoughts were drawn to the Wood. "Do you have a minute for a medical question?"

"Yes, but not if it's too personal. I don't think I'm ready to know more about you than I do about Dane."

He poked at her side and she laughed. "Selina's acting strange," he said, "and I've been having these headaches, so I was wondering if the proximity of magic could cause—"

"Headaches," came a man's voice, refined and clear. "The true plague of the people."

They turned to see a tall man dressed in a crisp, gray dinner suit walking towards them. He seemed to be all legs, moving with the lightness of a bird as he adjusted the round, charcoal-rimmed glasses atop his sharp nose. Rieka stood there frozen, her eyes wide, her breath caught in her throat.

"Doctor Pember," Aren said. "May I introduce Lady Rylilith-Terpin Rieka."

At the sound of her name, Rieka blinked several times. Then, remembering her manners, she bowed her head. Her bare shoulders glowed, the marks flickering then vanishing.

"You must be Counselor Darc's daughter," the Doctor said, seeming to take no notice of her marks. "A pleasure. Your father is most esteemed. We had an interesting conversation over dinner regarding the turbulent history of the truffle."

"My father dabbles in exotic cuisine," she managed to say. Aren raised an eyebrow at her; he had never seen her so dumbfounded and speechless. Her voice was faint and she seemed unsteady.

"Now what is this about headaches and magic?" Doctor Pember asked. "It turns out that genetic mage traits are my specialty."

A doctor from Illithe who specialized in mage traits; Aren's curiosity was piqued. Lady Illithe said he was a geneticist and that Vir had requested he come to Tiede. Aren's mind wandered back to the message he had brought from the river.

Whatever ailments or shortcomings you have must be overcome. These are small obstacles for you, Lord Vir.

"I'd rather not trouble you with my problems," Aren said. He looked at Rieka and smiled, recalling some of the subject matter that he and Dane quizzed her on for her tests. "I wonder, though, can the marked come down with incurable illnesses that the unmarked would be immune to? I've been transcribing an old scroll, and people were very superstitious a long time ago. I wonder if there was any basis for their paranoia."

Rieka passed a questioning glance to Aren. Her suspicion seemed to break her from whatever spell was laid over her, because she cocked her head and said, "There are very few recorded instances of illnesses that can be attributed to the mage trace in the marked genome. In fact, as much as ninety-eight percent of cases that were once thought to be related to the markings were later found to have no relation to the mage markers."

Doctor Pember looked down at Rieka from over his glasses. "Your father didn't mention that you were a student of medicine."

Her cheeks flushed. "I'm apprenticing in Tiede until I can qualify for Illithe's guilds."

"I'd say you might be ready," Doctor Pember smiled, his lips thin. "Perhaps we should have a talk before I return home. My particular school will have an opening for another apprentice soon."

Her eyes widened again, and she bowed from the waist this time, both hands over her heart. "I would welcome the opportunity, Doctor."

Doctor Pember inclined his head, then turned to Aren. "There you have it, Apprentice. Perhaps she has a potion for your headache as well."

Aren bowed, then Doctor Pember continued across the courtyard towards the guest rooms. As soon as he was gone, Rieka punched Aren hard in the abdomen. "You could've warned me! Gods, he must think I'm a fool! I could throttle my father for not telling me Illithe was coming! And you! Why didn't you tell me?"

Aren rubbed at the spot where she had punched him. "How was I supposed to know? Is he important?"

She gripped his forearms, her nails digging. "Doctor Pember is renowned in the medical field for his breakthrough work on molecular expressions. He's done so much toward advancing the areas of mitochondrial ancestry, not to mention all the *dabbling* he's done in reproductive charting and testing against organs with mage-traces!"

"He looks like a stork."

She punched him again. "You weren't really curious about mage illnesses, were you?" she asked, her hand still curled in a fist. "You were setting me up!"

"You're welcome?"

"Aren! Is dinner over?" a woman asked, entering the courtyard.

The Guard who let her in had a large, goofy grin on his face, and he bowed low to her before waving at Aren and returning to his post outside. The woman smiled, pulling down the dark hood of her traveling cloak as she walked towards them, revealing her beautiful face and loosing her silky, black hair.

"Master." Aren couldn't help but smile as he bowed his head.

"I really insist you call me Lake," she said, then looked from Aren to Rieka then back again. "Am I interrupting?"

"Not at all." He tried to stop smiling but couldn't, and he could feel Rieka's eyes boring into him. "This is Lady Rylilith-Terpin Rieka; she's like family to me. Rieka, this is Master Vesila Lake of Tennar."

The two women exchanged pleasantries, and Rieka raised an eyebrow. "Aren didn't mention having a new friend. I see he's been working his magic."

Lake looked at him, and by the expression on her face, he guessed that she was imagining marks on his shoulders. "She's joking," he said. "'Working magic' is a sort of colloquialism we use in the west."

Lake laughed and addressed Rieka, "Aren offered to show me the Library. He's so kind to sacrifice his time. I suppose this is the magic you're referring to."

"Our Aren is all about sacrifice," Rieka said, reaching up to pinch Aren's cheek.

"I was just going to change into my robes first," he said, ignoring Rieka.

"You go change, brother. I'll keep her company until you return."

He laughed, the sound of it false, staged. "Dear Rieka, I wouldn't dream of troubling you. I'll change later. You fetch your father's keys; I know you have a lot of studying to do."

Rieka was about to reply when Lake put herself between them. "You're both being silly. Aren, go change. I'd love to chat with Lady Rieka if she has the time."

He glowered at Rieka, whose shoulders emitted a soft glow that made her blush, then he walked away towards the stairs, glancing over his shoulder once to catch both women waving at him. He really needed to work on keeping himself closed up in the Library more often. Lounging about in the courtyard seemed to bring him nothing but trouble.

FOURTEEN

"Apprentice, I don't know where she is!" Nianni said, her voice high and panic-stricken. She had stopped him just as he left his room, nearly tackling him in the process.

"Calm down, Priestess," Aren said, sucking at his finger. He had been securing the pin that fastened his robe and ended up sticking himself when she grabbed his arm. "Breathe and speak slowly or you might explode, and I'll get skewered by all the silver that goes hurtling outward. Greater detail this time."

"I hate you so much!" she seethed.

"Your attitude isn't going to make me want to help you," he pointed out.

"Selina. Is. Missing." Nianni enunciated each word.

"What do you mean she's missing? You took her back to your room after dinner, didn't you? I thought she was asleep."

"She was! I laid her down, then stepped out to finish my chores and tend to my duties. I'm still expected to do my regular tasks in addition to babysitting," she said, getting defensive. "Head Priestess is going to kill me!"

"How could you lose her? Where have you looked?"

"Both worship rooms, the dining rooms, the kitchen, the parlor. The Library was locked, and two women were talking there, but I didn't ask if they had seen her."

"Maybe she's moving," Aren said, wondering which hallway he should venture down first.

Nianni twisted at her bracelet. "I can tell the Head Priestess, if you think that would be best. Maybe the Seer…"

Aren turned his head, his brows furrowed. He put a hand up to Nianni to quiet her. He had the sensation of being at a show, when the lights dimmed and every person seemed to turn to the person they were with to say, "*Shhh…*" Something was troubling about the thinness of the sound, the way it drifted like smoke and pulled his attention in different directions. His head was starting to throb the way it had by the river.

"Do you hear that?" he asked, his voice less than a whisper.

"Hear what?"

He held a hand up again, listening to the hissing sound for a few seconds, then said, "The roof." He started down the hallway heading east, and Nianni followed after him, trying to keep up with his long stride.

Aren's chest began to hurt, and he pressed a hand over his heart as if it would ease the sharp pain. Broken memories rushed at him, and he knew that the discomfort he was feeling was a bad omen. He hurried towards a hidden alcove, and when he felt the draft, he rushed up the stairs, taking the steps two and three at a time. The strange echoes that inhabited the secret, forgotten places of the House descended on him as if he were prey, and he growled as if to scare them away. He was only vaguely aware of Nianni whimpering as she hastened to keep up.

The door at the far end of the landing was ajar, and he wasted no time in pushing his way through and climbing the remaining steps up onto the rooftop. The sea winds blew more roughly up here, and his robes caught, threatening to hurl him off the roof. He grabbed at the robe's edges and held them close, then turned as Nianni emerged.

"Stay here! I'll be right back."

He followed the narrow walkway that had been integrated into the structure, glimpsing the skylight that led into Aalae's worship room, as well as the high arches that indicated the Library. The hissing voices were stronger, and he pushed on until he reached the incline that led to a spire where one could see the Laithe to the east and the Wood to the south. Selina stood close to the spire, her white robes held close to her little body, her raven hair whipping in the wind. Aren made his way to her, then lowered himself so he could look at her face. The moon shone in her eyes.

"They're asking for you," Selina whispered. "This is what you hear. This is where your headaches come from."

"They aren't calling you, are they?" he asked.

"No, just you."

Aren dropped his head in relief. Thank the stars she wasn't affected the way he was. He looked out in the direction of Tiede Wood. The wind traveled over the strange, dense treetops, causing the whole of it to shimmer in the moonlight. Aren didn't know what to say. On the one hand, he was relieved to know that he wasn't the only one who could hear the voices; on the other hand, what did it mean that Selina could hear them? Was it this whole mess with the goddess communicating with her? He kissed Selina's forehead and took her hand. "It's time to go back to bed now. Priestess was very worried about you."

Nianni surprised him by not asking any questions. "Thank you," was all she said before leading a drowsy Selina back to their room.

Aren ran his hands through his hair. He needed to get back to the Library. There was more research to do on Tiede Wood. Maybe there was something he had overlooked—something in a tale or a legend. Who was it that said Lady Elleina had gone mad? Maybe there was a record of illnesses, an historical list of people who suffered from headaches, visions, delusions. He crossed over towards the stairs leading to the courtyard just as Geyle was coming out of her room.

"Apprentice! Are you all right? You look tired. Everyone is talking about the little Priestess and what happened over dinner. Is she well?"

Aren pushed his hair away from his eyes and looked at the Lady standing before him. He went to pay the proper respects, but she placed a hand on his shoulder to stop him. He gave her a lopsided grin, and she giggled.

"Again, you make me smile," she said, her fingers playing with the ribbon that flowed from the sash around her waist.

"You should more often. It's a lovely smile." Stars, what was he saying? This. This was the sort of thing that got him in trouble.

She stopped fidgeting and smoothed out the skirts of her dress, her cheeks flushing. She looked in the direction of her room, then back at Aren. "I heard that Vir invited you to council. Is it because of the little girl?"

"Selina," he clarified. "Yes."

"Did Vir mention anything else? About Rose or Illithe?"

"My Lady, it's not my place to—"

She bit her lip, then moved closer. Aren, caught off-guard again by her casual manner, moved a step away, pretending to make room for her. Not seeming to notice, she leaned in and whispered, "Lady Illithe doesn't care for me. She's not said one word to me this whole night. I know she thinks I'm not good enough for Vir, and maybe she's right. She's here to tell him to be rid of me. You'll tell me if they talk about me, won't you?"

"Even if Lord Vir said the moon was brilliant this evening, I couldn't tell you." Aren watched slow tears linger on her cheek before falling. "What are his councils to you anyway? Matters of House, that's all. These things you speak of are more personal, not something Lord Vir would discuss with his Counselors and especially not me." Without thinking, he reached out and wiped away a tear with his finger. "Please don't cry." She smiled at him, her cheeks burning and her blue eyes watery. Stars, how did he get himself into these situations?

FIFTEEN

Aren found Rieka and Lake where he had left them. The women were talking in hushed tones, and as soon as he approached, they ended their conversation and turned to smile at him. He raised an eyebrow, but Rieka only stepped over to place a chaste kiss on his cheek. She made her way out through the courtyard, leaving Aren and Lake standing by the Library doors.

He gave Lake a smile as he unlocked the Library and launched straight into the grand tour. He took her through the deep archives and the vaults, showing her the ancient, prized scrolls from the first ancestors of Tiede. He pointed out interesting facts about the architecture and explained where different types and subjects of books could be located and how they were indexed and organized.

She asked questions as they went along, showing a sincere appreciation for the Library's historical significance. She was a wealth of knowledge, making suggestions on the cross-indexing techniques Elder had set up and advising on the care and protection of those volumes from Tennar that used a strange type of acidic wood-pulp paper. Aren pulled out his notebook and jotted down her recommendations. He enjoyed walking through the Library with her and found that he wasn't even thinking of her amorously. He wasn't wondering what words he should use to impress her or even what she thought of him. All that mattered was the conversation, the exchange of thoughts and ideas between them, the mutual respect for knowledge. He could talk to her all night.

"Thank you again for being so patient with me," he said as he led her back towards his desk. "I know you don't have a lot of time before you have to go. I got carried away showing you everything, and I feel bad that I made you wait so long for me to return earlier." He offered her a chair, then took a seat next to her.

"I got just as caught up as you did. Tiede's Library is everything I've heard tell of and more, but you never did say why you were gone so long."

"My little sister Selina, the newly chosen Priestess…" He fiddled with a pen on his desk for a moment. "It's a long story. We're not blood-related, but I'm all she has and she was having trouble sleeping."

Lake looked at him, smiling with admiration. "It sounds like you had good reason to be delayed. If I finish my research quickly, perhaps you wouldn't mind sharing your story. I know it's late, but I've nowhere to be until morning. I understand, though, if you're tired. I have a room at the inn I can return to."

He looked up from the twirling pen, stilling his fingers. "I can share a story if you'll tell me what you and Rieka were talking about."

"We'll see." She winked. "Let me get started on my research. Maybe you can get some work done too, and your evening won't be a complete waste."

Aren couldn't fight the smile on his face. "I'll ask the kitchen to send us some coffee."

There was a resonating click, followed by the groan of heavy, ancient wood as the doors to the Library opened. Aren and Lake exchanged glances before he stood up to greet whoever was visiting this late in the evening.

Vir strode towards them, still wearing his dinner attire. "Apprentice."

"My Lord." Aren dropped to his knee, bringing his fist to his chest. Lake rose to her feet next to him, bowing her head in respect.

Vir made a motion with his hand to tell Aren to get up. "And *you* are?" he asked Lake curtly.

"Master Vesila Lake of Tennar, Lord Vir," she said, her voice calm and steady. "Elder Lyte Tanda invited me."

"Welcome to Tiede, Master," Vir said, his suspicions disappearing at the mention of Elder's name. He turned his attention back to Aren. "Elder is in Council, so I need your assistance. My father once spoke of an ancestor who had a fighting technique that involved two special blades. I want to make sure that such a thing exists before I call on the Guild."

"I know exactly what you're talking about," Aren said, thankful for the easy question. "I'll get the reference for you." He disappeared into the stacks and reemerged a moment later with one of Tiede's historical volumes, flipping through the pages and placing the book on his desk to point out a section with various anatomical diagrams.

"It was originally used to behead mages. Your ancestor, who invented the technique in conjunction with an unnamed Fighters Guild Master, was Lord Tiede Mar," Aren explained. "It's called Uniting the Heavens. It's no longer used because it's impractical to fight with two blades. Those few who do it seem to do so for show."

"It would take too much discipline," Vir mumbled. "Strength is one thing, but to wield two long blades in harmony for the purpose of battle would take much more effort than mastering one long sword."

Aren hesitated, then said, "I can demonstrate the basics, if you'd like. There's a ritual to it; for example, aligning your blades to Night and Light, channeling both energies from your *kal* evenly into each blade—"

"You've studied this?" Vir raised an eyebrow, looking over the illustrations.

"Master Gerrit required his children to learn all the blade techniques," Aren explained, "even the so-called forgotten ones. If it existed, we had to learn it. Fighter Gerrit Gryf is set to be the first Master of the dual blade in decades."

Vir scrutinized Aren. "You can fight with two blades?"

Aren felt heat rising to his face. "I'm no expert, but yes I can, my Lord."

"Show me," Vir said, releasing the saber at his side and tossing it.

Aren caught it by the pommel and shrugged out of his robe, draping it across the back of his chair. "I don't have another blade at the moment—"

"Crescent Fire then," Vir demanded, referencing one of the older, lesser-known exercises.

Lake took a step back. Like Vir, she seemed to have no idea that a bookworm like him could use a blade. Aren moved to the clear area in front of the desks. "Crescent Fire" was one of the most artful of sword stances, used for show by average swordsmen, but a graceful and deadly combination when executed by a Master, even if it was labeled an exercise. Aren was no Master, but he knew how to handle a sword. He just hoped he wouldn't end up putting a tear in his pants or accidentally stabbing Vir.

Aren took a breath, slashing at the air to loosen his wrist. He went through the series of sword stances and exercises that Gryf had taught him at least once a week, but he still felt rusty.

May as well get this over with, he thought. He ran through a series of graceful moves that showed off his precision with the blade as he turned one way then another, as if fighting some imaginary opponent. His long body was agile and swift, as his mind guided each muscle. When the blade had completed its crescent arc, his sword hand settled close to his outstretched ankle while his other arm was positioned out to counterbalance. The entire sequence happened in the space of eight heartbeats.

Vir nodded and signaled for Aren to rise. He closed the book on the desk and picked it up. "I'll send for Master Gerrit's son. I'll want you there as well. The Messenger will notify you. If Gerrit can teach, I'll need you as a sparring partner."

"Yes, my Lord," Aren said, handing the saber over.

Vir took the weapon, then studied Aren for a moment. "How long have you been apprenticed to Elder?"

"Six years to the day."

Vir stared at him a little longer. "As the most senior apprentice in this House, it's time you took a more active role. You won't get very far hiding behind these books."

"Yes, my Lord."

Vir turned to give Lake a slight nod. "Good evening, Master." She returned the gesture and they watched him leave the Library.

Lake tilted her head at Aren, a wide smile on her face. "I'm impressed."

SIXTEEN

Kaila liked this young mortal far more than the man who had taught her cards in Kaishar. When she had followed Aren around Tiede last night, he seemed so distracted, uncoordinated, and naïve, but in the little time she had spent with him so far, he had proven to be intelligent, funny, and very charming. He was also graceful with a blade—beautiful even. Her memories spun back to their first meeting on the road near Tiede Wood—she as a swan and he as a sleepy fisherman. He had revealed his true skill then, his swiftness and his mind's ability to sense changes in his surroundings. He was an enigma.

Aren had cleared a space for her at his desk, and he busied himself with shelving stacks of books and answering research questions that Elder had left for him. She watched him every now and then from the corner of her eye, fascinated by how he had immersed himself in his work, determined to give her the space she needed.

She looked over her notes. The little Priestess couldn't be more than six or seven, and the images Kaila had seen—which she could only imagine were memories—were still fresh in Selina's mind. The rainstorm images had been the most prevailing, so she narrowed her search to the most record-worthy storms of the past five years.

She noted the storm that had resulted from the fight with Alaric during the autumnal aurorae. Tiede's records had much to say about it. The lower harbor area had flooded, and one fisherman had lost his life at sea. The storms were strongest the first three days, but continued on for several weeks. The aurorae, however, had been the most beautiful ever witnessed in Tiede.

She found it strange to read what the mortals thought of the incident. Beautiful, they had said. To her, it was one of the most terrible fights she had ever had with Alaric. It wasn't often he would turn demon, and "beautiful" was not the word she would have used to describe those evenings.

"Is everything all right?" Aren asked, leaning back in his chair, a small leather-bound book open in his hands, a look of concern on his face.

Kaila was taken aback, and it took her a second to snap out of her reverie. He closed his book and sat up, raising an eyebrow at her. "I was reading about this storm," she said. "It says a fisherman died, and I was just thinking of how awful that must have been for his family."

Aren moved closer to read the text she was referring to, then leaned back in his chair again. "No one knew that the rains were coming or that they were going to come down so hard. The seas were violent that morning, and the skies lit up bright as day, despite the dark clouds. We'd all hoped it wouldn't last because it was the height of the aurorae, and it's a tradition in Tiede to sit outside and watch the evening skies."

"You must have been so disappointed," she said, recalling her own anger and sadness.

"I don't know if you've ever seen the aurorae; I know they aren't visible from Tennar, but in your line of study, you must've traveled to see it. It's spectacular, and no one has a better view than Tiede."

She smiled at the pride in his voice. "I've seen it from Illithe, but my goal was to return to Tiede this coming autumn to view them from here."

"Come see me when you return. I know a nice spot in this House to view them where no one will bother us."

"Let me guess." She pointed up. "The roof?"

"Some of the servants who don't fear the heights and winds go up there, and most people like to go to Crescent Park or the Harbor and Guild Districts to take part in the festivities. If I'm not with my family, I go to the House baths to watch. I take a bottle of wine and lean out over the wall. Between the sea and the sky, there's so much peace."

"And you're inviting me to this inner sanctum of yours?"

"I'd certainly consider it," he teased. "I'm sure you have some interesting stories you could tell based on your studies. I might be willing to share a bottle of wine with you for a few good stories."

She laughed, leaning back in her chair and crossing her legs. Her heart felt lighter, and she was surprised that he could have this effect on her. The pain of her memories had a tendency to linger and cloud her mood, but with a few words he had brushed the pain away.

"Anyway," he said, "everyone spent the day inside, praying the rains would end, but it got worse; thunder shook the cliffs and lightning tore up the sky. People swore up and down that the world was ending. Then night fell, and rain or not, people began peeking out their windows and looking to the heavens. Sure enough, the aurorae appeared, brilliant as jewels against the blackened skies. Everyone wandered out of their houses and into the streets just to get a better look because fat clouds cut a horizontal line through the aurorae. You'd think that'd make for a terrible show, but the clouds were lighting up! So you have these amazing drapes of color, then bursts of white light erupting all over it. I stood by the baths, drenched from the downpour, but I couldn't stop watching. It was brilliant." Kaila stared at him with fascination; the wonder and amazement on his face made him look like a little boy. "I'm sorry. I talk too much when I'm comfortable." His cheeks grew red, and he turned his gaze to the book in his hand, a smile playing on his lips.

"I'm glad to get this firsthand account from you," she said so that he wouldn't feel embarrassed. "So often I read of these events, but there's not much substance without knowing how people were affected."

He looked at her and nodded. "There's only one other storm I can think of right off that really impacted me. It was the night I met Selina."

Kaila perked up. This was the event she was searching for. She took her cup of coffee and sipped a little. It was still hot and helped ease her excitement. She hoped her hands weren't shaking. "I think it's time for that story you promised me."

He laughed. "I don't recall a promise, only an exchange."

She flashed him a coy look. "If your story is good enough, I think an arrangement can be made," she said, referencing his willingness to trade stories for wine.

"Get comfortable, then. You're about to take a peek into my peculiar world."

"I expect nothing less," she said, reaching over to push stray strands of hair away from his eyes.

SEVENTEEN

Aren felt dizzy and wished with all of his heart that he could just lay down for a minute. He was tired, he reasoned. He had traveled all the way from the river the other day, running through the Wood to save his and Selina's lives. Then, he had stayed up late last night and was up late again this evening. That's why he was all out of sorts.

Who was he kidding? It was this woman. Her fingertips had brushed against his temple when she moved his hair aside, and he wanted nothing more than for her to touch him like that again. There had been no meaning in it—nothing seductive or mysterious or suggestive. So why did he feel as though his chest would explode?

"Are you well?" she asked.

He started to respond, then stopped, clearing his throat. "I'm fine. I bumped my head the other night, and—"

"I didn't want to be rude"—she indicated his left eye—"and ask when Elder introduced us. It looks like you took a beating."

He nodded, his eyes downcast. "I don't recall what happened, but there's this thing in Tiede that's been killing people. It hasn't been caught yet, and I think I'm the first person who's seen it up close and survived." He slid over the book he had been reading. "It said things to me I didn't understand. I was hoping this book would help; it has some of the older dead languages in it."

She picked it up and opened to a random page, skimming the words. "Were you able to figure it out?"

"My knowledge of old languages isn't terrible, but I'm far from being an expert. How are you on old languages?" he asked, pulling his notebook and pen close.

"Fair enough. What did you hear?"

He wrote the words on a blank page as she looked on. "I think I figured out enough to know how to spell it, based on key markers. *Shiijanh* is one of the words. The other is *nafhakur*. But it makes no sense. They sound like words in Ancient, but I've not been able to find a meaning."

"If you have the sound of the words, and if you isolated the key, then I'm sure you can figure out the rest," she said, taking his pen and correcting his writing. "It's not Ancient. Try this: *T'jand. Niaf'kur.*"

"Old Magic," he breathed, surprised. "I never would've guessed! I was so focused on using Ancient."

"So now do you know what it means?"

"Don't laugh if I get it wrong; my Old Magic is horrific," he said, squinting. "One who brings. A messenger?"

"That's right. *T'jand* refers to one who carries something from one place to another."

"And *niaf'kur* is something along the lines of 'one of our own'?" He scribbled a sentence. "So the last thing I remember translates to 'offering is good'—whatever that means."

"You are awfully young to know so much about the old languages." She winked at him.

"Look who's talking." He nudged her knee with his. "You just saved me hours of research." He looked her in the eyes, loving the genuine happiness he sensed in them. "Thank you. I don't know why this creature said these things to me, but I'm a step closer."

"Does this mean you're going to tell me that story?" she asked, closing the book on languages and placing it on the desk.

He took a deep breath, exhaled. "You have to promise you won't laugh or think I'm crazy."

"Is your story really that outlandish?"

"Some might think so. There was this woman..." He stumbled to explain. "It was three years ago. I was at the Mermaid's Song waiting for my brother Dane."

Aren sat at their usual spot near the back of the tavern, waiting for Dane to show up. He was almost through with his first beer that evening when Gryf came over. It wasn't unusual for Gryf to join them every now and then, and Aren pushed a seat out for him with the toe of his boot.

"Hey," Gryf said, punching Aren's shoulder.

"Hey. Joining us tonight?"

"Can't," Gryf said in his usual curt manner. "Just came by to tell you that Dane won't be either."

"Is he in trouble?" Aren asked, half joking.

"Yes. Father's got him chained to one of the work tables in the forge to make sure he doesn't try to get out of his chores."

"Thanks for letting me know. Guess I'll just head back to the House."

As Aren watched Gryf disappear through the crowded pub, a barmaid caught Aren's eye, and she pointed to a glass to see if he wanted another drink. He shook his head and drained the rest of his beer. She winked at him and he smiled, debating whether or not to talk to her.

He pushed his chair back as he stood up, bumping against someone walking by behind him. He turned to apologize, but the words never came out as he gazed upon the most beautiful woman he had ever seen. She wore a traveler's cloak of heavy, sky-blue velvet lined with matching satin, and her hood fell back to reveal silky, straight flaxen hair that fell to her shoulders. Her eyes were a shiny jade, and she had the gentlest slope of a nose. Her lips were the color and lushness of pink rose petals, parted slightly as if waiting for a kiss.

She seemed to glow. He was speechless.

"I was in your way." She smiled.

"Not at all, my lady," he finally managed to say. "I apologize, I can be an oaf. Are you hurt?"

"No, I'm perfectly fine."

"You're not Tiedan." It was the only sentence he could put together.

"I'm traveling through, and your features say you aren't Tiedan either."

"Yes and no. I'm Aren," he introduced himself.

She held a hand out to him in the style of the Old World, and he reached out to touch it to his lips, thanking Elder in his mind for the lessons on Old World traditions. She was about to say something but at his touch pulled away as if he had shocked her.

"Your blessing," she said at once, clearing her throat. "To which god do you belong?"

He groaned on the inside but kept smiling. "I belong to no one."

"You tease me." Her smile was coy and she poked a slender finger at his chest.

He grabbed her hand, held it close, feeling dizzy and crazy and not quite himself. "If you insist."

"Aren," she said his name, as if tasting it, then tugged at him to follow. "You are very tempting, but I was just leaving when you bumped into me. Walk me out?"

He took a smattering of coins from his pocket, laid them down in front of the barmaid, and followed the beautiful woman out into the night. They stood in the wash of the lamplight. She pulled her hood over her head and seemed to shrink into her cloak.

"Are you cold?" he asked, unfastening his own cloak to give her. "Where are you going? I'll walk with you."

"It's the night," she pouted, touching his hand to keep him from giving up his cloak. "I don't care for it. Also, if my brother sees me unattended, he'll have a fit. I need to go before he finds me; he would kill me if he knew I was here."

"I'm not afraid of him. Stay a while longer."

"You should be afraid." She looked up at him, clasped her hands behind her back. "In all seriousness, which god do you belong to?"

"Is it that important to you?"

"Humor me." Her smile was dazzling. "I like to read fortunes, and part of it requires knowing which god you belong to."

He folded his arms across his chest and shrugged. "I wasn't blessed at birth. What does your fortune-reading have to say about that?" He didn't mean to sound so clipped and rude, and he wished he could take it back. Seemingly unoffended, she took one of his hands into both of hers. He felt a warmth wash over him.

"It says nothing." Her voice was silky and sweet. "There's something familiar about you. I just can't put my finger on it—"

A deep rumble interrupted her, and Aren thought he could feel the ground shake. They both looked around and within seconds, lightning tore up the dark skies to the southeast. He could hear the shattering sound of rain rushing towards the town center. Within seconds, a torrential downpour was upon them, and he pulled the woman back under the protective awning of the tavern.

People were rushing to find shelter, surprised by the sudden violent storm. The winds began to pick up, throwing the water in all directions, and it was all Aren could do to shelter the lady. Within seconds he was soaked, and the storm showed no sign of letting up.

"Do you have a room at one of the inns?" he asked, raising his voice to be heard above the thunder. He leaned close to her ear and said, "I can see if there's a room available here—"

"I'd like that..." she started, but her voice trailed away as she looked out at the dissipating crowds. Her eyes widened.

Curious, he turned to see what she was looking at. A tall, shadowed figure of a man in the distance was running towards them. Aren wasn't sure if the eerie flashes of lightning were playing tricks on him, but the man's eyes seemed to glow.

"My brother," she giggled. "I guess he found me. I have to go!"

Before Aren could register what was happening, the woman ran off into the rain. He watched her pale-blue cloak drift further away from him, illuminated here and there as she passed under the biolight of the streetlamps. Then the man ran past, swift as a deer, his long black hair trailing behind him.

It took several seconds for Aren to realize that the woman of his dreams was about to disappear forever. He ground his teeth, then took off after them. Why did this sort of thing always happen to him? He couldn't imagine any man having the terrible luck he did with women, and he was determined not to let this one get away.

He never even learned her name.

The rain and the darkness made it difficult to see, and soon he lost sight of the woman's pale-blue cloak and the man's black cape. He paused to catch his breath, slicking back his hair, which was plastered all over his forehead and dripped into his eyes.

As he trudged through the rivers of water filling the streets, his eye caught movement to his left in the alley between two Guild houses. Calamity, a stray black cat that often wandered around town, had knocked over a lid to one of the trash bins in her search for food. Aren was about to move on when he saw a figure pick up the fallen lid and hold it up over its head.

Stars, it was a child!

Aren ran down the alley, dropped to the child's level. The skinny little girl's black hair was matted, her green dress tattered and soaked through. She was crying and her eyes glistened, though he couldn't tell her tears from the rain. "What are you doing out here?" he asked, scooping her up and rushing her back to the awning he had been standing under with the woman earlier. He set the girl down, and her little fists rubbed at her eyes as she cried. He dropped to his knees so she could see his face. "You're all right, sweetheart. I won't let anything hurt you. Where are your parents?" he asked, pushing his wet hair back from his eyes and rubbing a sleeve across his face.

A rumble of thunder was followed by a long stretch of lightning that split the sky in two, and the little girl screamed and threw her arms around his neck. He hugged her tight, picked her up, and looked around. He didn't see anyone frantically searching for a child; in fact, the streets were deserted. She was so small; she couldn't have been older than three or four.

"Are you lost?" he asked.

"Don't know," she mumbled into his shoulder.

If he left her out in this downpour, she would get sick. He had to find somewhere for her to dry off and get warm, and she probably also needed food, considering how thin she felt to him.

"Damn," he said under his breath. He wanted to search for the woman of his dreams, but she was long gone. Aren decided to return to the tavern. At the very least, he could get the little girl some food and something warm to drink. Calla, the tavern proprietress, would have towels and a fire. He readjusted the girl in his arms and prepared to run through the rain back towards the tavern.

"What's your name?" he asked.

She looked at him with big, violet eyes. "Selina."

Aren looked at Lake, trying to gauge her expression. If she thought he was being ridiculous, she didn't say it; in fact, she seemed to hang on his every word. He took a drink of coffee before continuing.

"I spent the entire evening with Selina, then went to the Harbor the next day when the rains died down. When I asked if any foreign ships had docked recently, the harbormasters shook their heads. I even returned to the tavern and asked the barmaid if she'd seen the beautiful woman in the blue cloak. She was annoyed and said she didn't pay much attention to the women I was flirting with."

Lake laughed at this, then at his perplexed expression. "Charming," she said. "Rieka says you work magic, but I'm beginning to think you have no idea when you're doing it."

"No magic. Three years is a long time, and I've grown up since then. I hope I have, anyway."

"You were so naïve," she said. "Precious and naïve."

"Well, I haven't forgotten that you said you'd share whatever conversation you had with Rieka."

"In a minute. We have all night, and your story has piqued my curiosity."

EIGHTEEN

Kaila knew this was the story behind the images in Selina's head. There was more to it, though, and she was beginning to put together the pieces to a much larger puzzle. It seemed she was not the first from Mytanth to have dealings with Aren, and she wanted to know why that was.

"Did you ever find Selina's family? Were you able to figure out anything about her background?" she asked.

"No on both accounts, and she still has no recollection of her life before that storm."

"And the woman? You never learned her name? Never heard from her?"

Aren began twirling the pen on the desk again. "Nothing. For a while I couldn't get her out of my head." He shrugged. "But I became more involved with helping Selina get settled and taking care of her, and the memories of the woman stopped haunting me."

Kaila stilled his hand and he looked up at her. "Does it bother you still? I'm sorry I brought it up."

He laughed a little, turning his hand so that he held hers. His thumb stroked the skin of her wrist, and she sensed a curiosity in him, as if he were simply wondering what she felt like. He had long fingers and strong hands, rough in places from years of manual labor and, she imagined, swordplay. She felt like a kitten in his palm.

"It doesn't bother me," Aren said, letting go of her. "As I said, it was a long time ago."

Sensing that he was done talking about the woman, Kaila redirected the conversation. "This storm took place three years ago?"

"At the height of the summer solstice turn."

She flipped through one of the books she had pulled to do her research, scanning the different entries. Aren leaned in next to her and pointed at the section that referenced the storm they were discussing.

"Unpredictable...without warning..." she read out loud.

"I didn't know this." He read, "A strange darkness was recorded in the southern Tiede region, primarily in the southeast over Tiede Wood. At one point, the Wood looked as though it would be swallowed whole by the blackness, and strange, beastly noises emanated from it."

Kaila closed the book and tapped the cover with her fingers, the memories of that evening coming back to her in full force. It had been the last time she had fought alongside her siblings—when they had brought down the heavens.

"Do storms play into your study of celestial activity?" Aren asked.

"The big ones do. I'd say a strange darkness in the sky descending over a particular spot classifies as celestial phenomena." Kaila stretched her arms out in front of her. "I'm in your debt, Aren. Not only was I able to get research done, but I also had a lovely evening."

"The feeling is mutual." He smiled at her. "Now, the conversation with Rieka?"

She rolled her eyes. "It was just the sort of thing women talk to each other about. She asked if I was married, and she talked about her beau, your brother—"

"Are you married?" he interrupted her. "There's no ring or sign that I noticed."

"There's a man," she said, her eyes downcast, "who claims to be in love with me, but I'm conflicted." Kaila looked up to face him, her feelings numbed and confused. Why was she opening up to this mortal? "I don't know what I want anymore."

"Does he suit you?"

"He's intelligent and handsome, as you are," she said, causing him to cast his eyes downward this time. "And I find you to be quite suitable."

"Now who's doing the charming?" He chuckled. "He would be wise to do whatever it takes to win you over completely."

"Perhaps he will. Right now it's irrelevant. We have books and stories and pleasant company. It does please you, does it not?"

"It does. Do you have to leave in the morning? Stay one more day; let me show you around Tiede."

"Let's not try to change what's already fated to be. Tell me more about Selina and your brother and the rest of your family," Kaila said, placing a hand over his. "I'd love to hear about them and you, and our time together is fleeting."

For a moment Aren seemed to study her, and she found herself mesmerized by the glittering green of his eyes. Then he nodded, accepting that she wouldn't be staying, and began another story—one about a little boy who was found by the edge of the Wood.

NINETEEN

Catar sat on a bench in Crescent Park, a book open on his lap, the hood of his apprentice robes drawn over his head. It was too late in the evening to be out, which might arouse suspicion, but he needed to connect to someone. He needed to know that the plan was working, that his brethren were in place, and that they believed everything was going well. He felt his will faltering because his brother was dead. He had received confirmation via a scribbled note from their colleague in the House, and that news caused his resolve to weaken.

I've seen the staff. It's in the Library.

His brother was dead. Catar needed strength right now, so he took a chance at finding one of his own. He only needed a few minutes. He knew that fellow mages would be on this mission, but he didn't know who they were or how many they numbered. He followed the gossip about mages and monsters as it flitted through the streets. That was when he found one of his brethren.

The mage was unreadable, but Catar had followed him after their monster's attack on the town center last night. People were running and screaming, but this man continued to walk as if nothing was amiss. Catar followed him to the tall, obsidian monuments that were known as markers for the dead, where those who had passed could still be heard—another lie the Priestesses fed to the foolish god-worshippers.

There, away from the biolight and shrouded by the confusion that the monster was causing, Catar watched the mage slice open the throat of a young woman who had been drugged, bound, gagged, and left there as part of their ritual. There was a gasp, then a gurgle, then nothing but the sound of blood spilling, feeding the currents of magic in the earth. The mage removed the strips of cloth that tied and silenced the woman before concealing his knife and moving on to the next sacrifice.

The man was called Mercer. He also donned the gear of the alchemist apprentice, but he did less to hide his features. Mercer wasn't surprised when Catar had approached him, and they traded information about where and when they could meet, and who else might be with them.

They sat on a bench now, close enough to talk but far enough so that no one would think they were together. "How can my brother be dead? The message was delivered," Catar said. "If it hadn't been, we wouldn't have been able to raise the beast."

"You know the Harbor was closed. The sacrificial killings backfired on us. The only way into Tiede was through the southern gates. Somehow, they managed to convince someone else to get the message into Tiede Vir's hands," Mercer explained. "Focus on the mission. You brought the beast to life. If you can sustain it for a few more days, it'll be powerful enough to kill Vir without any issues. The man has too much protection around him, but once he's dead the chaos will be so complete that when our armies come from the east, Tiede will fall easily."

"Life requires life," Catar said. "We need to let it out to feed again, and I admit I'm worried about how much power he needs in order to get past all the skilled fighters in the House."

"Don't worry, they're all mortal. Products have changed hands?" When Catar nodded, Mercer continued. "Then, just be patient. Vir will die one way or another. I'll let you know when we can let the monster out again; it had a minor setback in that last attack. I don't know if you noticed."

"Setback?"

"It smelled something it thought was magic, but according to the information the girl gave me, the man's no mage," Mercer said.

The news made Catar uneasy. "It isn't supposed to get confused. If the victim survived, and he's not a mage, then what is he?"

"I don't know yet, but if we get rid of him, we won't have to worry about it." Mercer stood up to leave. "We just need more time; the creature is still growing, still learning. Don't worry; everyone will get a chance to die, even the Apprentice. Rumor is he's the one who killed your brother."

SECRETS

ONE

Aren went through his morning routine in a daze, and as he sat in the hot salt baths, he smiled. He and Lake had spent the entire night laughing, exchanging stories, and playing copper and dice. They talked about smithing, stargazing, and fishing. He taught her how to play a simple whistle flute, and she taught him how to fold tiny paper stars.

When the coffee was gone and his desk was littered with stars, she wished him a good night—what was left of it. He took her hand in both of his and pressed it to his lips, asking her to stay another day. She declined. Perhaps their paths would cross again, she had told him. He stared after her, and at the Library doors she turned to look at him. Her eyes were shiny and she bowed her head and placed two fingers over her heart before leaving.

Aren sighed. There was no point in dwelling on her departure. He finished his bath and returned to his room to get dressed to spar with Lord Vir. A note regarding the training session had been slipped under the door to his room earlier that morning. The sound of the paper sliding against the floor had awakened him, and he cursed his inability to fall into a deep sleep.

He cut through the courtyard and was stopped by two servants, men younger than himself whom Aren had seen a handful of times. The taller one was the servant he had seen in the garden pouring water for Lady Saris.

"Master!" the shorter man said. "I need your help! We're low on House oil, and we put in an order at Wethern's, but his apprentice told us that they were behind because of the deliveries stuck at the Harbor. Lord Vir's been working late into the night, and we can barely keep up."

"Just Apprentice," Aren corrected him. "Not Master. There was a delivery yesterday, and I set it all aside for Lord Vir. Take whatever you need. I'll ration what I have left for the Library until Wethern's catches up."

The young man bent low from the waist. "Thank you, Master! Thought for sure we'd get thrown into the dungeon for this!" The taller fellow, garden-lemon-water-boy, remained quiet, his eyes downcast as if afraid to look at Aren.

"Are you both new here?" Aren asked.

"Dekney, I am. And this is Horin," said the short one. "Oh, and cook said if we found you we should bring you this." He handed Aren a small cloth sack and bowed again before they hurried off towards the storage room. Aren peeked into the bag. There were a few slices of warm bread, a little brick of cheese, and pre-harvest pipe apples. He had time to get to the *kasan* and have a leisurely breakfast before warming up. He might even have some time to read. So far, he was having a brilliant day.

Aren entered the *kasan*, prepared to kick off his shoes, when an arm struck his midsection. He felt the air leave his lungs as a fist came into view to greet him. He twisted to dodge but felt the knuckles glance off his chin. He dropped low, hoping that his attacker would continue to aim high. His opponent was ready for him, and he felt the point of a knife under his chin.

"I failed to mention." Aren grinned. "I guess you got the message."

The knife disappeared, and an open palm whacked Aren against the back of his head. "A little warning would've been nice," Gryf said, grabbing Aren by the upper arm to haul him up. "Imagine my surprise when a Guild Master told me Lord Vir requested I come in to conduct some training thanks to the Historian's Apprentice. And you need to stop being so predictable; I could've killed you."

"Is that food?" a muffled voice called out from within the *kasan*. "Bring."

Aren looked over to the figure lying face down on a wooden side bench. He raised an eyebrow at Gryf, "You brought Dane?"

"If I'm training, I need another dummy who knows what he's doing for you to demonstrate technique with. You hand my head to Lord Vir on a silver platter, and I take both of you with me as side dishes."

Dane ambled over and grabbed the sack from Aren's hands. He peered inside, reached in, pulled out some bread, and began to eat. "Rieka told me about the woman," he said between bites.

"Purely platonic," Aren said, taking off his shoes and pushing them against the wall. "Her name's Lake and she's already involved with someone." He rolled up his sleeves. "But even if she weren't, she had to leave this morning anyway."

"And if she didn't have to leave?" Dane asked.

"I'd rather not speculate."

"You can't do it. Chasing after the wrong woman is like a drug to you," Dane said.

"Speaking of women," Aren started as Dane rolled his eyes, "Trista came by the House last night. One of the servants—you know, the one always calling me Lord—came up to me in front of Lord Vir to tell me that Trista demanded to see me to talk about our betrothal."

"What was she thinking?" Dane asked, incredulous.

"She's lost her mind," Aren said as Gryf shook his head.

"I don't know why she's so fixated on you. It's not like you bedded her." Dane paused, then looked at Aren. "You didn't, did you?"

Aren whacked his brother's head hard. "No, you idiot. Even if I didn't have this so-called curse on me, I wouldn't have."

Dane rubbed his head, laughing, "Maybe you should've tried to. Your curse would've killed her, and you wouldn't have to deal with her anymore." Aren lunged at him and they began to wrestle and punch each other.

"I'm going to have Lord Vir beat the stars out of the both of you," Gryf said.

Vir arrived not long after the food was devoured, and the three brothers took a knee, fists over their hearts. Vir took off his shoes and shirt, then entered the *kasan's* arena. He was alone. No assistant or Guard or Hunter escorted him. In any other House this would have been odd. He regarded them, then addressed Gryf, who had the Fighter Guild's fire crest inked into his upper left arm. "The Apprentice said you were one of the rare few who could execute the technique Uniting the Heavens, and your Guild Masters agreed."

"Yes, my Lord. I've asked our brother Dane to join us. He's skilled with the sword and can help demonstrate."

Vir nodded. "I trust your judgment. You're not a full Master yet?"

"I've been sworn in as Blade Master and Fist Master among other disciplines, but I'm still working on full Master for all the combat arts."

"Blade Master, then. The Apprentice also led me to believe that the dual blades, when used by one with experience, is not merely for show."

"It's a fighting technique and that's how I'll be teaching it. Unless you were hoping otherwise."

"The blade is not intended for show," Vir said. "Let's begin."

When they had finished, water and fresh towels were brought in. Aren had managed to get a long cut on his forearm, which he wrapped to staunch the bleeding. They wiped their brows and necks in silence as Gryf sat by the sword rack, taking a soft cloth to each blade they had used. The blades had been very well kept, and Dane had silently pointed out the Gerrit mark on each one, though his brothers had already noticed.

Aren thought it surreal to cross blades with the House Lord. At first Vir was reserved and kept a grave expression on his stone-like face. After a few blows, though, Aren could see glimpses of the flesh-and-blood man who had worked all of his life to create the mask of power that all of Cordelacht expected to see attached to the name of Tiede.

"What next, Master?" Vir asked.

"Watching you spar with my brothers has revealed your skill level," Gryf said. "If you have time, I can start teaching the technique later today. Otherwise, late tomorrow."

"Why not now?"

"In the hands of a virgin, the dual blades can't meet until the sun crosses her zenith," Gryf said, folding the cloth he had been using, a broadsword across his lap.

"It's an old superstition among Fighters," Aren explained when he saw the confused expression on Vir's face. "Anyone who engages in a dual blade technique for the first time is called a virgin of the twin blades. The very first time a Master under a Night House instructs you in this technique, the sun must be past the high point in the skies during daylight hours in the summer season. The blades represent the god and goddess, and if you want them united, one can't be wholly dominant over the other. You can't learn how it feels to have balanced *kal* between two blades until you experience it."

"Superstition," Vir said.

Aren shrugged. "It's the way of the Fighter. No Master will teach unless it's just so. After the first time, the rule no longer applies because you'll know what it feels like to achieve that balance."

"Very well. I'll have my Messenger send word, and then..."

Gryf's head shot up as a robed figured burst into the room. He immediately jumped to his feet, the broadsword in both hands, moving with fluidity as he rushed across the *kasan* floor. The movement caused Dane to perk up, and he took up the blade he hadn't yet put away. Dane pulled a knife from the sheath at his hip and tossed it to Aren, who caught it by the handle. Without thinking, Aren grabbed Vir by the arm and put himself between Vir and his brothers, who were approaching the edge of the *kasan's* arena.

The robed figured pointed a staff in Vir's direction and let loose a rain of radiant red light. The explosion of magic hit Gryf's broadsword and the brunt of the force was deflected. Gryf winced as long, thin flakes of a glasslike substance bit the skin on his arms and the side of his face. Blood trickled from the wounds, but he kept a tight hold on his weapon.

The figure struck the floor with the bottom of a staff, and rivers of dancing light traveled across the floor and into the staff, coalescing at its blunt, gnarled tip. Muttered words crept out from the mage's dark hood, and the magic began to transform, ready to be unleashed again.

Aren held Vir back, shielding him completely. Vir resisted once, and Aren addressed him in a low, authoritative tone. "You are the last of Tiede's bloodline. Still yourself."

Vir obeyed.

The magic traveled in a stream of red again, and this time Gryf angled his blade to deflect a majority of the fragments. "Now!" he grunted, and Dane rushed the figure.

Dane brought his sword up to bring it down on the mage's head. The mage brought up his staff, blocking the attack, but Gryf was a heartbeat behind his brother and swept the feet out from under the mage. The figure landed on his back with a hard thud and a small cry, hands still locked tight around the wooden staff.

The hood fell back, revealing the face of a young man who couldn't have turned from boyhood more than a year ago. His face was contorted in pain, but he tried to roll onto his side and engage the staff again. Gryf crushed his wrist with the heel of his foot, causing the boy to shriek, and the staff clattered to the floor.

Aren and Vir then walked over to where his brothers stood looking down at the mage. "Horin?" Aren said, recognizing the garden-lemon-water-boy.

"You know this traitor?" Vir asked, raising an eyebrow.

"Ran into him and another named Dekney on my way here."

Vir signaled for someone to pick up the boy, and Gryf handed the broadsword to Dane before grabbing the young mage by the front of his white shirt and lifting him to his feet. Aren pulled the robe off to make sure he had no hidden weapons, then took the length of cord Dane offered and secured Horin's hands behind his back.

Vir stood in front of Horin, his eyes burning with anger. "Do you act alone or did someone send you?" The boy didn't speak; instead, he responded with a malicious glare of his own, and the marks on his shoulders began to glow. Vir's fist connected with Horin's face, and blood began to flow out of the boy's nose, the glow dimming. "Who sent you?" Vir demanded, his voice rising. A moment of silence passed and Vir punched Horin in the stomach. Horin began to cough, and tears streamed from his eyes and watered down the blood that flowed from his nose.

"Vir!" a woman cried out as she ran into the *kasan* with a half-dozen Guards and a Hunter. "Gods, Vir! Are you hurt?"

Two of the Guard stepped behind Horin, but they didn't pull him away from Gryf's hold. The remaining four Guards blocked the doorway, two facing in and two facing out, waiting in silence for Vir's command.

Aren watched as Geyle rushed up to her husband and looked over his angry face, relief washing over her features. Her attention then moved to Aren, and she gasped as if he had caught her by surprise. Her cheeks reddened and she turned to look at the other men in the room.

"How did you know?" Vir asked her, his voice hushed.

"I felt magic being summoned. Thank the gods you're not hurt; I was so worried."

He studied her for a moment, then said, "Tell the House doctor to ready the infirmary. Master Gryf needs medical attention."

"Vir!" They all turned to see Lady Illithe peering into the room. "Gods, what happened? Your Hunters are all over the House."

Vir indicated Horin with a nod. "Everything is fine, Aunt Valine, but if you could have Doctor Pember help our doctors with the wounded, I'd be grateful. I can give you the details afterwards. Is Gran Kente all right?"

"Yes, he's fine." Valine seemed to study Gryf and Dane, then her eyes fell on Aren. "He's just worried about you, of course." Aren dropped his gaze under her scrutiny.

"Please let him know all is well," Vir said, and Valine inclined her head before leaving. Geyle lingered for a second, then hurried out of the room. When she was gone, Vir gave a slight nod, and one of the Guard followed her. "Two of you," Vir addressed the remaining Guards as he rubbed his knuckles, "take him to the dungeons. The other three, find the servant called Dekney and arrest him. Someone get this room cleaned up." Gryf handed the boy over, and the Guards went to work, leaving the four men as they were before the attack. A

Hunter remained by the door, waiting for Vir. "I'm in your debt," Vir said, addressing them all but looking at Gryf.

"It is our obligation and our honor," Gryf said, bowing and bringing his fist to his heart.

"So it is for every citizen of Tiede, yet none have to act on it." Vir opened and closed the hand he had used to punch Horin. "Get to the infirmary. We're fortunate to have the renowned Doctor Pember from Illithe, who specializes in magic-related medicine." Gryf nodded. "Apprentice," Vir said, turning to Aren. "Find Elder and meet me in my study in an hour. You may as well have the Doctor look at that cut too."

"Yes, my Lord."

When Vir left, Gryf pulled on his boots and said, "I'll be in the infirmary; my skin burns like the mists of Aum. Try to stay out of trouble; that goes double for you, Aren."

"What's going on with Lady Tiede?" Dane asked as Gryf left the *kasan*. He put the longsword into its proper place in the rack. "I saw the way she looked at you, not to mention the message we got yesterday about you not being able to come home because the Lady required your presence."

"It's nothing. She's just lonely."

There was a space of silence as they gathered their things, then Dane said, "Lord Vir is better than I thought with the blade."

"He trains once a week."

"You're still the better fighter, and he shouldn't have managed to cut you. Where was your head?"

Aren looked down at his bandaged forearm, his mind overcome with conflicting thoughts and emotions. He recalled the note that had been buzzing in the back of his head no matter how much he tried to ignore it. "I got a weird note; something about how somebody saved my life but that I needed to stay away from 'her'. It was written in Ancient, but I know it wasn't Elder."

Dane joined him at the *kasan's* entrance, where they pulled on their shoes. "It doesn't matter who it was from or what it's about. If Lady Geyle falls for you, she'll be your undoing."

TWO

Aren squeezed his bandaged forearm. Doctor Pember had said it looked worse than it really was, then passed him over to the House doctor, who cleaned and dressed the wound. Doctor Pember had trickier wounds to tend to, such as the ones covering Gryf's arms and the left side of his face. Rieka had heard news of the attack from her father and rushed to the House, worried about Dane and his brothers. The Doctor said her timing was excellent and asked her to assist him in his work. She was relieved to see that Dane had managed to walk out of the *kasan* unscathed and was sitting at Gryf's side, providing moral support.

The shards of magic that peppered Gryf had to be extracted one by one. When each shard was removed, the wound released a horrifying stream of blood. Doctor Pember checked the flow by applying pressure, then Rieka used a minty salve to seal the wound. There were numerous shards, but the Doctor did the work without complaint, pointing out bits of medical interest to Rieka.

Aren frowned. "Should he be in this much pain?" Sweat dripped out of Gryf's every pore as he clenched his teeth throughout the procedure. "We've pulled thorns out of our feet before, and we've never made faces like that."

"We're extracting magic poison," Doctor Pember said. "The intent was to kill Lord Vir, not make him feel uncomfortable."

"Doctor," Rieka said, "have you ever let a wound of this nature bleed out?"

Doctor Pember raised an eyebrow, considering. After a moment he nodded, then said, "I think I understand, but let me hear your theory."

She pointed at the mess of towels and blood around Gryf. "Each time we pull out a fragment, the wound bleeds so much that our reaction is to staunch it immediately. What's odd is that even though many of these shards haven't hit any arteries, the amount of blood is significant. What if the body is trying to purge itself of the toxin?"

Doctor Pember nodded again and used the back of his wrist to push his glasses up on his long nose. "No one's considered it because the amount of blood loss is substantial. We would need a transfusion ready."

"Does that mean you're going to try it?" Dane asked. "She's not even an apprentice yet."

"She's my apprentice now. Her theory is intelligent and worth trying, especially with a strong, healthy specimen such as the

Fighter." Looking over the remaining shards in Gryf's arm, Doctor Pember said, "Master Fighter, are you willing to try this procedure?"

Gryf looked at his brothers, who made subtle signs of no. "If Lord Vir trusts you, I'm game."

"Are either of you willing to donate blood? You both look healthy enough to spare a few pints," Doctor Pember said.

"That's a ridiculous question," Dane said. "We'll both do it."

Rieka shook her head. "Just you, Dane. As much as Aren is your brother, we know for sure that you and Gryf share the same blood type."

"Aren's the same," Dane mumbled. "Just no one's bothered to check."

"Isn't Lord Vir waiting on you, Aren?" Rieka exchanged a look with them that said she would beat them within an inch of their lives if they interrupted the Doctor's work again.

"Do you need me for anything, Gryf?" Aren asked.

"Need you to arm yourself. Something wasn't right about that attack. They'll try again."

Aren nodded, then left the infirmary, reminding himself to check on Selina after meeting with Vir. She was the one who had said the mages were coming, and he guessed that that was what Vir wanted to talk about.

He was walking past the parlor when he spotted Geyle at the bar mixing a drink. He paused to watch as she poured out two fingers of Cloud, two more of the clear Ryme, and a splash of Frost. Then, she reached into her skirts and pulled out a small glass vial shaped like a teardrop. *Damn,* Aren cursed to himself. *Never thought I'd see that again.* Two iridescent, pearl-like drops fell into the drink, plunging through the layers of alcohol. She took a glass cocktail stirrer to it, then held it up to the light for inspection. That was when she caught Aren in the parlor doorway, staring at her with curiosity and disappointment.

"I don't drink much," she said. "I forget Tiede's toast."

"*Tse frie,*" he said, his voice catching in his throat.

She put the stick into a glass of water and smiled. "*Tse frie,*" she said, raising the drink. She took a sip. "Perfect." Her eyes watched him, fixed on his face as she moved towards him.

Aren snapped out of his daze, then bent from the waist. "Apologies, my Lady; I didn't mean to interrupt."

She stood before him, glass in hand, and touched his shoulder to indicate he should straighten up. "Don't you think that you and I are beyond formalities?"

"That could never be possible."

She waved a hand at him. "You are ever the gentleman and the hero. I owe you my gratitude for saving Vir's life. But what about you? What happened to your arm?" She ran her small fingers over the bandage and he flinched.

"A sparring accident," he said, taking a small step back. He was beginning to think Dane had a point about not allowing the Lady to get too close. He was sure that she was harmless, though. Over the years, she had become lonely and homesick, perhaps even bored. Her husband was always busy, so she found solace and companionship in the young man whom she believed the gods had sent to keep her company. He had been in the wrong place at the wrong time, and again the message from Rose flitted through his head.

The blood of Tiede and Illithe run through you, and so Illithe has made its peace with Tiede. Yet, you and Geyle are independent entities joined by ceremony and fragile promises.

"I have salves from Rose I can apply to your wound," she said, touching his arm again. "All natural and very potent. We have the best herbalists—"

"Aren!"

Little feet pounded towards them from the hallway. They turned towards the girl's panicked voice, and Selina threw herself at Aren's legs and held on tight.

"Selina!" Aren laughed, trying to maintain his balance. "What's gotten into you? Lady Geyle was talking." He turned to Geyle. "I apologize. I haven't yet taught her all the formalities of the House, and..."

Geyle raised a hand. "Hush. I'll not hear another word of your formalities." She left them by the parlor entrance, carrying her strange drink away with her.

"Selina, you can't behave like that in the House," he said, getting down on one knee to look her in the eye. "Where's the Priestess Minor?"

"Probably looking for me," Selina sulked, "but I heard about the mage and the fight, and I was worried that you were hurt!" She sighed. "And the Wood is getting louder..."

Aren tried not to stare at the glass on Vir's desk, but he couldn't help it. The clear liquid was swirled through with the telltale Cloud, wisps of the opalescent liquor floating through the drink like vapor on a cold day. Vir cleared his throat and brought the drink to his lips, taking a healthy swallow. Aren half expected him to fall over dead.

"The Guard have captured Dekney," Vir said, interrupting Aren's thoughts.

"Has he said anything?" Elder asked. He sat in the large leather chair in front of Vir's desk, walking staff in hand.

Aren stood next to the chair, feeling out of place in his sparring clothes, which were covered in sweat and masonry dust and blood stains. He began to wonder if he smelled.

"He claims to be innocent," Vir said.

"If my Apprentice hadn't spotted him walking with the one called Horin, I would be inclined to believe him. Freno Dekney comes from a simple family, and his father and grandfather have served the House. They've always been loyal to Tiede. This Horin, however, isn't familiar to me at all. He might have tricked his way into the House."

"It's still possible that Dekney's innocent." Vir shrugged, took another drink. "But I'm not taking any chances. Let him sweat in the dungeon with the night wraiths for a while. He'll break as others have before him. No one even needs to lay a finger on him." Aren thought about the wraith stories and the wandering ancestors of Tiede then shivered as a chill gripped him. "There's also the issue of the staff," Vir said, reaching over to the weapon standing against the wall next to him.

Aren's eyes widened. "That's the one I brought in."

"I thought I'd seen it before." Vir passed it to Elder. "How did Horin get it?"

"I left it in the Library," Aren said. "I didn't think anyone would be interested in it—especially not in the House."

"Now we know better," Elder grunted, studying the marks on the staff. "This is no language I know of."

"I think they're arcane symbols," Aren said. "I stumbled upon the topic about a year ago, and I've been meaning to do additional research."

"Copy the symbols," Vir said, "then have it destroyed."

They were silent, and Aren was mesmerized by Vir's drink and the swirling eddies floating within it. He debated saying something about the way Geyle prepared it. She was a magic wielder; could she have cast a spell on him to keep him silent? He had seen her weave spells without a staff.

"Are you thirsty, Apprentice?" Vir asked, raising an eyebrow at Aren, who was still staring at the drink.

"No, my Lord. I was just thinking that regardless of Freno Dekney's guilt or innocence" —he felt the words roll off his tongue— "it wouldn't hurt to do a House search. Mages need a staff to summon magic."

"You're suggesting that if a person has a staff in their possession, it means they're guilty?" Elder asked, knocking the bottom of his staff loud against the floor a few times to make a point.

"No, but it makes them worth checking. Are you marked, Elder? I just realized I don't know that about you."

"And you never will, boy!" Elder exclaimed, sweeping the staff around so fast that Aren caught it just as it was about to make contact with his groin. Vir brought his drink to his lips to hide his smirk.

"Just curious, Elder." Aren did his best to keep from smiling.

"Have the Guard do a sweep of the House," Vir said. "I'd rather err on the side of caution. We need to do what we can before even considering detaining the marked as Rose has."

Before he could stop himself, Aren heard himself say, "It's fortunate Lady Geyle isn't in Rose. They'd probably lock her up too." He opened his mouth to explain, "She's made no secret of her marks; it's the only reason I mention it." Aren thought about explaining himself further but bit his tongue.

Vir looked hard at him, swallowed the rest of his drink, then exchanged a look with Elder that Aren couldn't decipher. Vir lifted the piece of paper on his desk. "We covered the Freno boy, and we're going to search the House for staves. Next is the Priestess; has there been any word on her?" Aren shook his head. "Visit with her for a while today," Vir said, checking the item off his list. "She might receive more messages. I say it's about time; the gods have overlooked this House for far too long."

"Yes, my Lord."

"I understand Doctor Pember won't allow Master Gryf to teach today, but I want you and the younger Gerrit to show up anyway. The two of you have proven to be better sparring partners than my own swordsmen. You don't seem afraid to hit me."

"Not at all, my Lord," Aren stammered when Elder glared at him. "I mean, you know how to fight, so it's not as if…"

Vir leaned back in his chair and held up his empty glass. "Tell my wife to make me another. There's been a burning in my throat and the drink helps. You're dismissed, Apprentice." Vir summoned the servant hovering at the door, who was carrying flasks of oil, to refill the lamps.

Aren took the glass and stared at it for a moment. There was nothing left but a trace of Cloud particles clinging to the inside of the glass where they were swirled around. Even the strong scent of Ryme was gone, and he wondered how he would be able to tell if the drink had been poisoned or not. He also wondered if now was the time when Vir's head would meet his desk. Perhaps another second or two before the poison worked. Vir and Elder watched him with curious expressions, then Elder stomped his staff against the floor. Aren flinched, then bowed before leaving the room.

THREE

"Horin was clumsy," Catar said under his breath, talking towards his book. He was leaning against a wide tree near the markers for the dead.

Mercer watched as his companion, a big man called Copen, flirted with the Tiedan girl. "Clumsy, but it works to our advantage," Mercer said. "The House will think they've caught their monster."

"Will he talk?"

"Even if he did, what would he say?" Mercer directed his words at the tall slabs of shiny black glass. "This is why we try to remain isolated from each other. We don't need any one of us ruining the entire plan. The most they'll get out of Horin is that he was sent to kill Vir."

"Even if that were true, he failed on all accounts." Catar glanced at his colleague, who ran a hand over the stones.

Mercer laughed. "You didn't really think he'd be able to kill Vir, did you?"

"No, but he should've been able to kill the target we sent him after in the first place." Catar sighed, trying not to let his worries impact their mission. "Also, whatever wild magic is bleeding from Tiede Wood is affecting the creature. It needs to feed, but controlling it is proving more difficult that any of us could've imagined."

"We'll increase the sacrifices. If it makes you feel better, I hear Vir has been growing ill, so at the very least his slow death is assured."

"How did you hear this? We have another man on the inside?"

Mercer's eyes glittered with mischief. "A woman, actually."

FOUR

Wearing black from collar to toe, Kaila pulled her hair up into a long tail, then headed towards the sitting room, where a demon told her Alaric would meet to discuss the night's activities. The Keep was buzzing with news and rumors of Trum, but none of that was important to her. The new Priestess was the key, and all be damned if she didn't do the right thing by blessing that little girl.

Kaila summoned all of her confidence and strength and entered the room. Taia sat alone on one of the large, plush sofas, reading the various reports that came in, fed through the spells she had woven throughout the land. Kaila paid the proper respects, but Taia didn't acknowledge her, so she took a seat on the sofa opposite the woman, who looked more solid today than usual.

"You're looking well this morning," Kaila said.

Taia looked up from her papers. "Where have you been?"

"Tiede."

"Tanghi will risk his life at Trum while you lounge in a fountain."

Kaila forced herself to remain calm. "Even if I asked to go to Trum, Alaric wouldn't allow it."

Taia set her papers down and leaned forward to confront her. "Why do you think Alaric protects you? Do you honestly think it's because he values your mind? Do you really think yourself that clever?"

Kaila's thoughts rushed back to her time with Aren, when she was searching out the story behind the little Priestess. She had relinquished her powers and sat down with a mortal for an entire evening, tugging at threads of stories so that she could find out why Selina was so important. Aren had given her such clarity and insight into what had happened the day of that terrible storm, and she could now connect that storm with magic and possibly with Aalae.

Aren had thought her very intelligent.

"Alaric bonded with me for my power," Taia said, interrupting her thoughts. "He needs my mind and my strength. These are not traits he expects of you."

Kaila wasn't sure what to say. She couldn't dispute that Taia was smart and powerful, and it was true that Alaric relied on her for her spells and her ability to decipher and predict complex fate lines. So what was it that Alaric wanted of Kaila?

"You make him laugh when the entire world is falling apart. You're like a stupid pet that doesn't know any better. You're a self-centered, conceited child," Taia said, answering Kaila's unspoken question.

Kaila kept her gaze on the stone floor, studying the minute fissures that had been filled in with stardust. She knew it was only a matter of time before Taia confronted her, but she never imagined it would hurt this much. She took in small, slow breaths to calm her nerves. "I was in Tiede, trying to help," she said, unable to project the strength that she had felt before she had come into the room. "I was watching the new Priestess, and I learned—"

"This is how blind you are to your own stupidity," Taia interrupted. "Alaric never asks you to do anything but watch; sometimes, if he knows you won't be in too much danger, he'll have you fight. So if you can't fight for him or counsel him, what use are you?"

Kaila drew in a ragged breath. She knew she was more than what Taia thought of her, and some rational, tiny part in her heart told her that Taia was speaking out of jealousy. But if that were the case, then why was she never asked her opinion on important Realm matters? Could it be that she really was blind to what Alaric thought of her?

Taia picked up her papers and leaned back in her seat. Her form flickered once, then remained solid. She sighed as if she were tired. "It's about time you grew up and opened your eyes to the truth. Your flirtatious infatuation with my mate is revolting."

"I'm not," Kaila whispered. She couldn't think straight, couldn't fight back and address each accusation. She felt as stupid as Taia accused her of being. She tried to bring the topic back to what she had discovered in Tiede. "I found out things about the new Priestess. She's just a child, but there's great power in her."

"I can't wait until you let Alaric know," Taia said, a large, empty smile on her face. "I would bet my existence that he'll act fascinated and tell you to keep watching her, even though Aalae already knows that the Priestess is just a child and thinks the whole thing a joke."

"Why are you lashing out at me now? After all this time?" Kaila managed to ask.

"The fate lines are realigning."

"I don't understand."

"Of course you don't, foolish girl. I won't explain the intricacies of fate lines to you, so let me be clear: stay away from Alaric. I don't know what tricks you're pulling, but I won't allow you to take him away from me."

Kaila lifted her eyes to look at her, and the disdain on the woman's face hit her hard. The tears Kaila tried to hold back trickled down her cheeks, and she wiped away at them, worried that the rains might fall.

"Tell Alaric what you found out about the new Priestess," Taia dared. "I could use a good laugh."

"Is Tanghi home yet?" Kaila asked, drying her eyes. Tanghi was good at keeping her steady and rational, especially when Taia was pushing her.

Taia ignored her, returning her full attention to her papers. At that moment, Alaric strode in and said, "Taia, did you not hear her?" Taia started, surprised. They hadn't heard the familiar stomp of his boots. "Panther." Alaric smiled. "I think more clearly when I prowl." Barefoot, he dropped the boots he was carrying. "Tanghi is on his way. I sent him to Thell earlier." He smoothed out his pants and buttoned his shirt, then took a seat next to Taia and began to pull the boots on. The room was quiet, save for the sound of the buckles on the leather straps that secured his boots. As he worked, he glimpsed from Taia to Kaila and back again. "Am I interrupting something?"

"No, my love," Taia said. "Kaila was just telling me that she was in Tiede."

"Good girl. I know you find it boring, but Tiede must be protected."

Kaila seethed inside and had to bite her lip to keep from lashing out. Taia had been right, though; Alaric wanted her to stay in Tiede, where nothing was happening. She couldn't tell Alaric about Selina. If he wouldn't take her seriously, then the information on the blessing, the storm, and the powers the girl might have would mean nothing to him, and it would only enrage him that she spent her time with a mortal.

Tanghi swept in through the open window, his fiery wings disintegrating to ash as he took on his god form. "Thell is safe for now, and I've spread word that Trum has fallen to the mages," Tanghi said, taking a seat next to Kaila. "The rumor flew quickly and Thell sent scouts to confirm the news. Their army isn't as strong as Tiede or Kaishar, but at least they're prepared, unlike Trum."

"I thought you were going to allow Thell to fall," Taia said as she turned to Alaric. "The rest of the Night Houses are far enough away and can get defenses up long before the mages move west. It's not worth bargaining with Aalae."

"I can't watch Thell fall without a fight. If anything, we decrease the number of mages who move on."

"Tiede might send armies to Rose because of Vir's marriage," Kaila pointed out. "Stifling the mages before they turn on Rose will be a good thing."

"Not necessarily." Taia shook the papers in her hands. "Rose has already heard rumors of the mage uprisings and has begun detaining anyone who is marked. If Tiede goes to their aid, they could lose Illithe's support. Illithe has little tolerance for such injustices."

"What a mess." Tanghi was exasperated. "Do you want us to fight in Trum or not? I've no patience for tracing fate lines and debating the outcome of a war based on the color of gree shit on the solstice turn."

"I want you to go to Trum," Alaric answered. "You'll help get the Priestesses out."

"Will you send me as well?" Kaila asked, her blood pulsing hard in her neck as she waited for his answer.

"Not yet," Alaric said. He softened his tone and took her hand. "I know you're eager to fight alongside the others, but until I know just how dangerous it is, I want you to stay away from the east."

Taia had been right all along, and the smile on her face only made Kaila feel worse. If Alaric insisted on keeping her as a pet, Kaila was determined to find ways to slip from her leash when he wasn't looking.

"Yes, my Lord," she said, lowering her gaze.

"My beautiful Kaila, you do please me."

FIVE

Aren and Selina sat at his desk in the Library, a heavy book open before them. He flipped through the pages, skimming the various stories that had been transcribed from Ancient in his hand. Selina watched him, fascinated by his precise script and the speed at which he read the strange words.

"You're not going to find it," Nianni said. Aren had set up a chair for her on the other side of his desk so she sat facing them. She was reading through a prayer booklet, her elbow propped on the desk to support her head. "It was a guarded secret until it was revealed to Selina."

He continued to rifle through the pages. "I thought it was alluded to in another story."

Nianni rolled her eyes. "Why would a well-guarded secret be alluded to?"

He looked at her, a grin on his face. "That's the best kind of secret, isn't it? The one you know you've heard hints about and people talk about until it becomes legend. Now, you've disguised the truth." Aren turned to Selina. "So the Fire god gave the Priestess a gift to show how thankful he was that she found the Water goddess's sash?" he asked. Selina nodded. "That's some tale!"

"It's no tale, it's true," Nianni said without looking up from her book.

Aren brightened, then flipped to a different section of the book. "Here's another story about the Water goddess. Fishermen have always told tales of how you can trap the goddess on Cordelacht if you steal her robe or sash or ribbon or slippers while she's bathing. The stories say she can't return to Mytanth without her things."

"*Those* are just tales," Nianni pointed out.

"Yet you believe the vision Selina had about the Fire god gifting a Priestess for returning a sash. Why would he give a mere mortal a gift if that sash wasn't important?" Aren shot back. "These stories are all related. I'd file it under Water Goddess's Weaknesses." He added to Selina, "All powerful beings have weaknesses. It's supposed to make them more relatable."

Nianni slammed her book shut. "I will praise the gods with such exultation on the day that I am elevated to House Priestess and can return home and never have to see you again," she said, glaring at Aren.

"You don't really mean that, do you?" he asked, pulling open one of his desk drawers to retrieve a small wooden container. "I took the time to bathe just so I wouldn't offend you."

"How has anyone not killed you yet?"

Aren responded by picking something out of the container and throwing it at Nianni's face. She put her hands up just as it bounced off her forehead. "Too slow, Priestess," he said as he threw another paper star at her.

"Stop it!" Nianni complained. "Selina! Make him stop!"

Selina laughed as she scooped out the stars and began throwing them at Aren, who gave her a look of mock horror. "My sweet little sister! Traitor!"

They continued to laugh and pelt each other until the Library doors opened. Nianni straightened up as if she had just been struck by lightning, while Selina froze mid-toss. Aren put down the box, winked at Selina, then stood up to meet whomever was visiting. Her eyes darted to Nianni, who motioned to Selina to return the stars to the wooden container. She scooted off her chair to pick up whatever had fallen to the floor while Nianni pushed the stars to one spot on the desk.

Selina peered to see who had entered the Library. "I think it's a Messenger," she whispered as she put the stars back in the box.

"Where'd he get all these little stars anyway?" Nianni asked. "Is this what he does all day?"

Selina opened the drawer to put the box away but paused before closing it, having caught sight of a piece of paper with beautiful handwriting. She ran a finger over the lettering, and Aren, having returned from the Messenger, slipped it out of her hand and placed it in his pocket. "Secrets, little one." He winked at her.

"I couldn't read it," she said, giving him an apologetic look. "It was in the old language you like to read."

"Ancient."

"You read and write dead languages?" Nianni asked.

"It's part of my job."

"Like folding paper stars?" Selina asked in earnest.

The corner of Aren's mouth lifted in an impish smile, revealing a dimple. "A friend taught me how to make those last night. That's not part of my typical workload."

"Was it Dane?" Selina asked.

"You haven't met her yet," he said, reorganizing the drawer. "She had to leave this morning, but should she ever return, I'll introduce you."

"Is she pretty?"

Aren narrowed his eyes at her. "What are you getting at, silly girl?"

Selina shrugged, giggling. "I was just asking! She must be pretty! I bet you love her!"

Aren lunged at her, tickling her sides as she laughed and screamed for him to stop. "You're the pretty one!" he growled.

Nianni stood up and slammed a hand on the desk. "That's enough! This is inappropriate behavior for a Priestess!"

Aren stopped and Selina collapsed into her chair. He leaned forward on the desk towards Nianni. "Do you want a turn too?"

Her face reddened beneath her dark complexion, and her eyes widened in shock. "How dare you even think of touching me!"

Aren was about to comment when he squeezed his eyes shut. He pinched the bridge of his nose with one hand and gripped the desk with the other. Nianni frowned and looked to Selina, who jumped out of her chair and grabbed his wrist.

"Apprentice, this isn't the time for jokes!" Nianni said, fidgeting with a bracelet.

Selina felt the panic rise in her chest, and she held onto Aren as his entire body seemed to convulse. He fell into his chair. She had never seen him in this much pain before. "Aren!" she cried. "What's the matter?" Selina gasped as blood began to trickle from his nose, and she whipped her head left and right to find something to stop the bleeding. Nianni rushed around the desk with a delicate white kerchief. She hesitated for a brief moment before handing it to Selina, who pressed it to his nose. Nianni reached out to help, then pulled back, wringing her hands.

"Dane!" Selina said. "Dane will know what to do!"

Nianni nodded, rushing towards the doors leading out to the courtyard.

"I'll be fine," Aren said, barely above a whisper. "Messenger came by to check on you. Head Priestess and Lord Vir want to make sure you're well." He tried to smile. "It's my job to take care of you, sweetheart."

Selina noted the tears that fell from his eyes as she held the bloodied kerchief in place. "I'm scared," she said.

He let go of his desk and squeezed her hand. He hushed her, keeping his eyes closed. "It's just a headache."

SIX

The headaches were getting out of control. Aren hadn't suffered this much since before he was apprenticed, and he was determined to not get kicked out of the House because of his ailment. The headaches were the reason he had gone on his most recent fishing trip, but thanks to the messenger, he didn't have time to figure out how to let the illness run its course. There was only one way he knew of to fix this quickly, before it began to affect his job.

Aren sped through Tiede on the back of Bontan, whom he had borrowed from the House gree stables. His speed elicited a few stares, but it didn't matter; the closer he got to Tiede Wood, the less his head pounded, further convincing him that he was doing the right thing.

He rode towards the eastern cliffs. The wall on the east that protected the town from a thousand-foot drop to the sea came to an abrupt end at the point where the Wood began to become more dominant. Bontan managed the perilous white gravel without care and delivered his rider to the Wood's edge. Aren dismounted and secured him to a tree trunk. He removed the pouch of water that was strapped close to Bontan's neck and poured it into the gree's waiting mouth as if he were nursing a cub. Aren stroked the top of Bontan's nose, and the gree purred deep with satisfaction. "I don't intend to be long, but if you get a feeling that something bad's happened to me, feel free to cry out and let someone know, all right?" Bontan snorted as if in agreement.

Aren's headache had diminished to an annoying throb, and as he took his first steps into the mossy darkness, even that was beginning to fade. He took another look at the sun sitting high in the late-afternoon skies and hoped he'd be able to find his way back out. He knew a quick peek wasn't going to cure him. Whatever was calling wanted him to stay awhile, have tea. A few more steps—his boots pressing into the soft, leaf-and-needle-covered earth—and he was in near total darkness. He looked back again, feeling fairly certain that he could find his way back out.

Stars, what was he thinking? There had to be other ways to cure a monstrous headache. Maybe even the Illitheien stork doctor had an answer; all he had to do was ask. Aren took a deep breath. Maybe he should stop kidding himself; something masochistic in him wanted to go into the Wood.

The air was cool under the canopy of trees, and the smell of dirt and moss and wet things filled his nose. He ran a hand through his hair and made his way towards a small clearing where slivers of light managed to filter through. This place felt familiar. He took note of the trees that ringed the clearing—the flaky, dark-gray bark and the odd mark slashed into each one, revealing white wood inside. If the mark was some sort of character, he didn't know it. Perhaps they were symbols, runes. Had he put them there?

He rounded a worn boulder, his hands drifting over the surface where the strange marks were also etched. He wasn't sure if there was something he had to do or some ritual he had to perform. If he could remember his past experiences, that might be helpful. Instead, he stood among the mushrooms and flowers feeling like the biggest fool in the world.

"You called and I came!" he yelled. "What do you want from me?" The Wood stopped breathing. Feeling a knot in his gut, he spun around, panic beginning to overtake him. "Let's get it over with!" There was nothing but the thick silence. His breathing became more rapid, and he had to force himself to remain calm.

What are you doing here? a small voice asked in the Ancient tongue. Aren spun around, sweat breaking out all over his forehead.

Another small voice, from a different direction, spoke, *You're past the age of reason. You shouldn't be here.*

"Who are you?" he asked in Ancient, whirling around. "Were you the one who called me?" He forced himself to slow his movements as his eyes continued to adjust to the varying degrees of black. A flicker of vapor illuminated the clearing. Aren held his breath and watched as the vapor shifted then materialized into two children: a boy and a girl. They stared at him through the dark midnight-blue eyes of the Tiede bloodline, their bodies semi-translucent and mist-like. Aren felt his heart go out to them, and he asked in Common, "Do you need help? Where are your parents?"

The little girl giggled. *You're the one who needs help.* Her head changed from that of a child to an owl and back. Aren took a step away from them.

Are you here because of the threat to Tiede? the boy asked in a grave tone. *The magic is being pulled in all directions. Is that why you're here?*

Aren thought his legs might give, and having to translate was threatening to give him another headache. "I'm here because someone is calling me. Was it you?" His mind raced as he watched the children, their hands clasped, their faces innocent one moment, then owl-like masks with frightening, blinking eyes the next. He recalled the old sigils of Tiede, began to match the sigil to the names and the stories. "Lady Tiede Lis and Lord Tiede Lars," he breathed. "You died hundreds of years ago in a fire that consumed the nursery during a mage uprising. You're alive."

Im. Na nasbolv Tiede, the boy said before proceeding to explain what had happened to them.

"The Tiede curse killed you?" Aren held up a hand, overwhelmed. "You don't happen to know Common, do you?"

The children looked at each other, then back at him. *The Lady taught us,* little Lord Lars said in Common. *We didn't call you. Perhaps it was the Lady.* He paused. *You're Aren, then.*

Lis let go of her brother's hand and approached Aren. He backed away again, and she clasped her hands behind her back. *My dolls are in the secret space. Could you bring them?*

This is no time to think of toys, Lis. He has to listen to the magic, listen to the words and the name. Maybe the Lady called because he can understand it.

"I don't understand anything right now," Aren mumbled.

The girl took another step closer, her eyes wide and flickering. *But you have to try. Tiede's in trouble.*

Aren was torn between reaching out to them and running away. He was about to step forward when a tiny orb of green light began to dance towards him out of the darkness.

Lis! We have to go! The magic! Lars said, grabbing his sister's hand. He locked eyes with Aren, then said, *Listen. You have to listen! A'ars Tiede.* They disappeared, evaporated into nothingness as if they were a figment of his imagination.

"Protect Tiede," he muttered, his brain catching up to translate the boy's last words. "If this isn't madness, I don't know what is." Aren started after the children, then stopped, distracted by the green light again. He stared, mesmerized by its lilting movement, the glow surrounding it chasing away the shadows that were slithering towards him. The light grew and he wanted to shield his eyes but couldn't. He watched, mouth slightly open, as it paused in front of him. "Did you call me? Are you the Lady?" he whispered, hypnotized. "What do you want from me?"

The light began to spread until it seemed to mingle with the darkness, and then standing before him was a fae. Her head reached no higher than his chest. Thick, shiny green hair tumbled to her knees, covering her lithe, naked body, her spring-green skin. She looked up at him with large, dazzling green eyes that slanted upwards with thick lashes.

Her slender arms reached up and around his neck to pull his head down towards her, and she kissed his mouth with a passion that was eerily familiar, if not altogether strange. Aren felt a strange rush of euphoria as his headache disappeared, then everything went dark.

SEVEN

Aren felt his heart pounding hard in his chest as green images flashed through his mind and strange noises rang in his ears. Where was he? Was he dead this time? The air was filled with the heady scent of dream flowers. His vision was clouded with silver and mist, but he wasn't sure if his eyes were open. He felt as though he were falling off the high white cliffs of Tiede into the inky sea below. He clawed for purchase and felt loamy soil and crispy, dead leaves crushed between his fingers.

Arguing. Voices were arguing about something; a woman was pleading, crying. *I had to call. I hoped he wouldn't find out, but you're the only one who can save Tiede.* Her voice was like an embrace.

He remembered fae folk and faeries. Coy, lovely faces peeking out from the shadows of trees, flirtatious eyes looking him up and down, naked skin in pastel shades making him curious and bashful all at once. How long had he been unconscious? Was he dreaming?

"What do you want from me? Are you the Lady the children were talking about?" Was he screaming? He couldn't tell. He wanted to run, but which way was out? Would his legs work? Stars, he was going to be trapped here forever. What did he do last time this happened? It was so long ago.

Tiede is in trouble. The magic is too strong. You have to warn —

The woman was screaming again. The sound of it wrenched his heart to pieces, and he thought he would die. He covered his ears and fell to his knees, begging for the pain to stop, begging whomever it was to stop hurting her.

As if in answer to his wish, every noise ceased, save his own ragged breathing. He looked around, vertigo seizing him as the tiny orbs of faerie light swirled in his periphery. He felt the eyes of the gorgeous faerie nymphs on him, surrounding him, watching with indifference and amusement.

"Talk to me," he breathed. "Tell me you're all right. Where can I find you?"

No answer came, except for the bubbly giggles of the fae folk. He cursed them under his breath as he gritted his teeth and puzzled over how to escape this hell. The woman must be part of his imagination. The Wood was torturing him, playing to his weaknesses. As if on cue, the green fae who had kissed him earlier walked towards him, a tantalizing swing in her hips. He inched away on his hands and knees, trying to keep his eyes on her face. She smiled as if she could read his mind.

Run, Aren!

He squeezed his eyes shut and doubled over, his head reeling with pain. His senses felt heightened, and he detected the slight give of earth as the fae stood over him. As she ran a small hand through his hair, a sigh of pleasure escaped her.

That was when the ground shook and the trees quivered.

The fae eased her way behind him, pressing herself against his back. She ran a hand over his jaw, then cupped his chin, forcing him to look up into the canopy of trees, where darkness layered over darkness, and steel and fur and bone seemed to form from tree and rock and shadow.

Was he dead?

The voices had returned but were muted now. Aren opened his eyes and tried to adjust them to the movement of shadows. The air felt cool on his skin and he bolted upright. His shirt was missing, and there were cuts across his chest and shoulders. In the strange faerie light, he could see bruises the color of leindra blossoming on his skin, and the bandage he was wearing over the cut Vir had given him was gone.

Angry noises came from the depths of the Wood, and the faerie light was moving through the darkness. Had he escaped somehow? He couldn't remember. He hoped he hadn't hurt that beautiful green creature.

What was he thinking? Who knows what she had planned to do to him? Still…

A knife was thrust in his face and he cried out. Then a dirty, calloused hand with fingers like small sausages was clasped over his mouth. His eyes widened as he let out a muffled yell. He fought against every urge to run as the knife hovered between his eyes.

EIGHT

Dane swore as he stared past the tree line into the blackness of Tiede Wood. He had sworn earlier when the stable hand told him that Aren had taken Bontan to run an errand, and he had sworn again when he found Bontan napping by a tree at the Wood's edge.

He tied his mount next to the other gree and checked his weapons. Then, he took a long pull on his flask before returning it to the small pack he had thrown together. He followed the tree line west, away from the cliffs. He kept his blades sheathed. When it came to swinging a sword, he didn't have to question his gut, and as he walked, feeling the pull of shadows, he realized he didn't have to question the path he was taking now.

He stopped at one of the larger trees, a wide ghostwood whose smooth, white bark had felt the burn of magic at one point in its ancient history. He looked up to see the jagged, crimson-and-black scar that marred the bark deep and long on its southern side. Dane traced an imaginary line from the scar to the tree roots, where he knelt down to brush aside the years of leaf and nut and needle that had collected in the pockets and crevices. Half a dozen trees along this unmarked path had similar scars, so he wanted to make sure this was the right one. The last time Aren had gone into a trance, Dane realized that he always ended up in this particular area near a mossy boulder. When he shared this information, Aren suggested they establish some sort of marker system, and this tree was the first marker—or so Dane hoped.

When enough of the forest debris was cleared away, he brushed at the dirt along the spot of the trunk where the thick root rose from the ground like an octopus tentacle curving up out of the water. Carved deep into the wood were the distinct points of the Guardian constellation, connected by an unbroken line. He ran his calloused fingers over it, then stood up, taking a deep breath as he stared into the dark.

"You're going to owe me for this, little brother," Dane mumbled before walking a straight line in search of the next marker.

NINE

Selina sat on the white stone bench beneath the large window in Aalae's worship room. As the ocean breeze swept in and ruffled her hair, she could almost imagine Aren was there, mussing her hair as he always did. But almost wasn't good enough, and she was on the edge of her seat, hoping that Dane would find Aren soon.

Goddess, please watch over him, she prayed. She tried to imagine the Water goddess, but she was so distressed that her mind could only conjure an image of Aren fighting off a mage and a unicorn.

Crina and Min stood by the altar, speaking in hushed tones as they plucked pale-pink petals off the roses gathered in a heap before them. Selina couldn't hear them, but she thought she heard Aren's name at least once. She wondered what they were saying.

Nianni joined her, setting down a large wicker basket as she took a seat. She pulled a square white linen cloth and began to fold it.

Selina watched, then tried to mimic her, placing the folded cloth on the bench between them. "Try not to look so sullen," Nianni whispered. "You don't want anyone to know the Apprentice is missing, do you?"

The Priestesses said Aren's name again, and Selina asked, "Why are they talking about Aren? Why does Head Priestess seem so annoyed?"

Nianni grimaced. "I imagine anyone talking about the Apprentice must have reason to be annoyed."

Selina narrowed her eyes at her, then gave up on folding. She looked over her shoulder out the window, noting the pale-blue sky and the faint wisps of clouds smeared against it. The sun was past its zenith, but it wouldn't set for several hours yet. That was good. Dane could get Aren out before the Wood woke up.

"You can see the Laithe from here," Nianni said.

Selina got on her knees to have a better look. The sea winds tugged at her hair, and she pushed the strands away from her face. The bright-blue Laithe sparkled far away, a beautiful mask concealing the wreckage of ships and the drowned enemies of Tiede. She leaned out, wondering where the Water goddess had fallen to the fisherman's spear.

"Away from the window!" Crina's voice was stern and sharp, whipping through the silence like a lash.

Selina turned, setting herself down. Were Priestesses not allowed to look out the windows? She trembled as Crina made her way towards them. Nianni, who seemed just as startled, was on her feet, her head bowed. "I'm sorry," Selina apologized. "I didn't know I was doing anything wrong."

"More for your own good," Crina said, craning her neck to look out the window. "It's a long fall."

Min remained by the altar, plucking petals. In her calm, even tone she said, "You can see Tiede Wood from here, and some people claim to have visions while looking on it. The visions send them to do mad things like jump out of windows."

"Cursed magic," Crina growled as if to scare the magic away.

Curious, Selina turned back to the window, angling herself so that she could see the Wood. Crina didn't stop her this time, lost in her own thoughts and memories. Selina could only see part of the Wood and was disappointed that she couldn't see Aren. The Wood was too large and she was too far, but she tried to picture him anyway, walking away from the Wood, safe from harm. She wouldn't mind that sort of vision at all.

The treetops shuddered, shadows and light chasing each other across the leaves and branches. Selina imagined the sound it made— something like rushing water, only thinner, more fragile. She thought she could float right out the window, and she reached for the ledge, feeling the warm stone under her hand.

"Trum," she felt the word escape her lips before she realized she had spoken. "It's very bad. The dead are laid out on the streets like refuse, their skin burned and littered with magic. The entire city is on fire, and the mages have converged on the House." The words were not her own, and in her mind's eye she saw the handsome prince of the Night Realm. His hair was a black cascade, and the endless depths of his dark eyes seemed to stare back at her with sadness and loss. How could anyone be so beautiful in sorrow, she wondered.

Nianni's voice was far away, high and panicked, but Selina heard the way her silver jingled, felt the girl support her, laid her down on the bench.

Selina fought for air, overcome with emotion and the sounds of wailing and breathless fear. "Watch the House, children. The Wood says it's playtime."

TEN

Aren forced himself to breathe, then met the slate, watery gaze of the thing that was holding him at knifepoint, uttering low, gruff words. Upon seeing who it was, Aren thought he would cry in relief, and as every muscle in his body relaxed, the soil-scented sausage hand uncovered his mouth. The squat, familiar gnome stood next to him, a grin on its whiskered face.

"Pretraun, I never thought I'd be this happy to see you!" Aren choked on his emotions as he grabbed the gnome and pulled him into a fierce hug. Pretraun hugged him back, then pulled away. A dozen or two strange words fell out of its mouth, and Aren strained to find the pattern in the language.

Pretraun, seeming to sense Aren's frustration, held the knife in front of his face again. The gnome pointed at the marking engraved into the blade just above the bolster: the simple, yet stylized lines of the Guardian constellation. Aren took the knife and ran a thumb over the clean Gerrit mark. It was the blade that his siblings had given him;

the same knife Gryf insisted he carry at all times. The gnome had
sense enough to unstrap it from Aren's boot.

"It protects me, doesn't it? When I'm actually holding and using
it."

Pretraun nodded, then helped Aren to his feet. The gnome pushed
at his legs, and Aren began to run away from the voices and flickering
lights. He wanted to ask Pretraun how he had survived the unicorn
attack, but his head hurt like it had just been squeezed by an octopus,
and strange dots of light swam in his vision. He couldn't understand
the gnome's mushroomy words anyway, so he pushed on, propelled
by the strange cries and chanting that seemed to be nearing him no
matter how fast he moved.

The woman's voice reached out to him. *Don't look back, Aren. Tiede
needs you, so don't look back.*

Aren was delirious with exhaustion. His lungs were burning, and
every muscle in his body ached. No matter how fast or how far he
ran, the eerie noises kept following. He cursed the fae and their wings
and magics. Pretraun ran beside him, bouncing up and down like a
ridiculous squirrel. Aren had to make a stand; there was no way he
could keep this up. He had the knife and he had Pretraun; it might
not be enough to hold the fae back, but he had to try. He wasn't even
sure he was running in the right direction.

He stopped at a smattering of moss-covered boulders, leaning
against one of the larger rocks with one hand while keeping a firm
grip on the hilt of his knife with the other. Sweat dripped off his brow
and slicked his torso. Heat radiated off his skin, yet his body seized
in shivery fits, and he felt as though icy fingers were trying to take
hold of him. He wiped at his brow with his forearm and looked down
at Pretraun. "I can't," he rasped, his throat dry. "I'll have to try to
fight them off."

Pretraun didn't seem surprised or perturbed. He tugged at his
cloth sack, twisting it so he could dig around inside. Aren leaned back
against the boulder, his legs shaking, no longer able to hold himself
steady. He slid down against the rock until he was seated against it.
Pretraun produced a small flask, unscrewed the top, then pushed it
towards his face.

"Water?" Aren asked. The gnome nodded, nudging. Aren smiled,
closing his eyes as he declined. "You drink it. I've a feeling I'm not
going to make it out this time." Pretraun pressed the flask to Aren's
lips and poured. Aren sputtered, choked, then swallowed, shoving
the gnome away. Pretraun nodded, satisfied. "I thought you were
trying to help me," Aren managed to cough out. When he could

breathe without feeling like he was drowning, he leaned his head back against the rock, closing his eyes again. "I've been so tired, friend. I just want to sleep. Stars, I just want to sleep."

Images of fae and strange symbols danced in the darkness of his mind. He felt Pretraun smooth the hair back on his head, like a father would a child, then sensed the subtle shift of earth around him as the gnome moved away. This wasn't how he'd expected this expedition to turn out. The chanting and strange music were getting closer.

"I'm sorry, Selina," he said as the strong pull of sleep took over.

ELEVEN

Aren's eyes opened wide, the muted sound of guitar strings and wind chimes bringing him back to life. He sat up and found that he was clothed and indoors, sunlight shining in through the open windows. He squeezed his eyes shut, counted to ten in Ancient, then opened them.

The sitting room was small and tidy, and he was lying against a heap of pillows on a sofa of bright-blue velvet. He could smell the ocean breeze and wafts of fresh citrus.

"Dane," he called, not trusting his voice. The music stopped and the strings protested as someone gripped the guitar by the neck. Dane entered and set the instrument against a wall before taking a seat on the ottoman next to him. "We're at Rieka's," Aren stated, wishing it were a question.

"You could've told me you were leaving," Dane said. "I wasn't prepared for the state you were in."

"So I was ass-naked again?"

"No, just your shirt was missing this time, thank the gods," Dane grumbled. "But something had a grand old time beating you; all I could do was clean the cuts. You still have a high fever, though not as bad as when I found you, and—"

"You found me." Aren felt pieces of his memory start to come together, though at the cost of a throbbing in the back of his head. "You were able to use the markers? Where was I?"

Dane leaned forward, elbows on knees, fingers rubbing his temples. "I found the first and third markers. When I didn't find the second one, I thought I was lost for good. Then, I found you near the fourth marker. I thought you were dead."

Aren noted the weariness in Dane's tone, as well as the reined-in frustration. He wasn't sure what he could say or do to make it better. After a moment, when only the sea winds rustled between them, he said, "Thanks."

Dane looked him in the eye. "I'm just glad you're alive. We need to get Rieka to look at your cuts, properly dress them. There's also your fever we need to take care of."

"What time is it? We're supposed to spar with Lord Vir again."

"He canceled. The Doctor told him to rest because he's ill."

"And Gryf?"

"Pissed off and worried, but otherwise healing just fine thanks to Rieka's bleeding-out theory. We thought you had finally fallen asleep in your room once the nosebleed stopped. Gods' sakes, you couldn't even open your eyes for the pain."

Aren swung his feet off the sofa and felt his blood rush, unbalancing him for a moment. He kept the pain and confusion to himself, feeling guilty for what he had done, but the voices were gone.

Dane handed him his boots. "Selina had a feeling that you left. She said the Wood's gone quiet. That's how Gryf and I found out. She's frightened for you, and I would've taken you straight to the House just to ease her worry if you hadn't been so beaten up. You're in really bad shape."

Aren pulled on his boots as Dane stood over him, waiting. There was nothing else to say. There was too much to process, and they both knew that if he tried to remember what had happened, fierce headaches would seize him up again. Aren stood up, making sure he felt steady before moving again. He held a hand out and Dane pressed the hilt of a knife into it. Aren ran a thumb over the Gerrit mark. "Saved my life."

"I know."

TWELVE

"Aren," Kaila whispered, not wanting to startle him. She had found him at his desk in the Library with his head down, an arm for a pillow. Every now and then a fierce shiver would seize him. Aren didn't acknowledge her, so she crept closer. His breathing was ragged, his skin sallow. "What happened to you?"

He was mumbling in his sleep and she pulled up a chair. His words were unintelligible, and every now and then he winced in pain. Kaila bit her lip, not sure what she could do for him without her powers.

"Magic," he said, clear as a bell.

She cocked her head, then leaned in closer, hoping to make out more words, when she smelled something out of place. Something dark lingered on him. She recalled how he had smelled the other night: like the sea and the invigorating salt-tinged air. His scent was masculine, intoxicating. She leaned closer still, her cheek grazing his jawline. As he mumbled about a swan, she closed her eyes and concentrated, willing her dulled senses to focus, and her mind began to filter through aeons of history, testing and forming connections in the space of a heartbeat.

Her eyes opened wide as she sat up. "Wild magic," she breathed. "Why did you return to the Wood? How did you get out alive?"

"Trouble," he murmured. "Tiede...trouble..."

Kaila bit at her lower lip again, gazing at his pallid, troubled face. First, there was the little Priestess. Then, there was the storm connected to events in Tiede Wood. Aren seemed to be the key piece in the puzzle. What fate line had she stumbled upon, and where was it leading her?

She reached out to push stray strands of hair away from his face, and he stirred. His eyes, shadowed by dark circles and bruises, blinked open, lazy and hesitant. His head didn't move but his eyes began to focus, and she smiled, letting him take his time returning to full consciousness.

"Lake?" he rasped, his voice straining to escape his barely parted lips. "I must be dreaming."

"You'd dream of me?" she asked, her smile widening. He began to straighten up, but grimaced and squeezed his eyes shut. She reached out to help steady him.

He took a deep breath and exhaled slowly, his lips moving without words to accompany. When he opened his eyes again, he said in a sleep-slurred voice, "Stars, my fever must be bad. I thought Lake left this morning. When she said goodbye, I wasn't sure if I'd ever see her again."

"What was she to you anyway? Just another in the long line of women in your life."

"She was my friend." He lowered his eyes. "I let down all my defenses with her." He let out a laugh. "And she's mistaken if she thinks there are so many women. I haven't even—"

She put a finger to his lips to silence him. "Friends. It makes me so happy to hear you say that," she said, her heart leaping with inexplicable joy. He took her hand, pressed the back of it to his lips, and held it there. His touch was hot, feverish. "I don't think you're following Old World customs when you do that," she pointed out. "You aren't fooling me."

He shrugged, letting her go, a sheepish smile on his face. "I'm really not dreaming?" She shook her head, laughing. "Then, I apologize for my physical state. I must look like the dead."

"You're not far from it," she teased. "What happened to you?"

"I'm not sure."

A comfortable silence followed as they stared at each other, eyes locked, reading and seeking the unspoken. She noted the confusion, fear, and embarrassment in his green eyes.

"Lake, I know we've only had one night to get to know each other, but I—"

She pressed a finger against his lips again, afraid of what confessions he might make. He took her hand, kept it close to his mouth, breathing in her scent. "I made it as far as the farmlands," she said. "My contact received word that travel isn't safe, so I'll spend a little more time here. I have field research I can do out on the western cliffs."

"What you're saying is you can't stay in the Library with me every day while you're here," he said, a smile lifting the corner of his mouth, exposing a shy dimple.

"I thought it would be best if I put it out there before you started working your charms on me." She slipped her hand out of his.

"You're the one with the charms," he said. "Go ahead, I'll let you work them on me."

"You are incorrigible."

"You never told me about your beau, your lover—"

"Nikken," she said, her eyes meeting his, holding him. "His name is Nikken and it's not entirely what you think."

He must have noted the frustration in her tone and sensed that she didn't want to talk about it. His voice softened. "You don't need to say another word."

"Aren, I—"

"I really do feel much better now that you're here." He laid his head back down on his desk, closed his eyes. "Will you stay with me? I'll send for coffee."

She smoothed his hair back away from his face. "You aren't making this easy for me. You need to go to bed."

"Come with me. We'll go upstairs. Plenty of room under my covers."

"Aren!"

"Did I say that out loud?" His voice was getting faint, but she could still hear his smile. "I'm delirious with fever."

She rolled her eyes as she continued to smooth his hair. He didn't speak again, and she began to hum a lullaby that the women of the Kailen Islands sang to their babies. An overwhelming sense of serenity filled her as she watched him sleep. She leaned over to place a kiss on his forehead, then stood up, wondering how she could get him to go to his room and rest. She recalled how strict Elder was about the Library, so she imagined there must be keys to lock up. She was about to go through his robe pockets when she felt the change in temperature, a disturbance in the air. She whirled around, pulling the dagger hidden in her cloak as she did so.

The young man unsheathed a blade almost as fast she did. There were two of them, and she cursed herself for not hearing them approach. In her haste to see Aren, she had forgotten to close the doors behind her earlier. How could she have been so reckless?

The shorter, more muscular man spoke first. "That's our brother," he said. "If you mean him no harm, then none will come to you."

He hadn't drawn a weapon, but the power emanating from him was palpable. The dozens of small cuts all over the left side of his face and neck were covered in a clear salve and still healing. His clothes were dirty and shredded in places, allowing Kaila to glimpse the full marks of the Fighter inked onto his upper left arm.

Kaila reached out with her spirit as best she could, knowing now what to look for. Their fire blessings connected to her. She lowered her weapon, sheathed it. "You caught me by surprise. I apologize for being so paranoid."

"You've every right to be," said the Fighter. "The House was attacked this morning, and two people were killed in the lower eastern district earlier this evening."

"The House was attacked?" Kaila put a hand to her heart. Tiede was in more trouble than she realized.

"It's been a rough day. You must be the Master from Tennar," the taller of the two men said, sheathing his blade. "Aren and Rieka mentioned you. I'm Dane and this is Gryf."

"Lake." She inclined her head.

"Aren said you left."

"It's a long story and it's not important. Aren shouldn't be lying here like this. He's burning up, he should be resting."

"I'll carry him," Gryf said.

Her brows furrowed as Gryf picked up the unconscious Aren and walked away towards the stairs. Aren was so tall compared to his brother, yet Gryf carried him as though he were merely a sack of grain. Aren, dead to the world, played the part.

"What happened to him?" Kaila asked, turning to face Dane. She noted the anxiety in his eyes despite his calm demeanor. "Don't answer that," she said before he could say anything. "You don't know me, and to be honest, Aren doesn't know me as well as he thinks he does."

Dane nodded, then led her towards the stairs and out the second floor so he could lock the doors. "Aren is fond of you, whether he admits it or not, but he said you were already involved with someone. Like you said, I don't know you, but you seem nice and Rieka said she enjoyed your company. Aren says you're smart, and anyone with eyes can see how beautiful you are." Kaila was about to speak, but he held a hand up. "Maybe he's already fallen for you, but don't lead him on. You might break him."

THIRTEEN

Elder Tanda stood in the hallway, listening to the twinkling sound of the piano mingled with the singing and giggling of ladies. He peeked into the parlor, hoping that the time Vir was spending with his wife would ease some of the growing tension in the House.

Geyle stood by the black grand piano as Saris played a merry tune reminiscent of Rose. Another lady sang the lyrics in a high, sweet voice that seemed to lift the gloom that had settled over the House since the attack that morning. Geyle was laughing and clapping, and every now and then she'd turn her gaze to her husband, as if to make sure he was still there.

Vir sat in one of the high-backed chairs, a drink in his hand. The young lord managed to force a partial smile. He looked worse as the day wore on, more pale and haggard, and Tanda wondered if he could convince Vir to rest for a few hours.

"Is everything all right, Elder?"

He turned to find Crina approaching. He took a few steps away from the parlor to meet her, keeping his staff from thumping against the stone floor. "I don't want to disrupt. He has very little time for her anymore."

Crina sighed, feeling the weight behind his words. The Head Priestess, while still beautiful and graceful as always, looked tired and a little out of sorts, which was uncharacteristic. It seemed as if the entire House had been upended within a matter of days.

"What do you need to bother him about?" she asked in that regal tone of hers.

"My Apprentice." He grimaced. A knowing look passed between them, and he thought the mere mention of Aren had drained her of whatever energy she had left.

"He's been trouble since before he was born." She rolled her eyes before alighting a hand over her heart. "I have news of the little girl that I need to share with Lord Vir, but it can wait. I need to confirm some things before I talk to him, so I'll leave you to it." She walked away, her soft footfalls and white, gauzy dress making her seem like a ghost.

Tanda took a deep breath, then made his way into the parlor. The music and singing stopped at once, and he hated having to drag Vir away from this temporary respite.

"Continue." Vir waved a hand at the ladies as Tanda took a seat next to him. The women hesitated, but Geyle indicated that the songs begin again, only softer.

"Please tell me you've found the Apprentice," Vir whispered. "I would rather be in my study right now, and truth be told my wife would rather have his company."

Tanda forced a small, tight-lipped smile. "He's not well, he's caught a virus or something. Perhaps it's the same one you have. In any case, you should try to enjoy yourself. You don't really want the Apprentice to have her attention; he's just a boy."

"Boy or not, he's better company than I am. I belong in my study, where I've been holed up since that damned message arrived. People are gathering outside the gates, demanding to know what I'm doing about the menace in Tiede. What news on the interrogations? Did the traitor finally break?"

Tanda declined the drink Vir offered. "It didn't take long to break him," he said, recalling the clinical, detached report from the Hunter. "The Guard is in a particularly patriotic mood. They've beaten the prisoner far more than was necessary."

Vir took a swallow of his drink. "Let them. They've every right to be angry about the House being infiltrated on their watch. They're lucky I don't have them beaten instead."

"We have the names of others associated with Horin whom we can question. The Guard is rounding them up now."

"Good. I want answers."

"Yes, my Lord." Tanda shifted in his chair. "Horin's motives, however..." Vir waited, and the music quieted to the point that it seemed it had stopped altogether.

"What is it?" Vir urged.

Tanda looked into the dark-blue of Vir's deep-set eyes. "You weren't Horin's target. He was trying to kill Aren."

FOURTEEN

Aalae sat at the wrought-iron table on the roof of her castle, sipping on tea and nibbling on lemon cakes. Angels stood nearby, diamond white against the purple ivy overgrowth that clung to the stone walls and latched onto every crook and crevice. The angels waited like porcelain statues, with only their feathers and garments moving in the caressing breeze.

Aalae frowned. A week ago, this would have made her happy. Instead, she felt infuriated by the peacefulness of it. She had to contend with the mages and one of her Houses being destroyed. If she and her brother did manage to quell the uprising this time, how would she resurrect the House and restore balance, never mind dominance?

She made a dismissive motion with her hand. Two angels cleared the tea and cakes, and another placed a small glass of rosewater before her. They rushed away and two more replaced them, standing by to fulfill her every desire. What she desired was a way to kill the mages with her own two hands. She needed a way out of this mess and off this planet. She needed...

"Geir." She said his name as if it were a curse, and willed him to her side.

The breeze stirred and strengthened, and the angels moved to maintain their balance. Aalae leaned back in her chair, folded her arms across her chest, and waited for the Wind spirit to materialize. When he did, he was covered in black magic and blood. He dropped to one knee before her.

"Speak," she said.

Without standing or lifting his head, he said in his low, soft voice, "The House Lord has threatened to kill the Priestesses if they try to escape without him. The mages have a real army this time around, and when you kill one, there are a dozen more to take its place. Without the use of our powers..."

Aalae growled. "Will nothing go my way? Tell me you've found some kind of weakness in their ranks."

"They're fighting two battles," he said. "They fight the House's army and they fight their own power source. Small *istoqs* open when they use too much magic, and they're forced to divide their power between fighting Trum's army and closing the *istoq*. They learned to close the *istoq* with their magic, but it does take its toll."

Aalae thought about those dark gateways they had encountered over the centuries. The working theory Taia had come up with was that the *istoq*, or gateway, belonged to the planetary god whom Mahl had defeated and imprisoned within the planet's core. The excessive use of magic opened an *istoq*, which allowed the planetary god to send frightening creatures through. The *istoq* had to be closed; otherwise the beasts would run rampant and devour the mortal souls, weakening both Aalae and Alaric.

"I don't know how the *istoq* can be used to our advantage," she said.

Geir offered no opinion or insight; didn't speak unless she ordered him to. Part of her was pleased that he was under her control, but something else told her that he was only playing her game, biding his time. That unknown element unsettled her.

Rafi's presence broke through her thoughts. She turned to watch him come up the last two steps and walk past the angels towards her. He gave Geir a cursory glance, then returned his attention to Aalae, leaning over to place a kiss on her mouth. "I can return later if you're busy," he whispered.

She motioned to the chair beside her. There was a brief look of scorn on his face as he glanced at Geir again. "Will you at least look at your goddess?" she said, kicking Geir's knee. He lifted his face towards her, and she noticed the shards of magic embedded on one side of his neck, and the blood and grime that streaked his blindfold. His jaw was tense, and she wasn't sure if he was in pain or trying to keep from lashing out.

She reached down to wipe the dirt from his lips with her thumb. A softness there conflicted with the harsh angles of his face, and she found it alluring. She half expected him to bite her finger off, but he remained as still as the angels. "My beautiful Geir," she said as if talking to a child, "what am I to do with you?" She used her thumb to part his lips and felt the warmth of his breath against her skin. He didn't speak and she was tempted to strike him. He must have known it, because a tic worked in his jaw. She pulled away, cleaning her fingers in the rosewater. "Wait in the infirmary," she ordered. "If we don't remove the magic, you'll be useless."

Geir bowed his head, then stood up, summoning the winds. In an instant, he was gone.

"Taia just sent word that Alaric will send Tanghi to Trum," Rafi said as soon as they were alone.

"And what of Geir?" she asked.

He laughed. "Well, he didn't bite you. I treat the magic-inflicted wounds whenever he returns. The salve is working, it's in his bloodstream. Just give it time. If I try to make it any more powerful, he'll notice. I'll apply more as soon as I return to the infirmary."

"My patience wears thin, love," she said, gripping his hand. "We are losing this war and I need him broken."

Rumors

ONE

*A*ren's memories assaulted him in bits and pieces as he sat in the hot salt baths. His fever had broken overnight, but he felt weak and pains went from skin down to bone. It reminded him of when he and Dane were sent to the Fighters Guild to earn their blade mark—something Gerrit Derin required of all of his children, regardless of what they went on to study later. The marks signified knowledge of the basic combat arts and gave you the right to wield varying degrees of weapons. As far as the Gerrits were concerned, if it had an edge, they were more than qualified to wield it.

At the time, Aren and Dane hadn't even gone through the rites of manhood, and they joked about how getting their mark was going to make them very popular with the girls. Their sister Lana had warned them not to get cocky. She told them about the time she earned her mark and how ruthless the Guild Masters were. She also reminded them that Kel Bret had failed to earn his mark on his first try. The boys only laughed at her, and she left them to their foolishness. "At least," she had said before leaving them, "I had the luck of not having to fight Gryf."

That had silenced them.

Lana hadn't exaggerated in the least. The Guild Masters pitted the boys against their most prized Fighters, the toughest among them being Gryf. They were beaten down then forced to get up and fight again. At the end of eight days, Dane was able to earn his mark, while Aren had to return a month later to try again. In that month, Gryf trained Aren around the clock to make sure he didn't fail. Until then, Aren had no idea that pain could reside so deep in his bones and in the air he breathed—no idea that pain could linger in his bloodstream.

He touched the small, black, eight-pointed star with the single blade piercing it that had been inked onto his upper left arm, reliving the honor that had been bestowed upon him after passing the Guild trials. Then, he submerged himself in the bath, allowing the heat to permeate every fiber of his being. When he resurfaced, he imagined the illness leaving his body, the water cleansing and healing him. He leaned his head against the pool's edge, letting the morning light spill onto his face, the chill of the sea winds balancing out the heat.

"You look much better than you did last night."

Aren almost fell into the water in surprise and barely caught himself. He turned his head to look at the woman who had spoken, lowering himself so that the water came up to his chin. "Lake! Not that I'm not happy to see you, but what are you doing here?"

"A very groggy, grouchy Dane answered the door to your room. He didn't give me anything to go on except 'blargh,' so I went to the Library, where Elder told me you were probably having your first beauty bath of the day."

"This is embarrassing."

"Nothing I haven't seen before." She laughed, gathering the skirt of her dark-blue dress and lowering herself so that she sat at the pool's edge, her bare feet splashing in the water.

He smoothed his hair back. "But you haven't seen me before."

"Are you blushing or is the water too hot? If it makes you feel better, I can't see a thing for the churning. Besides, I don't know why you're being so shy, considering the offers you were making last night."

"Stars," he said, uttering the rest of a curse under his breath. "Please tell me I didn't say something that would've caused you to slap me."

She gave a little kick, splashing him. "I think I'll just keep that to myself." He shook off the water and grabbed her ankle, causing her to squeal. "Don't you dare, Aren!"

He pretended as if he would pull her in, but squeezed her calf and let her go instead. "You're lucky I'm naked or you'd be wet," he said. She gave him a look. "That didn't sound the same out loud as it did in my head." Lake's laughter was infectious and Aren found himself laughing as well. He reached to grab one of the towels he had laid out and handed it to her. "Put it over your head." She rolled her eyes at him but did as he asked. Pulling himself out of the pool, he used one of the other towels to dry off then wrapped it around his hips.

When he pulled the towel off her head, she let out a fake cry of terror. "Oh, the horrors! It's a naked man!" He dumped the towel back on her head before sitting down next to her. She laughed, removing the towel. "You're more modest than I imagined."

"Well, now you know something new about me." He grinned, leaning back on his hands. He was about to ask her to share something he didn't know about her when he realized she was examining him.

"What happened?" Her fingers reached out, brushed at the wounds on his chest, leaving goosebumps in their wake.

He wondered if he would ever not feel like he was falling from the heavens whenever she touched him. "Nothing's broken." He poked the long cut on his forearm. "I guess immersing my wounds in a hot salt bath might not be the smartest thing I've ever done, but the stinging only killed me for a little while and no one heard me scream."

She traced the length of the cut. "Either it wasn't so bad or you're a fast healer. Are these from the other night when you got attacked by that monster?"

He wasn't quite sure what to say or how to explain his odd behaviors. His head was swimming with broken images and noises. Then, he remembered her stroking his hair, humming a song. He remembered her speaking to him, asking him questions. His brows furrowed and he turned to look at her. "How did you know I was in Tiede Wood?"

"What are you talking about?" She bit at her bottom lip.

"You said something about Tiede Wood last night. I think you asked why I went back?"

"You were very feverish. You must be confused."

He closed his eyes for a moment, as if it would bring clarity to his memories. "Are you sure? I felt you, felt your face close to mine. You were looking for something."

She placed a hand on his jaw, turning his head to face her. Her thumb grazed the stubble there, and his train of thought vanished. "I was looking at the bruises on your face, and I asked what happened to you. You didn't respond, but you were talking about things like the Wood and magic. I leaned in so I could hear you."

"When I try to remember, I get really bad headaches." He was proud of himself for being able to put together a sentence. Her touch was such a distraction.

She changed the topic, letting him go. "I have to do some field research today; I just wanted to check on you."

"You can stay in the Library all day and just ask me about Tiede," he offered. "The way I tell it, you'll feel like you're standing on the cliffs, only you'll have a glass of wine in hand and me at your beck and call. Why bother traveling?"

She nudged him with her shoulder. "I'll come by later this evening, though I won't keep you up all night this time." She gave him a wink.

"You can keep me up anytime. And don't worry, I'll be clothed next time you see me," he said. She laughed, kicking at his leg in the water. He turned to look at her, ready to tell her anything just to hear her laugh again, but her eyes were downcast, her fingers fiddling with her dress. He stilled her hands and rubbed the satin fabric between his finger and thumb. "When something's on my mind, I write it down," he said. "Then, I cross it out when I'm done thinking about it. What do you do? Other than worry at your clothes like this."

She gave him a sad smile. "I usually go for a swim. I'm fine, really. Just worrying about my siblings."

"I didn't know you had siblings. What're they like?"

"One brother is fierce, and the other a quiet enigma. My sister is a warrior queen. They're all older than me and think I'm an annoying, over-emotional troublemaker," she said with a huff. "Don't get me wrong, I love them all."

"I'm the youngest of five…" His mind was getting cloudy, filling with the blurry images. "I remember being scared of fire…my little sister and I…" He shook his head.

Lake looked at him, her brows furrowed. "Are you all right?"

He shook his head again as if the motion would clear it. "Just confused. I grew up around fire, and my sister's about ten years older than me; this memory isn't mine." His head was starting to hurt again, and he blinked as images of a little girl and boy trapped in a room engulfed in flames assaulted his memories. It wasn't his memory, but the fear and desperation suffocated him and he felt his waking senses begin to extinguish.

"Aren!" Lake's voice. The sound of water as her legs moved out of the pool. The strength of her arms cradling his shoulders as darkness began to take him, as his spirit detached from his bones. "Aren…" Her breath on his cheek as she took his weight and laid him down. "I've got you." The hard, cool touch of stone. Her soft hand against his face, brushing over his eyes, his nose, covering his lips.

Like falling asleep in water.

TWO

Aren wandered from his room in a daze. He couldn't remember what had happened with Lake. He had passed out, which embarrassed him to no end. When he had awoken, he found that he was lying by the pool's edge. Lake was sitting next to him, her eyes closed as if in meditation. His voice was hoarse as he whispered her name, and she flashed her gorgeous smile for him. She said that he might not have fully recovered from his illness and that he should rest. He didn't argue or ask questions as she walked him back to his room.

He pulled out his notebook and thumbed through the pages, hoping to find some thought or note that he had jotted down to set him straight. A slip of paper fell out and he stooped down to pick it up.

Keep your distance. I only saved your life for her happiness.

That wasn't helping anything. He tucked the threat back into his notebook and continued wandering through the halls. He recalled something about fire and his sister. No, not his sister. Why was it so hard to remember?

He was walking past Vir's study when a voice called out, "Apprentice!" Aren peered into the room, spotted Vir pacing by a bookcase, then paid the proper respects. "Ask my wife to make me another drink." Vir passed an empty tumbler to him, and Aren bowed before taking his leave. He was thankful for the distraction.

He found Geyle by herself in the parlor, lounging on a deep blue, velvet chaise, a small leather-bound book open in her hands. He was about to bow when she spotted him and frowned. "I would prefer it if you stopped doing that," she pouted, closing the book as she placed her bare feet on the floor. "I see you so often that it's tiring to have to watch the formality every time."

He gave her a smirk as he made a show of straightening to his full height and bowing from the waist with a flourish. "The formalities are what keep us civilized. They are an outward reminder that you are the Lady of the House and I am but your servant. Besides, Lord Vir sees me more often than you do, and he doesn't tire of it."

"Do you tease all women or just me?"

He walked to where she was sitting and presented Vir's glass. "I'm not teasing. I act as Lord Vir wishes, and he wishes me to ask you to fix him another drink."

"You are forever the humble servant." She patted the spot next to her to indicate he should sit. He remained standing and presented the empty glass again. His brothers would be proud. Geyle sighed as she stood up and took the glass. She reached up to cup his chin with one dainty hand. "What am I to do with you?"

He gulped, still not accustomed to her informal attitude towards him. He took her hand from his chin, where he felt it had lingered a little too long, touched the back of it to his lips, and released her. "The House shall do with me as it wishes."

She paused, her freckled cheeks burning bright and pink, then managed to laugh. She took up her rose-colored satin skirts and made her way to the bar, leaving her book behind. Aren moved closer to the chaise to see what she was reading, but he couldn't make out the faded title.

Geyle fanned at her face with her hand. "Did the drink help Vir's cough? He won't even listen to Doctor Pember's advice half the time, which I find odd because he's always so impressed with Illithe's medicinal advances."

"I think he found the drink helpful," Aren said, distracted. As she poured and stirred at the bar, his mind ran through the books in the Library with worn titles and bound in sable leather. He differentiated the fiction from the nonfiction, then began eliminating Houses that he knew didn't use such binding. "Genethew Farista, Herbal Remedies and Potions," Aren murmured, his mind locating the book title. "House of Tennar."

"Did you say something?" she asked, stopping and replacing the various liquors she had used.

"No, my Lady," he stammered. "Just talking to myself."

"Am I not interesting enough to talk to?" Her smile was coy and it made him uncomfortable.

"That's not what I meant. I tend to remind myself of my tasks out loud."

"Oh! Have you read that book before? It's fascinating! Tennar has a lot of plants that you can only get in the southern mountain regions, but their healing properties are amazing."

Aren picked up the book and leafed through it, confirming that it was indeed the book he thought it was. He also found it completely un-fascinating—so much so that he had fallen asleep while cataloguing it years ago. When Elder had checked on his progress and found that there was very little, he had ordered him to go out and bring back a sample of every plant native to Tiede that was mentioned in the book. The results of his scavenging had made the herbalists grateful at least.

"I'm not very smart on plants," he admitted as he watched her out of the corner of his eye. She had that mysterious vial out again, and he glimpsed two perfect pearls of liquid falling into the drink and disappearing. As she stopped the vial and slid it into the folds of her skirts, he returned his full attention to the book. He then made a show of clapping the book closed and returning it to the chaise. He forced himself to smile and noted how flush she seemed.

"*Tse frie!*" Geyle raised the glass, then brought it to her lips.

Aren's mind was working. She had assured him the first time he caught her putting drops into Vir's drink that it was harmless. He wanted to trust her; stars, he wanted to trust her.

"Shall I take it to him?" he asked.

"I'm perfectly capable of bringing Vir his drink," she said, licking her lips and moving towards him. "Besides, he's been so busy it'll probably be the only time I'll get to see him until he comes to bed — if he comes to bed." She stopped in front of him. "If you were my husband, you'd come to me every night, wouldn't you?"

His gut tightened. "Well—"

"You don't know what it's like, do you? To feel so alone and isolated..."

"My Lady," he said, his emotions torn, "I know exactly what it's like."

"Trust me, Aren." Her voice was soft and she didn't look at him. "I'm going to make this work. Then, we'll all be happy."

Before he could speak, she swished her skirts out into the hall.

THREE

A Messenger notified them that there would be no sparring with Lord Vir today, as he was still feeling under the weather. Dane decided he'd spend the time with Rieka at her parents' house. Aren walked him out, and they took the long way from the *kasan*, through the courtyard and to the other end of the House, past the kitchens, the storerooms, the greenhouse, and out to the gardens. They could hear Tiede's people outside of the gates, rattling tin cans and sticks against the iron, calling out to Vir, asking him to do something about the killings.

Dane talked about how scared everyone was, and said that rumors were circulating about the end times and the fall of Tiede. Aren, still not feeling entirely well, didn't talk much. The headaches and fever had drained him, and he had too many other things on his mind. Dane seemed to sense his mental agitation. "You and Rieka were right. Your new friend Lake is a goddess," he said as they paused by one of the garden fountains.

"You think so?"

"Don't act like you didn't notice."

"I didn't want to notice." Aren reached out to touch the tip of a glass star suspended over the fountain. "But she started talking about scroll preservation and celestial phenomena and the dead languages. Maybe she's Elder's idea of a practical joke."

"Elder is tricky like that. Maybe he taught her how to get to you, but she must be a Fighter. She's ridiculously fast on the draw; uncanny the way she knew Gryf and I were there when I'm positive we didn't make a sound."

"I guess she's got a lot of talents I don't know about," Aren said, trying to sound nonchalant.

"Did you tell her about your episodes?"

"No." Aren rubbed drops of water between his thumb and middle finger. "I don't need to scare her off." It was bad enough that he had passed out in front of her. "I hear voices and I'm compelled to go to the Wood. When I come out—rather, when you save my ass—I have no idea what's happened to me. I've lost my mind."

"You think that'll scare her? There's a monster on the loose, and not a single soul has any idea what it really is. Lord Vir's been attacked in his own House by a mage. Selina's hearing voices and having premonitions. At this point, only Gryf showing up to spar in a yellow summer dress would be more frightening."

Aren looked at Dane with a quizzical expression. "Why yellow?"

Dane shrugged, then patted him on the back. "I'll be back later to check on you, make sure you aren't dying or doing something stupid."

Aren was about to tell him not to bother, when Vir entered the gardens, Geyle at his side. A smile lit her face when she saw them, and Dane exchanged a look with Aren before they took a knee.

"Gentlemen." Vir stopped before them and motioned for them to stand. "Doctor Pember recommended I take a break from sparring until whatever illness I have passes. I trust you got the message." Vir's complexion was pale with dark circles under his hollow eyes. He hadn't shaved and his jaw was covered with a considerable amount of black stubble. His limp hair was slicked back, and the veins on his temple and forehead seemed to throb. "It's good that you're here, though," Vir said, addressing Aren as the young men straightened up. "I need a word with you, Apprentice. Young Gerrit, if you wouldn't mind escorting my wife around the gardens for a moment."

Dane inclined his head and offered his arm to Geyle. She took it, looked wistfully at Aren, then back at Vir, her smile fading as she allowed Dane to lead her away.

Vir proceeded to have a coughing fit, and he signaled a nearby servant for a drink. The meek girl, with her brown hair tied in a black ribbon, came forward with two glasses of water. She handed them to Vir and Aren, then bowed, taking her leave. When Vir was done coughing, he asked, "Apprentice, is there anyone you know who might consider you an enemy?"

Aren's first thought was the mysterious note. It was threatening, but what was he going to say? *Now that you mention it, I received a note written in Ancient. I have no idea where it came from, or who saved my life, or who I'm supposed to keep away from. Do you have any advice?* Ridiculous. "No, my Lord," he said instead. "Why do you ask?"

"The mage who attacked the House admitted he was trying to kill you, not me."

Aren was taken aback. Why would anyone want to kill him? He was a nobody and he didn't remember pissing anyone off. "Is it possible he's lying so that you might spare his life? I only met him once before the attack."

The mage was Horin, the tall boy with the yellow hair who didn't speak a word to him. Aren's mind raced to make connections. He had seen Horin once, before running into him with Dekney. The boy had poured water for Lady Saris. Garden-lemon-water-boy.

Vir interrupted Aren's thoughts. "Perhaps there's a girl he was fond of who might have shunned him for you? What about that girl the other night? The one who came to the House to discuss your alleged betrothal?"

Aren's mind was spinning. "Miss Crilys Trista misunderstood my intentions, and I apologize for her behavior. I'll keeping thinking, though. If there's someone who might want me dead, I'll let you know."

Vir nodded, handing Aren his empty glass. "I hope you will. We can't have your drama endangering everyone in this House." He turned away, looking to see where Dane and Geyle had walked off to. "Are you ill, Apprentice?"

"An overnight fever of sorts."

"Doctor Pember didn't think I was contagious, and Elder seems fine, as does my wife." Vir watched as Dane led her back towards them. "A handful of servants have fallen ill as well."

Aren was about to offer up some theory when the sound of a staff pounding against the stone caused them to turn around. Elder marched up to them, frowned at Aren, then addressed Vir. "My Lord," Elder said, his face grim, "news on Trum. Also, one of the ill servants has passed."

Vir rushed back into the House, Elder several paces behind him, pumping his staff up and down.

Geyle left Dane's side, gathered her skirts, and made to run after them, but slowed herself when she reached Aren. "I suppose he forgot we were going to spend some time together." Her voice was small, and tears gathered at the corners of her eyes. "It shouldn't be this difficult."

Aren looked to Dane, who was standing a few feet away. Dane gave him a look that he interpreted as: "Just walk away, you gigantic imbecile."

Aren began to think of excuses, ready to leave with his brother. Geyle could return to the House and find her ladies, spend time with them. Instead, Aren offered his arm and said, "I'll walk with you if you like."

FOUR

After walking through the House gardens, Aren managed to excuse himself from Geyle's company by using the growing angry mob outside of the gates as a reason for her to return indoors. He had been able to make her laugh a few times, which he much preferred over the crying. He never realized she could be so emotional, though he supposed he might get a little choked up if he were trying to poison his spouse.

She's not trying to poison him. My imagination is out of control.

During the walk, Vir's news about Horin targeting him was buzzing in the back of his mind until something clicked. He wrote a note for Elder, left the House, and headed for the northwest district.

When he arrived at the Morning Light, a high-end jewelry shop, he peeked through the spotless window. He associated the shop with bad memories, with feelings of inferiority and worthlessness. A few seasons ago, his father had asked him to pick up an order of precious stones from the shop proprietor, Gem Master Crilys Ire. That was when he met the Master's daughter Trista, and Master Ire had cursed and insulted him for casting his Unblessed and unholy shadow upon her establishment. Sometimes he wondered if Master Ire's attitude towards him was what made him flirt with Trista in the first place. Part of him felt guilty about it, but he felt that he had paid for his sins by putting up with her.

From his vantage point at the window, he saw Trista napping on a green chaise in the sitting area, where her mother entertained serious shoppers, plying them with mediocre wine as she laid out brilliant gems for consideration. The bells over the door tinkled clear and bright when he entered the shop, and Trista was startled awake. Her movement disturbed the lint in the velvet, and dust motes floated into the light, drifting like snow. Aren tried to smile but couldn't find the energy, so he closed the door and waited for her to say something.

She stood up, rushing to straighten her pink dress. He watched her eyes move from his face to the point between his collarbones where the silver clasp fashioned in the Tiede crest kept his robes fastened. Her expression darkened; she knew he was on House business, and he knew she hated him for it.

Aren waited to see if Master Ire would appear from beyond the dark-green draperies behind the locked glass cases displaying her wares. He didn't come here to be insulted, and he was more than ready to head back to the House if he saw her sharp, disapproving face.

Trista cleared her throat. "Are you here to see me?" He nodded and her smile was so wide and genuine, he hated himself for coming.

She gestured to the chaise but he declined. "I can't stay long." He held up a hand to refuse the glass of water she offered, moving to stand behind an armchair, gripping the top of it, wondering how to begin. He was compelled to look towards the cases again, worried that the Master would come out when he least expected it.

"My mother left for market days ago," Trista said, as if reading his mind. "My father is caring for the shop, and he went to deliver a necklace to the wife of some Counselor."

"The shops and markets always seem a little off-kilter this time of year. With the mess at the docks, it's worse than usual." He indicated the door with a thumb. "You should keep that locked."

"I will." Trista seemed surprised at his concern. "All the danger is around Crescent Park anyway, and the whole area south of that."

"Actually, the House was attacked yesterday," Aren said, watching her reaction. She was nodding, and she folded her arms across her chest, pushing up on her bodice and revealing ample cleavage. He turned his head to look out the window instead. "If the House is vulnerable, then everyone else is even more so."

"You aren't invincible," she said. "Did you come out of the big House just to check on me?" The sass was starting to creep back into her tone, and he questioned his decision to confront her.

Aren hadn't been attacked on the way to the shop, so it was possible Vir's information was wrong. If he were being tortured as Horin was, he'd probably say crazy things too. There was no reason he could think of for anyone to want to kill him—not since the mage after the river, the unicorn, the smoke creature with the red blade, and that thing in the Wood.

Maybe leaving the House was a bad idea after all.

He returned his gaze to Trista, concentrating on her face. "I want to know why you came by the House the other night." Her face reddened and she moved to retrieve a glass of water from a side table and took a sip. "Don't throw the betrothal lies at me," he added.

"It was the only way to get the Guard to take me seriously," she said, setting down her glass. "How else am I supposed to get in touch with you?"

Aren let out a laugh, not meaning to. "The reason you can't get in touch with me is because I didn't give you the means to. If I wanted to talk to you, I'd come find you like I did just now."

A gloss of tears filled her eyes. "You're such an ass," she said through gritted teeth. "Why do you have to be so mean? Why don't you just leave me alone?"

Aren felt his patience wearing thin as he recalled every conversation they'd had and how it always ended up in an argument. "Leave you alone? You're the one who came calling at the House, spreading lies about us getting married. Did you just happen to forget that it was Lord Vir's House and not mine?"

Trista averted her gaze, looking down at her ringed fingers. "I needed you."

He leaned against the back of the armchair, dropping his head. Why did he torture himself like this? "Needed me for what?"

"For everything!" she cried. "I want you to smile at me the way you did when you first met me, to hold my hand against your lips, to tell me I'm beautiful, to twirl my hair around your finger."

Aren felt as though a blood vessel in his forehead might rupture. He peered at her from behind the locks of hair that fell over his eyes. "What about your new friends? All those things you want from me you might willingly get from them."

"Mercer is handsome but he's not like you." Tears spilled from Trista's eyes.

Why in Aum was every woman crying around him? No wonder he enjoyed Lake's company; she wasn't ever on the verge of an emotional breakdown. "Of course he's not like me," he said. "I'm not like him either, I'm sure."

"I don't mean it like that. He's selfish, and when we..." The tears fell in earnest now, and Aren was taken aback. He reached into a pocket and pulled out a kerchief, walking over to hand it to her. "Copen is even worse."

"Then why do you keep their company?"

Trista threw up her arms. "They're fun when they're in a good mood." She looked straight into his eyes. "It's also nice to feel wanted sometimes."

Aren didn't flinch under her gaze. "I suppose you should put up with their selfishness then."

"Get out," she seethed. "I'm tired of your condescending attitude. Just leave me alone."

"I'll be glad to," he said, "provided you leave me alone as well." He put on a large, fake grin. "No more visits to Lord Vir's House, okay honeypot?"

"It wasn't my idea to begin with!" she yelled. "Now, get out!"

He was about to storm out of the shop, but he paused. "If it wasn't your idea, then whose idea was it?" He walked back towards her.

She shuddered as if a cold had seized her, and she clenched the kerchief in one hand as she toyed with her hair with the other. "No one," she said with less force than before.

Aren had a bad feeling in the pit of his stomach; she was clearly hiding something. He wouldn't have pissed her off so completely had he known there was more to her story. He took a deep breath. He was going to hate himself for what he was about to do, but if he rationalized that he was kissing her for the sake of the House, maybe he'd be able to live with himself.

He calmed down and told himself that Trista was just a girl who was infatuated and that her feelings had clouded her judgment. One day, she'd look back on all this and have a good laugh.

"Someone asked you to do it," he said, his voice softer now. "I know you; you never would've come to the House on your own for such a silly reason." He focused on her pretty face, her blue eyes, which seemed grayer in the early-afternoon light that poured in through the windows. She seemed transfixed by his change in demeanor and blushed under his gaze. The kerchief fell from her hand, and her fingers began to twist at her hair.

Aren stepped in, reached out, then drew back as if approaching a flame. His hands seemed to hang suspended between them as they contemplated each other, then he pressed his lips together and touched her. She didn't stop him as he put a gentle hand on her face, tilting her head back, didn't protest as he moved her fidgeting fingers away with his other hand. He brushed a thumb along her jaw and was surprised when she flinched. He frowned, studying her skin, the heavy application of powder.

He traced a line from her ear to her neck with a finger. She gasped and her eyes fluttered, as if anticipating his lips, but his thoughts were elsewhere and he frowned at his discovery. He could make out the discoloration now. The bruises formed a chain around her neck, and as he let her go, she grabbed at his hand with both of hers and looked up into his eyes. "What have you gotten yourself into?" he asked, his voice just above a whisper.

"It's not what you think." She smiled for a fraction of a second before her true emotions took over, and she stifled a sob.

"There's no excuse for this. Why would they do this to you?" There were marks on her arms as well.

"It's my own fault. Sometimes I have too much to drink. They say I get annoying, asking for you, talking about you all the time." She choked on what sounded like a laugh. "You think I'm annoying."

Although he did find her irritating, he would never hurt her. He picked up the kerchief and handed it to her. She let go of him to dab at her eyes, sitting down on the chaise as she did so.

"Your friend Mercer asked you to go to the House, didn't he?" When she didn't answer, he asked, "Why? What do they want from me?"

"I don't know," she said at last.

"Think!" he snapped. "Where are they from and how did you meet them?"

"I met them at a party while you were away."

"Are they marked?" he asked. She didn't look at him, and her unspoken answer hit him straight in the gut. "Did you ever meet up with a boy named Horin? Have they talked to anyone at the House?"

"I've never heard of Horin," she huffed, getting irritated again.

"Did they ask you to go to the House? To ask for me?" he pressed.

"What is this about?" She stood up to face him, fury coloring her features.

"It was a mage that attacked the House yesterday." His memories bubbled to the surface, and he could almost smell the sweat and blood, the wood and stone, the burn of magic. "I don't know any mages, but I got a bad feeling from your friends, and from the looks of things, my instincts were right on target."

"Rieka's marked," she shot back. "And everyone knows Lady Tiede bears the marks."

"So you can't help me," he said, turning to leave.

"That's right, turn your back on me again," she cried. "Run back to your books and hiding places!"

A tingle ran over Aren's skin. "A hiding place," he breathed, his memories from that morning assaulting him. He bolted out of the store, back towards the House, Trista's sobs hastening his departure.

FIVE

Selina wandered into the darkness as Aren lifted the oil lamp to illuminate the musty room. Shadows came to life, stretching across the floors and slithering down the walls. He indicated the sconces by the door, and Dane pulled out a tin of fire magic, his lips reciting the incantations as he lit the old wicks.

"What are we doing here?" Nianni asked as Selina began to poke around the cold, forgotten room in the upper level of the House. A layer of dust covered the sheets draped over the furniture and books and mementos of a past long forgotten.

"I'm just following Aren to make sure he doesn't do anything stupid," Dane said.

"We shouldn't be here," Nianni said, keeping near the door. "This is Lord Vir's House and these rooms could be private."

Selina thought the room was more than private; it was abandoned, and it felt gauzy and haunted. This room was lost in time, looking nothing like any of the other rooms she had seen in the House. Vir favored heavy tapestries in rich tones, massive oil paintings against stone walls, floors of dark wood and plush rugs. In this room, streaks of black marred the floor, and the windows were boarded shut. What was left of the curtains was merely the raiment of ghosts, thin and tattered, edged in soot. Black streaks like angry claw marks scarred the walls, and wood, now decayed and crumbling, had been put up to cover the stone. The wood had once been painted over, and in some areas Selina noticed where wallpaper might have been hung, the paper now peeled and shredded, exposing dust-coated glue.

"I don't like it in here," Nianni said, voicing Selina's feelings.

"Come on, Priestess," Dane urged. "How often do you get to see what kind of junk the House Lords kept around?" Nianni remained by the door, twisting at the silver band on her upper arm.

Selina returned to where Aren was moving boxes. "What are you looking for?"

"The wall," he said, ruffling her hair. "My memory is hazy, but I think there's a secret in here." He pulled a piece of paper from a pocket in his robe, unfolded it, and smoothed it out on the box he had just moved. On the scrap of parchment was a rough sketch of the third level of the House. His finger traced a line around two adjoining rooms. "A very long time ago, this room was part of a nursery," he explained. "I think in one of these rooms is a hiding place."

Selina stared at the drawing for a while, wondering why this was so important to him. His behavior was odd.

"You all right, sweetheart?" he asked, folding up the piece of paper, breaking her trance.

She looked up into his tired eyes and wondered when he had last slept. "Why did you go to the Wood?"

He was quiet for a long time, and it seemed to magnify the sound of the flames dancing along their wicks, Nianni fidgeting with her silver bracelets, and Dane grunting as he rearranged the heavy boxes.

"I know you're upset about it," he said at last. "It's not an excuse, but I was in so much pain; I was desperate. I really am sorry that I made you worry so much."

"You should've taken me with you."

"I could hardly take care of myself. It's best I didn't take you, and I'm not going to apologize for that. If you had gotten hurt—"

"But I'm supposed to take care of you!"

He looked at her, a curious expression on his face. "It's my job to take care of you, not the other way around. I will never forgive myself for what happened in the Wood with you—for all that happened with the mage and the unicorn."

She looked down at her feet, at the perfect, white satin slippers that had replaced the old, worn boots she had been wearing just days ago, when they were running for their lives. Life had changed so quickly that she was caught unaware. She wondered if this was the goddess's doing.

"Why do you hear the voices?" he asked, his own voice hushed. "Have you always heard them?"

Her brows furrowed as she considered his question. She didn't know, but it didn't seem strange to her. She just accepted it as another aspect of her life, as strange as ending up in Tiede and being found by the one person she felt she had been bound to since gaining consciousness.

"I always hear the Wood," she said. "But never like it is now, the way it calls your name. It used to have a whispering sound, peaceful like a sleeping kitten. Then, the other night on the rooftop, I heard your name carried on the wind."

Aren studied her for a minute, then stood up, returning to the task of moving crates and furniture away from the walls. "For as long as I can remember, it always called me with urgency, with a desperation that makes me ache inside." He paused in his work, glanced down at her. She was surprised to find so much fear in his usually serene eyes. "That's why I will never take you with me when it calls. So, please don't ask again."

She turned away as he occupied himself with shifting a desk. She understood his desire to keep her safe, but he didn't seem to understand that her very existence was tied to his—that if she couldn't watch over him and keep him alive, then her safety was of no value.

"Aren!" Dane called out. He wore a tall, silly hat covered with long feathers, and was standing in the small path he had made, boxes and furniture on either side of him, looking down at the wall. "Were you looking for a tiny, secret door that leads to Aum?"

Aren and Selina went to have a look, and even Nianni was curious enough to follow behind them, standing on her tiptoes to try to see over the piles of stuff. Aren squeezed in next to Dane as Selina crawled through their legs, making her way to the wall. The worn, decorative paper was peeling back and revealed an outline of a door smaller than Selina. There was no knob or handle, only space enough at the bottom for little fingers to fit and pry it open. Selina crouched by the door and put her fingers in the space.

Aren lowered himself as much as he could into the cramped space, edging Dane back. He said to Selina, "You don't have to do this. Let me move some boxes and I'll be able to fit."

"Your fingers are too big. I can do it, I think I feel a latch."

"What are you expecting to find here?" Dane asked.

Aren furrowed his brows. "I'm not sure." He looked at Dane. "Was Lana ever scared of fire?"

Dane frowned, pulled his neck back like a rooster. "Lana? Our sister? The Fire god incarnate?"

"Blasphemy," Nianni whispered, more to herself than anyone.

"You're right," Aren laughed. "I don't know what I was thinking. My memories are still a mess."

"Open it?" Selina asked.

Aren nodded.

SIX

Kaila paced the precipice overlooking the sea, just under the Keep's looming shadows. She had been torn about returning home. She knew that returning would ease Alaric's mind and not rouse his suspicions. On the other hand, staying in Tiede meant learning more about Aren and simply enjoying his company.

Their last meeting at the baths had been dangerous. When his body had slumped to the ground as if dead, she had cradled, covered, and protected him. She had watched as his spirit seemed to shut down to protect itself. But protect itself from what? She wondered if it had anything to do with his experiences in Tiede Wood. What was his connection to that place?

Her mind, her logic, had screamed at her to leave him. He would get up on his own, and he would think it was all a dream. Yet, her spirit was compelled to reach out, to heal him. Something in her needed to protect him. While he was unconscious, she had resumed her powers and taken some of his pain away, enough to ease his suffering. It was such an infinitesimal amount of energy, easily masked in the salt baths, in her element so the gods would never know. Her willful disobedience of the Realm's Laws of Divide was punishable by exile to Aum, but when Aren had awoken and stared up at her with his beautiful, deep emerald eyes, she felt it had been worth it.

She would have done it again in a heartbeat.

"What is wrong with me?" She stopped pacing and shook her head.

"Quit talking to yourself and do something useful." Taia's voice was cold and Kaila spun around, surprised by her sudden appearance.

"I would if Alaric would let me," Kaila retorted.

Taia considered her, flickering once before her form stabilized. "He wants to see you in his study. Maybe he'll ask you to sit in a lagoon."

Kaila ignored the comment and took in Taia's blood-burgundy riding outfit, flowing wool cloak, high-cut leather boots. "Where are you going?"

"Dusk, on a task for Alaric. Try not to seduce him while I'm gone."

Taia turned towards the path leading away from the Night Realm, singing a spell. The darkness gathered, rushing towards Taia until it materialized into a wild, black stallion with stars for eyes beneath her. Then, the spell weaver was gone.

Kaila took the long route along the cliff and over the waterfall. She swam into the underground caverns, dressed in layers of long silk robes in aqua and blue and green that trailed behind her. She wrapped a wide sash in golden orange around her waist, and pulled her hair up in a messy sweep of curls, the fallen locks framing her face.

Alaric's study was empty when she arrived, and she wondered what he wanted to see her about. He might ask what she had been up to. Flirting with a mortal in Tiede.

By Mahl's holy name, she had to stop thinking of Aren.

She walked to Alaric's desk and examined the odds and ends lying around: trinkets, scrolls, jewels. He liked to have objects to connect to, things that held meaning and memory scattered about like stars in his skies. She ran her fingers through the stardust littering Alaric's desk, her wavy lines like drawings in sand. Then, she picked up a small vial and held it up to the moonlight to reveal the clear liquid. Perhaps it was a potion stolen from Rafi, a secret ingredient expelled from some flower, or the separated blood of an angel or demon. She was about to set it down when Alaric entered. He took the vial, holding it between his thumb and middle finger, examining it as she had.

"Your tears," he said, answering her unvoiced question. "When you were dying from the fisherman's spear, and I took you home. You said you were so happy that at the end of it all, mine was the last face you'd see. You were crying and it broke my heart. I closed your eyes and put you to sleep so that we could heal you." He smiled. "You look beautiful this evening."

She blushed, hugging herself as she turned and took a few steps away from him. "You'd keep a memento of that incident? When I was feeling better, you spent the next several weeks castigating me. We argued and screamed and said horrible things to each other," she reminded him.

"I didn't turn demon."

"I was surprised," she admitted.

He leaned against his desk, sifting a handful of stardust through his fingers. "We can go through the worst trials yet still love each other at the end of it all." She gave him a nod and he continued. "The lines are changing faster, the patterns more intricate, the lattices unraveling then rebuilding in fractal compositions we've never seen before. These will be the worst trials yet."

"The end times." She heard the words before she realized she had said them. The words were like a curse, a clock on the verge of stopping.

Alaric shook the stardust off his hands and made his way to the fireplace. He picked up a lick of flame sitting on a silver dish on the mantel, then walked towards her. "I received a message from Tanghi earlier." He suspended the flame between them, then passed his fingers through it, causing the fire to swirl, expand, then reveal a window with Tanghi standing at the center of it. He was covered in sweat and grime, the black powder of magic, and blood.

"Geir found a tunnel but it was no good. We're also having some trouble with the House lord, but Sabana says she'll take care of it." Tanghi let out a heavy sigh as he wiped his brow with the back of his hand. "The mage threat is no threat and their number is great. We weren't paying enough attention. The planetary god's been biding his time, but with one land mass left, he has little to lose." Kaila wanted to join her brother, to fight, to do something more than just stand here, waiting for Alaric to let her out of her cage. Tanghi's eyes glowed gold as he stared at them from the ruins of the House of Trum. "We need to look at the rules again, find a loophole that allows us to use our powers around mortals. Maybe Taia can find a key or a spell; maybe there's something about her lost staff. If we don't figure it out soon, there will be no god-life left." He paused and they could hear Sabana calling for him. "They're waiting on me. Tell Kaila that I need to talk to her, that I spoke to Geir."

Kaila stared into the space Tanghi had been in, as the window turned to black, and the flame returned to Alaric's hand. He walked back to the mantel to return the fire to its silver platter. The sound of his boots released her from her trance, and she moved towards the window overlooking the sea, hoping the air would help her think more clearly. Tanghi spoke to Geir. Her heart began to thrum in her ears as her nerves tangled.

"There are things going on under my roof that I'm only marginally aware of," Alaric said, returning to his desk and leaning against it. "I'm trying to keep an entire Realm from collapsing, so it's hard to pay attention to the details sometimes." His tone was mocking, fed up. "I know that you and Taia had a very bad fight." She opened her mouth to explain, but he held up a hand to silence her. "More foreign to me is whatever is going on between you and Geir. Why would Tanghi be so concerned?"

"I'd been talking to Geir," she said, fingering the thin scales on her sash. She had to play this right. She had to give Alaric the news about Selina before Tanghi did. "I hadn't seen him in a long time, and I talked to him about things that Tanghi probably feels I should've shared with him first."

"Tanghi would be in the right," said Alaric. "Especially if these things you spoke of could betray a weakness in my Realm."

"Geir would never do anything to hurt us," she said, clenching her sash.

"He was," Alaric stopped her, "*is,* one of the most powerful spirits ever known to exist, even before he was pulled out of the Plane of Distant Echoes and given his god form." He picked up a handful of stardust, tossed it into the air in front of him, and countless spiritual planes appeared, bright and glittering against the backdrop of Night. "You were once spirit before I summoned you," he said, locating the swirling Plane of In-Between with a finger, bringing it into view, cradling it like an egg. "Tell me, were you and yours anywhere near as ruthless as the spirits of Echoes, never mind the legendary Geir?" When she didn't answer, he said, "Why do you think Aalae chose him?"

"Those same legends tell of Geir's honor and empathy, his sense of justice."

Alaric slashed at the images, and the dust fell to the floor. "He belongs to Aalae. She has taken whatever legend he was, whatever joy and love he's known, and broken him. She will have everything he is, and anything you share with him becomes hers. Do you understand?" She nodded once, keeping her eyes averted, not wanting to hear any of it. "What did you tell him?"

Kaila sighed. What choice did she have? Best he heard it from her and not, gods forbid, Aalae. "I found out that the new Priestess was Unblessed." Alaric froze as he considered her words. His eyes, cold and dark, locked onto hers, and she felt she was on more familiar ground again. "I blessed her," she said with all the confidence she could muster. "I felt compelled to bless her, and she hadn't yet reached the age of reason, so I had the right to my powers. She's linked to the Night Realm now, and Aalae can't touch her."

"What kind of blessing could you place that would link her to us?"

She had hoped he wouldn't ask that. "I'm not sure. It just sort of happened, but I know she's linked. I can feel her."

He shook his head and laughed, but Kaila wasn't sure if he was happy or not. "These truly are the end times. You were the one rearranging the fate lines I was following."

"I did? I was?"

"Everything was a disaster. All the lines pointed to the destruction of Night," he said. "Taia and I kept reworking the lines. We thought Aalae was on to something with the Priestess count. It turns out you changed something, and now the Realms are balanced again, though it's a tenuous balance to be sure."

"I did the right thing?"

"For now, yes." He gave her a smile. "This is why you can't keep secrets from me. I'm trying to save the world, remember?"

Geir was right. She had nothing to worry about. She did what she had to do, and she had done the right thing.

"Taia's still not so sure about it," Alaric said.

"She mentioned the fate lines when we argued last," Kaila said, eager to keep the conversation away from when and how and why she had blessed Selina. "She didn't tell me what it was I did, but she was very angry."

Alaric let out a sigh, and the demon marks flitted across his features. "She is angry with me as well. Something in her reading shows that events are driving us closer, and she's threatened by that."

Kaila felt her heart race. "Does she have good reason to feel threatened?"

"I'm not sure if it's related to what you did with your blessing or not. Tanghi says it's because of the way I treat you. He says I should be less obvious." Alaric's eyes met hers, held her. "I'm not like my sister; she weaves intricate lines to get what she wants. She'll mask her emotions, present different faces to different people. You never know what her true motives are or what she's really thinking." He crossed his ankles and studied the buckles on his boots, releasing her from his hold. "I am enraptured by you. I can't hide that. I won't pretend to believe that I can change the promises I've made or alter my destiny, but what I do know is that I'm miserable when you aren't near me."

Without considering the consequences, she said, "We can never be together. Why do you continue to lead me on and try to make me believe that if I just wait long enough, something will change?"

He lifted his gaze to look at her. "What if it does? The lines—"

"And what if it doesn't? We've been playing at this since the beginning, and I thought at some point Taia would let you go. Now, you're telling me that something is happening to drive us together, and she can't stop it. You'd make me believe again…" She trailed off. "It feels like it really could be the end times. One continent left and the mages bringing about our destruction just as the lines bring us together."

He joined her by the window. His power emanated from him like waves of velvet, wrapping around her, caressing. "Am I supposed to see the end times and not know what it's like to be with you?" he asked, his voice like an evening breeze.

"Alaric—"

"Kaila, do you love me?"

She studied his face, the endless depths of his midnight eyes. These times were rare lately, when they didn't talk about the next battle or an upcoming council—when he didn't treat her like a child and she didn't feel the need to push her boundaries. He was gentle, almost shy. He was made up of dreams and starlight and barely whispered promises.

Alaric closed the space between them, and slipped his hand through her hair. He pulled her face towards his, and she felt the cool rush of night as he kissed her. His lips were desperate, persistent, passionate. She placed her hands on his shoulders, intending to push him away, but instead succumbed to his touch.

SEVEN

"It's a good thing this place is clean, boy," Elder said under his breath. "Where were you this afternoon?"

"Looking for manuscripts in the storage room," Aren said, feeling a chill in his veins as he recalled the semi-charred, soot-covered items hidden behind the tiny door that Selina had opened. He pushed the images out of his head, then parted the heavy midnight-blue draperies that separated the second floor of the Library from the balcony that faced out from the front of the House. Elder narrowed his eyes, then stepped onto the balcony, joining Counselor Helmun. Vir stood next to Aren, peering through a gap in the drapes. Even with the heavy silk and velvet muting the noise from outside, they could still hear the chants from the growing crowds, demanding that Vir do something about the monster and the recent string of deaths.

"They wouldn't carry on like this if I was out there," Vir grumbled.

It had been decided that Vir was in no condition to address his people. He had the complexion of a dead fish, with hollow eyes to match, and he could barely finish a sentence before coughing fits seized him. The people needed to see the strength and power of Tiede, and Vir was far from inhabiting his ruling persona at the moment. Counselor Darc, the next best choice to represent the House, was needed in a meeting with the elite Hunters and high-ranking army officers. His logic and tactical thinking were best put to use trying to get a handle on the mage and monster situation. That left the softer, slower Helmun to address Tiede, as his rank held prestige even if his stature didn't inspire. His wife, Saris, was invited for the occasion, and she was more than happy to provide company to Geyle while ogling Aren.

"Any more visions from the girl?" Vir asked, taking a seat near his wife. He leaned his head back as if it took too much effort to hold it up.

"None, my Lord," Crina said. She stood close to where Geyle and Saris were sitting. Her gauzy white gown billowed in a wayward breeze, and she brushed a hand against her midnight-blue sash. "We are still unnerved by Selina's visions of Trum."

Vir frowned. "She couldn't have known the extent of what was going on in Trum. No one aside from our Illitheien guests, Elder, and me knew the details reported by Illithe's scouts."

"Do you know if anyone in the House survived?" Crina asked.

Aren glanced at Illithe Kente, who was being swallowed up in a chair by the wall, quiet and content to be a part of the hubbub. Valine took up a seat next to him, staring at the draperies as if she could see past them to the people yelling outside of the gates.

"The House was surrounded at the time of the report, and our scouts had to retreat," Valine said without turning away from the drapes.

"So there mustn't be any survivors," Saris said, clutching at the gold and emerald pendant hanging from her neck. "The House is lost."

The conclusion didn't sit well with Aren, and he imagined the House of Trum, its protective stone walls, the battlements and high towers. He imagined an army of mages around the ancient House. "There must be survivors, otherwise the mages would be inside the House, not surrounding it," Aren blurted out. All eyes turned to him, and he wondered if there might be some sort of herbal remedy to keep his mouth shut. He thought about slipping out onto the balcony to face the angry mob, instead of having Vir reprimand him for his insolence in front of his guests. "If I were in the House of Trum, I would try to get the House Lord and his family to safety," Aren said, hoping it would soften the impact of his outburst.

"That's very noble of you," Crina said, a smirk on her elegant face. Aren wasn't sure if she was mocking him or being dismissive.

Illithe Kente laughed to himself, and Valine squeezed his hand to calm him. "How will you save us?" Kente asked in his paper-thin voice.

Vir coughed, and the servant girl with her hair tied up in a black ribbon hurried to bring him a glass of water. She glanced at Aren, then blushed deep red before rushing away. Aren wished he could leave with her.

"Even if there are survivors there would be no way out," Crina said. "It's just a matter of time."

"They could go under," Aren said before he could stop himself.

Vir took a drink of water, then said, "Would you dig a hole, Apprentice?"

Damn it all to Aum. Why did they have to be in the Library? This was his sacred space, the one place he was free to speak his mind because only Elder was ever there to hear him. Aren let out a nervous laugh, backing into the draperies. "Not a hole, my Lord. I'd look for an underground passage."

"Is that so?" Vir set down his glass.

"The Eighth Lord, Trum Pernius, was rumored to be a licentious man. I've found old journals that tell of how he visited brothels, favored the more aggressive sexual practices of Kaishar." Aren wondered if his ability to say all the wrong things was a result of not being blessed by the gods. He had to say something to cover up his inappropriate rambling. "Not that I would know about such things."

Saris giggled behind her hand, and Crina looked as though she wanted to stab him in the forehead. Aren wished she would. Kente was laughing and wheezing so hard, Aren hoped the old man wouldn't wet himself.

"Elder read some of Trum's history to me when I was young," Vir said. "Lord Pernius hated to be alone and never left the House unattended."

"That's true," Aren said, puzzling the pieces of history. "So if you're trapped in that House with mages outside trying to kill you, wouldn't you grasp at the old rumor? Your life is on the line, and your only hope is that Lord Pernius used secret passages to get in and out of the House without being noticed."

"Let's imagine for a moment that whoever is trapped in the House manages to escape. Then what?" Vir asked, his tone daring.

"If the surrounding farms and villages didn't get sacked, it shouldn't be difficult to find horses. I'd choose Syrn for refuge first, especially if I have Priestesses. My second option would be Illithe."

"Why not Thell?" Vir's voice was raspy and dry. "It's closer."

Aren wanted to clear his throat, but swallowed instead. "If the mages are serious, Thell would be the next sensible target. You'd be escaping Trum to go through the whole ordeal all over again."

No one spoke, and the pained look on Geyle's face told Aren that he should learn to control his tongue. Now would be a good time for one of his skull-piercing headaches that caused nosebleeds. Then Aren could blame illness.

The drapes parted, and Elder stepped into the Library. His brows were furrowed, his frown long. He clutched at his staff as if he were ready to take someone's head off, and Aren took a step away from him. "They aren't listening," Elder said, referring to the crowd outside. "They want their Lord or no one at all."

"This is a farce," Vir growled. "What shall I do? Cough up a lung for them to ponder?"

Aren's mouth opened before he could stop himself. "What about Lady Geyle?" he asked. All eyes turned to look at him, and he was quite sure that even the servants were wondering what had come over him. He tried to smile, felt like a clown, then cleared his throat and said, "Tiede has always had a soft spot for her Lady." Geyle shook her head a little as if the motion would stop him from continuing. A nervous laugh escaped him, and he said, "Not singular as in just Lady Geyle. Ladies. All of them. Of the House, rather. The history of." Did he just sound like he was reading one of his indices? "Ladies of Tiede. A reputable account, not a squalid…"

Aren considered excusing himself, wondered if he could make himself vomit on the spot to prove he was sick, but Vir held up a hand and said, his voice almost surreal in its patience, "Apprentice, start again."

The servant girl with the black ribbon appeared at his elbow and handed him a glass of water before disappearing. Aren was sure he was hallucinating, but took a drink before setting down the glass. "The Lords of Tiede have always been a symbol of great power, but if you really study Tiede, you'll notice the Lady holds a revered spot in the hearts of the people." Aren steadied his breathing, focused on the books, the tone and message behind and between the words. "The Lord Tiede protects his people, but the Lady Tiede nurtures them. In no other House is the symbolism of father and mother so clear as it is in Tiede." He took a few steps towards Geyle to address her. "We talked of how Tiede celebrated your marriage, how grand the parties were, and how welcome you felt when you arrived." He turned back to Vir. "The accounts I've read of your mother, Lady Elleina—she was adored by everyone."

"You believe that these angry people will be still for a woman?" Vir asked.

"What would it hurt? To see Lady Tiede is to know that all is well. She hasn't been hidden away for her safety, and therefore there's no reason for anyone to panic," Aren countered.

Geyle stood up, twisting at her sapphire ring. "Apprentice, speaking of Lady Elleina is one thing, but..."

Valine stared at Geyle with cold, stone-gray eyes. "My sister was regal, beautiful, and had a heart big enough to love Tiede more than she might have loved Illithe. You are right to doubt your ability to achieve what she did."

Geyle cast her eyes down and was about to sit, but Aren took her hands in his and had her take a step towards him. "I didn't have the honor of knowing Lady Elleina, but all you have to do is open a book on Tiede or walk through this House and see her portraits. She is the pinnacle of what Lady Tiede is expected to be, and how difficult that you should be the one to have to follow her," Aren said, his tone soft and kind. "But you also have the potential to love this House as much as you love your Lord husband. The people need to see you."

"Do you think so?" she breathed, her glossy blue eyes gazing at him as if under his spell.

He studied her for a moment, her hair braided and crowning her head, woven through with a string of creamy pearls and silver stars. Her dress was high-collared and covered her shoulders, and therefore the marks. "Yes." He passed her hand to Elder. "And so well suited you are, dressed in Tiede's midnight blue." *The only thing more perfect would be if you were swollen with child to give Tiede hope of an heir.*

Elder stared hard at Aren, then looked at Vir, who nodded. Elder patted Geyle's hand, then said, "If the people quiet down long enough, I will tell you what to say."

Geyle nodded, cast one last look at Aren, then allowed Elder to lead her out onto the balcony. The roar of the crowd intensified when the drapes were pulled back, and Aren clenched his fists with fear, feeling the gravity of his actions hit him like a splash of cold water after a night of drinking with Dane. As Aren made a show of smoothing the drapes, he wondered what had possessed him to do and say the things he did. Perhaps now would be a good time to vomit. His gut was knotted enough to make him sick.

The gears in the Library clock rotated in their measured way— soft, rhythmic clicks mocking the erratic beating of Aren's heart. Vir looked at him as if waiting for an apology or an excuse. Aren blinked, feeling the sweat gather at his hairline.

Silence.

All eyes turned towards the balcony as if they could see through the drapes that divided them, as if they could see Geyle in her long midnight gown with her hands folded before her.

Silence. Then, her voice.

"My dear people," she said, gaining strength and volume with each word, "I thank you for your patience, as I have been trying to find the right words to say. Then I realized that all I need tell you is what is true. My beloved Lord husband cannot speak to you as he had hoped. He has been working tirelessly, seeking a way to be rid of this terror that threatens us all. He has worked himself ill, yet pushes on because of his love for this House." She paused, and Aren wondered how much of the message was coming from Elder. "All I ask is that you listen…"

Aren felt every muscle in his body relax. He was pushing his luck these days.

Kente chuckled in his chair, tears rolling down his eyes. "That's a poppy," he wheezed.

Then a thundering boom shook the House, and the people began to scream.

EIGHT

The Hunters worked with a precision that Aren envied. They were levelheaded, quick, and focused. They were separate from each other, yet they moved as if they shared a collective mind, anticipating one another's moves, not questioning the decisions made but reacting to each action in a way that propelled them towards the end goal. One Hunter moved Kente, Valine, Elder, and Helmun and his wife to a well-protected corner of the second floor of the Library, away from the balcony, which a Guard promptly secured. Two other Hunters took Crina and Geyle, setting off with them towards another part of the House. The servants were told to scatter and hide.

"Lord Vir, please come with us," a Hunter with silver hair said, then faced Aren. "Apprentice, you can stay here or—"

"Hunter Tenley, he can come with me." Aren turned to see Gryf accompanied by Dane. Gryf addressed the Hunter as he handed Aren a sword. "He's fought the monster where the rest of us have not, so he'll be useful in tracking it down. Hunter Illana agrees."

"Monster?" Vir frowned. "In my House?"

"Yes, my Lord," Tenley said. "We need to secure you right away. We've already secured the Priestesses."

Vir growled deep in his throat, then turned on his heel with Tenley and two others escorting him.

"I thought the House exploded. Did anyone see the creature?" Aren asked as he and his brothers scrambled out the first floor of the Library and into the courtyard. There were two bodies, Guards, by the main House doors. Blood pooled on the stone floor, and magic burns scarred the columns nearby.

"I was just tagging along with Gryf. Thought I'd see if you had time for a beer," Dane answered as they surveyed the damage, trying to determine which hallway to investigate first.

"Guild sent me," Gryf explained when Aren looked at him.

A high-pitched scream came from the direction of the parlor, and Aren felt his heart lurch as he led the way towards the sound. As they ran, they could hear boots stomping off in a different direction. He wondered why the Guards weren't marching towards the parlor as well, but then they heard the scream again.

"Careful, Aren!" Gryf called out.

Aren was several strides ahead of his brothers and arrived first. He burst into the room and began to scan it when a bright stream of red light came hurtling towards him. He felt a curse escape his lips as he was tackled to the floor, the sword falling out of his hand.

"Do I have to beat you to get you to stop being so damned predictable?" Gryf growled, keeping Aren's head down.

"There!" Dane threw a knife at the dark shadow slinking around the room. The knife managed to nick what might have been a shoulder, resulting in a fine spray of black against the fireplace mantel. Dane reached for another knife.

The monster's form began to take shape beneath the swirling, black smoke that outlined it. Yellow reptilian eyes shrouded in black tendrils swept the room. It was taller than Aren, and curved spikes rose out of its calves, points like daggers jutting out where elbows might be. A long tail trailed behind it, the point of it a vicious barb the width of two large hands.

Gryf let go of Aren and stood up, his eyes never leaving the wraith. They seemed to size each other up, waiting for the next move.

Aren lifted his head from the floor and caught movement in his periphery. He saw a servant girl, not much younger than himself, crouched behind one of the velvet chairs, hugging her knees close to her chest, trying her best to control her sobs. Shards of magic were embedded all over her face, her right shoulder, and her chest. A black ribbon was tangled in her brown hair. She had come here to hide when the Hunters gave the order to scatter. The girl caught Aren looking at her and gasped, her tears renewed. Aren brought a finger to his lips to silence her.

Gryf was pointing his sword towards the ground, waiting to see what the creature would do. He and Dane were the only ones between it and the door, and Aren wondered what was taking the Hunters and Guards so long to arrive.

Aren moved on his hands and knees towards the girl, keeping an eye on the monster. "That's definitely the thing that attacked me the other night. It moves like smoke."

"Wonderful," Dane said as he and Gryf switched places.

Aren moved forward another few inches. "It can speak and understand Common, but prefers an old language I don't know very well. No preference for right or left. It uses an unnatural blade." The wraith screamed, turning towards him.

"It likes you," Dane said.

When it opened its mouth to wail again, Gryf attacked, his sword moving so fast that it seemed to create a vortex in its wake. His blue steel met a lustrous blade of deep crimson that the wraith pulled out of the air. Metal crashed on metal, grinding as each fought for the upper hand. "Stay near the door! Don't let it out if it gets past me!" Gryf ordered through gritted teeth.

Aren was mesmerized, locked on the fierce, feral eyes, searching for some clue, some hint as to what it might be. It looked bigger than when he had fought it in the alley, more developed. Gryf grunted and pushed, throwing the beast back. It stumbled and hissed, then dematerialized. Dane let out a curse, turning his head left and right, but the creature reappeared behind Gryf, stabbing at his side with the red blade.

Gryf dodged as if it were the next choreographed step in a well-rehearsed dance. "You're just as predictable as my brother," he said. He stepped into the beast and sent his blade into the creature's thigh. Metal scraped against bone, but the monster vanished again, this time reappearing next to Dane. Dane held his sword up in a defensive stance, waiting for the strike, but the creature didn't move. The room hummed with tension and the summoning of magic.

Aren scurried over to the frightened girl, who let him wrap his arms around her. She pressed her face against his chest, and he could only imagine how frightened she was. He knew her skin was on fire from the inside, yet she squeezed herself close to him despite it.

Guardians, the beast hissed in Common. *Baby guardians at that. You've no idea the powers you trifle with.*

"Guardians? What's it talking about?" asked Dane.

The wraith chuckled low in its throat. Spidery veins of red light burned through the rich, dark-blue rugs beneath them and raced up the creature's legs, through its center, and towards its spindly fingers, where the magic coalesced. Aren narrowed his eyes as the red light illuminated strange symbols below the smoke that concealed its flesh and bone.

"Your magic is limited," Aren said, hoping to stall the beast, "and you don't know how to find Lord Vir." His mind began to run through the symbols. It wasn't Ancient—possibly something older. He drew the signs in his head, traced them again and again until they were burned into his memory. He recalled the staff with the strange symbols that he and Selina had brought back to Tiede. "You used magic to enter the House, to bypass the crowds of people outside. You used magic to kill the Guards when you came in, to attack a defenseless girl, to attack us when we came through the door. You're just now able to summon it again," Aren said. "I'm willing to bet the Guards can't find us because you're clouding their senses with magic, throwing them off because you can't fight all of us at once yet. Now you're low on power. You weren't meant to attack the House yet."

Its eyes darkened and the air around it began to waver. The symbols began to pulse again, and Aren caught the scrollwork of a stylized leaf, its elaborate petiole curling and winding. He had seen the sign before, and he strained to remember where.

"Now!" Gryf commanded, lifting his sword.

Dane threw a knife. It plunged straight into the creature's abdomen, and the monster screamed as an inky liquid spurted from the wound. The magic convulsed, then dimmed. Gryf brought his sword down in a diagonal cut from shoulder to waist, but all he caught was smoke and tail. The momentum of his blow caused him to strike the floor, but the tail fell with a thump before crumbling into bone and dust. The shadow slipped out of the room, leaving a trail of sticky fluid.

"Damn it!" Gryf growled. He and Dane rushed out the door, colliding with a handful of Guard who looked lost and confused. "That way," Gryf ordered. "We'll follow the trail towards the courtyard, surround it. Someone take the girl to the infirmary if it's safe."

Aren nodded at his brothers, who returned the gesture and rushed out of the room in pursuit of the beast. Aren picked up the bloodied girl and brought her to the one Guard who had stayed behind. "We'll have a doctor take care of you, all right?" he whispered close to her ear. He started to place her in the Guard's waiting arms, but she clung to him, unwilling to let go. "Look at me, sweetheart," he spoke as if to a child. The girl—a young lady, really—turned her tear-soaked, bloodstained face towards him. Her breathing was shallow, her skin clammy, and her eyes struggled to focus. It would be a miracle if she survived this. A muscle in Aren's cheek twitched, and he fought back the dread that threatened to consume him. He smiled for her. "You're safe now, and as soon as this is over, I'll come see you." She hesitated, then gave him a slight nod. Aren placed her in the Guard's arms, then kissed the top of her head. She blushed despite everything. "Travel away from the courtyard," Aren said.

"Watch yourself," the Guard said before leaving.

Aren picked up his sword, then took a deep breath. He moved towards the door, ready to join his brothers, when a noise like the crackle of fire perked his ears up. He spun around to see what had caused it. The creature was standing in the center of the parlor, its entire being charged with burning magic. He couldn't see the outline of its mouth, but there was no mistaking the gleeful look in its yellow eyes.

Aren took in the position of the rattled and tumbled furniture, the distances towards some kind of cover. Everything looked so shoddy and breakable when he imagined the firepower the creature was about to loose on him. Then, he saw the hilt of Dane's knife, still stuck in its belly. He estimated trajectories and concentrated on the knife and the glowing symbols that sent light streaming through the creature's smoky tendrils. It opened its mouth and emitted a high-pitched cry as it extended its arms and sent a barrage of magic towards him.

Aren dropped under the light, rolling towards the beast. Tiny flecks of magic nipped at his cheek, burning little tracks as they tore and settled. The massive energy coursed out the door, crashing into the wall of the hallway. The sound of destruction reverberated down the hall, filling the air with chalky debris. Aren sprang to his feet and reached for Dane's knife, pulling it out of the monster in an upward arc, sending more black fluids spewing out. He shielded his face as the hot, inky substance made contact, burning his skin.

The wraith reached out and grabbed Aren by the throat with its massive claws, lifting him off the ground as if he were a weed in a garden. It screamed into his face, and Aren thought he'd die from the stench of its breath. He kicked out, clawing at the vice around his neck, struggling to get air in his lungs.

The creature met Aren's eyes with a furious glare, then hissed in Ancient. *You tricked me with the scent of magic on your spirit, but I'll not be tricked again. You are not T'jand!* It sniffed at Aren's hair before continuing. *I will drink your blood and drape your entrails around my shoulders. I will consume you from the inside out, suck the marrow from your bones.*

Aren's vision was getting dark around the edges, and he found it difficult to believe that this was how his life was going to end: as an intestinal necklace. At the very least, he thought he'd die with a sword in his hand.

The wraith convulsed and cried out, staggering backwards. Aren wanted to ask what was happening but found he had only enough energy to hang from the creature's grip like a rag doll.

Not yet! the beast said as its body began to vanish. *I want his power, his blood! Let me go!*

Gryf and Dane rushed into the room, covered in stone and dust. Gryf charged at the beast, catching a slice of bone as it vanished and Aren dropped to the floor. Gryf uttered a curse.

"Mother's going to wash out your mouth," Aren rasped as he tried to catch his breath. Dane crouched on the floor next to him, helping him sit up.

"I didn't count on him coming back here," Gryf said. "That's what I mean when I tell you to be unpredictable."

NINE

Aren sat at his desk in the Library, flicking the paper stars he had scattered. His heart was heavy, his mind numb. His face was covered with little cuts that burned beneath the surface. Rieka was shocked to learn that he had been hurt, and she did her best to treat him while the doctors dealt with the more seriously injured. He looked worse than he was, and when Rieka removed the magic, he didn't bleed out anywhere near as much as Gryf did. They said he was lucky.

Aren folded his arms on his desk, rested his head on them, and stared at the little stars as they blurred out of focus. His ears were filled with inhuman wailing, sobbing, stone and marble crashing, magic humming. He closed his eyes, and in the darkness of his mind, the memories were still so clear.

Are you really here to see me?
I told you I would.
You've always been so kind, my Lord.
Please call me Aren.
You're so kind, my Lord. I've always loved you.

Aren fingered the black ribbon he had tied around his wrist when the loud, familiar click of the Library doors made him sit upright. He swiped at his eyes with the back of his hand, sniffling and clearing his throat. One heavy door creaked on its hinges, opened a little, then closed again. He gathered the stars on his desk, pushing them into a pile to return to the little box he kept in his drawer.

There were footsteps, unobtrusive and respectful of the silence. Then, her voice. "Aren?"

"At my desk." He pushed the stars into the box and perched it on top of a leather-bound journal as Lake reached his side. He looked up at her, registering the blueness of her dress and her raven hair spilling over her shoulders, but was unable to rise to his feet or voice any pleasantries. He just stared up into her concerned face, tried to find some tranquility in her aqua eyes. She cupped his face in her soft hands, and he felt the tears rise again. He willed them not to spill and turned his gaze away from her.

Without a word, Lake stepped into him, pulling his head towards her body, cradling him as if he were a child running into his mother's arms. His hands reached for her small waist, then his arms were wrapped around her, squeezing as if letting go would send him into an abyss. She stroked his hair and cooed soft phrases that felt like she had tugged them out of his very being. "My heart shatters," she whispered, "and the pieces are as the stars in Alaric's skies."

"A piece to watch over you," he said, hardly recognizing his own voice. "Another to light your way."

"A handful more to tell a story of my love for you."

"For time ever after," he finished. After a beat, he asked, "Where have I heard that?"

She continued to stroke his hair, not trying to break free of his grasp. "I don't know where you've heard it. I know it from the old songs passed down over time in the Kailen Islands. I heard it in a song so beautiful it was woven into my memory." There was silence as he considered this. "Why has your heart broken?" she asked, her voice echoing the innocence of a child's.

Aren remained quiet, contemplating songs that Dane would sing, revisiting books filled with old tales, wondering where those words had come from if not his bones. At last, he let go of her and stood up to offer his chair, clearing his throat and drying his eyes as he did so. He pulled Elder's chair over and took a seat next to her. "I'm sorry about all this," he said, rubbing his nails together, his eyes focused on the floor between them.

Lake reached over, lifted his chin with two fingers so that he would look at her. "I was so worried about you. Tiede's streets are full of soldiers, and the people are frantic. There was rumor of an attack on the House, and when I arrived, the Guard told me what happened."

"There are eight dead."

She dropped her hands into her lap. "I am so sorry."

"I knew them all. There was a girl—she was always so shy, never got my title right. She was in the wrong place, probably startled the monster. It attacked her, and I..." He paused, the noises filling his head again. "She was hurt and when I went to see her all she could do was smile and tell me how kind I was. I wanted to laugh. How was I kind to her? I never stopped to get to know her or thank her for everything she did for me every day. She was a familiar face. She was a little black ribbon scurrying around the halls. I couldn't even tell you her name before this evening. I held her hand and I wanted to take the pain away, but I was so powerless and her skin was so cold. She said she loved me, and I felt the life leave her body."

TEN

"What happened?" Mercer asked through clenched teeth. He watched as Catar paced the length of the parlor. Every now and then, Catar would stop at the large, stone fireplace, pick up the poker, and push at the dead logs.

"You shouldn't be here," Catar said at last, putting down the poker and moving towards the armchair, gripping the top of it. "If anyone sees you—"

"What happened?" Mercer repeated, unsure why he was asking. They both knew what had happened. Catar had lost control of the creature, and it had attacked the House before it had been ready. The element of surprise was lost.

"There's too much conflicting magic in Tiede because of the Wood. It loosened my hold on the creature," Catar explained. "It hasn't reached full maturity, but it's eager to fulfill the spell that woke it. When it broke loose, it went off in search of its target."

"Eager or not, it must wait for you to command it. It might be strong, but Vir has a powerful retinue of Hunters. We haven't come this far only for the creature to fail because it couldn't be controlled."

"I repeated the rituals using the original sacrifice, since that was the blood that first woke it. I was able to pull the creature out of the House with the sacrificial magic, and I have it under control again," Catar said. "It's not pleased."

Spittle flew from Mercer's mouth as he shouted, "I don't care if it's pleased or not. Do whatever it takes to keep it under control."

"It's hungry and the sacrifices are barely enough anymore," Catar said. "The spell will hold, but the magic required to sustain it without producing an *istoq* is draining."

"We'll perform more sacrifices," Mercer said, leaning against the love seat. He had no problem killing every last person in Tiede, but would it be enough to keep the beast under their control? It had grown in stature and power, but what did that matter if it wouldn't bend to their will?

Catar interrupted his thoughts, bolstering Mercer's doubts. "We didn't plan on the proximity of wild magic leaking from the Wood, didn't plan on the House being as secure as it is, and we most certainly didn't plan on the Apprentice."

Mercer wanted to pull his hair out at the thought of Aren. "The girl said he's not marked!"

Catar shot him an angry glare. "She must be mistaken. Why else would the creature be so conflicted?"

"I don't know!" Mercer yelled, louder than he had intended.

As if in response, a muffled moan came from the adjacent room, but neither of them paid it any mind.

"It's just a matter of time before we're discovered," Catar pointed out.

"Leave it to me," Mercer said, his decision made. They could fix this if they eliminated the variables. "I'll find out what the Apprentice is, and I'll kill him myself if I have to."

CURSE

ONE

Kaila stood by the window in the room she had booked at the inn. She didn't need the room, but not having one would arouse suspicion. She watched as the rain fell in a misty drizzle, and she held an arm out to gather the droplets to her. A few people were still walking the streets below, their parasols keeping them dry. Soldiers were patrolling in groups of four, swords in hand. The sound of their boots marching in unison echoed off the cobbled streets and stone buildings. The fear and uncertainty was palpable, and it was a very different Tiede from the one she had arrived in just a few days ago.

She changed from her dress to her black battle gear. She checked the long daggers in the vambraces, the smaller blades at her boots, the blade strapped to her outer thigh. Satisfied, she pulled her hair up. If Alaric knew what she was up to, he'd lock her in the Keep. The kisses they shared wouldn't change the way he treated her, and she berated herself for letting it happen. It wasn't the first time, of course, but she wanted it to be the last.

She returned to the window, then climbed onto the sill, hefting herself up onto the roof. This whole affair would be easier if she could use her powers, but there were too many mortals. It was a good night for shadows, though. The evening skies were thick with clouds, veiling the moon's light, and fear had kept most people indoors.

She traveled along the rooftops, lithe and silent as a cat on the hunt, until she reached the main road. The lower district was her best bet for finding the creature, and she crossed the wide stretch of pebbled road after a detachment of soldiers marched their way back to the barracks.

The lights that lined the streets in the area known as the Wedge were dim, and from this distance the House shone like a jewel overlooking the city. Kaila kept close to the old buildings, watching for the curious eyes that would peek out of the derelict structures. The moans of the hungry and the haunted shrieks of the addicts assaulted her ears, and she understood why the creature could find easy prey in this part of the city.

The street opened up to the park that served as a buffer between the various parts of the western districts. The lamps that marked the park borders shone with a dull, pulsing glow, and she sprinted past them into the cover of trees, keeping away from the walking paths. She noticed a few foolish mortals who must have thought they were safe from any rumored monster. She cursed their stupidity, their presence preventing her from taking in her powers.

She moved deeper into the park, listening for something that didn't fit into the familiar patterns of evening sounds. With or without her powers, the night was woven into her very being, and as the rain began to drizzle around her, she allowed her muscles to relax and feel the night embracing her, connecting her to the entire Realm. That was when she felt the hum of magic and the cold chill of darkness. It wasn't the comforting, velvety darkness of Alaric's night; there was an emptiness to it, a feeling of foreboding and malevolence. She drew one of her long blades, then prowled towards the low humming currents of magic, glancing at the ground to see traces of liquid light rush past. She heard a whimpering cry, muffled and weak.

When she reached a point where the vibrations were so strong they seemed to repel her, she crouched behind a tree and peered around it. She strained to make out the litter of boulders upon which sat a shadow with feral, yellow eyes. Symbols in a line from what she guessed to be collar to elbow glowed red. In all of her years, she'd never seen anything like it.

The rocks and grasses were covered in splashes of dark liquid, and the sickening scent of raw flesh tinged with metal filled the air. The creature jerked its head upright, and she ducked behind the tree. She waited, wondering what made the creature powerful enough to sense her presence. It hissed a chain of words in a language older than she was, words tied to the planet's tongue. This creature was Old Magic that had been twisted somehow. It spoke again, this time mixing its words with Ancient.

I smell you, it breathed, and Kaila heard the click of bone and saw a slither of smoke as it moved from its perch to walk a circle, searching for the intruder. *You smell of power.*

She pressed herself tight against the rough bark of tree, listening for the whoosh of smoke to approach. She mouthed a silent incantation to bless her knife with the Realm's power.

Join me? it asked, and she could hear the grin on its face. *I've not finished eating yet.* There was a cold snap, then a flash of red before a faint glow illuminated the area. There was that whimpering sound again, and she couldn't stop herself from peeking around the tree. Lying in a pool of crimson was a Tiede soldier, his arm missing, his legs broken, his head and face covered with blood.

He was still alive.

Kaila gasped and turned away, the heat of anger burning her cheeks. Allowing her fury to fill her, she stepped away from her hiding place, prepared to fight, to end this senseless carnage.

There you are, it chuckled.

"What are you?" she asked, her blade at the ready.

The creature tutted, then said, *No, my beauty, the question is: What are you? I wear no disguise, pretending to be something I'm not, while you are more than you seem.* It approached with its arms open as if to embrace her, and she thrust her blade at it. It spun out of her reach and produced a blade of red. They circled each other, the creature with its ghostly movements and Kaila with her liquid grace. *You must be of the Heavens,* the thing said, its tone rising as it made the connection. *Your laws bind you and your powers when mortals are near. Kill him, and you'll be free to fight in all your glory!*

She spared a glance at the dying man. Tanghi and Sabana would have done it; they would have killed him and justified it with the fact that he was near dead anyway. Maybe Alaric was right to treat her like a child.

The creature laughed. *The gods are weaker than I would have imagined.*

Furious, Kaila threw her blade and it stuck in the creature's chest. She launched herself at the beast, and it reacted in time to cut a thin line below her ribs, to her waist and lower back. She moved through the pain as she grabbed the blade at her thigh and reached for where she imagined the creature's neck might be. Her hand passed through black vapor and settled on scale-covered flesh, rigid and cold to the touch. Her arm wrapped around its throat.

Surprised, the thing's sword dissipated and it clawed at her arms, which were protected with tough scale vambraces. She pulled it close, the smell of smoke and death filling her nostrils, then pressed the tip of her blade under its chin, staying inside the sharp spikes of its elbows and calves.

The creature laughed and stopped trying to fight back. *You're fast. I've never fought anything so fast.*

"What are you? Who summoned you?" she demanded, pain searing through the cut in her side.

Let me go, it said. *You might not have your powers, but they are inherent to your very being. I can feel it in your blades and smell it in your blood. Only magic and mortals can kill me.*

"Who summoned you?" she repeated.

Kill me, and the force of magic combined with the powers you hold will open an istoq.

"You lie," she hissed, pressing her knife into the creature's throat. Black fluid dripped and sizzled out of the wound.

The red symbols glowed brighter, and Kaila felt her powers tugging from the cuff around her upper arm. The creature laughed harder and she reluctantly let it go, pushing it to the ground. It coughed and sputtered, laughing all the while. She kicked it onto its back and pressed a boot to its chest. It looked up at her through slitted, yellow eyes, then disappeared. The blade she had driven into its chest fell to the ground.

She rushed towards the dying man and knelt by him, ignoring the burning wound in her side. "It's all right," she whispered as she squeezed his bloody hand. She could feel his soul slipping away, fire burning at the edges of it. "I will pray for your spirit and intercede on your behalf, son of Fire."

"Thank you, my goddess," he breathed.

She let her tears fall, choking on her sobs, then placed her blade against his neck and recited the Priestesses' prayers for Tanghi in the forgotten Ancient, the power of the words coursing through her body and into the blade. Kaila steeled herself, then bled him clean with one swift stroke. He shuddered, then stilled, and she wept alone in the pouring rain.

TWO

According to the demons, Kaila had left Mytanth, wanting to be alone. Tanghi spent hours searching the seas, rivers, and islands without any luck. He wondered if she had relinquished her powers because he couldn't pinpoint her location or feel her presence. Annoyed and just about ready to give up, he decided to see if she had returned to Tiede.

It was possible she was keeping an eye on the new Priestess. Kaila didn't have much experience with blessings, only submitting what graces were required of her for the Priestesses to bestow birth blessings and other routine favors. A direct blessing could have powerful, lasting effects, and for one as inexperienced as Kaila, creating such a link might make her feel compelled to watch and protect the new Priestess more often than not.

Tanghi appeared then disappeared out of the various fires lit within the House of Tiede. The House was silent and in chaotic ruin. The courtyard was a disaster of broken marble and shattered stone stained with blood and burn marks; only the mermaid fountain remained intact. The dead were laid out in Alaric's worship room, cleaned and covered in oils and leindra petals, an elemental token laid on the forehead of each. Tanghi spotted a flat firestone on one, and he beckoned the spirit out, calmed it as best he could under his current circumstances, and instructed it to return to Mytanth.

He paused, studying the tokens again. Firestone, feathers, gold, and seashells. He whispered an incantation, calling forth the two souls promised to Kaila, only to be answered by silence. *She's freed them already. She was here.* Tanghi retreated into the flames and left with more questions than he had started with, and still no idea of where Kaila had gone.

He did manage to find the little Priestess. Tanghi was shocked at just how young this initiate was, and for her to also be Unblessed there had to have been a mistake. Still, it wasn't for him to worry about. She was tucked into her bed, journeying through Alaric's dreamscapes, and Kaila was nowhere nearby.

He continued to travel through the fire to other rooms. He found Geyle crying in her bedchamber. He found guests from Illithe. The old, Illitheien House Lord was mumbling about poppies in his sleep. In another room, Illithe Valine sat at a desk, writing letters to her brothers by candlelight. He wondered what the Illitheiens were doing in Tiede.

He was relieved to find Vir with the Elder and the full council. Vir looked sick and weak, but he was alive. Tanghi listened as they argued over what to do with the marked, the mages in their dungeons, the monster roaming the streets.

What on Mytanth was going on in Tiede, and why hadn't Kaila said anything about it? Alaric had ordered her to watch the House. She must have known what was going on. Tanghi hated himself for doubting her, but the evidence against her was overwhelming.

He wandered into a lamp in the Library. A boy sat with his head on his desk, tears and a distant look in his eyes as he pushed little paper stars about. Every now and then, the boy would wince in pain and curse in the old languages. The Library door creaked. "Aren! Come quick. She's been hurt—a wicked slice from her rib all the way around…"

Tanghi had had enough of mortals and didn't stay to hear another word. He was too upset about Kaila, and it concerned him that he hadn't been able to find her. He left the House, reemerging in the small, eternal flame the Master Blacksmiths kept in an altar in the forge. He turned into a firefly and made his way towards Tiede Wood.

THREE

Kaila reached the top of the stairs and stood at the edge of the town center. She was thankful for the rain, which washed the blood from her hands and face. The downpour kept the streets empty, and with an arm clutched across her midsection, she hoped no one would notice her injuries. She stood in the shadows, debating what to do next. She couldn't return to the inn. With the magic embedded in her wound, she was in danger of succumbing to the same poison that had almost killed Tanghi long ago. Then, she recalled that the girl Rieka was a student of medicine, and if Aren could trust her, perhaps she could too. The only problem was that Kaila had to figure out where to find her.

Kaila steeled herself against the worsening pain in her side and straightened up when a familiar sensation like the warmth of embers cut through the rain. "Is that you, Master Fighter?" she asked, recalling the Fire blessing she had sensed in him the other night.

The stocky man stepped out of the shadows and into the biolight. He was dripping wet but didn't seem bothered by it. "Gryf, my Lady. What're you doing out in this weather?"

"I was just taking a walk, and…" She looked down at the tight, reptilian fabric of her black bodice and pants, the high boots with the knives strapped to the sides, the bloodstained blade pressed against her thigh. She peered at Gryf through long, wet lashes. "Aren was in mourning, so I went to see about a monster."

He raised an eyebrow. "Many a woman has done crazy things for that boy, but please tell me you're joking."

She moved her arm and turned slightly, revealing the gash in her clothing and the wound beneath it glittering with magic, oozing blood. Gryf closed the gap between them and put a hand on her shoulder, staring hard at the injury.

"I didn't do it for Aren. I'm a scholar. I needed to see this thing for myself." She smiled in the hopes of wiping the concern off his face. "I thought maybe Rieka could help."

"That cut is deep. Can you walk?" he asked. She nodded, wrapping her arm around her waist again. "Rieka's staying at her parents' house this evening. I'll take you."

Kaila was relieved for the help, but she walked on her own strength with Gryf keeping watch beside her. She appreciated that he hadn't volunteered to carry her or anything equally gallant. "What are you doing out on this lovely night?" she asked, trying to keep her voice cheery.

"Just finished paying my respects to the dead. Decided to take the long way back to the Guild." He placed a hand on the hilt of the broadsword at his hip. "Thought I might see about a monster too."

She laughed a little. "Don't bother, it's disappeared again."

They soon approached a home on the western edge of the upscale Council District. It was dark blue, its windows and doors framed in white. A turret jutted out of the right corner, and Kaila noticed that the lights were still on inside. They climbed the stairs to the covered porch, and Gryf used the large iron knocker to announce their arrival. After a few moments, the door opened and Rieka stood in the soft biolight, her braids undone, her long black hair falling in soft waves around her.

"I hope we're not intruding," Gryf said.

She looked from Gryf to Kaila and back again. "Not at all. Please, come in. Give me a moment and I can get you something to dry off with." She stood aside for them to enter.

Gryf touched Kaila's shoulder, nudging her forward. "Master Lake needs your help, but I'm needed back at the Guild. Is Dane here?" Rieka nodded as Dane came up to the door, a glass of amber liquor in his hand. Gryf motioned with his head. "Let's go. I'll walk you to the House to get Aren."

"Why? What's wrong?" Dane asked as Rieka took his drink.

Gryf and Kaila exchanged looks, then she revealed the wound flowing with blood and rain.

FOUR

Aren tried not to push Bontan so fast that he'd leave Dane and his gree behind, but he felt anxious and a little guilty. If he hadn't spent his evening moping about and locking himself away from everyone, this never would've happened.

By the time they arrived at Rieka's parents' house, the rain had calmed to a soft drizzle. They tied the gree to a hitching post on the porch, and Dane let them in. They removed their shoes and made their way to the sitting room, where they found Lake lying topless on her stomach across a large ottoman that Rieka had draped with a dark sheet. Aren did his best to keep his eyes away from Lake's bare shoulders, the small of her back, the curve of her waist to her hips. He tried not to imagine those parts of her that were pressed against the ottoman, swallowed up in sheets. He focused on the satiny, star-metal cuff still wrapped to her upper left arm.

"You didn't have to come," Lake said, a sleepy smile on her flushed face. She winced as Rieka pulled another shard out of her back and dropped it into a small bowl, where it made a little clatter.

"She's doing surprisingly well, considering how deep the wound is," Rieka said. "She's like you, Aren; she's not bleeding out the way Gryf did."

"Tennari are said to have faint traces of magic in their veins. It helps us heal faster," Lake said, her words slurred.

Aren took a seat on the floor, positioning himself in front of her, and tucked stray strands of raven hair behind her ear. He traced the contours of her burning cheek with a thumb. "You've been drinking."

"Rieka said it would help dull the pain because she has no other anesthetic," she said, flinching as Rieka worked. "I'm sorry to make you worry. You were in mourning. You shouldn't have come."

"This is what friends do." He perched his elbows on his knees. "What were you doing out on the streets when you knew this creature was on the loose?"

"I wanted to see this thing for myself, and it infuriated me to see you so distraught."

"My distress isn't something for you to risk your life over," he said, raising his voice a little. "People I knew died. I wasn't sad as a way of encouraging you to avenge them."

Rieka stood up and wiped her brow against her forearm. She made a show of taking off her spectacles and putting down her instruments. "I'm going to take a break to relax my eyes," she said. "I want to make sure I don't miss anything. Dane, come with me? Our guests could use some drinks."

"Aren's no guest," Dane scoffed as he followed her.

When they were gone, Aren said to Lake, "What were you thinking? You could've gotten yourself killed."

Lake stared at him out of misty, cerulean eyes, and he studied the way her pupils adjusted to the light as if they had a life of their own. His words had angered her, had hit some kind of nerve.

"Why does everyone insist on trying to keep me out of harm's way? I'm not helpless and I'm not a child."

Aren sighed and leaned forward to rest his chin on the ottoman so that their faces were inches apart. "I never said you were helpless," he said, lowering his voice to a whisper. "I just care about you. Tell me you're going to go after a monster, and I'll tell you you're being irrational. I'll try to stop you, but if you end up going anyway, at the very least I want to know where I can find you if things go wrong. I just want to be there to pick you up if you fall." He took a peek at her wound, then said, "Or take you to get medical attention if you get sliced open."

A silence settled between them, during which they could hear the clatter of dishes and hushed conversations coming from the kitchen.

"The symbols you mentioned earlier," Lake exhaled. "I wanted to see them for myself. I've read a lot about arcane magic."

Aren perked, surprised at how quickly their argument had ended. He was almost sure that he'd have to spend the next day or two apologizing for something he wasn't so sure he was wrong about. On top of that, she thought the symbols were important—that he was on to something.

"Did you see them? Do you know anything about them?"

Lake lifted her head, supporting herself on her elbows, then winced at the pain in her back. "I did see them, but I don't know what they mean. It looks like Old Magic. Have you heard of the *istoq*?"

Aren cocked his head. "The word is Ancient for a doorway into another world. It's a device or method used in stories to explain the unexplained."

Lake closed her eyes for a moment, allowing a wave of pain to wash over her, and Aren placed a hand over hers, wishing he could take the pain away or give her more strength to endure it. "What if I told you the *istoq* is real?" she whispered. "I've found enough evidence in my research over the years to conclude that such a thing exists."

"Could I look at your notes?" he asked, feeling as giddy as a child being handed sweets. "We could bring up your references, and you could show me how you came to that conclusion." He furrowed his brows, then said, "But what does the *istoq* have to do with the symbols?"

"The *istoq* is a very old idea," she said, opening her eyes again, smiling at the excitement in his voice. "It deals with magic, which is what we happen to be dealing with with this monster."

Aren raised an eyebrow at the tight, armored pants she was wearing. "Not to change the subject, but you didn't tell me you were a Fighter."

"I'm not, but I can hold my own." Lake winked. "Just not so well against magic-induced creatures."

"We should spar sometime," Aren suggested, nudging her arm with a fist. "I'd love to have you kick my ass."

FIVE

Kaila found it odd to wake up next to someone other than her brethren. Last night, without her powers to heal her, her body had succumbed to mortal exhaustion and she had fallen asleep where Rieka had tended to her. She remembered Rieka draping a blanket over her, had fuzzy recollections of the girl checking on her throughout the night. Kaila woke before dawn and when her senses pieced together her location, she sat up, holding the blanket close, concealing herself. The cut in her side was more of a dull annoyance that she hoped would be completely gone once she resumed her powers. She also had to sneak home at some point to let Alaric know she was alive.

Kaila was about to set her feet on the floor when she realized Aren was asleep there. He had spent the night next to the large ottoman, a pillow in his arms and a blanket tangled at his feet. She suppressed a laugh, then searched for her top, hoping she wouldn't wake him.

"It's on the armchair," Aren mumbled, "but I don't mind if you choose not to wear it."

"You're awake?" Kaila whispered.

"No."

"Is anyone else up? Did Rieka's parents come home?"

"Counselor Darc was in emergency sessions all night, and Admiral Mila is still at sea." Aren turned onto his back. He was hugging the pillow against his chest, but his eyes remained closed. "Rieka and Dane are still in bed. Don't tell her father."

Kaila turned away from him so she could get fully dressed. "I'll make breakfast before I go. It's the least I can do."

"Before *we* go," he corrected her before yawning. "I didn't know you could cook."

"There's a lot you don't know about me, Aren."

After a quick meal, Aren brought her back to the inn via gree. Kaila found his friendship with the animal charming and realized she had never ridden one before. He waited in the tavern while she went to her room to clean up and change. In private, she absorbed enough of her powers to heal herself and regain her strength. Then, she relinquished them in a silver bracelet she slipped onto her wrist.

When they returned to the Library, Kaila sat at Aren's desk as he pulled references she suggested from the shelves. She flipped through the books, wondering if she'd be able to find anything on the symbols she'd seen on the beast. The symbols were so old, it was a wonder they had been resurrected at all. Unfortunately, Tiede's Library, as impressive as it was, might not have the information she was looking for.

Aren placed an armful of scrolls on the desk and took a seat next to her. He wasn't happy about her working in the condition she was in. He had tried arguing with her, but she wouldn't hear it, and at last he dropped it altogether. "These are the oldest we have that reference any kind of symbolism," he said. "I'm not sure what's in it because I haven't even begun to transcribe and catalog that entire section." He thumbed over his back in the direction of the disorganized shelves.

"See if you can find anything on the *istoq*. The symbol looks like a circle partially overlapped by a dark oval. You're well versed in Ancient?"

"Not well versed but I can get by," Aren said, unrolling one of the scrolls and using a weight to pin it open on his desk. He studied the parchment, skimming over the strange words as if it were second nature, while Kaila picked up the paper on which he had sketched the symbols he had seen.

"This one, the leaf," Aren said, looking at his sketches. "Gives me a headache every time I look at it. I know I've seen it before, but I can't figure out where."

"Leaves can symbolize any number of things," Kaila mused, handing him the paper. "Renewal, change, shelter, strength."

Aren wrote the words as she said them, his clean script flowing across the parchment. "It could also depend on the type of leaf," Aren said. "Is it poisonous or from one of the noble line of trees?"

"Maybe that's not the leaf of a tree. Maybe it's a shrub like the leindra. Leindra leaves are wider than this, but you get my meaning."

Aren moved some books around his desk, looking for one in particular. "Leindra is symbolic of holiness, purity, divinity," he said. He opened a book with faded lettering on the sable cover, then flipped through the pages to find the beautiful purple flower. "Have you read this? It's Tennari; Lady Geyle was reading it yesterday."

Kaila wrinkled her nose. "I've not read it but I've heard of it. Plants and seeds and such. I like plants but this book is dull."

Aren laughed. "I couldn't agree more." He then added, so softly that she strained to hear him, "Why are you so perfect?"

Kaila placed a hand on his shoulder so that she could lean in and take a closer look. "What was Lady Tiede reading it for?"

Aren shrugged. "She has a lot of interest in plants and their medicinal properties. Rose is renown for their adhesion to all things natural."

Kaila flipped a page and pointed at a simple white flower with silver leaves. "Look at this beauty: 'Snow Lady, of the *nim* family of poisonous, flowering plants. Common to the western Relythaun Wood and the surrounding lowlands. The toxin can be found in all parts of the plant, and if ingested can lead to severe illness or death.'"

"Stars," Aren breathed. "It's found near Rose."

"So it says." Kaila flipped to another page.

Aren stilled her hand, turning back towards the poisonous flower. "Have you heard stories of the Curse of Tiede?" he asked.

"Terrible fates befalling the Lords and Ladies of Tiede; everyone's heard of the curse, but they're all just stories and coincidence. Why?"

"With everything going on, I just wonder if it couldn't be true." Aren was silent for a moment, and she wondered what was going through his head. "If you're promised to someone, is it normal to become interested in someone other than your mate? Sometimes I wonder if Lady Geyle is happy." Kaila thought about Alaric and the kisses they shared, and a sense of shame overtook her. She removed her hand from Aren's shoulder. He must have realized he had hit a nerve because he closed the book and turned to face her. "Did I say something wrong?"

Kaila sighed, hugging herself. "No, I just have a lot on my mind."

"Does it have to do with Nikken?"

She faced him. "You remembered his name."

Aren smiled, revealing his dimple, and fiddled with a black ribbon tied around his wrist. "I'm just a little envious of the man. Don't worry, I won't let it get in the way of our friendship, and I'm sure whatever exhilarating sensation I get whenever I'm around you will fade eventually."

"Are you trying to complicate my life?" Kaila laughed, nudging at his shin with the toe of her shoe.

"I'm really not," Aren said, reaching for her hand and placing it back on his shoulder. "I like this. It's comfortable and I won't complicate it."

Kaila rolled her eyes and gave in, bumping her shoulder against his, causing him to knock his notebook off the desk. He reached down to pick it up, and she retrieved the slip of paper that had fallen out. The writing was in Ancient, and she recognized the sweeping, perfect strokes of the fine lettering and had to keep her hand from shaking.

"I'm sorry." She blushed, handing it to him. "That was probably personal."

He frowned as he looked at it. "It might be if I knew what it meant." He held the note so they could both see it. "I translate it as 'Keep your distance. I only saved your life for her happiness.' Is that how you read it too?"

"Yes, where'd you find it?"

"Under the door to my room," he said, tucking it back into his notebook. "I've been meaning to figure out who it came from, but with everything going on, it's remained a mystery. It's probably just someone's idea of a joke."

Kaila was about to offer up some vague guesses as to what it could be when she sensed a diminishing trace of holy Fire in the air. Tanghi had been here. Why had he come to Tiede when he should have been in Trum? For Tanghi to seek her out in Tiede was dangerous. If he found out about Aren…

She had to leave, had to find Tanghi. She had to come up with a story to tell him, to keep him away from Tiede.

SIX

Aren leaned against the balcony wall, looking out over the sea. His brain needed a break. Ever since he had returned from the inn, he had been poring over the texts on his desk, scribbling notes about the *istoq* and symbols. Lake had given him a lot of information to work with, and he wanted to do as much research as possible while it was still fresh in his mind.

"It's a lovely day."

Aren turned, then bowed his head, surprised to see Lady Valine. Her long, chestnut hair was shot through with silver, but in the sunlight it held a coppery quality that was pleasing to look at. She wore it loose and it carried on the wind, but she didn't seem to mind. She walked over to him, leaning against the wall, as he had, to look out at the sea.

"After the rains last night, it's a welcome sight," Aren agreed. "Were you looking to be alone? I can leave if you like."

She put a hand on his arm. "I'd prefer if you stayed. I dislike coming to Tiede, wandering these rooms."

"It's not an easy journey," he said, turning back towards the sea, trying to ignore her casual demeanor.

"The trip itself is not so bad. I had to come, to tell Vir of the mages. Our Houses are connected by blood, by Vir, but we are still on opposite ends of the chronos. Sometimes, my brothers have difficulty remembering the blood between our Houses. I come to remind myself so I can remind them."

Aren lowered his head. "I've read and heard so many wonderful things about Lady Elleina. I forget that she was your sister."

"My foolish little sister," she sighed. "She deserved better, should have married an Illitheien or at least a lord from another House of Light. But Tiede Ren was so charming at the time; it was easy to forget about the curse."

Aren's ears perked up. The curse again. "How did she die?" he asked, hoping she wouldn't think him rude.

Valine laughed, but it sounded like the false sea echoing within a shell. "Only she and the gods know. Perhaps Ren knew but he's dead too. My brothers and I imagine Elleina's fear of Ren's temper sent her into the Wood. She was lost for well over a year, and when she found her way home, she was not the same. She got better in time, and Ren seemed kinder towards her. I stayed for as long as I could—two, almost three years—and she convinced me that she was fine. I should have known better. She was going mad but I wanted to believe her, so I returned home. A few months later, we were mourning her death. Her body had washed up on the Laithe. The rumor was that she had jumped into the sea."

"I have no words that can express how sorry I am for your loss," he said. "It's all history and stories to me, but she was your sister, not a historical figure."

"She was both, and a legend in her own right. Not a lot of people wander into Tiede Wood and live to tell the tale—though she couldn't remember a thing about it. I think people are pulled into the place, people who are too curious. Any book on Tiede tells a story of some soul who was lost to the Wood. It's as dangerous as the stories claim."

Thinking about the voices he heard the other day, Aren wondered if Elleina had heard them too; he wondered if she had gone off alone because she didn't want anyone to worry about her.

"Vir seems immune to the call," she said.

Aren nodded, concentrating on the sound of the sea as it rushed and crashed against the cliffs. She was still talking to him—about Illithe, the grandeur of her House, how different from Tiede it was. "My nieces and nephews have children now, and they run all throughout the House," Valine said.

Run, Aren.

He imagined himself walking into the darkness of trees and moss, and he looked around. There was a light, small and green and coming towards him. He recalled a beautiful fae with long green hair. *She kissed me and everything went black.* Footsteps approached behind him, but he didn't turn around. The sea rushed and crashed, over and over.

"Aren?" a little girl's voice.

A little girl and her brother, scared of fire.

"Good day to you, little Priestess."

"Good day." A pause. "Lady Illithe. You can call me Selina if you want to."

Aren felt her little hands grab ahold of one of his. A bright light filled his vision, and then he saw the Wood again, each tree and twig and leaf outlined in a brilliant white. He saw himself standing in the Wood, surrounded by faeries peeking at him from behind trees and rocks. He felt the knife in his hand, the fear in his chest. It was hard to breathe.

There was a man. The man was a tree, then he was a bear, then a man-beast warrior clad in fur and claw and bone. He wore a helm of iron and gold with horns like spires that vied for the skies. He carried a blade the size of a mountain, held it tight with fingers ringed in uncut ruby and onyx.

Aren remembered a fight. Remembered hands that beat him, gems that cut him. Was it a god? A guardian of the Wood? What quarrel did he have with Aren? Aren shuddered, dropped the knife.

"Aren! Why is he shaking? What's wrong?"

Selina? How did she get to the Wood? He told her to stay put at the House.

"He seems to be in a trance. Apprentice, can you hear us?" Valine was here too? Damn it, how was he going to protect all of them from this beast-god? "I'm going to count to three; when I say three, you'll return to us in the House, on the balcony, in the sitting room overlooking the sea."

The bear-man lifted his sword, and Aren fell to the ground, fumbling for the knife.

"One."

He couldn't stop shaking. He was a dead man if he couldn't get that knife. He laughed, all he had was a knife.

"Two."

He looked up at the great sword, half-ready to accept his fate. The sword began to glow with a green light that traced the curves and points along the length of the blade. Scrolling lines like vines raced along the flat of the blade, the light emanating from it, pulsing in the darkness of the Wood. The lines tried to rearrange themselves in his head, tried to communicate something. His eyes widened before the wind tore through the trees. Leaves rushed in its wake, and he forced himself to isolate one leaf in his head. It was slender, covered in a fine fuzz, with a long, elaborate petiole scrolling in an unending line, growing and wrapping around his neck until he thought he might choke.

"Three."

A blade sliced through the air before his eyes, loosing him from the leaf, locking with the man-bear-beast-god's blade. He struggled to breathe.

A piercing cry rang through his ears, and he opened his eyes again. He was in the House. Valine was gripping his arm and Selina was pointing at the sky. A falcon, its wingspan exceeding the height of a full-grown man, circled the House. It called out, screeching as the wind grew, and the waves crashed harder against the cliffs.

Aren put an arm around Selina, who seemed magnetized where she stood, and herded her and Valine into the sitting room, where

Geyle was stumbling in. They had escaped the growing windstorm only to enter another one inside the House.

"The god!" Geyle called out over the noise, trying to hold her hair and skirts in place. "All the fire in the House has gone out!"

Aren looked over his shoulder, out past the balcony where the falcon circled. Then, he blacked out.

SEVEN

Kaila sat on one of the deserted beaches on the Kailen Islands, trying to come up with excuses. She would tell Tanghi that she was in Tiede Wood. She could admit to relinquishing her powers just as Geir did. The lack of her powers, plus the intense, raw energy of the Wood, was more than enough to mask her location. Tanghi would be upset with her for mimicking Geir, but his fears would be assuaged.

She would have to tell him about the attack on the House as well, and why she hadn't told Alaric right away. Lies were so hard to keep up with, and Kaila wished she didn't have to deceive the ones she loved. But what else could she tell them? That she had it under control?

A breeze lifted Kaila's hair, and she couldn't help but smile despite her worries. She felt the shift in the sand as Geir made his way towards her and sat down. He looked out at the open waters without seeing them, and she imagined he was thinking of great ships and sails, and majestic birds taking wing.

"I can't stay long," said Geir, his bare feet covered in a rush of water. "But I'm happy to see you again. What's wrong? You called because you're in trouble."

Kaila sighed. "Why did you tell Tanghi about the blessing I placed on the girl?"

"I didn't tell him anything about that. You said you'd tell Alaric when you were ready."

Kaila recalled the message that she and Alaric had watched, Tanghi saying he had spoken to Geir. "Then, why was he so concerned—"

"I told him that I'm in trouble with Aalae again," Geir cut her off. "That's all. I regret saying anything." Kaila's brows furrowed but he pushed on. "I don't have a lot of time, Kay. Tanghi is with Sabana in

Trum, and they think I'm out looking for horses." He brushed off some of the black, magic powder that covered his arms.

"Has Tanghi said anything about me being missing?" Kaila asked as she picked a feather out of his hair.

Geir leaned back on his hands. "No, but the fae of Tiede Wood told me he was looking for you. If I don't get back soon, he'll be looking for me too. We should convince him there's something going on between us."

"You could have any creature in all of creation; the most beautiful gods and goddesses ever to exist would want you as soon as they laid eyes on you." She nudged him with her shoulder. "Besides, you're too old for me." He smiled, making her feel warm inside. If only he would be like this all the time, the way he used to be. "When did you talk to the fae?" she asked.

"This is a nice respite," he said. She was about to repeat her question, but he went on, "So why would Tanghi venture into Tiede Wood? He hates trees."

Kaila moved to kneel in front of him. She needed to look at his face, even if she couldn't see his eyes. "Tanghi knows I was in Tiede, but he didn't know I relinquished my powers to be there. There are things in Tiede that I can help with, and if I succeed, maybe Alaric will take me seriously, but I don't want anyone to know that I relinquished my powers to spend time with mortals."

Geir sighed. "I'm the last one to tell you what to do, but you know how dangerous mortals can be. I've warned you to keep your distance."

"Is that why you left that note for the young man in Tiede?" she asked. She couldn't see his eyes, but the movement of the muscles in his jaw told her everything. "Since when did you get involved in the affairs of mortals?"

"He didn't listen to my advice," Geir managed to say, "and you remained in contact with him. I saved his life because I knew it would hurt you to see him dead, but I was hoping that the note would scare some sense into him. Most mortals would retreat back into whatever comfortable hole they came from; this one charges into trouble with reckless abandon. No mysterious note from some stranger is going to stop him from flirting with danger."

"How did you save his life?"

"After you mentioned him, I decided to see what he was about, so I followed him around Tiede that night. He attracts chaotic magic. The first time, I alerted him to a creature's presence in an alleyway. The second time, I physically picked him up and brought him back to the House after he was knocked unconscious." Geir exhaled, as if he had been holding his breath. "I thought that all you felt for the boy was a temporary curiosity bolstered by your sense of compassion. I wasn't betting on you altering the course of the fate lines by having feelings for him. The more you interact with the mortal, the more your line tangles with Alaric's."

"You knew I had feelings for him?"

"Not until you told me you saw the note," he said, and she grimaced. "You can't lie to me, Kay."

"Alaric will lock me up if Aalae learns about Tiede. Please don't tell her," she begged.

"Aalae already knows about Tiede. She's keeping Alaric distracted so that it might fall on its own. She even has counter-spells in place so that Taia isn't alerted. But don't worry, she doesn't know about the mortal," he assured her. "I don't know what this boy's actions are doing to the lines, and now it's too late for me to undo what he's done. I probably should have let him die. This would all be less complicated."

She took his hand. "You did the right thing by saving his life. He would never hurt me, I know he wouldn't."

"Kaila, there is no future with—"

"I know!" she cut him off a little too harshly. She continued, softer. "I mean to say I need to see my work through to the end to face Alaric. The new Priestess, the conflicts in the House, the magic…"

A darkness settled over Geir's features, and a sadness she couldn't explain clouded his aura. "You need to let him go," he said. "Whatever it is you have to do in Tiede, finish it and say goodbye. Your line tangles with Alaric because he will kill the boy with his bare hands if he ever finds out about him." Kaila couldn't stop the tears from flowing, and her body was racked with sobs. "It hurts, I know it does, but if you care for him at all…" Geir reached out to touch her but pulled back. "If Aalae finds out, she will use the mortal to control you. Alaric can't afford that and neither can I. If it came down to it, I would kill the boy if it meant saving you. I don't say these things to hurt you, but you have to understand if you want to save his life." Geir cupped her face. "If you can cut all ties with him, I will do my best to assure his safety and keep him hidden from the gods. I promise."

"His name is Aren," she whispered as Geir finally pulled her into his arms. "No one can know about him."

"I swear on Mahl's holy name that no one will hear of him through me."

EIGHT

Aren stood outside of the Mermaid's Song, waiting for Dane. His brother said he'd meet him as soon as he delivered the latest sets of daggers to the Fighters Guild. As Aren leaned against a lamppost, he pulled two burned dolls from the pack he carried. Their rigid, ivory bodies were cracked, and their painted faces faded. He fingered the threadbare clothes covered in soot and examined the little shoes made of bone.

When he had woken in the sitting room, the connections had become clear. Valine and Selina were sitting next to him, conferring with Elder. Aren had begun talking at once about monsters and magic and how he had to help the ghosts find their way home, how he had to listen to the voices and protect Tiede. That was when Geyle gave him some tea to calm his nerves.

Valine and Geyle began to argue, then the room dimmed. When he had woken up again, he was in his room. Elder had left a note with express instructions to stay in bed, but he left anyway. *How am I supposed to stay in bed when there's a monster trying to kill us?*

Aren tugged at his black vest, then glanced at his pocket watch before looking down the street. Still no sign of Dane. What was taking him so long? All the good ale was here at the tavern, so he couldn't have stopped between the Guild and here.

"Well, if it isn't the luckiest man in Tiede."

Aren turned towards the mocking voice, wondering which drunken apprentices were going to go at it today. Before he could figure it out, a fist caught him square in the jaw. He lost his balance and fell to the ground. The dolls in his hand clattered to the pavement, and he cursed as he recovered himself, looking to find his assailant as a few onlookers gasped and scattered, the fear of killers and monsters driving their actions.

A kick landed on Aren's ribs, knocking him back, his arms coming up to shield himself from another blow. The next kick was aimed at his face, and he rolled before the boot could connect, pushing himself up into a defensive crouch. When the next kick came, he was ready for it, blocking and preparing his defenses again.

"Aren't you just full of surprises," the man said, the black hood of his apprentice robes dropping back to reveal Trista's friend.

Recognition blossomed in Aren's brain. "Inra Mercer. What do you want with me?"

"I want you dead, asshole," Mercer attacked again, but Aren managed to block the strikes. He pointed at Aren's shoulders. "Let's see the marks. I know Trista was lying to protect you."

"We're going to talk now?" Aren scoffed, his arms open wide. *"Kiakt'i gu'rd!* Come on, hit me again. Give me a reason."

Mercer looked hesitant, but there was no mistaking the frustration and anger in his eyes. "Show me the marks!" Mercer demanded.

"Aren! What's going on?"

Mercer took a few steps back as Dane came running down the road and joined them. Aren rattled off a string of curses, gesturing at Mercer, and Dane gave his chest a few pats with the back of his hand. "Calm down, brother. In a non-dead language I can understand."

Aren pointed. "They are trying to kill me."

Dane looked at Mercer and raised an eyebrow. "Not with a stance like that. Who is *they* anyway? And why you?"

"That's what I was trying to find out, but he keeps telling me to take off my shirt."

Dane shook his head and began to pick up the ivory dolls, the broken limbs, not bothering to acknowledge Mercer's presence any further. "Why are you carrying these creepy things around?" He replaced them in the pack. "Is this what you wanted my help with? To play with dolls?"

Aren let out a breath, put his hands on his hips as he hung his head. "I need to take them to the Wood."

Mercer yelled something and Dane put a hand on Aren's back, leading him away. "Calla's probably called for help," he said, referring to the tavern proprietress. "We don't need to be here when the Regulators arrive."

Aren looked over his shoulder to find Mercer backing away towards the town center, hatred contorting the man's features.

"Next time you want to fight me, bring the big man!" Aren yelled.

Dane put him back on course, and they walked towards the stables on the other side of the inn. Vir's information was on target; someone really was trying to kill him. But why? If Mercer believed he was marked, why would he want to kill a fellow mage?

"Shouldn't we have him arrested?" Aren asked. "That's why Trista came to the House the other night: to get me out in the open."

"Arrested? On what charges?"

Aren put a hand to his ribs. "He beat me and I think he's behind the first attack on the House."

Dane stopped to examine him. "He hardly touched you, you big baby. Gods, you better not tell Gryf. He'll beat you just to remind you what a beating is." Dane put a hand on Aren's shoulder and they continued walking. "Just so you understand, I'm only going with you to the Wood because it's already in your head to do it. It seems every time I leave you alone, you get into some kind of trouble. I'd start to believe that Tiede's curse attached itself to you if I didn't already know you had your own special kind of curse."

They approached the stables, and Aren gave him a droll stare. "That's only when it comes to women."

"Speaking of which, how's Lake?"

"Doing well, I think. She and I were working this morning, but she had some pain so I took her back to her room so she could rest." They greeted the stable boy and pointed out two of the younger gree. "I owe Rieka a huge debt for taking care of her."

"Don't mention it," Dane said as they watched the boy prepare their mounts. "It's given Rieka a huge boost of confidence, and I personally enjoyed waking up to a fully prepared breakfast. Also, not that Rie needed it, but the gold pieces were a very generous token."

"Lake left gold?"

"She most surely did," Dane said as he and Aren herded the two gree out by the scruffs of their necks. "She must be rather well off herself. Seems to me there's still quite a bit you don't know about your beautiful friend."

NINE

Aalae watched with annoyance as Rafi applied salves of wintermint, aloe, and papaya to Geir's wounds. Rafi winced at the sight of the raw, open burns that raked Geir's chest, but Geir only clenched his teeth, waiting for Aalae to tell him to return to the fighting in Trum.

"Have you nothing to say for yourself?" she seethed.

Geir turned his face up as if to look at the bright, white ceilings that turned and bounced the light that shone in through the glass walls of the botanical. A thin layer of black powder covered his skin, shadowing and accentuating his muscles, making him look almost demon. He looked out of place, a broken beast surrounded by the vibrant greenery of plants and trees, the saturation of flowers.

A breath escaped his lips. "Why must you have me followed? Are you afraid I'm off worshipping someone more beautiful than you?"

"You can't bait me," she snapped. "Why did you meet with Kaila? What did you give her?"

"My love. Something you will never have." He gave her a cocky grin. "Ask me another question."

Aalae reached out to form her whip when Rafi touched her hand and gave her a look to remind her that their problems were bigger than Geir's madness.

She made an irritated noise, then said, "Did you tell her about the counter-spells over Tiede? Have you ruined everything I've put in place?"

"If only it were so easy," he sighed. His speech was getting slower, and he looked as though he were having difficulty holding up his head. "No, my Lady. I have bled to keep your secrets safe. Kaila is just..." he trailed off, smiled, then continued, "She just needs me sometimes."

Aalae glared at him. "Whose side are you on?"

"There once was a time long, long ago when there were no sides. There was one timeline, one unbroken cycle of Light and Night with four major Elements supporting it. There were eight continents and one imprisoned yet quiet planetary god." Geir's voice was soft, lulling. "Now, we are being strangled in countless fate lines with an angry planetary god who is trying to free himself and destroy us."

"Your point?"

He laughed and she wanted to slap him, cut open his beautiful face. "No point, my Lady. I forget who I'm talking to." He smiled but his fingers gripped the treatment table with enough ferocity to turn his knuckles white. He shook his head and gritted his teeth.

Rafi held a hand up to her, and she tried to rein in her temper. He gave her a slight nod to let her know that the potion he had mixed into the salve was finally starting to work.

"What were you doing with Kaila?" Rafi asked. "Did Alaric send her to you to get information?"

"No, she just..." Geir turned his head left and right as if looking for something. "She missed me and needed to talk."

"About what?" Aalae pressed, her patience wearing thin again.

"She's in love."

TEN

Nothing happened when Aren buried the dolls. There were no ghost children, no glowing lights. Granted, Dane didn't allow Aren to go deep into the Wood. They stayed within sight of the first marker, the ghostwood with the Guardian constellation carved into the base of the trunk. Dane asked if they were going to perform any rituals. Maybe it had all just been a bad dream.

They stayed in the Wood for a while, close to the tree line, since it was still light out. Aren sat on a mossy log, breathed in the scent of soil and wood and green, and felt a calm that he hadn't known in a while spreading over him. Dane leaned against a tree, peeling the bark off a fallen piece of branch while Aren recounted his conversation with Valine, the images that assaulted his memory, and the strange experience with the falcon.

"Rumor is, the Wind god paid a visit to the House," Dane said, examining the stick. "I wasn't nearby, but they said you could feel the gusts all the way out to the town center and midway down Guild Row."

"We had rain yesterday," said Aren. "It could just be a prelude to more storms." He found it odd how people always explained things away by blaming it on a god.

"Could be, faithless Apprentice," Dane chuckled, and Aren shot him a wry look. "I choose to believe that the gods are paying attention because Tiede is in serious trouble. Nothing this bad has happened in Tiede for as long as I can remember."

Aren hated to admit it but his brother was on to something. "Not since Lady Elleina died. Before that, there was an assassination, some strange illness, a disappearance. All the incidents revolved around the Tiede family and their spouses and offspring." Aren looked towards the cluster of rocks where the dirt had been newly turned. "There was the fire that killed those two Tiede children. I think I met them. I think that's what my brain is trying to piece together."

Dane whistled a note. "I'm not sure which is crazier: meeting ghost children or burying their creepy dolls." He whistled another note and looked down the length of the stick. "Are the ghost children going to give you a reward?"

Aren laughed as he stood up, brushing the dirt off his gray trousers. "I just want them to be at peace."

They rode the gree back to the stables, talking about normal things like how their parents were doing, how quickly their nieces and nephews were growing up, and when Dane was going to ask Rieka to marry him. By the time they reached the town center, the sun had loosed her grip on the sky, leaving a melting trail of pinks and golds as she slipped over the horizon. The Fire god would be sitting on the highest peaks of Tennar with his bow soon, stringing his fire-tipped arrows and shooting them into the darkness to sparkle throughout the night.

After stabling the gree, they parted ways and Aren checked his pocket watch before making his way towards the town center and up the curving stairs. His vision was swirling with symbols and leaves and a bear-man ready to cut his head off. That explained the growing headache.

Looking up into the expanding blackness of night, he caught sight of the moon dangling high and far. He remembered that it was on these steps that he had been attacked. It was where he had been knocked unconscious, where a stranger had picked him up to take him to safety. He paused, looking around, trying to reconnect himself to that night, to the events that took place around him.

"Out of the way," someone on a gree called out.

Aren pressed himself against the wall and let them pass. A Guard returning to the House for duty wished him a good evening, asked him why he was blocking the stairs. *No one can feel it,* he thought, watching everyone go about their business, a few raising their eyebrows at him for just standing there. *It's like a small fissure with a leak, like time and magic frozen in one spot.* He swiped a hand through the air in front of him. Nothing happened.

Stars, he was going insane.

He continued the rest of the way up the stairs and went to the wall that overlooked the town center. He wanted to see the twinkling lights of the city spread out below him like a reflection of the night stars. He wanted to see the great gears of the city at work, find his place among the mechanics of it all, feel connected for once and not like the out-of-place oddity he really was.

"You must have a lot on your mind this evening," said a woman sidling up to him.

Aren looked over at his company, and a smile overtook his face. "I was hoping I'd get to see you tonight. How are you feeling?"

"Better than earlier," Lake said, imitating his posture on the wall. "How was your day? No monsters, I hope."

Aren turned so that his back was against the wall. "No monsters other than the ones in my head." Lake frowned, so he tried to explain. "Memories from my forays into Tiede Wood are coming back to me in strange, broken images that make no sense. The logical explanation would be that my mind is confusing reality with things I've read."

"But there's more, isn't there?"

Aren's head started to hurt again. "I was on the balcony talking to Lady Illithe when Selina came out to find me. I felt Selina take my hand, and when she did, the visions became vivid, scary." Lake was looking at him with concern, and he realized he hadn't told her everything about his odd connection to the Wood. "You and I never got to talk about my strange episodes. In short, I hear voices from the Wood. They call me and I'm compelled to obey. I understand if you want to say goodbye and never see me again."

Lake turned back towards the city below, and Aren felt that something was off about her, though he couldn't place it. She forced a smile to her face as if she knew he was watching. "Tiede Wood is a strange thing."

Aren nudged her. "You're taking my confession awfully well. Shouldn't you be backing away from me?"

Lake winked at him. "You forget that I study celestial phenomena and things that most people find impossible—like the *istoq*. Did my notes help?"

"More than you know. I'm going to figure this out, find that creature's weakness. Then, Gryf and the Hunters can kill it, and I will take you out for dinner to celebrate."

"You have no idea how wonderful that sounds." Lake was smiling but her eyes were full of sadness.

"Great!" Aren said, hoping to cheer her up. "Are you busy this evening? I could use your brain to help me puzzle through the symbolism."

"Lying in bed all day has made a slug out of me. I don't know how useful I would be."

"I guess that means you missed the House event of the year." Lake gave him a quizzical expression and he chuckled. "I was on the balcony overlooking the sea when out of nowhere, the wind grew so powerful that even the ocean seemed to be carried into the air. I rushed to get Lady Valine and Selina inside, but the wind was coursing throughout the House. Fires were put out and people had to seek shelter."

Lake's expression changed, her face paled. "What?"

"Everyone's saying it was the Wind god. I don't know that I believe it." Aren shrugged. "A few of us spotted this massive falcon flying out over the Parthe. The Priestesses documented the event as a god sighting. I don't know what hard evidence they have, but I will admit that I have never seen a bird so enormous—bigger than the golden cranes of Syrn."

Lake choked on a sob as she hung her head. Then, she turned her face to the night skies, her eyes glossy, her fingers gripping the wall. He put an arm around her shoulders, wondering why she was so upset.

"Lake, is something wrong?"

ELEVEN

"Please talk to me." Aren's voice was soft and soothing. "Are you hurting? Or did I say something stupid?" He tried a little smile, but that only made her feel worse.

Kaila had to get this over with. The sooner the pain hit her, the sooner she could begin to heal. His arm was around her shoulders, and she turned into him. As naturally as breathing, he took her in his embrace, and she tiptoed so that she could take in his fresh, salt-tinged scent one last time. The light stubble on his jaw tickled her cheek, and she could feel his warm breath near her ear.

"Aren, we have to say goodbye," Kaila whispered. His arms tightened around her in response. "I'm so sorry." He didn't say anything, but she felt the quickened pace of his heart mirroring hers. Aren held her close and his body was so warm. She had wondered what it would be like to be in his arms like this, and now that she knew how perfectly she fit there, it hurt all the more to have to leave him. "I received a message from home and I'm leaving tonight," Kaila said. "I only came to say goodbye."

Aren loosened his hold so that he could look at her face. The hurt in his clouded green eyes was undeniable. "The first time you said goodbye, we'd only spent one evening together. I was disappointed to see you go but I accepted it."

"Maybe I should've stayed away—"

"But you came back and we spent more time together. I felt like something clicked between us, and before I knew what was happening, you were in my head all the time. I promised I wouldn't complicate your life, but—"

"As much as I've let you in, I've had to put up that many defenses," Kaila said, and he wiped at her falling tears with a thumb.

"You're handsome, intelligent, and absolutely charming, but I can't stay."

Aren leaned over, put his forehead against hers. "I've never met a woman who didn't make me feel like there was something wrong with me. Being around you is so easy. No one talks to me about books the way you do. You get my sense of humor..." His desperate fingers tangled in her hair, then moved to cup her face. "You kept coming back. I thought that meant something, that maybe you felt something more between us too. So why do I get the sense that I might never see you again?" He touched his lips to her forehead.

"There's still Nikken, and he would be very angry if he knew about you," Kaila said. "In time maybe everything will make sense, and I'll make things right by both of you. I don't know what the gods have planned."

Aren seemed to consider this, and she hoped that bringing up Alaric would help ease the blow. "I don't know why it matters what the gods have planned," Aren blurted out, irritated.

"Only they have any control over our fates."

"Never mind the gods. Let *me* change your fate."

Kaila felt his lips, soft and light as a feather, brush against hers, and her heart stopped. It wasn't a kiss, it didn't qualify. It could be labeled an accident. The fate lines fell in a massive tangle around her.

No one, aside from Alaric, had ever touched her lips.

Aren's forehead was against hers, and his breathing was shallow, ragged. "I'm sorry," he whispered. "I wasn't trying to...I want..."

Kaila took his hands in hers, placed a kiss in each palm, then pressed his hands against his chest. "In the Kailen Islands, it means I'll keep you in my heart—"

"Until we meet again," he finished for her.

"Goodbye, Aren." Kaila wiped the tears from her eyes and ran down the stairs.

Friction

ONE

Aren was numb as he watched Lake leave him. He was convinced that she had cast some spell to keep him rooted to this very spot, destined to stand here for all time as his senses replayed over and over the sweet promise of her lips and the truth and finality of their goodbye behind her salty tears.

It had taken every fiber of will in his being not to kiss her; he wanted to satisfy the curiosity that plagued him every time he saw her face. Yet, he managed to stop himself, and he wasn't sure whether he should feel proud or extraordinarily stupid. It wasn't as if Nikken, Aren's personal demon, was watching. He respected her too much to just take from her. If she had wanted him, she would've taken the kiss he offered, let him know that she felt the same way, but for whatever reason, she couldn't, and her will had been stronger than his. He supposed he should just be glad she didn't slap him.

He watched until he could no longer see her, then mapped out the path she would probably take past Guild Row, through the Harbor District, then down the multitude of steps to the harbor. The Harbor Master, charmed by her beauty and kindness, would let her break Vir's rule and allow her to leave by boat.

He was sure she'd made arrangements for transport to the Rail. Maybe she'd hire a coach and try to get some sleep, or maybe she wouldn't sleep until she was on the train which would take her as far east as Rose. She'd need supplies, food, a few new books to read. She'd hire another coach to take her to the borderlands of Tennar.

In his head, she was already a world away.

He turned to walk back towards the House. He'd bury himself in his research again, hide among the books and papers. He walked a few feet before he was knocked hard to the ground. He tried to get up, but something heavy had him pinned and was throwing punches at his face. He brought his arms up to protect himself.

"I brought 'the big man' like you suggested," the familiar voice said with a smile. Mercer. Aren managed to block some of the punches, but he could feel the blood dripping from his nose.

"He's not so tough," the big man said, pausing to cock his head and look at Aren.

Aren felt numb, thought about moving, but let his head fall back against the ground. What was the point anymore? Nothing ever seemed to go right for him, and it was getting really old. He turned to the side, spit blood, then looked up at his attackers. He began to tremble. "What the fuck do you want with me?" he erupted, his senses and manners leaving him.

"Do it, Copen."

The big man pulled a knife from within his robes, and Aren's instincts made him squirm and try to get out from under his weight. He grabbed at the man's wrists, trying to keep the knife away, but Mercer stepped in and caught his arms. Copen yanked at Aren's collar, lifting him off the ground, then slipped the knife under the fabric of shirt and vest, tearing Aren's clothes apart at the shoulder seams. Aren felt the blade bite his skin in the process, and he hissed as the blood burned and spilled.

"Nothing." Copen shrugged, baring Aren's shoulder to the night air.

"I don't understand," Mercer mumbled. Copen repeated the tearing on Aren's other shoulder, exposing it as well.

"I told you I wasn't marked." Aren tried to slow his breathing.

"What does it mean?" Copen asked, as if Aren hadn't spoken. "The beast smelled magic. He should be marked."

Mercer indicated that Copen should cut open the sleeves. He did as instructed, and Mercer pushed the fabric away to examine Aren's forearms in the biolight.

"I'm not marked!" Aren repeated, his agitation growing. "Has it never occurred to you that magic and all its properties might be a little beyond human comprehension? If you want to kill me, be done with it."

"This wasn't about you to begin with," Mercer said, "but you got in the way, changed everything."

"What do you want to do with him?" Copen asked.

Mercer spit. "Pompous pretty boy. Finish him."

As soon as Mercer loosed his hold, Aren moved, his fist connecting with the underside of Copen's chin. Mercer scrambled away, but Copen regained his balance and went for Aren's throat. Aren struggled to pull the big fingers apart, and his abdomen tightened as he strained against the man's weight. His vision was blurring and breathing was becoming difficult.

"Selina," Aren whispered. He wasn't sure why he thought of her in that moment. He seemed to fail her at every turn. He had assured her that she should never worry about him, yet here he was dying. Again.

And what could you possibly do to protect me, little one?

His strength began to leave him, and he dropped one of his hands, clawing at the ground.

"Let's see how well you comprehend death, Apprentice," Mercer said.

TWO

Aren's legs continued to kick out as he suffocated. He imagined the Night god grabbing him by the ankles to drag him off to Aum. Part of him was ready to let go and be done with it. He never thought he'd be broken-hearted to the point that his will would shatter so completely. It wasn't as if he and Lake were lovers. They had been friends, and on more than one occasion she had asked him not to complicate that friendship. He was a fool.

His fingertips were growing numb, but he continued to scrape at the ground. He imagined that he could feel the roots of Tiede Wood even here, tangling, reaching, creating its secret network of magic under the city. If he could just get some air, he could...

He heard a voice on the wind, different from the Wood—softer, colder. *This death is kinder than the gods would deal you,* the man said in a whisper. *I warned you, did I not? If you want to live, let go of her.*

You left the note, Aren thought, surprised at how clarity seemed to hit him when he was at death's door, but the voice left him, carried off on the breeze.

Aren! Hold on! I'm trying to help...

Selina?

Stars, he had been so wrapped up in himself that he hadn't considered the consequences of his death. He was a huge disaster, but Selina still needed him and he couldn't leave her, not without a fight. He concentrated, making the most of the air left in his lungs.

He summoned what little energy he had left, pulling what he could from the power he felt below him, from the tangle of roots that spidered like veins beneath the rock. A pulse of soft green light flowed up through his hand, warm and tingling. He thrust it at Copen's chest.

"What—?" Mercer choked on his words as Copen was knocked back several feet.

Aren pushed himself up, gasping for air. His clothes were torn to pieces; he was bloody, dirty, and broken. The green light he had imagined was gone, but in its place was an anger so feral that he was even ready to challenge the voice on the wind that had threatened him.

Mercer sensed the anger, and he began to back away as Aren got to his feet. Aren could feel the sizzle of magic like lightning over his skin, and he had to look at his shoulders to confirm that he had no marks. Copen was on his knees, holding tight to his midsection, wailing in pain.

"What did you do to him?" Mercer breathed.

Aren flexed his hands open and closed. He had no idea. His ears perked up. Footsteps hurrying towards them, slippers and boots. Priestesses and Guards. Selina.

He strode towards Copen, grabbed a fistful of the man's dark hair, pulled his head back. "Look at me," he growled. Copen sobbed, still holding his middle. "I said look at me!" Aren's voice was loud and rough, as terrifying as any god. Mercer ran off, tripping twice over his robes.

Copen begged, "Mercy, please!"

"Mercy for information. Do you control the beast? Where is it? How do I stop it?"

"I don't know," Copen choked. "I...One person never knows all the details."

"You must know something!" Aren seethed. "Why attack me? What is it you think I know?"

"Aren!" Selina called out. She and the others were closer now, running towards him.

"Look what you did to me!" Copen cried, releasing his hands from his chest and abdominal area. His robes and clothes had disintegrated, and whatever had burned through it was now eating away at his flesh. A fuzzy, moss-like substance covered the wound. Blood dripped through Copen's fingers, fell to the ground.

Aren let go of his hair, and the man fell to his knees. Aren backhanded him, sent him sprawling onto the cobblestones.

"Aren! Stop!"

Selina, I can't...

"Please, I'm an Unwanted like you, Unblessed. I lived with the *Naspa* until I met Mercer. I just wanted to belong to something."

"I'm not like you." Aren wrapped his fingers around Copen's throat and squeezed.

The voices were calling him again.

THREE

Alaric rubbed his temples as he listened to Taia reading the evening's reports. She sat at his desk, her papers laid out before her. Trum was going to fall.

Tanghi entered the study and took a seat, and Alaric moved to stand next to the armchair opposite him. "Do you know where Kaila went?"

"I thought she was in Tiede." Tanghi's tone was cold, distant. "I can try to find her if you want. Chances are, she's snuck off to see Geir—which wouldn't happen if you just let her go. She feels like she's being treated like a child, and she does everything in secret to circumvent you."

"She is a child," Taia piped up. She was diagramming fate lines based on the latest reports. "Tanghi's right. If you put her to work instead of fawning over her, she might actually grow up."

"Your tongue," Alaric growled. "Silence it."

"She argues every decision you make," Taia burst out. "If Tanghi did as she does, you'd have him punished!"

Alaric glared at her. "Do not concern yourself with my business!"

"It's become my business!" she argued, walking towards him. "You promised yourself to me because you needed me to help you gain power. I've done nothing but obey every word, every thought you've conveyed, even when I thought you wrong."

"I didn't realize at the time," he said, his voice low, "that there was more to existence than power. Maybe my promise was a mistake."

Tanghi stood up, putting himself between them. "This is not the time for arguing."

"You made a promise to me before the gods!" Taia said, her form flickering.

"What more do you want?" Alaric asked, pushing a surprised Tanghi out of the way. "I'm promised to you and I can't break it. My body, my soul, my destiny are all tied to you. What more do you want?"

"She wants your heart," Kaila said.

Not having seen or heard Kaila come in, they all stared at her in silence. Kaila took a hesitant step towards Tanghi, and he met her halfway, staring into her eyes as if seeking answers. She mouthed the words "I'm sorry," and Alaric had never seen such conflict cross the Fire spirit's face.

"Now is not the time," Tanghi said, recomposing himself. "First the mages, then we fix this." He indicated all of them with a sweep of his arm.

Alaric and Taia looked at each other, trying to reach some sort of temporary resolution but failing. Taia returned to the desk, and Alaric threw himself into the armchair. He could feel the darkness growing within, pulsing and pushing at his nerves. He leaned back, taking in deep breaths.

Kaila made her way to Alaric, got down on her knees before him. He sat up, then leaned towards her as if seeing her for the first time. Her hair was wet, clinging to her flushed cheeks. Her eyes were dark and solemn, the playful aqua he was accustomed to clouded over with such hurt that his instincts went on alert. Something was wrong.

He pushed her hair away from her face, and as she lowered her gaze, he could feel his heart beating harder, the demon blood churning, waiting for a reason to break free.

"I've kept a secret from you, my Lord."

FOUR

Leaving Aren had been harder than Kaila had thought it would be, and it hurt even more that she had to do it so that Alaric wouldn't kill him. She sought shelter in a lagoon near the Keep as her body was racked by sobs.

When her tears were under control, she left the tranquility of the lagoon and entered the Keep flickering from spirit to god form, drifting through the halls like a wraith, leaving a trail of water in her wake. Her work in Tiede wasn't over. Aren still needed her help, and if she didn't do something soon, either the monster or the Wood would kill him.

She had to laugh a little. The boy was in a world of trouble, and that was without the wrath of a jealous god on him. Her smile felt foreign on her face, but it reinvigorated her. Why was it that just thinking of Aren could lighten her mood?

She reached the study and heard the arguing well before she entered the room. Alaric and Taia were at each other's throats, and Tanghi was trying to keep the peace.

Kaila settled on her god form and knelt before Alaric, feeling the tension in his hands, the trembling in his thighs. She did this to him. She made him worry, made him paranoid. She hated herself for it because she did love him. "I've kept a secret from you, my Lord," she said. It was time to ask for help, even though it would prove that she was an incompetent child. It was all she could do for Aren now.

Alaric leaned towards her. "I knew you were keeping something from me, and I won't deny that it hurts to know I was right." He reached out to stroke her jaw, and she felt the cool of twilight on her face. "What is it?"

Kaila hesitated, hoping that she was doing the right thing. She took a deep breath and exhaled. "There's trouble in Tiede," she said. "I wanted to take care of it myself. I wanted to fix it so that you would trust me, so that you would send me anywhere you're willing to send Tanghi, but I failed." Tanghi took a seat and listened, his concern mirroring Alaric's.

Alaric's voice was steady as he prodded her for more information. "What's going on in Tiede? Taia's not noticed any disruptions in her spells."

"She hasn't noticed because Rafi placed a counter-spell," she said. "I just found out from Geir."

Alaric sat up and turned to look at Taia, who stood before opening another book, paging through the spells at a frantic pace.

"The mage threat has already made it to Tiede, and Aalae was hoping you wouldn't notice," Kaila said. "The House has been attacked; mages captured, questioned, and executed or imprisoned. What's worse is there's some kind of beast loose in the city. It's been killing people, and it attacked the House." Alaric clenched her hand, and she rushed to add, "Vir is safe. Three young men promised to Tanghi drove out the monster. They happened to be at the right place every time. Blacksmiths."

Tanghi grunted as he nodded. "Must be Gerrit clan. Guardian blood runs in their veins."

"Is the beast still alive?" Alaric asked.

"Yes, I tried to fight it, but..." She hesitated, then moved to lift the black, reptilian skin of her armor to expose the long scar, which was still healing. Alaric let out a hiss as he reached out to run his cool finger along the length of it.

"Kaila, what were you thinking?" he asked, raising his voice. "You could've been killed! This is why I didn't send you to Trum, but apparently you can find danger regardless!"

"I got out of it just fine," she muttered, pulling her top down.

Alaric stopped her so that he could point out the areas that still pulsed crimson. "You were infected with magic!" he said. "Taia, look at this." She drifted over and peered at the wound. He glared at Kaila. "How did you get the magic out? You couldn't have done this yourself."

She looked down at her hands. "Geir," she whispered. "I made him swear not to tell anyone."

"I would've helped you," Tanghi's low voice cut in.

"You would've told Alaric," she mumbled.

"Get to Tiede, find this thing, and kill it," Alaric said to Tanghi. "I want its bones."

"You can't!" Kaila said. "I mean that none of us can kill it. It sensed my power even though I relinquished it. Our powers in combination with magic that strong will open an *istoq* to rival the one we dealt with in Tiede Wood" —*on the night Aren found Selina*, she added to herself.

"You relinquished your powers to fight? Damn it, Kaila!" Alaric said, rising to his feet so that she had to move out of his way. He took a few steps towards his desk, then turned and pointed at her. "This is why I worry. This thing could've killed you, and now we have to figure out how to stop it before it goes after Vir again."

"I thought I could take care of it."

Alaric ignored her. He said to Taia, "Check her wound. I don't doubt Geir did a good job, but it doesn't hurt to be thorough. Then, I want that damned spell of yours fixed." He turned to Tanghi. "Trum can wait, I want you in Tiede. Watch the House, look for the creature. Make sure your Guardians are protecting Vir. I'm going to check his fate line."

Kaila rose to her feet feeling sad and uncertain. "And what would you have me do, my Lord?" she asked. She had a good idea of what his answer would be.

"You are barred from leaving the Keep until I say otherwise," Alaric growled. "I could have lost you, Kaila."

FIVE

Aren had a fitful night's sleep. He was plagued by nightmares of plants reaching out to strangle him, moss that ate at his flesh, beautiful flowers that kissed and poisoned him. He remembered his hands around a mage's neck, strangling. Bitter rage had consumed him, blinded him, and he wanted the bastard dead.

He remembered Selina rushing towards him, screaming at him to stop, begging him to let go of the mage. She had seen his eyes, and the expression on her face was one of fear and heartache. She threw her small arms around him, pleading for him to come back to her.

Between the stabbing pain all over his face and his inability to put Lake out of his mind, Aren was up most of the night staring into the darkness. At one point, he stumbled over to his desk, lit a candle, and began writing letters to Lake in his notebook. He wrote about the vast emptiness of the evening and how all hope had drained out of his being. He referenced passages from old texts regarding shattered stars and the ghosts of unrequited love. He had never written such a personal letter to anyone in his life, and it embarrassed him that he was pouring his heart out to her now. He had no intention of sending her his prose or having it otherwise see the light of day, but something was cathartic about scribbling his soul onto parchment. He'd bury it in the chest at the foot of his bed, then pull it out decades from now and laugh at himself. Maybe he should burn it.

Eventually, exhaustion overtook him and he dozed off naked at his desk. When he woke up, his head was pulsing, his ears were ringing, and his chest was aching from the empty void that Lake had left in his heart. Despite feeling out of sorts, he managed to draw a bath, wash up, get dressed, and pull on his black robes. He half-stumbled out of his room, and a Guard caught him before he could fall. The Guard offered to escort him to the Library, which caused Aren to laugh so hard that he doubled over in pain.

"Gods, Aren, what do you think you're doing?" Dane asked, rushing over. He gave the Guard a nod, then helped steady Aren, who was walking like a drunk towards the Library.

"Going to get some work done before someone or something else decides to choke me," he said, the dizziness subsiding. "Why in Aum would I need an escort to the Library? Have I been arrested?"

Dane sounded irritated when he said, "You were beaten badly, and Lord Vir doesn't want someone trying to kill you—if only because part of him believes that mother will burn down the entire city to protect you. She's beside herself with worry. You're a disaster. Have you seen yourself?"

He had. And he didn't care. "I'm sorry I made you all worry, but you can return home. I have a lot of work to do." Aren took a deep breath, then turned in the direction of the kitchens. "I need some coffee."

Dane stopped him. "Gryf and I saw the mage in the dungeons— the one who attacked you. How'd he get to you? He's big but I know you're faster than he is. What is wrong with you? The truth, brother."

Aren refused to look at him. He felt stupid hearing these words spoken aloud. "Lake's gone and she's not coming back."

"Gods, Aren. Really?" Dane dropped his head, put his hands on his hips, and didn't say another word for several heartbeats. "How old are you?"

Aren shoved him out of his way. There was nothing like a big brother metaphorically kicking you in the balls to get you back on your feet.

"I'm sorry." Dane caught up to him. "I know you had feelings for her, but you knew that it wasn't going to work, that there was someone else. I liked her too, but no woman is worth you getting your ass handed to you."

Aren glared at him. "It might not have happened if you had taken me seriously for once when I told you mages were trying to kill me."

"You want to wallow in self-pity? Fine." Dane met his glare. "Get back to hiding behind your books. I'll get your damned coffee for you."

They parted ways without another word.

By the time the kitchen delivered a carafe, Aren had managed to file a stack of books and pull more sources for his research. He thanked the young woman with a nod, unable to bother with any pleasantries. He felt terrible about his argument with Dane and sick over Lake's absence.

The Library doors opened with their loud, familiar click followed by the deep creak and moan as the heavy wood was pushed open. Aren swore under his breath and gulped down half of his coffee, scalding his tongue and the roof of his mouth. His eyes watered, and he moved the cup containing the remaining coffee into an unused box in the very back of the bottom drawer on the left side of his desk and hid the carafe.

"I need the scroll on the treatise with Rose, the two volumes from the Illitheien medical collection on mage markers, and indices four through eight on Tiede's war history," Elder called out. "Now."

Aren pushed his chair back and went to get the medical records. He had filed several Illitheien works recently and knew it would be most efficient to get those into Elder's hands first. Elder grunted his approval, then began to page through the contents. Aren rushed to get the volumes on Tiede's history and the treatise with Rose.

"Fighter Gryf and the Hunters can't find the mage that ran away or that cursed monster," Elder mumbled. "Gods help us." When Aren returned with the rest of the material, Elder took the scroll and peeled the parchment back across the desk. "I was surprised to find the doors unlocked; I wasn't expecting you to be working."

"I'm well enough to work," Aren said, using a hefty marble stone to weigh down the top corner of the curling scroll. "Lake and I stumbled on some possible links between plants and symbolism, so I might be making some headway there."

"That's very kind of her to help. You seem to get along very well."

"She left last night." The words sounded as if someone else had said them. "I know what you're thinking: I'll get over it."

"You will never know what I'm thinking," Elder corrected him. "I'm not concerned about whether or not you'll recover from a broken heart. You will do your job as well as you always have. In fact, you'll probably throw yourself completely into it to dull the pain. I would thank her for leaving if only I wouldn't miss her charm and conversation."

"I appreciate the concern," Aren said sarcastically.

"I'm thinking there are secrets and stories that have been woven into your soul that have yet to be unraveled," Elder said, ignoring him. "I'm thinking that you need to start figuring out who and what you are and accepting it instead of trying to hide or fit in."

Aren fidgeted. "I saw what I did to that mage, but I swear it wasn't me. There are a lot of crazy things about me, but I don't have any kind of magic, if that's what you mean."

"*Krinn a'tmor.*" Elder's voice was low, and the Old World accent came easily to his speech.

Aren's mind raced to translate. Why did the old man like to quiz him when his brain was pulp? "Something not derived from fear," Aren puzzled out loud.

"Truth," Elder answered for him. "Truth for what it is, and not created from or derived from fear."

"Meaning?"

Elder sighed with the knowledge of a thousand whispering winds. "You hide from what you are because you're afraid. What truth are you willing to accept about yourself?"

SIX

Vir was exhausted.

He buttoned his shirt as he looked out past the balcony that extended from his bedchamber. The sea was tumultuous this morning, churning under a sad gray sky. The threat of rain hung over the House, and he recalled stories Elder would tell him about the Night god calling out to the Water goddess, trying to find her as she hid her lovers from his jealous wrath. She tossed them into the sea, turning them into sharks and mermen, building up an army of her own so that one day she could rebel against the Night and be freed from his overzealous love for her.

Vir sighed. He had no time for stories. He needed to finish writing his reply to Rose Gaithus, telling him that Tiede, at present, could not come to Rose's aid. Tiede had its own mage problem to contend with.

The servants continued to work in silence as he slipped on a charcoal-gray vest and black shoes. They fixed his bed, took his laundry, and laid out hot tea, cubes of sugar, and cream in the sitting area. He noted their concerned glances, heard the whispers that swept through the halls.

Lord Vir is ill. Lord Vir is dying. There is no heir to Tiede.

He took a seat as he prepared his tea. The servants put on polite smiles, exiting as he stirred, the gentle clinking of the spoon against porcelain signaling for them to leave.

Vir hadn't planned on dying anytime soon, so while he knew he needed to produce an heir, he hadn't been in any hurry. At first, he wasn't sure what the problem was. He and Geyle both seemed healthy enough and still young. After a year with no success, and the House doctors baffled, he began to call on Illithe.

And still there was no heir.

Vir stared at the empty bed as he drank his tea, savoring the heat down his throat. He didn't get to bed until near morning. The Apprentice's brush with death had left him troubled, and he spent most of the night discussing it with Elder. When he finally did make it to bed, Geyle was sound asleep, and when he woke up she was gone.

Vir swallowed the rest of his tea and was about to pour another cup when he decided that one of Geyle's concoctions would be preferable. His throat and lungs were irritated, and the only thing that seemed to ease the pain was the burn of liquor. He left the room without putting on a tie, wondering where his wife would be by now. He heard Geyle's voice coming from the drawing room, but as he

approached, he heard the Apprentice as well. He paused, torn
between barging in to ask her to make his drink and returning to his
study while the Apprentice kept his wife occupied.

"Aren, please sit awhile!"

Vir could hear the smile in her voice. It had been a long time since
she had sounded like that when talking to him. He also noted how
informal she was around the young man, and Vir moved to stand by
the door, out of view.

"Gods, look at you. What happened?"

"Apologies for my current state; I had a rough evening," Aren
said, sounding cool and formal. "Your maidservant said you needed
my assistance, but I'm afraid I can't stay long. Elder has me on
important tasks."

"I'll steep some of my special tea for you. I use it for headaches,
but it should help with any pain."

"That's kind of you but unnecessary." Aren paused, then said,
"The last time you gave me tea, I blacked out."

"You were in a frantic state. It was necessary to calm you down.
Valine thought you were hallucinating, and she would have dragged
you off to Doctor Pember to have your blood drawn and pills forced
down your throat."

"What's done is done, my Lady. What service do you require of
me?"

Vir peered into the room and watched as Geyle floated about in
her pale-pink gown.

"I have a confession to make," Geyle said, walking towards Aren.
She kept her eyes focused on the intricate patterns on the rug. "I've
been in Tiede a while now, but these past few days, in those few times
when it's just been the two of us, I've never felt so comfortable. I'm
not sure what power it is you have over me"—she laughed a little—
"but I do like it."

"My Lady…"

She held up a hand, finally looking at him. "I know Vir has a lot
going on right now, and he doesn't have time for me."

"I'm more than happy to entertain you," Aren said, wincing at his
word choice. "Keep you company. Rather, I'm happy to be a
companion." He paused as if to rearrange his thoughts. "I'm glad
you're comfortable with me, and I'm sorry it's been difficult for you
with Lord Vir being so busy."

"You are more than company," she said, almost pleading with
him to understand. "I can confide in you, tell you things I couldn't
tell anyone else."

Aren seemed to consider this, then said, "If you think so much of me, then I need to ask a favor."

"Speak it."

"I need you to tell Lord Vir." Aren stared hard into her pale-blue eyes, and she angled away from him. "Everyone can see he's sick, and I fear the only ones who might know why are standing in this room."

"Why can't you just trust me?"

"This trust feels very one-sided." Aren sounded strange to Vir, exasperated. "Do you have further need of me? I have other duties to attend to."

Tears welled up in Geyle's eyes. "The gods sent you to me. Isn't that enough?"

"Not for me." Aren's emotions were barely in check. To Vir, this was uncharacteristic. "I have done for you, but you've given me no explanations, no assurances."

She threw herself into him, clutching tight to his waist. "Vir is paranoid like his father, and he will lock me up if he suspects anything!"

Aren looked down at her as she cried into his chest. "My Lady, this is…"

They both turned towards the door at the sound of his footsteps, Geyle gasping as she released Aren from her embrace.

Vir's voice was raspy, his tone disappointed as he said, "I trusted you."

SEVEN

Selina was doing her best not to worry as she listened to Nianni explain some of the rituals that would take place during her initiation ceremony. It was hard not to worry when those voices were calling Aren's name again, and they seemed louder here in Aalae's worship room with the large window open.

"Let's go over the part where you get marked," suggested Nianni. "It'll seem scary, so it's best you're prepared for it."

"Why are Priestesses marked with plants?"

"It's a ritual that began long ago when the gods wanted to mark which Priestesses belonged to which gods. The gods send a vision to the Seer on how to mark each new Priestess. The designs, symbols, and flowers all hold special meaning," Nianni explained as she lifted the hem of her dress to expose one smooth, brown leg.

Selina traced the swirling design with her eyes, the aqua ink snaking its way up from the top of Nianni's foot, circling her calf, then over her knee and upwards. "What's the meaning of yours?" she asked.

Nianni turned her calf this way and that. "I'm not sure yet. We're supposed to learn about ourselves as we mature. I don't even know what kind of flower it's going to be."

"I bet Aren knows," Selina offered. "He's not very good at plants, but I'm sure he knows which books to look at."

Nianni curled her legs under as if Aren had just walked in. "I'm not letting him examine my marks!"

Selina lifted a finger and began to draw in the air. She could see the patterns before her, leaves of different types and varying textures. She cocked her head, tracing long green stems that wrapped around and around. Nianni followed the movements, perplexed and curious. "What're you doing?"

"They're leaves," Selina said, mesmerized by the pictures. "I don't know what kind, but I bet Aren knows. The goddess wants to help, but she can't come to Tiede right now."

Nianni was entranced. "The goddess is showing you pictures of leaves? What's that going to help?"

"Apple, nightshade," Selina said in a singsong voice. "Discord and magecraft. Aren knows. He's seen it."

"Seen what?"

"The secrets of the Wood," Selina explained in a voice not her own. "Aren can save Tiede."

EIGHT

Aren squeezed his eyes shut against the pain in his head as the Guard led him through the halls of the underground dungeons. The dungeons were dark and dank, hewn of stone and lit by torches lining the tight halls. The sound of water dripping and running seemed to echo around them, interrupted only by the wails of the prisoners and the hushed whispers of the wraiths.

He replayed the scene from earlier, wondering if there was any way it could have come out differently. Vir was standing in the doorway staring at Geyle, who had her arms wrapped around Aren. Vir had hurled question after question at his wife. "What did you ask him to do for you? What things do you ask of him that you won't ask of me? What are you hiding from me?"

When Aren had tried to speak, to explain everything, Vir demanded he remain silent. Geyle had refused to share any information. Her body had been racked with sobs, and when the marks on her shoulders began to glow, Vir had seized her by the arm and called the Guard.

Yet here Aren was, being led through the dungeons. It wasn't fair, considering he wasn't the one with the glowing marks, but he wasn't the one wearing a pink dress either, so it was probably more appropriate for him to be the one entering the bowels of Tiede. He tried not to feel too bitter about it. If Aren were in Lord Vir's shoes, he would probably choose to lock up the questionable Apprentice rather than his delicate wife.

The Guard unlocked a cell, and Aren entered. It was devoid of any furnishings, and the bare stone floor and walls made it chilly. It couldn't have been deeper than eight feet and even less wide. Even the ceiling seemed to press in on him. The Guard brought down the iron bar and locked the door, and Aren leaned against the wall, slipping down until he was sitting on the cold floor. He listened to the Guard's footsteps echo down the hall as he jogged back towards the exit, eager to leave the darkness and terrors.

Aren hugged his knees. At least the voices in his head dulled a little—enough to allow him to ponder his fate anyway. His mind drifted to Lake, and he smiled despite himself.

You left and my world imploded. I'd give it all up if you came back. I'd follow you to Tennar if you'd have me.

He squeezed his eyes shut. This wasn't helping. Lake was gone and she would have Nikken—an older, mature man who could provide for her if she wanted; a Master in whatever trade he chose, respected by his peers. He imagined her lover was a full-blood Tennari with lineage, someone promised to and blessed by a god at birth, and not some Unblessed, Unwanted boy who had no idea where he came from except Tiede Wood.

The fire, the water, the stars. What crimes have you committed, boy?

Aren's eyes bolted open at the hissing whisper in the Ancient language. A shifting form of mist and shadow moved to the back of the cell, cocking its head one way and then another. The vapor drifted and changed, the shape of its body resembling that of a human, but its hooded head that of a wolf, then a man. Aren stood up, keeping himself pressed against the wall.

You'll speak your crimes to me, and I'll pass judgment. A'bertrinn se'miq vihallc.

"I've committed no crimes against the House, Lord Hraf." Aren tried to keep the fear out of his voice. He didn't recognize the man, but the man's wolf sigil. Hraf was one of the earlier lords of Tiede, renown for his cunning in battle. *"Wils rengen a'eqistille."*

The wraith dropped his large fur hood, revealing a translucent, scarred face and a long, thick gray beard. His eyes were empty sockets, and a sharp grin was the only indication of what the man might be thinking or feeling. Aren stood his ground, reminding himself that the wraith could physically hurt him if it wanted to. Mentally, Aren was sure he was scarred for life.

It's been a very long time since I've heard anyone speak in my tongue, the wraith said in Ancient, his gruff voice softening just a little. *And you recognize me. What are you doing here, if you've committed no crimes? You say you are waiting—waiting for what?*

Hoping his Ancient was good enough to appease the wraith, Aren switched over to the forgotten language. "I'm waiting for Lord Vir to decide my fate. He thinks I've betrayed him."

Your accent is not bad, but it makes me laugh. You're waiting on Vir to predict your future. Aren was about to correct himself, but Hraf said, *Quiet. I know what you meant.* It floated closer, examining Aren. The air became colder, and Aren had to clench his teeth to keep from chattering. At last it stilled, its smoky form billowing. *There is power in you. What are you, boy?*

"I'm no one. Just the Apprentice in the Library, and that title might soon be stripped of me. My name is Aren."

The wraith drifted back a little, as if surprised. *You're the reason the Wood calls. You're the reason the god came.*

"I am not the reason for anything," Aren corrected him. "The Wood was creepy long before I was born, I'm sure. As for the god, I was merely present at the time a gigantic falcon flew overhead. Only the House Lord is able to call on the gods."

Hraf broke out into laughter so loud that it filled the dungeons, echoed down the tight halls, and caused the mortal wailing in the other cells to stop. He switched to Common. *You just said that you showed up as a feathered creature to give witness to the end times, and that the House Lord has the stamina to piss on the gods.*

Aren frowned, feeling flustered. He, too, switched to Common. "End times? Did I say that? I didn't think I knew the word for end times. I said *yvcas*, didn't I?"

You let the symbol slip out of your mouth, and it changed the word. Aren opened his mouth to respond but then closed it, not quite sure how to ask what he wanted to ask. This only made Hraf laugh again. *That's the trick with what you call the Ancient tongue.*

"Fine," Aren said, even though it wasn't fine at all. "How does a symbol get spoken? I didn't hear it."

Hraf had an eerie smile on his misty face. He reverted back to Ancient. *Sometimes, languages die because people fear the power in words, in the telling.*

"The language becomes spell," Aren concluded, his mind reeling. "The language became power."

Hraf's head shifted to that of a wolf with empty eye sockets, and Aren couldn't stop himself from shuddering. *Vir sends you here to be punished, but your being here is an omen.*

The wraith began to diminish, but Aren felt as though they still had so much to discuss. "Lord Hraf!" he called. He switched to Ancient in the hopes that he would linger a while longer. His mind was working now, the gears spinning so fast he thought they might be sent flying. "The power is in the symbols, isn't it? If I can decipher the meaning, then there's something in Ancient that can be spoken to neutralize the power, right? You said the symbol can be spoken."

The wolf head with the empty eyes stared at him, but the canine teeth glistened in a grin. *Ystve a'chyr. Tal tsiom.* The wraith dissipated.

Aren paced the cell, his hands squeezing at his temples. Stars, what had just happened? He had to get to the Library. There were books he had to pull, notes he had to puzzle through, and it wasn't going to be easy with the voices distracting him. When he heard the iron bar lifting, the sound of a key in the door's lock, he stopped his pacing. The door opened, creaking loud on its hinges, and Dane walked in, the earlier incident between them forgotten.

"Didn't I tell you?" Dane said, frustrated. "Didn't I tell you that something like this was going to happen if you let her—"

"How'd you hear?"

"The whole House is talking about it, but Lord Vir ordered your release. Everyone's afraid the curse is at work again, and half the city is cursing your Unblessed existence. I leave you alone for a few hours, and you get yourself thrown in the dungeon. Unbelievable."

"The curse," Aren muttered, following his brother and the Guard.

"People are talking about how Lord Vir's turning into his father," Dane said as the Guard led the way out of the dungeons. "They're comparing it to when Lord Ren killed Lady Elleina in a fit of jealous rage."

"No one knows that Lord Ren killed her. Even Lady Valine couldn't confirm it."

Dane shrugged. "The people who aren't cursing your existence are the ones who are completely in love with or pity you. Those people—and a lot of them are in this very House—know you wouldn't have betrayed Lord Vir. The Illitheiens went to him on your behalf too."

"That's ridiculous. I'm sure Lord Vir finally got the truth from Lady Geyle, and that's the reason he's letting me out. Have you heard anything about me being kicked out of the House?"

"No, but Lord Vir wants you in his study. It's getting bad. Two more servants are dead from some illness. Three more dead citizens found on Guild Row. People outside of the House are screaming and chanting; they want Lord Vir to do something. The pressure's too much. Between the attack on you last night and whatever the Lady's done, he's decided to put out the order for the detainment of the marked."

Aren stopped in his tracks, causing Dane to stop as well. The Guard turned to look at them, and Aren gave him a nod to indicate that he could leave. "How long was I locked up? It couldn't have been more than ten, twenty minutes?"

The look of concern on Dane's face worried him. "It's been hours. It's early evening."

Aren attempted to replay his conversation with Lord Hraf in his head. It wasn't that long, was it? Had he been asleep? Had it been a dream? Unsure what to think, he closed his eyes, pinching the bridge of his nose.

"Selina says they're calling you again."

"I felt a little safer in the dungeon," Aren said by way of confirmation. They walked in silence for a while before he realized how self-absorbed he was being yet again. He put a hand on Dane's shoulder to stop him. "Rieka. Is she all right?"

"Rieka and Lady Geyle are locked up in Alaric's worship room. She's fine."

"I'm sorry."

"Selina had another vision," Dane said, his voice quieting. "Apparently, the gods think you can save Tiede. They mentioned you by name. Could be that's why Lord Vir let you out."

NINE

Taia stared at Kaila with contempt. "Aalae is seething. She wants us to fulfill our promise and send Tanghi back to help stave off the mages until they can get the Priestesses out."

Alaric ignored her and asked, "What's going on in Tiede?"

Tanghi took a seat next to Kaila. "One of my Guardians is with Tiede's Hunters, looking for the beast. The other Guardian Kaila mentioned is in the House." He held up three fingers, then looked at her. "You mentioned three, but those are the only two I found working directly with the House."

Kaila shrugged, hoping she looked more nonchalant than she felt. Her heart was hammering at the thought of Aren. "Three young men fought together and addressed each other as brother."

Tanghi thought for a moment, then brightened. "I know who you mean now. He's not a Guardian, but the blacksmiths adopted him into their family when he was a child. He's not blessed; don't know much about him."

"As long as he's protecting Vir, I don't care if he's blessed or not," Alaric said, writing on the parchment laid out before him. "Return to Tiede. I'll stall Aalae as long as I can."

"Do something with me." Kaila wanted to beg, but she kept her tone even. "Send one of us to Trum and the other to Tiede. I can watch just as well as Tanghi."

Alaric only raised an eyebrow, indicating that it was a ridiculous request. He continued with his writing, and Tanghi returned to the hearth and disappeared into the flames.

Frustrated, Kaila explored the bookcases behind Alaric's desk, her fingers skimming over the spines. If she found more information on symbols, Selina could pass the message on to Aren. The connection she had made with the little Priestess was proving more beneficial than she could have imagined, and she was going to use it to keep Aren safe.

"What are you looking for?" Taia asked suspiciously.

"Books on symbols or marks. The creature had them along its shoulder, and since I'm not doing anything, I wanted to see if I could find some information."

"Anything with the capability to use magic bears marks." Taia sounded annoyed, but a look from Alaric forced her to move. She pulled out a book and flipped through it until she found what she was looking for. She pointed at the diagrams. "Mage with the silver marks, angels with marks carved into their horns, demons with marks covering their bodies." Kaila's eyes flashed to Alaric, then back to the book. "Even plants have marks." Taia's finger moved to an image of a leindra leaf swirled through with faint silver scrollwork.

"May I?" Kaila asked, and Taia dropped the book into her hands. She took a seat by the fireplace, skimming over the pages. There was a fair amount of information collected on the marks, but she had to figure out what would be most useful to Aren. She was so absorbed in reading that she didn't notice Alaric until he was sitting next to her. He leaned closer so he could see what she was reading.

"Marks are like spells," he said. "They redirect or subdue magic, give the bearer certain gifts. Under my father's realm, Tanghi was responsible for weaving those marks and spells onto the angels and demons. He's the one who wove them into my demon side."

Kaila frowned. "Then he should have the ability to unweave."

"It doesn't work that way. It's similar to the way the Priestesses are marked. Each being has a predetermined design, and I am no different. Tanghi made that design visible or accessible. He doesn't create them out of his own mind."

"But marks are different from symbols—like the symbols I saw on the creature."

"Magecraft," he said. "They're not inherent to the creature's essence. The symbols could be controls so that whatever summoned the beast could tame it."

"So if we could find out who summoned the monster…"

Taia strode over, a long, slender length of paper woven through her fingers like ribbon. She looked down at Kaila and said, "Once the summoner dies, the beast is free to do as it pleases. In fact, the summoner's death might provide vast quantities of power to the beast. In magecraft, blood and death give power."

"It's all right, darling," Alaric said, squeezing her hand. "Keep thinking; every idea leads to another."

She nodded as he stood up and returned to his desk with Taia close behind him. If only she could return to Tiede. Everything pointed back to Aren. She traced the outline of the eight-pointed star, symbolic of balance and harmony, adopted by the Fighters Guild to mark their successful initiates. She recalled the small star on Aren's deltoid, the sharp black points vivid against his smooth, tawny skin. She closed the book and stood up. "May I return to my chambers?"

"Yes, but don't stay away too long. I might need you nearby if Aalae decides to summon," Alaric said, glancing up from his work.

She nodded, then left to contact Selina.

TEN

Two more dead Guards were in the courtyard, and dozens more wounded outside. Vir stood in the middle of the courtyard, his wife conspicuously absent, as everyone in the House, from servant to Priestess to guest to Guard to Hunter, was ordered to congregate to listen to the House Lord speak. Aren and Dane, sweaty and just a little more banged up than before, stood close to Elder.

"I will not tolerate another attack like this in my House!" Vir cried out so all could hear him.

Moments ago, a mage had blasted her way into the House after attacking the protesting people outside. She had made it only as far as the courtyard when Aren and Dane ran into her. She sent volleys of magic at them, and they took cover behind the fountain. The distraction had given a Hunter enough time to get close enough to take her down, sending a blade into her heart.

"To that end," Vir continued, "I must ask you to trust me. Elder Tanda, Counselor Helmun, and House Priestess Min will be checking every single person assigned to this House for the marks. Anyone who requests entrance into this House will be checked as well. As you all know, the detainment of the marked has already begun. Anyone in this House who bears the marks will be asked to stay in Alaric's room until this threat passes."

This comment elicited some argument and frustrated responses.

Vir put up a hand for silence. "My wife is subject to the same rule and has already been moved to the worship room, along with Counselor Darc's daughter, Lady Rieka. I would not ask this of you if I didn't think it was for everyone's safety, and I assure you that they and you will remain comfortable." Then he said in a quiet voice, "Thank you," before walking away towards his study.

Elder rapped his staff against the stones to get everyone's attention, then Helmun began to speak on the details of Vir's plan. Elder herded Aren and Dane towards the Library. "Dane, see if Fighter Gryf and the Hunters have had any luck finding the creature. Aren, back to work. Time is not on your side. I just received word that someone smuggled some kind of pill or potion into the dungeons where the big mage was locked up. He's dead."

Aren felt his gut knot. He was hoping that Copen wouldn't die because of whatever he did to him, but it still didn't feel good to know that he was ultimately poisoned.

"And Lady Geyle?" Aren asked.

"She told Lord Vir everything." Elder let out a sigh that seemed to deflate him of his energy. "She wasn't trying to poison him as her actions would suggest. All that aside, he's still very sick, and the doctors are concerned."

"I never believed she would hurt him," Aren said by way of an apology.

"You took a chance, but your faith in people is naïve. You need to start seeing the darkness that exists in everyone," Elder said. Aren and Dane bowed to Elder, then clasped each other on the upper arm in the way of the Fighter before parting.

Aren opened his notebook, refilled his pen, and grabbed a few sheets of flat parchment. He breathed in, letting the air fill his lungs, relax his muscles. Then he began to redraw the symbols. According to the messages that Selina had "relayed from the gods" while he was in the dungeon, the marks were important, and he had to connect the marks to the summoner. What was he supposed to do? Check every mark on every person being detained? It was ridiculous.

He would concentrate on the leaf. The leaf was what had given him a bad feeling before, and it was part of the message that Selina had conveyed. He scribbled *apple, nightshade, holly, elder, aspen, iris, sage,* and *tansy*—the plants that Selina had recited. Then, he went to Elder's desk and dug out the book on plants that Geyle had been reading.

He started with the apple. Often left as food offerings for the dead. The leaf was too slender. Nightshade: mostly toxic, but it did have medicinal value. He looked at the illustrations of berries, roots, and leaves. The leaves were too wide. Holly. Aren thought all holly had barbed leaves, but the illustrations proved him wrong. The echols variety had small, slender leaves. Holly symbolized truth and hope. He marked it as a potential candidate.

Aren pinched the bridge of his nose, then reached into his drawer to pull out the cup of coffee he had hidden there that morning. He sniffed it, then swirled it around. Shrugging, he took a gulp, then made a face. Only five more to go, he told himself, looking at his list. What if these were just suggestions? With the myriad of plants out there, this could take forever. But who was he to question the suggestions of a god? He laughed to himself. When had his life become so strange? At least his headaches had dulled to a pounding sensation at the base of his skull.

The Library doors opened, and he looked up to see Valine gliding towards him, her elegant, dove-gray gown sweeping the floor behind her. He stood up and inclined his head. "I was hoping to find you here," she said in her smoky voice.

"Is there something I can help you with?" he asked, pulling Elder's chair out for her.

"I just wanted to see for myself that you were unharmed, but you seem to be a little bloodied." She took a seat and gazed straight into his eyes.

"My brother and I served as bait for the mage attack a little while ago." He grimaced. "I'm fine, though; thank you for asking."

"You are full of trouble. First, I heard you were attacked last night. Today, my father and I learned that you had been locked up, and we went to Vir on your behalf."

"I appreciate it, but I believed that Lord Vir would do the right thing."

"You're so naïve." She laughed a little. "Please, sit down. I don't like having to look up at you, dear." He did as she asked, and she continued, "Vir is Tiedan to the core, and Tiede blood is ruthless and rash. You can't live your life assuming the best in people."

"Maybe I am naïve. I've been told it enough times, but there are some things that I'm willing to be stubborn about."

"The copper and bones rolled in your favor. Still, you take too many chances, and you need to understand that Vir's mind was changed partially because he doesn't wish to make an enemy of Illithe. It's bad enough that he's decided to detain the marked."

"I don't dare flatter myself to think that Illithe would think me in such high regard." He was taking a chance in saying it, but he wanted to put it out there.

She leaned back in her chair and crossed her legs. "Go ahead and flatter yourself. The gods are in communication with Selina and have called you out by name—you, an Unblessed. The gods haven't had much to do with the Sacred Houses in years. Illithe isn't foolish; we'll side with the gods and whomever they chose." Aren was silent, not knowing what to say, so she continued. "I'm curious as to why the gods would call on you to save Tiede."

"Shouldn't you be more curious as to whether or not Selina has gone mad?" he asked. "In the past few days, that little girl has seen people die, was called to be a Priestess, and watched her big brother get beaten up. Gods communicating through her almost seems normal after all that."

"If you believe in that sort of thing," Valine added for him.

"If you believe," he repeated, his mind wandering towards the leaf again.

"And do you?"

"My Lady, the gods have had nothing to do with me."

"Maybe they're making up for it now." She smiled and stood up, and he followed her lead. "In Illithe, the elders have a saying, 'Sometimes, even the gods need to borrow oil from the mortals to light the stars.'"

"What does it mean?"

"It means that sometimes the gods need us almost as much as we need them, and it's beginning to sound like they need you—blessed or not." She reached for his hand and squeezed it. "I'll let you get back to work."

Aren watched her leave, curious about the whole exchange. He wasn't sure what to think of Valine. There was a mysteriousness to her that made him wonder if he could trust her. He did, however, like her father. The old man seemed so far off the deep end that it made Aren laugh inside.

He sat back down at his desk and tried to refocus, studying his leaf drawing again. Had he gotten it right? He took his pen and redrew the lines, going over them, adding bits of shading. The parchment swallowed the ink, and he let his hand do what it would, falling into his self-imposed hypnosis.

Remembering the man-bear-tree-god in Tiede Wood, he shuddered. He remembered the winds, fumbling for his knife, and the violent swirl of leaves. A leaf from Tiede Wood or a leaf carried on the wind from a faraway place? The pen loosened in his hand, and he found himself dragging out the petiole. It curled and whipped and wrapped and…

Aren froze. "The gods need us," he whispered to himself. He scribbled the Illitheien quote Lady Valine had shared with him.

Sometimes, even the gods need to borrow oil from the mortals to light the stars.

"Oil," Aren breathed, rising to his feet, pushing back his chair. He dropped his pen and grabbed his keys. It was already dark, so he had to hurry. He had to know if his eyes had shown him the truth.

ELEVEN

Aren watched the upper window of Wethern's Oil & Torch Shop from across the street. He should've acted on his suspicions at the beginning. If he had been wrong, no real harm done; it wouldn't have been the first time he looked like a fool, and it certainly wouldn't have been the last. He crossed the deserted street and walked up to the shop. Like last time, it was closed earlier than usual. He rang the bell, wondered if it sounded hesitant, then rang it again with more force. He stepped back into the light of the streetlamp so that Tun could get a good look at him.

The curtains of the upper window parted, and Tun's big head peeked out. Aren managed a smile and held his hand up in greeting. Tun made an effort of removing the frown from his face, then motioned that he'd be down in a minute.

That's odd, Aren thought. *Where'd my headache go?* He pinched the bridge of his nose, wondering if the headache was just stuck, lodged somewhere. Then, the three locks clicked and the door creaked open.

Tun stood in the doorframe scowling. "What does the House want now?"

"Oil, obviously." Aren shrugged. "May I come in? Lord Vir's using it up faster than usual. He's so sick that he ends up falling asleep at his desk, and all the lamps are burning. Then, he wakes up, realizes he still has a lot of work to do, so the lamps continue to burn. It's been chaos in the House." He wondered if he was talking too fast, or if he sounded nervous. "He hasn't bothered with electricity in some of the rooms, what with the devotion to the Fire god." They stared at each other for a few seconds, then Aren said, "I'm glad the state of my beaten face doesn't repulse you."

Tun moved back into the store, leaving the door open for him to follow, and like before, Tun lit a small lamp filled with rose-colored oil. Aren watched the light grow, pushing away the darkness and revealing white incense trails. The shop smelled of wood, perfumed flowers, and noxious smoke. He coughed and felt like he was suffocating.

"Something wrong, Apprentice?" Tun asked in his gargley voice.

Aren shook his head, wanting to vomit. "I'm allergic to incense," he said, hoping it sounded like a joke. Tun didn't laugh. "I hope you have some House oil left. I know we've been rather demanding."

Tun didn't say anything. He moved to the storeroom, and Aren looked around, searching for signs that something was out of place. He grabbed the matches that Tun had left on the counter, struck one with a flick of his thumbnail, then proceeded to light a candelabra display.

"Elder wants me to buy candles too," he called out. He moved around the store, lighting several more candles. "I might buy a few for myself. Maybe a little romantic lighting will help me win over this girl I like."

Tun's large head peeked from out of the storeroom, and his eyes widened to the size of dinner plates. "What are you doing?"

The store was brighter, but the shadows cast from the dancing lights were eerie. Aren said, "Wethern told me the items on display are for testing—try it out, see if it's what you really want, that sort of thing. He's especially lenient when it comes to the House." Aren weaved his way around the various lamps and torches, his eyes scanning the walls and floors. "How do you not cough up a lung? You've got enough incense burning to hide a rotting corpse."

Tun narrowed his eyes, then ducked back into the storeroom. "I didn't think the House would use so much oil. Maybe someone is taking from the crates I delivered specifically for Lord Tiede."

"Lord Vir doesn't stop," Aren said, noticing a tall, misshapen stick up against the far wall next to the doorway leading into Wethern's living area. A staff. Wonderful. "Tiede blood is powerful. In the stories, the Night god suckled the first Lords and Ladies of Tiede with the blood from his finger." Aren picked up the staff and noted the strange symbols that ran along the length of it. "It's said that those of Tiede blood don't need to sleep and can see in the dark because of Alaric's gifts."

"Stupid stories," Tun grunted from the storeroom, "about ridiculous gods."

Aren walked back towards the middle of the store, staff in hand. "I love a good story." Tun came out of the storeroom carrying two flasks. When he saw Aren holding the staff, he froze. "I'd like to hear yours, if you've got a minute. I'll help you start; children's stories have the best introductions. 'In times untold...'" Aren indicated that Tun should continue.

Tun put the flasks on the counter and stared hard at Aren. His breathing was labored, drowning. "If you've something to say, go on and say it."

"You want me to tell it? I'll try but I don't know it as well as you do." Aren cleared his throat. "In times untold, there was a mage from Pren-Holder who came upon the great House of Tiede. All across Cordelacht, the mages were beginning to rise against the gods. The mage from Pren-Holder was given the mission to kill Lord Vir, but it would be difficult because he's well protected. Several plans had to be put in motion, and a slow poison would be perfect. Let it work in the background while everyone is focused on the chaos." Aren paused for effect, then acted as though he had just had a revelation. "Ah, that's where the oil comes in!"

Tun folded his arms across his wide chest, his head bobbling a little. "You read too many stories."

Aren walked over to another set of candles on display and made a show of lighting them. The lights pushed back the shadows, throwing them against the walls. "So much is revealed in the light; makes it difficult to keep secrets." He raised an eyebrow at Tun. "You are marked, aren't you? Otherwise, what need would you have for this?"

Tun's eyes darted from the staff to Aren and back again. "I need it to walk."

Aren made a show of examining the symbols on the staff's dark wood. "There's no oil shortage, is there? I was stupid for believing that story. You were stalling in order to poison the House oil."

"Give me the staff." Tun held out a hand.

"I'm not that dense; I know what a mage can do with a staff. I've seen what Horin did, what that woman did just a few hours ago. Did your friend Mercer tell you that Copen's dead? You were all in this together, weren't you? Now, tell me who summoned the monster."

Tun gargled his words. "You're in no position to give me orders, boy!"

"Really?" Aren cocked his head, then pointed at the staff. "But I have this. Now stop talking to me like I'm an imbecile, and tell me the truth. You've been poisoning Lord Vir, and you know about the monster. Then, there's the leaf."

"The leaf," Tun said flatly. "What are you talking about?"

"The one inked onto your arm," Aren said, pointing with his free hand. There was a curling line there, peeking from under the edge of the loose sleeve. "I don't think you really understand the meaning behind it."

Tun stared at him, then slid his sleeve up. Aren flinched. There was the petiole, curling and winding this way and that; then the blade, slender and shadowed, laced with veins. Aren was surprised that he had been right, and he gazed at it, mesmerized and haunted by the image of it.

He still had no idea what kind of plant it came from.

Aren was in such a daze, he didn't see it coming and barely managed to dodge the flask of oil that Tun threw at him. It crashed into a display, spilling oil everywhere. The glass hit a candelabra and the oil caught fire.

"Still feel like playing?" Tun yelled, throwing the second flask. This time, Aren struck it away with the staff, but the splattered oil only added to the fire, causing bursts of flames to erupt around him.

Aren pushed over the displays, letting candles and boxes fall to the floor. He needed room; he needed a barrier from the fire. Stars, he hoped he wasn't going to die here. If he did, Dane would be really pissed off.

Tun grabbed the smaller vials that lined the wall behind the counter, throwing them without even bothering to look. Aren was able to dodge a few and deflect several others with the staff; a handful connected with his blocking arm, and he winced at the pain.

The growing fire now blocked the way out. Aren changed directions, moving towards the doorway that led to the living area. He needed to find another exit fast. There was a crashing noise behind him, and he heard Tun's large frame push through overturned tables. There was a roar of pain, and Aren looked back to see him trying to put out the fire that had caught on his pants. Aren pulled down more boxes and cases before crossing into the living quarters.

He found himself in a dark, narrow hallway that continued to his left and right. Just ahead was a staircase. He was sure the only way out the second floor was going to be through a window, and he didn't have a good feeling about how that landing would turn out.

"Give me the staff!" Tun yelled, throwing a box of glass tealight holders. It hit the back of Aren's head with a resounding thud, and he was propelled into the staircase railing, falling head first into it. He pushed himself up with a grunt and ran his tongue over the new cut on his lip, tasting the blood in his mouth. He was getting really tired of that flavor.

Aren passed what he guessed was a coat closet and ignored it, focusing on the doors to two different rooms at the end of the hall. He opened the first and found a washroom. With a curse, he closed it and tried the next. It looked to be a parlor. He entered, closed the door, then began to move the furniture to block it. It might stop Tun for a minute or two. From the hallway, Tun bellowed like a gree in labor.

Aren scanned the room. There was a large stone fireplace against one wall with bookshelves crammed with odds and ends on either side. The wall to the right revealed the only other door in the room. He stumbled past the love seat, hoping that this door didn't open into a closet. He pushed down on the handle, but it didn't budge. There was a banging on the other door, and he turned to see the armchair, ottoman, and console table rattling.

"Tiede Vir is a dead man!" Tun bellowed from the hallway. "But I'm going to kill you first!"

Aren wanted to respond but bit his tongue. This wasn't the time for witty repartee. Tun began to throw himself at the door.

Aren twirled the staff in the same manner he'd learned to use the staff-like *clai'bo* weapon, but it was slick with oil and he ended up dropping it. He cursed, picked it up, then swung it over his head and brought it crashing down on the door handle. Tun shrieked, then slammed himself even harder against the blockade.

Aren wiggled the door latch; it wasn't as strong as the hardware in the House. He wiped the staff against his shirt, raised it again, then brought it down harder. The handle came off, and he fumbled with the locking mechanism. He pushed the door open and closed it behind him when his nose was assaulted by the stench of waste, blood, smoke, and bile. He fought the urge to leave, and he clasped his free hand against his nose and mouth to keep from throwing up.

The room was lit by dying candles, dozens of them filling up the spaces on shelves, set up in random clusters on the floor. In the middle of the room, spread out on the charcoal-gray carpet, was Wethern Duv, his eye sockets empty, his face bloody and beaten. His limbs were broken, arranged at odd angles from his body, and where his feet should've been there were bloody, bandaged stumps. The strange leaf symbol had been carved onto his torso, a violent red against the pale gray of his skin. Aren stared in horror.

"Wethern…" Aren felt the name leave his lips, but he couldn't quite link the word with the thing laid out before him.

"Who?" Wethern's voice was so weak, Aren thought he had imagined the sound.

"You're alive?" Aren was so overcome with surprise that despite his initial repulsion, he knelt beside the man's body. "Stars, how are you alive?"

"Aren?"

"I've got to get you out of here."

"Just kill me," his lips barely moved.

There was a crash on the other side of the door, and he knew that Tun had made it through. Aren bolted towards the door and jammed the bottom of the staff into the space between door and floor. Then, he glanced around the room to look for something to block it, but found nothing.

He peered through the hole where the door handle used to be and saw Tun massaging his shoulder, bent over in pain. Then, Tun picked up a poker from the fireplace.

Aren cursed under his breath. "Think, think, think!" he growled, taking inventory of his surroundings: staff, candles, and a near-dead man. Wonderful.

The heavy iron poker thumped against the door three times, then Tun said, "Congratulations, boy. You've found my Goat. Now open the door so I can smash your head in."

"That sounds appealing," Aren called back. "Let me think on it."

Tun kicked the door and Aren gripped the staff hard, determined to come up with a way to get himself and Wethern out of this alive. There was a splintering sound as the door was kicked again. It wasn't going to hold.

"You're only making me mad! Open the—"

A deep booming noise interrupted him. They were silent for a moment, then the building rumbled.

Aren looked up at the ceiling. "The second floor is going to collapse," he said. "We're all going to die here!" There was another rumbling boom as the fire hit the storeroom. The building creaked, and there was a thunderous crash in the direction of the storefront.

"I'm not leaving without tearing your limbs apart!" Tun kicked the door again, and this time it buckled in its frame.

Aren lost his leverage and stumbled backwards as Tun came through and swung the poker at him. Aren fell to the floor, extinguishing a few candles with his body, but managed to bring the staff up with both hands to block the blow. Tun swung again, and Aren held the block, managing to pull his knee in and send his boot into Tun's groin. Tun clutched at himself, and Aren swung the staff around fast, aiming for his knees. Tun dropped a little, still holding his groin, and Aren's attack ended up connecting with the side of Tun's massive thigh. Tun roared in pain, but he made a grab at the staff, managing to hold onto it with one meaty hand.

Aren gripped the staff, knowing that it was the only weapon he had. He wrestled for it, pulling and twisting, but Tun's hand seemed to meld with it, despite its slickness, as if it were an extension of himself. Aren watched in frustration as Tun's shoulders began to glow under the fabric of his shirt. The symbols on the staff began to pulse its red light.

"I'm going to kill you for killing my brother," Tun growled. "How dare you keep his staff as a trophy!"

Aren was incredulous. "That was your brother? I didn't kill him; a unicorn did!" Why did everything that came out of his mouth sound ridiculous?

There was an explosion, and for a second Aren thought Tun had blasted him full of magic, but it was the sound of the second floor as it continued to collapse. The noise made Tun falter, and the crimson lights receded.

"Help," Aren breathed, and in his mind flashed images of the House, the city glowing at night, the sea in the morning light, Lake, his family, Selina. "Help…"

Tun's magic recovered and the staff began to pulse again. Aren could feel the power of it vibrating under his fingertips. *This is it*, he thought.

Tun grinned.

CONSEQUENCES

ONE

Eight Hunters and Gryf had tracked and fought the monster on the main road outside of the industrial district, and by the time it disappeared in a trail of smoke, six Hunters had been seriously injured. They returned to the House to regroup and tend to their wounds. They had worn the monster down, learned how it moved, how it could summon a sword out of thin air and generate a shield around itself. Now, they had to prepare to defend the House. The monster was going to recharge its magic, and when it did, it would likely go after Vir.

Gryf's twin swords had been scattered across the gravel road, and he picked them up, looking them over in the biolight. Once this fiasco was over, he'd spend a whole day cleaning his weapons. Then, he'd find time to get to the House and force Aren to do more sparring. He had forgotten how predictable Aren was in a fight, and how much chaos his little brother seemed to attract.

Gryf shook his head, recalling the brief conversation he had had with Hunter Illana as they converged on the monster's location. She had run into Aren before the hunt, and Aren was rambling on about Lady Illithe, the gods, and oil. Illana said Aren ran from the House as if he were being chased by demons. Gryf hoped that Dane was with him.

A sound like thunder caused Gryf to flinch, and he felt his skin prickle. He frowned, his eyes scanning the area and finding nothing. He looked up and noted a few ghost-like clouds. No rains. Then, the sky towards the west, in the direction of Crescent Park, began to glow orange, and black smoke rose like wraiths escaping the confines of Aum.

"Fire," Gryf heard himself say. Then, a sensation like ice water ran down his spine. "Aren."

He ran towards the nearest stables, borrowed a gree, then took off towards the western districts. When he arrived at the scene, a fire had consumed an entire storefront, the oil shop, and he couldn't see any way in. People were gathering in the streets, panicking, staring, doing nothing useful.

Gryf pointed to the man closest to him. "Get Fire-Control and Regulators. Have them block off this area." Then, he pointed to another bystander. "Get on a lark or find a messenger. Get word to the House to have the doctor standing by. The Historian's Apprentice might need medical attention."

Another citizen, who had snapped out of the trance of the fire, began to knock on nearby doors, telling people to evacuate. Satisfied, Gryf ran west towards the first alley, then turned and headed towards the back end of the block of buildings. He found the door that corresponded to the shop, jumped over the low wall, then kicked in the door. The kitchen was full of smoke, and he crouched low, allowing his eyes to adjust to the hazy lighting. "Aren!" he called out.

He headed into the hallway, where the smoke was thicker. He began to cough, then peeled off his black body armor, holding it over his nose and mouth. His eyes watered, but he took a step forward. There was an explosion and he ducked. The heat was intense and sweat poured down his face. The storefront was just to his left, and tongues of flames lashed out into the hall. There was a staircase to his right, but if Aren had gone up there...

Gryf stood frozen for a moment, thinking. The safest place, aside from the kitchen, was the other end of the hall, and he prayed to the Fire god to spare his brother's life. As if in response to his prayers, Gryf heard the sounds of a struggle, metal against wood, yelling. He rushed down the hall, past the open doors of a coat closet and washroom, and into a parlor. The door was cracked in places, and furniture had been moved and kicked. Aren was here.

The smoke was getting worse, so he had to act fast. He noticed the second door, awkward in its frame, its handle missing. He ran towards the room and saw the burn of red light through the smoky haze. He wiped a hand across his face to focus on the figures on the floor: one prone, its limbs not quite right, too short to be Aren. Two more, struggling over a glowing staff.

A man with a large head held the staff in one hand, his shoulders alight with the silver telltale signs of the magic wielder. He was charged and ready to loose a stream of magic right at Aren, who was gripping the staff with a twisted determination.

Let go, Aren! Gryf thought. *Damn it, let go and find cover!*

Gryf dropped his makeshift mask and unsheathed his swords, ready to rid the mage of his whopping skull problem. They hadn't seen him come in, and he lifted his blades for the strike.

"Meina Tiede gala gin mei!" Aren roared, his eyes seeming to look off into another world.

Gryf dropped to his knee as his arm shielded his eyes from the strange green light that filled the room, throwing the large man back several feet. Aren stood up, unaffected by the blast and looking possessed. He held the staff out with one hand, and the red light receded, replaced with a soft green glow.

"Keip tei ga jei," Aren growled, taking slow, confident steps towards the mage.

The mage was shaking his head, and Gryf didn't know if it was because of the hit he had taken or because he didn't know who Aren was anymore. Gryf wasn't quite sure who Aren was right now, and that sent all sorts of warning messages through his brain.

"Aren!" Gryf called out. "Aren, it's me, Gryf!"

Aren stopped, then turned towards him. Gryf stood up, holding his swords out in front of him as if in surrender. The clouds seemed to disappear from Aren's eyes, and he said, "Gryf? What're you—?"

Gryf sheathed one of his swords as he eyed the mage, who was getting to his feet. Gryf had had enough of magic. He strode towards the mage, slammed him against the wall, and pressed a blade to his throat. "My brother's enemy is my own," he growled, the sword's edge causing a fine line of bright red to blossom at the mage's neck. Gods, he wanted to kill him for what he had done to Aren.

"He's been poisoning Lord Vir," Aren said, putting a hand on Gryf's shoulder. His voice was cloudy, unsure. "We need to take him to the House."

Gryf paused to consider, then plunged the sword in just above the mage's knee, causing the man to scream. When he pulled it out, the mage cried again, collapsing onto the ground. He sheathed his sword and looked at Aren. "We need to move. We're going to die from breathing this smoke if the building doesn't collapse on us first."

"There's also Wethern," Aren said, using the staff to point at the disfigured man on the floor.

"He's dead."

"Actually, he's not."

Gryf looked at the man again. His limbs looked like they had been broken days ago. He had no eyes, no feet, and he had been cut up. There were wounds that looked like they were infected, and the man had been burned in various places.

Gryf looked at Aren. "He's one breath away from death, and this smoke will kill him before we get him out the door. He's suffering. He's been suffering for days, it looks like."

"Kill me," the disfigured man rasped.

Gryf looked at him again, and the empty eye sockets seemed to plead with him. "May you return to the gods," Gryf whispered, and in the space of a breath he drew his blade and plunged it into the man's heart. Aren stared at Gryf, horrified. "We still have to drag the mage to the House," Gryf said. "Let's go."

TWO

Kaila spent the evening in her room, reading what the Night Realm had documented on the *istoq*, the planetary god, and mage-summoned creatures. Unfortunately, there was no useful information on the latter, which made her feel frustrated and helpless. She didn't know when the creature was planning to attack the House again, and she worried about Aren.

By Mahl, what spell did Aren weave to make her think of him so often? She thought about contacting Geir. It was said that before he was given flesh, he could remove memory. Maybe he could help her forget.

Kaila felt a thump in her chest; Alaric was summoning. She stood up, slipped her feet into a pair of aqua satin slippers, when a little girl's voice echoed through her head. *Goddess, I need your help.* It was the little Priestess.

Kaila sat on the edge of her bed, closed her eyes, and concentrated. Selina sounded so small and terrified, and Kaila had to fight the urge to rush to Tiede to find out what was going on.

A messenger came to the House with news. There's a big fire, and Aren might be hurt. I heard Aren calling for help. I heard him in my head, but I didn't know what to do. I tried to talk back to him, but then everything was dark. The Priestesses tried to wake me up, and they were fussing about something. I could hear them, but I couldn't wake up.

Kaila took a deep breath and talked to Selina in her mind. *Where are you now?*

Asleep. Somewhere in the House. I feel tired, like I was running a lot.

I'm going to ask my brother to check on Aren. Try not to worry.

Thank you, goddess, Selina whispered in Kaila's mind. *Please bring him home.*

Kaila opened her eyes and ran down the halls towards Alaric's study but found it empty. She paced the room in front of the fire blazing in the hearth, trying to think of a way to get to Tiede, but her mind could only conjure an image of Aren calling for help.

"What's got you so worked up, darling?" Alaric asked as he and Taia entered the room.

Kaila gasped, caught off guard. "Worried about Tanghi," she lied. "That creature is powerful, and we haven't heard from him yet."

Alaric was about to speak when Tanghi stepped out of the fireplace. Alaric smiled at her, then squeezed her shoulders. Taia went to Alaric's desk where she set down papers and opened up the heavy logbook.

"This generation of Guardians is my best yet." Tanghi was grinning. It meant Tiede was still standing, and Vir wasn't dead.

"The creature?" Alaric asked.

"Still alive, but from what I witnessed, if anyone can kill it, Gryf can. And, if a mortal kills it, we needn't worry about the *istoq.*" Tanghi took a seat, resting his elbows on his knees as he leaned forward. "There was also a fire in the southwest district; that made it easy for me to get in and take a look around. The boy the blacksmiths adopted found the mage that's been trying to kill Vir. That's why servants in the House have been dying and why Vir was so sick; the boy found out he was being poisoned. Anyway, the mage tried to kill the boy, but Gryf showed up."

Kaila tried to look as disinterested as possible while still maintaining an air of concern regarding the situation as a whole. At least Aren was alive.

"They took the mage to the House for questioning, but no doubt Vir will have him executed." Tanghi looked thoughtful, and Kaila could see confusion flitting across his features. "There's something about the boy that strikes me as odd. The mage was one breath away from killing him, but in that final moment, the boy turned into something else."

Alaric frowned. "What do you mean? Not an actual transformation?"

"His eyes glazed over, and he began speaking in an old language I'd forgotten. When he spoke, the magic backfired on the mage."

"Is the boy marked?" Alaric asked.

"Other than the mark of a Fighter initiate, I saw nothing, let alone anything that would indicate any magical abilities."

Alaric turned to Kaila. "The boy he speaks of, did you see him when you were in Tiede?"

Kaila felt her cheeks flush. Could they see the truth on her face? That she had indeed seen this boy—naked, at that—and that he'd nearly kissed her? She pressed the tips of her fingers together. "Yes. Remember, I thought he was a Guardian as well? He was with his brothers defending Vir."

"He was raised by Guardian blood," Tanghi said. "He'll have been brought up well unless there's something else in his nature that would overpower that."

"The Unblessed," Taia interjected, nearly causing Kaila, who had forgotten that she was in the room, to jump. "They are as dandelions in the wind: of little consequence. Sometimes, mortals are able to channel energy when they are near death. It's not unheard of."

"When I was in Tiede," Kaila spoke up, "I overheard that the boy was researching symbols. I thought he might be on to something, which is why I was looking through your books. I thought I might find something to help Tanghi—"

"He's just a mortal with a small mind," Taia interjected again. "Tanghi says his Guardian can kill it. I don't know why we're bothering to discuss it."

Kaila faced her. "I fought that creature, and it's more powerful than you think! If it were really as simple as gutting it, it would be dead by now."

Taia huffed. "Obviously it's not just flesh and blood. We all know it uses magic. My point is that if Tanghi's people are wearing it down, at some point it'll run out of power."

"At what point is that?" Kaila challenged her. "Before or after it kills Vir?"

Alaric stood up and put a hand on Kaila's shoulder. "All right, that's enough." The women exchanged glares.

"Apologies, my Lord," Kaila said in a soft voice. "I'm still angry with myself for not finishing what I started. I really wish you would hear me out on this. It's going to take more than a sword to kill that monster."

Alaric looked to Taia, and Kaila watched as she rolled her eyes and slammed the logbook shut. He placed a kiss on Kaila's jaw. "Why don't you and Tanghi go for a walk, cool down a little. I think we all need some breathing room."

.

THREE

Aren followed two Guards, Lord Vir, Elder, and Counselors Darc and Helmun into the dungeon. As they made their way through the chilly corridors, Aren took note of the marked who were locked up, two or three to a cell, and one cell after another. For the most part, they looked terrified and helpless, and he tried not to look at their faces. He wondered how many of them were visited by Lord Hraf or another of Tiede's ghosts.

As they walked, the sounds of their shoes against the stone floors created a rhythmic pattern in Aren's head, punctuated by the thunk of Elder's staff at every measure. Aren slipped into a trancelike state, and it helped to dull the voices that had returned once he and Gryf had escaped from the fiery oil shop, dragging Tun behind them. He thought he could see the whispers of ghosts, their invisible trails made visible to his subconscious.

Vi hist aft, Aren heard the voice by his ear.

"I hope we're well met, Lord Hraf," Aren responded in Ancient. The party stopped, and everyone turned to look at him as he snapped out of his trance. "I was talking to myself," Aren stammered. After a moment, they continued down the corridor. Hraf was laughing so hard that Aren was tempted to yell at him to shut up, but he reminded himself that he was coming off like a lunatic as it was, and Tiede Hraf, while dead, was still a Lord of Tiede.

Vir spoke up, as if to normalize the journey. "I don't think it's a coincidence that the little Priestess woke up when you arrived, Apprentice. The Priestess Minor said the little girl said you needed help, was drained of color, then fell over."

"She worries excessively, and we seem to have some kind of connection," Aren replied from the back of the group. "Coincidence or not, I'm glad she's feeling better."

"The doctor says you escaped with some bad cuts and bruises, minor burns," Vir said. "But that seems to be the norm for you these days."

"I'm alive. I can't much complain about that."

"Not only are you alive," Darc broke in, "but you found the one responsible for trying to kill Lord Tiede. We owe you a great debt."

"It is my duty and my honor," Aren responded, as his siblings and parents had taught him. "As usual, the praise belongs to Gryf."

The Guards stopped in front of a room with a solid iron door with a small barred window. Vir nodded and the door was unlocked and opened. Each Guard lit one of the inner torches on either side of the door.

The cell was large, with chains that hung from the ceiling. Aren's eyes swept past the crude tables and instruments and stared at the far wall, where Tun was naked and chained, his limbs pulled so that he formed into an X. He had been beaten to a bloody mess, and it looked as though someone had given him a matching wound on the knee opposite the one Gryf had stabbed.

Helmun gagged, then ran out of the room to throw up.

"Did we learn anything from him?" Darc asked, as if he couldn't hear his colleague retching outside.

"He admitted to the poisoning," Elder said, "and to torturing Mister Wethern Duv. Fighter Gryf and the Apprentice have corroborated the latter part of the story. Unfortunately, too much was burned for us to learn anything more at the oil shop, but I'd say it was a mercy what the Fighter did."

"According to accounts from fire control, it wasn't just torture," Darc said.

"The Apprentice described it as a ritual," Vir said, his eyes studying the would-be assassin. Tun might have been staring at them, but it was hard to tell because one eye was swollen shut. "Is that right, Apprentice?"

Aren said, "My theory is he's the one who summoned that creature."

"The one we've lost track of," Darc said.

"I feel it's still enough to free the marked," Elder said. "Every piece of evidence points to this man."

"However," Helmun said as he reentered the room, his voice raspy, "we don't know for certain. We've already executed Horin. The mage that beat the Apprentice was killed, but there's at least one more the Apprentice claims is still out there. Then, there was the mage attack yesterday. We don't know which marked will attack next."

Darc said, "The ones who mean to do the House harm are in hiding."

"You want to free the marked because you have a personal interest, because your daughter is marked," Helmun said, keeping his eyes away from Tun.

"I know my daughter is innocent," Darc said, his voice steady. "I have no worries or fears where she is concerned. Perhaps the personal interest is yours." He fixed his eyes on Helmun. "It's hard to ignore the stories of how your wife favors young, marked men."

Aren cocked his head and raised his brows as he watched Helmun fluster.

"I've no intention of standing here and taking such abuse!" Helmun cried.

"You'll go nowhere, Counselor. We still have the matter of this mage to discuss," Vir said. "Do you have any argument, mage?" Vir asked Tun. "You can give us the answers we seek now or draw this out painfully. In either case, you'll die; it's only a matter of how much you want to suffer before you get there."

It was quiet, with the exception of the distant echoes of dripping water. As bloody and beat-up as he was, Aren wondered if Tun was even conscious. Then, the chains rattled a little, and Tun let out a cough as tangled as cobwebs.

"Question the mage under your own roof," Tun rasped, his less swollen eye glaring at Aren.

"Name these mages in my House," Vir ordered.

Tun snorted and blood dripped from his nose. "The pretty one next to you." All eyes turned to Aren while Tun's head rolled from side to side. "Did he tell you about his powers? How they bested mine? How he near killed me?"

Aren shook his head. "What powers? I—"

"He spoke magic," Tun accused. "Magic so powerful, I didn't understand it. Did you ever consider that he might be the one who summoned the creature?"

"I'm not marked. How would that make sense?"

"When did you come into your powers, mage?" Vir asked.

"Since a child," Tun breathed. "Parents died under Kaishar rule. I learned from other mages to help free Pren-Holder from the condescending god worshippers."

"And have you, in all your learning, ever heard of a mage without marks?" Vir asked.

Aren furrowed his brows as his memory churned through all the information he had read about mages. There was no such thing as an unmarked magic wielder.

Tun gurgled and blood and drool slipped out of his mouth. "Never."

"Nor have I," Vir said, turning to face the Counselors. "I'll order the interrogator to return this afternoon. We'll force an answer out of him sooner or later. He won't be allowed to die until we destroy that monster."

The Counselors bowed their heads and Vir made his way towards the cell door. They prepared to follow when Tun wheezed out a request. "Wait."

Everyone paused, but Vir didn't turn around.

Elder addressed Tun. "The time for bargaining is over. Did you summon the beast? How do we destroy it?" Tun was mumbling something in his phlegm-addled voice. Elder pounded his staff against the floor. "We can't hear you, mage."

Aren looked from Tun to Elder and back again. Tun didn't raise his voice; perhaps he couldn't. Aren strained to hear him, and in one ear Hraf whispered in Ancient, *Listen, boy.*

Aren murmured back, "He speaks in Old Magic!"

A'ars Tiede, Hraf ordered, his voice the growl of a wolf.

Adrenaline surged through Aren's body and he yelled out, "Cover!" as he moved to defend Vir. Instead of ducking, however, everyone looked at Aren, and no one noticed the scrolling leaf symbol animate, shooting its curling petiole out from Tun's arm.

Aren pushed both Counselors out of the way as he lunged forward. Darc stumbled but caught himself against one of the tables. Helmun hit his head against a wall and fell to the floor. Aren reached out to catch the lashing petiole before it could connect with Vir, and the plant caught on Aren's forearm, wrapping around it several times and dragging him towards Tun's sweating face.

"Guards!" Darc called out as he steadied himself and herded Elder and Vir out of the room.

Aren struggled, wrestling with what felt more like a vine than a leaf as it squeezed and pulled him against his will. He cursed as he reached for one of the chains that hung from the ceiling. He managed to grab one, but his grip didn't hold and he lost his balance, falling to the floor with a thud, making it easier for the plant to pull him.

The Guards came in and rushed to Aren's aid. One took a sword to the vine, but it wouldn't break. He struck again, without luck, then tried to pry the plant from Aren's arm.

The other Guard held a knife to Tun's throat, pushing his big face against the wall. "Release him!"

Aren grabbed at the vine with his free hand, let out a curse, then said, or thought he said, "*Tuin.*" The vine began to drain of color and loosed its hold. He pushed the twisting plant off his arm, then pushed the first Guard towards the exit. Aren called out, "Don't kill him. He has answers about the creature."

The second Guard nodded, let go of Tun's face, then moved, but as Aren turned to follow, the vine whipped back to life and flung itself at Helmun, who still hadn't gotten up. It wrapped around his neck, and he cried out as he was hurled towards Tun. It happened so fast that Aren didn't have time to think. He ran back to try to free the Counselor, but the vine tightened, and Aren heard a sickening crack as Helmun's neck was broken.

Aren stared, horrified as the vine-leaf thrust itself into Helmun's open mouth. The plant began to glow red, and Tun hung his head, a grin on his swollen face. When Helmun was nothing but a pale sack of bones, the vine retreated back to its owner.

Aren backed away, the signals from his brain to his muscles suffering from a serious disconnect. The second Guard, who had been standing by the door in a similar state, hit Aren in the arm to get him to move.

Tun raised his eyes, and he and Aren stared at each other. "I am the *Catar*, the final sacrifice. You'll never stop the beast now." Then, the red glow grew, the vines winding a pattern throughout his body. He chuckled, blood beginning to ooze from his lips. "*Catar cri covinen,*" he whispered.

Then, the vine pattern ripped the large-headed mage apart.

FOUR

Aren sat on the larger sofa in the sitting room that overlooked the sea. Selina's sleeping head was on his lap, and he stroked her hair as he stared out into the distance, where the Parthe Sea met the sky. His head was buzzing with symbols and long-forgotten words, images of death highlighted in red glowing lights. From his lips came a voice he felt detached from as he sang an old lullaby.

Sweet little child, close your eyes,
And dream of the stars in Alaric's skies.
If you lay awake and tearful,

The faeries of Tiede will come and steal you.

"What a horrible, frightening song," Nianni said from the chair close to the fireplace.

Aren smiled at her, then returned to his reverie.

I'll watch over you, my heart, in peaceful slumber.
Your wishes I'll turn into prayers.
In fire and water, your soul will find respite
Until death catches you unawares.

"You Tiedans are a morbid people," she interjected again. When Aren didn't respond, she added, "But you have a beautiful voice, considering how annoying you are. I didn't know you could sing."

"Thank you," he said at last. "Dane is the one with the voice, though."

Nianni seemed to perk up, eager for conversation. "Your singing got Selina to fall asleep, and that's enough for me. She was hysterical earlier. She said that you needed help, that she could hear you." She paused, as if reliving the events. "But you've heard this already."

There was a knock, and Aren looked over to see his brothers enter. They bowed their heads in greeting to Nianni, and she returned the gesture as she stood up.

"Are we interrupting?" Dane asked. He knelt down beside Selina, placing a hand on her head. Selina's eyes fluttered open, and she flopped her hand onto Dane's shoulder.

"Not at all," Nianni responded, refusing to make eye contact with Aren. "Let's go rest for a while, Selina. You can see the Apprentice again later."

Selina, too tired to argue, took Nianni's hand. She walked past Gryf, giving his leg a hug, then followed Nianni out of the room.

"Outside," Gryf said. Aren followed his brothers without question, and they leaned against the balcony's low wall, looking out at the sea, with Aren between them. "Elder told me what happened in the dungeons and asked if I knew what the mage was talking about. Something about accusing you of having powers."

"What happened to me at Wethern's?" Aren asked. "Tun sounded too confident to be lying, but it's ridiculous. I don't know magic, and I have no marks."

"When I found you, Tun had the upper hand. He was going to kill you, but you started speaking in some strange language. Whatever magic Tun was about to use on you got changed into something else."

Gryf's brows were furrowed, and he looked as though he didn't trust his own memory. "You were going to kill him."

Aren racked his brain, trying to find the memory, but without any luck. "Did you tell Elder?"

"No, just Dane," Gryf sighed, rubbing his eyes. "I told Elder that you and Tun were fighting for control of the staff, and maybe that's why Tun thought you were a mage. He seemed eager to accept that explanation. The Guards told me in confidence how you managed to break loose of the plant that attacked you in the dungeon. He said the vine had you but you said something and the plant loosened its grip."

"*Tuin*," Aren said, his throat feeling parched. "That's what I said, but the way it sounds right now isn't the way I said it." He narrowed his eyes as he stared at the horizon. "It means 'to drain or wither, to take energy from.' On its own, it has no power." He tumbled over his words as he tried to understand what had happened. "I can say it until I dry up and die, and it wouldn't do what it did to that vine."

Dane looked confused. "But it did."

"Because that's not quite what I said." Aren struggled to make sense of his own words. "Stars, I'm going mad." He looked at Gryf. "You can't keep this from Lord Vir. After that mess with Lady Geyle—"

"I'm not going to chance him locking you up again," Gryf said. "We don't need him to entertain the possibility that you have any kind of powers or that you could've summoned the creature."

"Of course I didn't! You're taking a big risk. If Lord Vir knew, he'd lock you up, and—"

"Aren," Dane interjected. "If they suspect that you have magic without being marked, they'll see you as a whole new threat."

Gryf grabbed Aren's forearm and held it between the three of them. "You are our brother. We protect you first."

FIVE

Aren read over his notes. He was running out of time. Every turn of the gears on the clock was one moment closer to an attack on Vir. Gryf and the Hunters were prowling the halls and rooms, waiting. Dane was also in the House visiting Rieka, and Aren felt terrible that they had to be kept apart. It made him think of Lake and how far away she was. He wanted to hold her, to see her smile. He wanted to talk about old books and stories, laugh until the sun began to peek over the horizon. He wanted to watch her as her eyes stared off into the heavens, her mind far away. He wanted to be the one to touch her, to bring her back home.

He reached into his drawer for his little box of stars, then spilled them onto his desk. He forced Lake out of his mind and returned to work, the fingers of his free hand fiddling with the paper stars. It was time to study plants again.

The tracing elder could be found all over northern Cordelacht, boasting clusters of tiny, white flowers. This particular type of elder plant had conflicting meanings. One reference said it symbolized a curse or revenge, but another book said it was used for protection. Then, there was the aspen. There were no aspens near Tiede, but Aren was intrigued by their meaning: fire, transformation, transcendence. This was probably not the plant he was looking for, but he'd mention it to Kel Bret and Lana. It might be nice to incorporate into a weapon design.

He skipped the iris just to narrow his list and looked up the sage. It symbolized wisdom and immortality. The leaf of the summer sage was close to the leaf he had seen on Tun, but not quite.

He sighed as he unscrewed his pen to refill it with ink. "Gods, if you're really listening, I appreciate the list of plants, but a few more hints would've been nice." He pulled an old, stained cloth from the box of pen supplies in his drawer and used it to wipe up any smeared ink. "I don't know if I'm supposed to eat these plants or shove them in the creature's eyeballs."

Next was tansy, one of the plants he had to hunt down for Elder years ago. The flowers looked like puffy, yellow buttons, and one of the herbalists told him it was wonderful for keeping flies away. Aren thought that the flies might also stay away if that particular herbalist stopped mixing up concoctions that smelled like gree shit. In any case, the leaves were all wrong. He crossed it off his list.

Aren picked up one of the paper stars, rolling it back and forth along his thumb and index finger. He continued to scribble his findings. Just one more: iris, a message. He flipped through Miss Genethew Farista's boring book and found page after page after page of iris. He dropped his head onto his desk with a thud. "The gods hate me," he muttered to himself as the Library door clicked and creaked. He guessed Dane was back from his visit with Rieka, and he hoped he was bringing a drink. He knew that the work was important, that the gods had placed the fate of Tiede in his hands, but why did it have to be plants?

He sat up. "If those cursed gods hadn't put the ridiculous idea in everyone's head that I'm supposed to come up with the answer to this mess, I wouldn't be here torturing my brain with illustrations and diagrams of leaves. Now I know they hate me."

"Every time you open your mouth, it's a blasphemy festival," Head Priestess Crina said as she walked up to him.

Aren cursed under his breath, then stood up, bowing his head in respect. "My apologies, Head Priestess. I thought you were my brother."

"It doesn't matter who you thought I was. The fact remains that you are a blasphemer," she said, weary and disappointed.

He straightened up, biting his tongue and putting on a smile. "Is there something I can help you with?"

"I'd like to talk." She took a seat, smoothing out the white chiffon of her dress. Then, she looked up at him with her severe, silver eyes. "It's regarding Selina. You are her guardian, even if it's not in any official capacity. It's plain to see whom she goes to for comfort, guidance, and protection. I still see you as an immature young man who has no business raising a little girl, never mind a Priestess; however, Elder Tanda has asked me to be patient with you."

"I see we're speaking plainly," Aren said, smoothing his hair back away from his eyes. "For the record, my sister Lana is Selina's legal guardian."

Crina ignored him. "Syrn believes Selina is very powerful and has a strong connection to the gods. We still don't know which god to align her to, but there's no doubt she must go to Syrn."

"If there's no doubt, and I have no business raising her, then why bother telling me? You'll do what you have to do regardless of how I feel."

If Crina was offended by his words, she didn't show it. "I'd rather we say what has to be said in private, instead of you making a fool of yourself in front of Lord Vir during the initiation ceremony."

"How kind of you," he said, not bothering to hide the sarcasm.

She gave him a hint of a smile. "I owe it to Elder. We've served together in this House for a very long time. Our respect for each other is mutual and deeply rooted." She cocked her head to the side, as if to examine him. "I'm not sure what he sees in you. I trust him but I don't see it."

"There's nothing to see. I'm devoted to my family and to the House. I'm nothing beyond that."

"Then let me say what I have to say, and we can move on with our lives. If the mages are rising again, Selina's ties to the gods make her a prime target. Once they find out about her, her life will be in danger. The sisterhood will protect her with their lives, and if you're as smart as Elder claims you are, then you know that Syrn is the safest place for her."

"According to legend, Syrn is a city built by the hands of the gods of both Night and Light," Aren said, leaning against his desk. "Walls that touch the skies. Syrites who believe their sole purpose is to serve the gods and to that end have taken up arms to protect the city at any cost. Priestesses gifted with forms of elemental power. Not even Tiede would dare challenge Syrn."

"Then, you see why Selina should go."

"She's safe with me too," he pointed out.

Crina looked like she would have laughed if she didn't think it was beneath her. "You have been at the center of battle with at least three mages in the past several days, not to mention that creature that still haunts our streets." She leaned forward in her chair. "I have never known a more dangerous young man to be associated with in my life, and I have lived a very long life, Apprentice."

Aren folded his arms across his chest, feeling defensive. "Then you haven't known very many young men. Besides, I'd never let anything happen to her. She's safer with me than the likes of you."

The Priestess's eyes blazed as if she'd been challenged. "Is that so?" she asked, her voice soft.

Aren was about to come back with a witty retort but then noticed the edge of his vision begin to go dark. "What are you doing to me?" he asked, his hands gripping the desk. The color was draining from his surroundings, everything beginning to blur. He tried to remain calm, but his heart was pounding in his chest. He was going blind and was on the verge of panicking.

"It's paralyzing when you lose one of your senses," Crina said, her voice no longer in front of him. His arms reached out as if trying to catch her. "I'm promised to Alaric, and this was his gift to me. Not all Priestesses come into their powers, and for the ones that do, it requires years of devotion and patience." Her voice was moving, and he could hear the rustle of her chiffon gown.

"That's wonderful," he said, his arms still flailing. "Now, please give me back my sight."

"What do you need it for? There's so much to learn from darkness."

He put his hands down, holding onto the desk, afraid that he'd fall over. "Lesson learned, Priestess. If you're trying to show me how well protected Selina will be, I get it." Light began to fill his eyes, bright and near blinding. It stung, and he squeezed his eyes shut, almost wanting the darkness back. He blinked, and his head swam, his surroundings saturating with color. Crina sat as if she hadn't moved. "Thank you," he said at last, more out of courtesy than actual gratitude.

"I told you that we wait years before we are gifted, but Selina is already blessed."

"In what capacity and by which god?" he asked, blinking a few more times.

"I admit I don't know, but she communicates directly with the gods, particularly the Water goddess." Crina stood up and took a step towards him. "Apprentice, if the mages find out about her, they will kill her. I just want you to understand why she must go to Syrn."

Aren sighed. Her logic was sound, and deep down he knew that the Priestesses could give Selina a life that he never could. With the Priestesses, she would live almost as well as the House Lords and Ladies. She might even be able to find out where she came from.

"By the expression on your face, I can tell you agree. I'll let you carry on with your work since everyone is depending on you. Strange how all our lives changed when you and Selina returned from your fishing expedition."

Aren didn't look at her, didn't watch her leave. He waited for the door to creak and the latches to catch. Then he slumped back into his chair, feeling drained and defeated. Had he heard the Priestess right? Elder told her he was smart? Aren chuckled, wondering what Elder had been drinking when he said it. He returned to his notebook. This wasn't the time to worry about Priestesses. He could do that after the creature was dead.

He picked up his pen and riffled through the boring *Herbs and Potions* until he got to the section on the iris. He selected a random page, then began to sketch the flower into his notebook, copying the diagrams and adding his own lines and shading. He wrote a line beneath it about how the iris symbolized a message. Then, he flipped back to the pictures of aspens.

He propped up his head with one hand and let his mind wander as he began to sketch the leaves of a fire aspen. The shape of it, so similar to a flame, intrigued him. He put down his pen and thumbed through a few more pages and learned that great clusters of fire aspen could be found northwest of Kaishar, northeast of Aum, and west of Syrn. He wondered how he'd never heard of this tree before, considering his family's strong ties to the Fire god. He was getting distracted, but he couldn't help himself. He leaned back in his chair and continued to read.

Aspens were renowned for lying dormant and sending off their shoots underground, waiting for the right moment to reemerge. A large stand of fire aspens had once been near Tiede, northeast of the River Taethe, but a strange disease had killed them off long ago and they never returned. Arboriculturalists had found the Tiede root colony, determined that it was still alive but asleep. Masters in Rose and Tennar continued to log the colony's status, but because of the inactivity had proclaimed the fire aspen of Tiede to be eternally dormant.

Aren turned the page and found sketches of the once living Tiede colony. There were pages of theories on what might have killed the once regal trees, but the one that caught his eye was the illustration of the vines wrapped around the trees, strangling them.

He sat up, fumbled for his pen. He began to scribble notes about vines and his experience with Tun in the dungeons. Then, he reread the aspen symbolism he had written:

Fire. Transformation. Transcendence.

"Rising, changing, rebirth, supremacy," he muttered out loud, tapping his pen against his notebook, ink splattering his desk, fingers, papers.

He mopped up the ink without thinking, then flipped through his writing. "A vine. A leaf." He stopped at his sketch of the iris, picked up his notebook, and turned it sideways, frowning at his drawing. Then, he took up his pen and drew the flower again, this time drawing only one petal. "It's not a leaf," he breathed. "It's a petal, a disguise. Iris. Message."

He dropped his pen as he stood up, pushing back his chair. "Stars, what've I done?"

He bolted for the doors. Like Crina had said, everything had been fine before he and Selina had returned. He had to find Lord Vir.

SIX

Aren ran across the courtyard and spared a glance at the mermaid when he collided with Dane. "Where's Lord Vir?" Aren's tone was urgent.

There was a piercing scream as the main doors were blown open. The creature had returned, taller in stature with twisting tendrils of black smoke surrounding it. It fixed its gaze on them and screamed again, causing them to cover their ears. Hunters swarmed the courtyard, pouring in from the myriad of hallways and rooms lining the overlook. Gryf ran up to his brothers, his great sword at the ready.

The creature spread its arms, and shards of magic sprayed out in all directions. Aren and his brothers dove for cover behind the fountain. "It learned how to use the front door," Aren said. "With great power comes great manners."

"Is it just me or does it seem stronger than last time?" Dane said, unsheathing his short sword. "Bigger too."

Three of the Hunters attacked, and Aren noticed the trace of arrows taking flight from the overlook.

"I think I found something on the monster," Aren said. "I need to tell Lord Vir."

"Go," Gryf said, preparing to leave his cover. "Take Dane with you. Once you find him, you can act as another layer of defense if this thing gets away from us."

Gryf's eyes were fixed on Tirren, the Hunter with the gun at the corner of the overlook. Tirren loosed eight shots, and the creature turned to seek out its attacker while deflecting sword blows. Gryf pointed at the nearest hallway, and Dane and Aren took off, hoping that the creature hadn't seen them.

They approached the Lord's quarters and Dane pulled him back by the shirt collar, before Aren took another step. "This is what Gryf means about you being predictable. You think a Hunter is going to let you just walk in?"

A Hunter stepped out of the shadows, as if to answer Dane's question. "What are you doing here?" she asked.

"I need to see Lord Vir," Aren said. "It's about the creature. I think I know where it came from."

"Follow me," she said, leading them down the hall. They entered the Lady's room, then walked to a door that connected to the Lord's chambers. She pushed on the latch and swung the door open. The room was empty and lit by streams of light pouring in through the windows and balcony. She pursed her lips and whistled a strange, short melody.

Aren watched for movement, and soon enough another Hunter revealed himself. The silver-haired man had been positioned just to the side of the door, and Aren jumped at his presence. "What's going on, Illana?" he asked.

"Tenley, take the Apprentice to see Lord Vir. I'm returning to the hallway to stand watch."

Dane said, "Put me somewhere I can be of use if that thing finds us."

Tenley grinned. "I do like you Gerrits." A woman came up behind them, and Aren jumped again. "Dane, follow Hunter Lyse; Apprentice, with me."

Aren had never been in the Lord's chambers, and he was awed by the size of it. It was filled with dark furniture covered in luxurious fabrics. There was a sitting area, a desk, bookshelves filled to capacity. Rich oil paintings and ornate tapestries hung from the high walls, and gilded mirrors echoed his passing reflection. It was a home within a house.

Tenley led him into another room, whistling a low tune over and over as they moved through the space. Aren began to see shadows shift and slide, and he could sense the presence of others. A massive bed fixed in midnight-blue silks dominated the next room.

Aren turned to see Elder standing just inside the doorway, and the old man assaulted him with questions as Tenley left them. "How did it look out there? Is the monster weakening at all?" Elder studied Aren's face. "Why do you have ink all over yourself?"

Aren wiped a hand over his face. "I've been working. I thought we could hear the fighting from here, but the sound insulation is impressive." He raised an eyebrow at Elder's narrowed gaze. "Where's Lord Vir?"

"What news?" Vir asked, stepping in from the balcony. "I can't stand being locked in here like a prisoner. Tell me my Hunters have disposed of that thing so I can get back to running this House."

Aren studied Vir for a moment, noting how much healthier Vir looked since they had been rid of the oil. His voice was still a little rough, but the cough was almost gone. His eyes were sharp and vibrant again, and there was color in his cheeks.

"I don't think they can kill it," Aren said. "Not by conventional methods."

"I know you haven't come all this way to give me bad news."

"That depends," Aren said, taking a deep breath. "Do you have the message I delivered from Rose? I need to read it."

Vir frowned at him. "That letter is personal. The only information you or anyone needed to know was in regards to Rose's detaining of the marked."

Aren felt jittery and was doing his best to keep still. "I'll hold the information in the strictest confidence, my Lord, I swear it. I'm just looking for markers or a code. I think the reading of the message triggered this whole mess," Aren explained. "I'm hoping that there's also another trigger to end it." Vir and Elder looked at him with doubt. "All this time I thought it was a leaf, but it's an iris petal." Aren waited for the light of understanding to fill their eyes. Nothing. "The iris is symbolic of a message. What don't you understand?"

"Why would the sender entrust such a delivery to a messenger who couldn't be bothered to deliver the message himself, and instead ended up giving it to a random boy fishing on the river?" Elder asked, pushing the tip of his staff into Aren's chest.

"About that..." Aren sucked in his lips, breathed, then said, "He gave me the message because he was supposedly being pursued by a mage. That's how I got the staff." Elder looked as though he could beat Aren on the spot. "The mage went after Selina and me, and that's why we were running through the Wood."

Elder knocked his staff against the ground, then said, "I will deal with your lies later. For now, tell us why a mage would want to stop the message that you say started it all?"

"Credibility?" Aren suggested. "After everything that's happened, I've come to the conclusion that I was duped. The messenger and mage wanted to get the letter to you, but when the Harbor closed, they were at a disadvantage. The messenger made it seem like he was being pursued, and the mage was there to ensure that I had the motivation to get the letter to you. The mage didn't like the change of plans and didn't think I'd succeed. There was too much riding on that message. It's a theory, anyway."

"Why didn't the mage or the messenger read it to activate the spell?" Elder asked.

Aren sighed. "I don't know. I can only guess that it takes a certain kind of person to read it. Maybe you need to have lived in the House or something? So many variables."

Vir spoke up. "Is Rose behind this?"

"I don't know." Aren ran his hands through his hair. "But that's why I want to read the message. Is it possible that Rose is behind this? Yes. Is it possible someone's infiltrated the House of Rose? Yes. Is it possible the message got intercepted between Rose and Tiede and cursed with magic? Yes." He sighed. "I need to read it."

Vir looked at Elder. "You've read it. Did you see anything odd?"

"I didn't, but I wasn't looking for any hidden meanings. What specifically are you looking for?"

There was an explosion, the sound of magic obliterating stone, and the House rattled. A Hunter peered into the room to check on them, then disappeared.

"I don't know," Aren said. "I'm going on instinct, and something is telling me to look at the message." Vir and Elder only stared at him. Stars, he hated being treated as if he were some sort of creature that had just wandered out of Tiede Wood. "Lord Hraf believed in me enough to protect you from that whipping vine this morning. What more do I need to do to prove myself? I don't want to know your secrets, I just want to—"

"Tiede Hraf?" Vir asked. "When did you speak to..." He looked at Aren as if seeing him for the first time. "That's who you were talking to in the dungeons."

Another boom shook the House.

"Now really isn't the time to discuss the dead," Aren said. "But yes, I was talking to Lord Hraf in the dungeons." One day, Aren hoped the words that came out of his mouth would sound sane.

"Wait a minute," Elder said. "There's evidence that the creature made appearances before you and Selina arrived, not after."

Aren hung his head, took another deep breath, then looked Vir in the eyes. "I read the message before I brought it to you."

Vir's usually composed face transformed into a mask of rage. "You what?"

Aren didn't back down. "I've read it, and I never told a soul. The seal was broken, and I risked my life to get back to Tiede just to get it to you. I wanted to know what I almost died for. I didn't even tell you about the unicorn—"

"I should have had you put to death!" Vir shouted, his face red.

Elder came between them, but Aren shouted, "Maybe you should have, because putting my life on the line as often as I have these past few days clearly isn't enough to appease you!"

"There were private things in that message," Vir started, his voice lowered, a finger pointing at Aren.

"And I didn't breathe a word of it to anyone. I've sworn my allegiance to this House, and other than the incident with Lady Geyle, I've done nothing against Tiede. In fact, after saving your life in the dungeons, I spent the better half of the day torturing my brain to figure out how to kill this monster. I might be on to something, but I need to read that message again." Elder looked like he was going to have a heart attack. "The Fire god's blood seems to burn hot in Alaric's people. You can have me executed after we kill this monster, all right?" Aren stated in a more conciliatory tone.

Vir's expression changed from one of outrage to confusion to frustration at being addressed so boldly. Aren didn't budge, meeting his stare. At last, Vir said, "It's in my study. We'll take my private stairs." Elder made to follow, but Vir stopped him. "Wait here, Elder. You'll act as witness if this fool errand gets me killed. Send a Hunter to catch up with us."

Aren followed Vir to the back of the bedchamber. In the corner, set off by a curved stone wall, a set of stairs wound its way to the study. The stairs were dark, the sconces along the walls extinguished. Vir navigated each step with ease, and Aren wondered if the blood of Tiede really could see in the dark.

Vir was already at his desk by the time Aren caught up to him, and the Hunter managed to close the distance to a handful of steps. Tenley swept past them to check the doors. They were just down the hall from the battle raging in the courtyard, and Aren wondered what madness had possessed him to put the Lord of Tiede in danger.

Producing a small iron key, Vir unlocked a compartment in one of his desk drawers. He reached inside and pulled out the message that Aren had once carried from the river and through the Wood into Tiede. Vir ran a thumb over the wax seal, contemplating his decision.

Aren looked him in the eye. "Your secrets are safe with me."

Vir pressed the note to Aren as if he couldn't stand to touch it any longer. Aren bowed his head as he took the parchment. He took a deep breath and unfolded the message, laying it on the desk. Then, he read:

This message is hereby addressed to Lord Vir of the House of Tiede.

It is written by the hand of Master Fern Grivel, House Pen, on behalf of Lord Gaithus of the Illustrious House of Rose.

Lord Vir, husband to Rose's most beloved daughter, it is with great distress and anxiety that I write you this letter. Word has reached us that the House of Trum has been infiltrated by mages. My scouts say that mages were embedded within the House, that mages who had walked the streets as one of their own had turned against them. Upon what gods are we to call now? Unleash what prayers and chants, hymns and sacrifices?

Trum is as good as lost to Cordelacht, numbering the remaining Houses at seven with the Night Houses outweighing the Light. What can a peace-loving House such as ours hope to do? The Rose is a symbol of the ideal. The Rose is trampled in battles and wars. Should mages raise arms against us, we would be even more defenseless than Trum. Once weakened, we will eventually be overrun by the ambitious Illithe from the north and the barbarous Kaishar on the western end of the Rail.

The fall of Rose is no good omen for Tiede. You, Lord Vir, are as kin to us now, and we would do what we can, not only to protect ourselves but also to ensure your long life with that of our daughter Geyle. We cannot chance mages rising against us, and so the Council has decided to begin detaining all the marked; it matters not who you are or what your class in our society. I am only thankful that Geyle is far from here, as the thought of having her locked away breaks my heart. You are her chosen, her protector. With you, I know that no harm shall befall her. Just knowing that you are Reading my letter. The Terror is kept at bay still longer.

I risk being bold and request assistance from Tiede. We need soldiers to keep the peace, to guard the detainees, to quell the riots. These are troubling times. These are changing times. This era is coming to an end. When the new one begins, will the Houses still be standing? Will the mages rule Cordelacht? Will our gods die with us? Of what can I be certain of anymore? The old texts of Rose speak of renewal by Fire, but not the same Fire as that of our gods. The mages seek to transcend our gods and end our current way of life. As far as Rose is concerned, you, Lord Vir, are our savior and martyr. It is Upon Tiede we place our faith.

While I am being bold, I would stress the apparent lack of an heir to Tiede. While I recognize your loyalty and fidelity, while I trust your word, I do not feel that our Houses are truly joined. The blood of Tiede and Illithe run through you, and so Illithe has made its peace with Tiede. Yet, you and Geyle are independent entities joined by ceremony and fragile promises. A child would seal that promise. Whatever ailments or shortcomings you have must be overcome. These are small obstacles for you, Lord Vir. Geyle must be made with child one way or another, and our doctors have ensured us that she is healthy and more than capable of conceiving. Should you be unable to plant your seed, we will have to seek out more creative solutions. This is no threat, Lord Tiede, only encouragement.

Please send Words back soonest on your decision. The House of Rose would be ever in your debt. Lord Vir, have mercy on your extended family.

In all things Light, I sign this letter with much affection as your father by marriage,
Rose Gaithus, Lord of the House of Rose

Aren read the message over and over, trying to ignore the watchful eyes of Vir over his shoulder. He supposed the whole section about Gaithus nagging Vir for an heir was the personal part. Gaithus wasn't shy about laying the blame on Vir—to the point of making subtle jabs at his manhood. It made Aren wince to read between the lines.

There was a rhythm to the message, a sort of singsong lilting. He looked up to see Vir glaring at him. "Is Lord Gaithus always so…" Aren trailed off, not wanting to offend.

"Long-winded?" Vir offered. "Rambling?"

"Verbose?" Aren couldn't help but grin.

"Our wedding ceremony took hours because of his lengthy speeches. Tiedan weddings are never so full of—"

"Words?" Aren cut in. The corner of Vir's mouth lifted in a rare smile. "There's something about the sound of it in my head that's jarring, though. Have you read it out loud?"

"I'm not in the habit of reading personal messages aloud so that anyone passing might hear me."

Aren ignored the sarcasm and muttered the lines in the first paragraph over and over. He frowned, then moved the fingers of his left hand as if counting them. He reached for the pen in his robe pocket only to realize he didn't have a pen or a robe. He spotted a pen on the far side of the desk and reached for it, his mind still turning the puzzle over in his head. His thumb rolled at the small copper gear near the pen's nib. He felt for the change of pressure when one gear pushed against the other, waited for the familiar resistance of a full ink tank. Satisfied, he drew a series of quick strokes on the back of his left hand. Then, he read the words again in a whisper. "Eight," he said after he was done. He blew his hair out of his eyes. "Twice. A special number."

Vir stepped closer. He tried reciting the words to himself as well. Then, Aren started as if he had just woken from a dream, and Vir had to take a step back. Aren scanned the large desk, its surface covered in volumes and papers. He moved a few of the books, his lips articulating a silent mantra while he rearranged the objects around him.

"Is this some kind of ritual?" Vir asked.

"Paper."

Vir opened a drawer and pulled out several sheets. He handed them to Aren, who grabbed them and began scribbling his notes before the paper even had a chance to settle.

Upon what gods are we to call now?
Unleash what prayers and chants, hymns and sacrifices?

"The rhythm is all wrong."

"What are you talking about?" Vir's tone was full of annoyance.

"And why comment on the number of Houses?" he said, more to himself than to Vir. "It's like a key that doesn't quite give itself away because the key is eight words, not seven."

"Apprentice," said Vir, "I'm about ready to strangle you—"

The House rumbled again.

"It could just be an explanation, not an answer." Aren frowned. He scanned the desk again and reached for the ornate silver box that was smaller than his hand. He opened it, and pulled out a pinch of fire magic. He replaced the box and muttered the incantation over the silky, black slivers in his palm. The flame appeared and he paused for a moment, catching the concern on Vir's face. He placed the fire on the parchment, and Vir stepped back, expecting the fire to consume it. The paper didn't catch, and the fire fizzled with nothing to burn.

"Magic," Vir breathed.

"Right, so there is a key; I just have to unscramble it." Aren scribbled two more sentences.

The Rose is a symbol of the ideal.
The Rose is trampled in battles and wars.

"That's just Gaithus being melodramatic again," Vir said.

"Maybe, but it fits the pattern. Look, it's falling into place."

Just knowing that you are Reading my letter.
The Terror is kept at bay still longer.
Of what can I be certain of anymore?
It is Upon Tiede we place our faith.
These are small obstacles for you, Lord Vir.
This is no threat, Lord Tiede, only encouragement.
Please send Words back soonest on your decision.
Lord Vir, have mercy on your extended family.

"You've pulled out random sentences. What does it mean?"

"They aren't random. They're the only sentences with eight words apiece in them. Also, why are certain words capitalized?" Aren pointed, then circled *Reading* and *Terror*. "Why does he address you as 'Lord Tiede' here"—he circled again—"but nowhere else in this message?" He drew another piece of parchment, then scrawled out more words, thinning out his list.

Upon, Unleash, Reading, Terror, Upon, Tiede, Words

The battle cries were getting louder, and Tenley made his way towards them. "My Lord, we should return upstairs. We have a better defense up there."

"Apprentice, we're running out of time," Vir said as he watched Aren work. Vir motioned for the Hunter to leave. Tenley bowed his head and returned to guarding the doors.

Aren pointed at the mess of connecting lines and circles. "I had to infer based on what we're given, but part of it says, 'Unleash the terror upon Tiede Vir.'"

"You said you had part of it. What's the other part?"

Aren returned to moving words around, crossing out parts of sentences. Then, he took a step back so Vir could read.

Upon the Reading of these Words, unleash the Terror upon Tiede Vir.

"It's a spell," Aren said, his brows furrowed. "I can't undo a spell, and if everything I've read about magic is true, then this creature won't stop until you're dead."

SEVEN

"Who cast this spell? Gaithus?" Vir asked, his anger rising.

"I've never read anything about Lord Gaithus having any gift for magic; I don't think he's even marked."

"The messenger who asked you to deliver this? The House Pen of Rose?"

"It could be either of them or none of them," Aren said. They stared at each other for a moment, the sounds of battle unceasing. At last, Aren said, "I know what you're thinking. It wasn't me." Vir was about to speak when Aren cut him short. "If it was me, why would I decipher it for you?"

"Because it's too late to make any difference."

"Unbelievable." Aren shook his head. "I work for you and fight for you—stars, I even talk to your dead ancestors. You know what it is? You don't trust me because I'm Unblessed."

"I don't trust you because my wife…" Vir exploded, grabbing him by the shirtfront.

"Your wife and your problems with your wife have nothing to do with me, Kel Vir." He pushed Vir's hands away. "We're wasting time. I'm going to see what I can do about modifying this so that creature might stop seeing your death as its end goal."

Aren returned to the parchment. Feeling the heat color his face, Vir was ready to draw his sword when he was struck by how Aren had thrown himself right back into the message as if nothing had happened.

"When you had me locked up, Lord Hraf talked to me about the Ancient language and the power of the spoken symbol," Aren said, as if they were two colleagues working on a Guild research paper. "If I can apply it here, it's possible I can change the message. What do you think their language was called back then? They probably weren't calling it Ancient, right? I like Lord Hraf, but he can be intimidating."

Vir snorted a laugh as he considered the young man's bravado. Aren was so peculiar. Vir knew he was loyal, and he had no idea what had overcome him when he'd accused Aren of treachery. Gods, was he that jealous of the young Apprentice?

"I've tried manipulating some of the words, but I'm not seeing any reaction," Aren said. "I have one last option, but I don't know if it'll work."

"What's that?" Vir looked down at the scribbling and stared in wonder at the way the parchment seemed to reject Aren's writing, causing any additions to disappear.

Aren cursed under his breath as he pushed his hair away from his eyes with one hand and opened the ink reservoir in the pen with his other. Vir opened a drawer and pulled out an inkpot, placing it on the desk.

"It doesn't want me to change the spell, but the fact that my writing vanishes makes me think it can be changed, given the right words." He refilled the reservoir with a deftness that impressed Vir. "Unfortunately, I don't seem to be using the right words." Aren paused and looked at the tool in his hand. "This is a really nice pen."

"You mentioned a last option," Vir prodded.

Aren looked at him, shrugged, then struck through the words "Lord Vir" from his chosen sentences and wrote in the word "Aren."

Once Vir realized what Aren was doing, he moved a hand to stop him. But it was too late. The lettering on the parchment rearranged itself, and Vir could clearly see the message that Aren had deciphered earlier, only now it said:

Upon the Reading of these Words, unleash the Terror upon Aren.

"What have you done?" Vir asked in disbelief.

Outside, the creature screamed so loud that glass shattered throughout the rooms.

Aren's face lost all its color, and he dropped the pen on the desk, taking a step back. "Well, I guess you have nothing to worry about now." He flashed Vir a weak smile.

"Hunter!" Vir called out. "We need to get the Apprentice upstairs, hide him well."

Tenley grabbed Aren by the upper arm and pulled him towards the private stairwell. There was a commotion of boots stomping down the halls. Then, they heard footsteps rushing and half-stumbling down the stairwell. Tenley pulled his sword out and put himself in front of Vir and Aren. To Vir's surprise, it was the younger Gerrit who emerged.

"It found the Priestesses," Dane said.

"Selina," Aren growled, then shoved his way past them, racing up the stairs.

EIGHT

Aren arrived at the battleground a few seconds after the Hunters did. Of the eleven Hunters who were with Gryf earlier, only four were with him now, and the anxiety of not knowing the fate of a fellow Fighter felt like a cold stone in Aren's gut. He felt awful for thinking it, but he was relieved to see that at least Gryf was still intact.

"Gods," Dane breathed, catching up to him. "What's it done?"

The entire wall to the worship room had been reduced to broken chunks of stone and glittery white powder. Covered in dust and rock, the two Hunters who had been guarding the Priestesses stood with weapons at the ready.

A Hunter came up behind Aren and grabbed his arm, turning him to face her. "What in Aum do you think you're doing?" Hunter Lyse hissed. "Lord Vir ordered us to protect you, now come back with me to the—"

"Lord Vir can come get me himself," he said, jerking his arm away. Lyse's fiery eyes narrowed, and it hit him that she could have him on the floor with his hands tied behind his back in seconds. He adjusted his tone. "Please tell Lord Vir that I'm close to unraveling the symbols. Tell him I need to help kill this thing." When she didn't move, he added, "Fighter Gryf will back me if you won't take my word."

She drew a knife so fast he didn't have time to register the movement before the tip of it pricked the skin underneath his chin. "Only because I respect your family. If Lord Vir doesn't like your answer, I'll be back and you won't be able to use your silver tongue to talk your way out of obeying me."

He gave her a toothy grin as she made her way back towards Vir's quarters. He pressed at the spot where she had pricked him and frowned at the blood on his fingers.

Two more Hunters emerged to join the melee. Eight Hunters now, plus Gryf, all moved towards the monster. They were unable to take down the creature in the courtyard with more power than this. How could any of them believe that it could be killed with something as simple as the strike of a sword, Aren wondered.

The monster's head swiveled one way, then another as it contemplated its situation. Then, its yellow eyes with reptilian pupils fixed on Aren, and it shot its long, bony arms at him. Aren stood frozen in place as the arms changed into vines, racing straight for him.

The vines killed the trees, was all he could think. He didn't have time to brace himself when Dane tackled him to the ground.

"Why didn't you move?" Dane growled. He had rolled into a crouch and already had his sword up, giving Aren time to recover.

"Look out!" Aren said as the vines whipped back around. Dane swung at it with his sword, but the vine seemed like steel, and his sword didn't manage to cut through it as it passed over them. Aren reached for his blade as he stood up, but found he didn't have one.

"If Gryf knew, he'd punch you, monster be damned," Dane said, handing him a knife. Aren gave him a sheepish smile as he took it.

Gryf ran over to where Crina, Estelline, and Teyna were picking their way over the debris and entering the battlefield. Their airy white gowns were covered in charcoal-gray dust, and their elaborately coifed hair was a tangled mess. Only their silver seemed to shine in the dimming light that washed in through the broken windows. Aren wondered what madness had overcome them.

"Where's Selina?" Aren felt his panic rise.

"She's fine," Dane said, his eyes never leaving the creature. The vines had turned back to limbs, and the creature raked at an attacker with its long claws. "You'd know if she wasn't."

Aren felt his grip tighten around the knife's handle, and he fought to keep himself still. *I'll only get in the way*, he reminded himself.

There was a sickening crunch as the creature wrapped a vine around a Hunter, then thrust its protruding elbow down on the Hunter's skull. The man's body went limp and the creature tossed it aside.

"No," Dane breathed.

"It wants me," Aren said, taking a step forward. Dane grabbed his arm and yanked him back hard. Aren faced him, pointing his knife at the fight. "I can end this."

"It. Will. Kill. You." Dane stressed each word. Aren was about to speak, but Dane cut him off. "Do you know how many Hunters are dead? They're the elite of the elite. If they can't kill it, what makes you think you can?"

"Who said anything about killing it?" Aren said, his voice hoarse. "Once it has me, the spell is broken. It dies with me." The creature roared, and a spray of crimson caught their attention. A Hunter staggered backwards, her arm torn from her body. A vine reappeared, snaked around her ankle, and hoisted her into the air before hurling her at a wall. Blood streaked down the stones as she slid then settled into a lifeless slump.

"If you think you're just going to give yourself over, you're stupider than I ever thought possible!" Dane growled, his fingers digging into Aren's arm.

The monster cried out with glee as it fed on the death around it. Then, mid-scream, it gurgled, lurched, and spasmed. Aren and Dane stared wide-eyed as the beast grabbed at its throat and tossed back its head. Dane brought his sword up, then lowered it again, confused.

The remaining Hunters seemed just as surprised, hesitant to attack, wondering if it was some kind of hoax. Bewildered, Aren looked at Gryf, who was still watching the creature's every move. Behind him, Teyna's mocha eyes were now an opaline blue. Her fingertips were touching, her palms a breath apart, and Aren realized that she was using her powers—her gifts, as Crina described them— against the monster. He imagined that, as one promised to the Water goddess, she was drowning it somehow.

Crina mimicked Teyna's posture, and her eyes began to swirl in that liquid silver that made Aren cringe. He knew she was calling the darkness, and seeing the beast thrash its head from side to side with one arm flailing about confirmed his suspicions.

Estelline placed a hand on both women's shoulders to add her strength to theirs. Aren felt his hope returning, and the corner of his mouth began to lift into a grin.

The Hunters were regrouping, seeing this as their chance to take the creature down while it was weakened. Tirren holstered his gun and drew a blade, lifting it high and crying out in Old Tiedan, *"Fyrsa Pato'um!"* For the dead. The others, Gryf and Dane included, echoed his cry, as they went in to finish the creature.

The darkness grew, and Aren wasn't sure if it was the setting of the sun or if Crina's powers were affecting him as well. It was enough to give the Hunters pause, and that's when Aren saw her, stumbling out from behind the rubble of the worship room, her face dirty, her hair covered in dust. Selina was running, tripping over stones and overturned urns; Nianni, Min, and the red-haired Seer were several heartbeats behind her, failing to hold her back.

"Stop!" Selina screamed, pulling at Crina and Teyna. "You'll make it worse!"

"It's too late," Aren heard himself saying. "The *istoq*!" he called out, pointing at the gaping black void that was taking shape near the blood-streaked wall where the dead Hunter lay. All heads turned to look, and a sound like the deep pulse before a magnetic boom filled the House. An ivory skull began to push its way through the void, and Aren yelled, "Drive it back!" as he charged towards the darkness.

NINE

Kaila met Tanghi at the hot springs when he called on her. The springs were nestled at the bottom of large, jagged rock formations to the southeast of Alaric's Keep, surrounded by a dense mist and silver, barren trees. From afar, the place seemed like a bleak, colorless wasteland, but once past the fog, the hidden waters were an inviting, brilliant aqua.

"Tanghi?" she called out, walking towards the water.

"Over here," he replied, dissipating the mist around him. The flames that encircled his arms were gone, and there was a strange quiet over his aura. When she reached him, he wasted no time on small talk. "What is he?" he asked in a rough, hushed tone.

Kaila frowned. "What is who?"

"The boy," Tanghi growled. "There's something about him you aren't telling us, and I'm asking you to tell me here, away from Alaric and Taia and the demons. What is he?"

She felt her blood rush and wondered if she could blame the flush on her face on the heat of the springs. She wasn't going to put Aren's life in danger. She had sworn to herself that she must protect him, and she would keep that promise. "What boy, Tanghi?" she asked in a tone as exasperated as his.

He threw up his arms. "The boy in Tiede. The blacksmith's adopted son. The Elder's Apprentice. You know damned well who I'm talking about!"

"You just stated everything I know about him." She paused for effect, then said, "Oh, and his brothers, your Guardians, called him Aren. Are you satisfied now?"

"No, I'm not satisfied!" he bellowed. "You were in Tiede, and you saw everything that happened, and you didn't tell me. I can't help but wonder what else you hid from me."

"I said I was sorry! The opportunity was there for me to do something and I failed. I guess everyone was right about me after all. Congratulations!"

"Kaila, enough," he said, his tone softer, though still exasperated. "I get it. I should've been the one to back you up. That's why you go to Geir; he supports you no matter what you do. You just can't imagine how it felt to know that you were hiding from me."

Her heart ached. She was torn between lying to Tanghi and protecting Aren. How in Mahl's holy name could she fix this?

"You mean the world to me, and I didn't mean to disrespect you," she said. "You're right; I should have come to you. I should always come to you."

"You can trust me. In my heart, you come before Alaric." He reached out and took her hand in his. "We have a lot to fix, but let's get through this mess in Tiede." She nodded, giving him a small smile. "The creature attacked the House. I was about to tell Alaric that it's not looking good, but the boy, Aren, found the spell. It's like you said; he was on to something with the symbols, and he found out that it all stemmed from a message Vir received from Rose."

Kaila did her best to restrain her elation at the news. "You mean he might be able to kill or weaken the creature?"

"He changed the spell. I think Vir is safe for the time being."

"Changed it how?"

Tanghi shook his head and laughed. "He managed to replace Vir's name with his own, making himself the target. The boy's strange, but he's got the balls of a god. He's out of his mind."

Kaila thought she would choke on the air she breathed. She had to get back to Tiede, back to Aren. What was the point of protecting him from the gods if the mages were going to kill him anyway?

"Are you all right?" he asked, cupping her face. "You look like you might be ill."

She had to reveal more in order to hide Aren in plain sight, and her connection with Selina might be the key. She held a hand out towards to springs, and the mist cleared; the aqua water turned into a one-way looking glass. Her eyes clouded and she could feel Tanghi move to support her, believing that she was under duress.

Goddess!

"The new Priestess," Kaila breathed. "I can't control the connection between us, the blessing I placed—"

Goddess, what's happening?

Tanghi placed his large hand on her shoulder and hushed her, feeding her power with his own. An image began to move into focus on the water's surface, rippling and shifting, then settling to glass again.

"Selina?" Kaila whispered. She wasn't sure what she expected to see: the inside of a safe room where the Priestesses were being kept, or maybe random, broken memories from Selina's head. What she hadn't expected was the scene of the battle. The picture was devoid of color, shadows pitted against shadows on a canvas of shifting grays. "You need to return to shelter where Tiede's Hunters can best defend you," Kaila said.

Currents of aqua and silver drifted through the scene in the mirror like colored smoke in a tinkerer's glass. Chrono-elemental gifts. The Priestesses were hoping to stop this monster with their powers, but they didn't realize that the powers of gods against a creature like this...

"By Mahl's holy name," Tanghi breathed, terror tingeing every word. "They can't—"

"Stop them!" Kaila ordered Selina. She was gripping Tanghi's hand in hers now. "Stop them or they'll open a portal to the Undergod's realm!"

Selina didn't respond, but the images began to change as the little girl rushed towards the Priestesses. Kaila could sense the confusion, anger, and frustration from the older Priestesses, but after a few moments the aqua and silver disappeared. Kaila bit her bottom lip, waiting. Then, the darkness began to spread over the vision, and she shook her head. It was too late!

The monochromatic image on the water's surface began to fade, but before it did, Kaila caught a glimpse of Aren, charging the *istoq* with nothing but a knife, the light in his green eyes cutting through the gloom.

Tanghi was right; Aren was out of his mind.

TEN

When Selina pulled on the Priestesses' arms, begging them to stop, she felt the surge of power flowing from them come to an abrupt halt. They didn't feel how their powers were clashing with the monster's magic. They didn't notice the lightning feeling that sliced through the air and made her hair stand on end. They didn't smell the inky, stale stench that began to fill the space around them.

Aren noticed.

When he called out and pointed at the darkness, which no one else had seen, she knew she wasn't imagining things. What she didn't know was that he would be the one to charge the skull monster that was coming out of the black hole. She felt her heart fall into the pit of her stomach when she saw that all he was carrying was a knife. Protecting Aren was proving to be as difficult as stopping the river from tumbling over Tiede Falls.

"Aren! No!" Selina screamed. Gryf was pushing her towards the Priestesses, but as soon as he heard his brother's name, he turned back towards the fight, a string of curses slipping from his mouth so quiet and quick that it resembled the hiss of a snake.

Aren stopped in his tracks, then took several steps backwards as the skull emerged from the darkness. It had a wide forehead with horns curled on each side. Large, empty eye sockets studied the wreckage of the room, and as it forced itself into the world of the living, it released a deep, rumbling roar.

"It's a gigantic gree," Aren said as Dane rushed to his side, "without a fleshy head." The skull creature managed to get one of its forelegs through. Its body was substantial, with rippling animal muscle beneath cream-colored fur.

"How is this possible?" Dane held his sword up, unsteady and uncertain.

The wraith let out a piercing scream as if to remind everyone of its presence, and that's when Gryf attacked. His broadsword seemed to weigh nothing as he swung it with two hands, aiming for its neck. The wraith was fast, and its hands with its elongated claws came up to block the blade. A red glow emanated from its core, acting like a shield, but black ooze dripped to the floor, sizzling on contact.

"Tenley!" Tirren, the Hunter with the guns, called out, and the man with silver-white hair rushed the monster with a sword that gleamed like fallen stars.

"Look out!" Selina cried.

Tenley either heard her or expected the monster's next move. He dodged the vines that lashed at him from the monster's sides and managed to hack one off. It fell to the ground with a lifeless thud. He swung low and his blade found purchase in a thigh. More inhuman cries. More black blood. Selina turned her attention back to Aren to keep from looking at the horrific violence.

"How do we kill this thing?" Dane yelled as he and Aren took turns distracting the half-bone, half-flesh gree.

"Help my brothers," Gryf demanded of the Hunters. The monster was still holding on to his sword, and Gryf proved to be just as stubborn, refusing to let go and putting all of his weight behind the weapon, hoping to break through the shield.

Knives cut through the air, and Aren swore as one whizzed past his head. Two knives hit the gree in the shoulder, and it roared. He turned his head to see Hunter Lyse pulling two more knives from their sheaths, as she rushed to help.

"Are you here to bring me back to Lord Vir?" Aren asked, raising a sweaty brow.

Lyse rolled her eyes at him. "Nice blade. Only one?" She rushed the gree as it thrashed in response to the pain in its shoulder, hoisting herself onto the gree's back as it bucked. She thrust a knife at the base of the skull, hitting nothing but air. The lack of substance was unexpected and shook her off balance, and in that moment the gree threw her. She rolled, her dark violet hair trailing her like a ribbon.

Tirren fired several shots at the gree's skull, and the ivory fissured. This only angered it, and it began to whip its tail and paw at the air around it, trying to take a swipe at its attackers with its bone-sharp claws. Lyse grabbed Aren and Dane by their collars and pulled them out of its reach.

"More monsters!" Aren called out, pointing at the dark hole. The yellowing skull of yet another creature was trying to push through. "We've got to close the *istoq*!" Aren ran past the thrashing gree towards the void.

Gunshots resounded again and Tirren cursed, holstering his weapon. "I hit it straight through the eye socket. Nothing! How do we kill something that's only half alive?" He pulled out a sword and ran to join Lyse and Dane.

Selina squirmed out of the Priestesses' hold and ran to Aren, who was crouched near the Hunter who had been slain nearby. His voice was hoarse as he closed her eyelids. "May you hunt the stars." Selina's eyes filled with tears and she turned away, trying to stifle her sobs.

Aren hadn't realized she was there, and when he heard her crying, he snapped back to the carnage and chaos going on around him. He stepped over the dead body to reach her, then pulled her close. "Sweetheart, you shouldn't be here."

"There's another monster coming out."

"I know. I have to figure out a way to close this." He put her down behind a large chunk of fallen rock, shielding her as best he could.

"Do you know how? Do you know what it is?"

"It's called an *istoq* in the Ancient tongue," he said, examining the feathery edges of the void. "The stories say it can swallow your soul. I don't know if it's true or not, but I'm not about to take any chances. No one knows what it is, but it's said to appear when an enormous amount of magic is used. The theory is the magic creates a tear that allows these creatures to come into our world. How did you know to stop the Priestesses?"

"The goddess told me," she said as she watched him peer into the darkness.

"Any luck, Aren?" Dane yelled from across the room. Lyse and Tirren had all but gutted the gree. Black ooze covered the floor, and the stench of decaying flesh filled the air. Still, it bellowed and thrashed. Dane jumped clear of the rake of a massive claw.

"Not yet!"

Selina swiped at her eyes with the back of her hand. She felt dizzy, and the smell made her want to throw up. She gripped the remains of the stone wall to keep from falling over. She looked up and saw Nianni stepping over the debris and positioning herself behind the broken wall next to her.

"Priestess, you need to get her to shelter," Aren said. "This creature will breach the *istoq* soon."

"The what?"

"Not important," Aren said. "Can you get her back to the worship room?"

"I think so. The other Priestesses said they could provide a distraction."

"No!" Selina interrupted her. "No powers."

"That's what caused the *istoq*—the void—to open," Aren began to explain.

Selina breathed long and deep, and in a voice not quite her own said, "Yes, that's what caused it to open. The Priestesses' powers, combined with the monster's magic, tore open a gateway to the Undergod's realm."

Aren and Nianni exchanged glances, and Selina could feel their surprise and fear almost as clearly as she could feel the grit of broken stone beneath her fingertips. "You must close the *istoq*."

ELEVEN

"The goddess!" Nianni said in awe. "Look at her eyes. Selina's not here anymore."

Aren grabbed Selina by the shoulders. "How do we close it? Stop hiding behind a little girl and close it for us."

Nianni slapped him and he winced, glaring at her. "You don't speak to the goddess like that!"

"Aren," Selina said in her trancelike state, "remember the symbols. Your brothers can't hold much longer. You're so close to finding the answer. If I knew myself what it was, I would tell you."

"What is she talking about?" Nianni asked.

"Symbols. How did the goddess know about..." He turned back towards the battle. Gryf and the Hunter called Jaye had taken the offensive and were now forcing the creature into submission, a furious barrage of blows from sword and spear raining down on it.

Meanwhile, Dane and Lyse were trying to take down the gree. They were covered in sweat, blood, and the inky-black tar that spilled from the gree's flesh. Tirren lay still on the ground in a crimson heap, and Tenley moved to cover the Priestesses.

"Symbols," the voice coming from Selina reminded Aren. "You're so close to finding the key." Then, she took in a sharp breath of air and crumpled like a wad of discarded parchment. Nianni caught her.

Selina took in another lungful of air and seemed to come back to life. She wiggled out of Nianni's arms. "I can do this," she said, looking at the void. "I know what to do."

There was a deafening cry, and they all turned to look at the wraith Gryf was fighting. It kicked out, and Jaye was hit hard in the abdomen. She was hurled down the hall, and there was an agonizing crunch as she hit the floor. Lyse left Dane to join Gryf's fight.

"Aren!" Dane called, dodging the gree's charge. "Did you figure it out yet?"

"You work on the symbols and I'll take care of this," Selina said. She placed one small hand on the edge of the darkness and another on the stone-littered floor. Her voice was soft as the susurrus of the trees as she spoke, "I seek the power of Tiede, the secrets of the Wood." Her eyes were glazed over, and a soft green light seemed to emanate from her hands.

Aren watched in awe as the *istoq* began to shrink and the creature that was trying to come out was pushed back. How was she doing it? Was this the work of the goddess? That had to be it. If the goddess could communicate with Selina, then she must be able to channel power through her as well. He didn't have to worry about Selina right now; the goddess was working through her. He needed to concentrate on the fight. Hunters were dead, and his brothers would die too if he didn't figure out how to kill the creature that was sent to destroy Vir.

It's out to kill you *now, dummy,* he reminded himself.

He stared at the monster made of black, smoky tendrils and glowing red symbols. It was a message; he had figured that much out. The message was from the mages. The Houses were being taken down. Transcendence. Destroying the gods. To destroy the gods, you destroyed their people. Well, that was one thing Aren had going for him: he didn't belong to the gods.

Dane cried out as he took a horn to the ribs. His sword flew out from his hands, clattering to the stone floor. The gree opened its gaping mouth and roared.

Aren glanced at Selina, who had managed to close the *istoq* to the point where it was only as wide as a man's hand. She was covered in dirt and sweat, and the effort and energy she used to continue closing the portal was tremendous. He ached for her.

"Go," Nianni said, her hands on Selina's shoulders. "I'll give her what strength I have."

Aren nodded his thanks and ran towards Dane, picking up the sword in passing. His brother was curled up on his side, his eyes squeezed shut as he dealt with the pain. Aren dropped the sword and put a hand on his brother's arm. "I'll carry you back to where Lord Vir and Elder are. You'll be safe there."

"No," Dane said through gritted teeth. "Be a Gerrit and pick up the damned blade so you can kill the gree."

"You're better than I am in a fight," Aren argued, lifting the sword. "How am I supposed to—"

"Glad to hear you admit it," Dane managed to laugh. "You're faster and definitely better at using your brain. Figure it out." Aren hesitated, and the gree bellowed again, lowering its head and preparing to charge. "Now! Before it rams us both!" Dane growled.

Aren steeled his resolve, then ran towards the gree with a knife in one hand and a sword in the other. He cried out as he charged it, hoping to pull its attention towards him and away from Dane. The gree complied, swinging its massive head and turning towards its new adversary.

"Aren, what are you doing?" Gryf yelled as he blocked the wraith's strikes.

"The eyes!" Nianni screamed at Aren as he sidestepped the charge. "Selina says it's the eyes! Actually, it's not quite Selina."

"The eyes," he echoed, watching the gree prepare itself for another charge. "Magic opens the *istoq*. The creatures are magic-fed. Magic is quelled by"—the gree lowered its head and aimed—"the gods," he whispered.

"Move, Aren!" Dane yelled.

Aren held out his blades, one shorter than the other, but it would have to do. He shifted so that his left hand—the hand holding the knife—was extended. "I was never blessed," he muttered. "But may the gods steady my hands now."

The gree was closing in, and Aren touched the sword to the knife, naming one Light and the other Night, then drew the sword back over his head, extending his *kal* evenly into the blades. The gree was on him, and he thrust the sword into the empty eye socket, following it with the knife to the other eye. He expected the blades to cut through the space the way Tirren's bullets did, but he hoped they would at least catch on bone as he rolled out of the gree's path. Instead, he felt resistance as the blades found purchase in the skull, and he was so surprised, he almost forgot to move.

"Is that...?" Vir asked. He had come out to assess the situation, unable to wait behind his remaining Hunters any longer.

"Uniting the Heavens," Dane responded, awe in his voice. "A rough and sloppy variation of it, anyway."

The gree roared in agony, and the black blood began to stream from its empty eyes like tears. Aren steadied his breathing, wiped his palms on the front of his pants, then rushed towards it. He jumped at the skull, grabbing at the hilts that stuck out from the creature's eye sockets, and pulled himself up and over its head. He straddled its bony shoulders and dug in with his heels. It tried to throw him, but he reached for the blades and managed to hold on.

When the bucking slowed, he pulled the blades out. Blood sprayed the halls and he wasted no time. He was moving on instinct now, and once again he touched the blades to each other. With a deep breath, he plunged them into the back of the gree's neck, into the space between the skull and the furry, fleshy body. It buckled, its front paws giving way, and calling on all of his strength, Aren ripped the blades away from each other, severing its head. The skull fell to the floor, cracking along the forehead and one of the cheekbones. The body fell to the side, taking Aren down with it. He didn't have the energy to tuck into a roll, and his left shoulder took the brunt of the fall, sending currents of pain coursing up to his teeth and head and down to his hip. He cried out in agony and thought he might black out.

"Apprentice," Vir's voice. He sounded close, and Aren wondered how that could be. "We need to get you out of here."

"Selina closed the void and you killed the gree!" Dane said.

Aren opened his eyes. Vir and two Hunters were looming over him. Dane was crouched next to him, his breathing ragged, an arm hugging his ribs. He looked bad, but the crazy grin on his face made Aren want to laugh. Instead, he coughed, tasting blood and bile in his mouth.

"Let's get these boys back to safety," Vir ordered.

"No," Aren choked. "Gryf..."

"You're in no condition to do anything, and they're trying to wear the creature down before it comes after you," Vir said.

"That monster can't be killed with a sword." Aren said, pushing himself up.

"Aren!" Selina cried out. They all turned to look where she sat slumped against the wall next to Nianni and the dead Hunter. "The goddess said to tell you that Magic is older than Ancient, but the faith behind Ancient is more powerful."

Every eye seemed to turn to Aren, and he furrowed his brows. "Tell the goddess to get her divine ass here right now—"

Before he could register the horror on Nianni's face at his blasphemous words, a vine lashed out, wrapped itself around

Selina's torso and whipped her small body back towards the monster. Aren yelled in protest as he jumped to his feet to attack. He got as far as Gryf, who held him back with one rough hand tight on his upper arm.

"He'll hurt her," Gryf mumbled, tightening his grip.

The monster held Selina close, the edge of its crimson blade pressed diagonally against her jaw and neck. Bright red blistered through her dirty skin, and she did her best to be still, stifling her sobs.

Aren, the sound slipped from the place where the creature's mouth might be, and it tilted its head to look at him. Its voice was as dark as the smoky tendrils that surrounded its decaying flesh, as rough and sharp as the bones and claws that were its weapons. It spoke in Ancient. *You play games with me, boy. You hide behind magic to trick me, make me believe we're of the same maker. You surround yourself with magic, and it protected you from me. The magic clings to you.*

"What are you talking about?" Aren managed to ask, able to speak only in Common.

You change spells, weaving the words as if the language was your own, but you used the power to save Tiede Vir. You betrayed me and our kind. You're an impostor, and you keep the company of gods and their pets. It narrowed its eyes at Gryf.

Aren looked to Selina, her frightened violet eyes full of tears. He felt something pressed into his hand. A hilt. A knife. It was warm, and as was his habit, his thumb caressed the blade's heel, finding comfort in the Guardian constellation engraved into the steel. He felt his resolve strengthen. "Your fight is with me, and you're bound by the spell. Let her go, and take me instead."

Why do you serve these weaklings? You're more powerful than they. The monster slid its blade across Selina's skin, and she cried out.

"Stop!" Aren choked. "My death, not hers, ends the spell."

I think her death would be yours as well, the creature said, switching to Old Magic.

"You don't need her to get to me," Aren responded, his mind racing to translate. "There must be some exchange we can make."

An exchange. I want this power of yours. Explain how you are magic, but not mage. Tell me where you're from.

"I don't know what you're talking about. I come from nothing," Aren said, wishing it would switch back to Common. His brain was trying to do several things at once, and the translating was slowing him down. "I was found near Tiede Wood. I was little more than an infant." The monster seemed to consider this, and as it did, the symbols on its upper arm glowed and burned. "My birth parents wanted nothing to do with me." He felt a pain in his chest as he said the words out loud, felt the truth of it reverberate through his bones. "You think I have power but you're wrong. I'm nothing and have nothing but that little girl and my adopted family. I have no history, no bloodlines. I have no blessings from any god, so even my fate, my future, is worthless."

You lie, boy, the creature said, this time with less certainty.

"Do I?" Aren did laugh this time, but it was bitter and full of a hurt that he had worked hard to keep locked up. His head was throbbing, and the voices were whispering to him again. Stars, this wasn't the time to be haunted by the Wood. He took a deep breath to let the voices pass through him, but still they whispered and he felt his anxiety growing.

Thank you, Aren! The voice belonged to a child, a little girl.

"Who said that?" he asked, looking around, waving the knife. The creature cocked its head at him. There were giggles and the happy sounds of small children playing, chasing each other through the halls. A shiver passed over him, and cold sweat rolled over his face.

"Aren," came Gryf's voice. "What's wrong?"

I'm so happy you found my dolls! Thank you so much!

"Lady Lis?" Aren half laughed, wondering if he'd finally gone mad. "And your brother? Lord Lars?"

Listen, Aren… The voice of the little Lordling. *Listen carefully…*

Aren complied as the currents of wind danced around him, bringing him messages from the Wood, translating the magic, bending the rules.

A name, Lars said. *The Lady says you can control it with a name.*

The creature screamed, cutting through Aren's delusions. *Tell me what you are before I gut you and the child!*

Aren felt as though the gears in his head had come to a screeching halt. The voices continued whispering, and he stared in pain as Selina's blood dribbled over the creature's blade. He felt raw anger rising within him. He had had enough. "I am nothing!" Aren yanked at the front of his shirt, tearing off the buttons. Then, he pulled a sleeve down to expose a shoulder and the cuts that had been reopened. "You say I have magic. Where are my marks? I don't belong, *Tsalmit*. I don't belong to the gods or the mages. Now, tell me I'm lying!" he screamed.

The monster's limbs went slack, as did the vine holding Selina. She fell to the ground with a resounding thud, and Aren rushed to her. Her skin was as white as the mermaid in the fountain, and blood spilled like water from the cuts on her face and neck. He dropped his knife, then pulled his shirt off and began to bandage the wound. Crimson flowered into the white linen, and he cursed, pulling her close to him. Her body was shaking.

"Selina," he whispered into her hair. "I'm so sorry, sweetheart. I'll fix this, all right? Just open your eyes for me. I'll fix this. Please don't leave me."

"Aren," Gryf said, placing a hand on his shoulder. "She needs a doctor. Give her to Lyse. Something's changed and I need you to focus."

Aren looked up as he swiped at his eyes. Gryf moved to a defensive stance, watching the creature, who seemed frozen in place. Lyse was crouched next to Aren, her arms open. He felt dizzy and wondered if he was going to black out again. Maybe this was all just a really bad dream.

The creature stirred and looked at them. *How did you learn my name?*

"Aren, if you want to save Selina's life, hand her to Lyse right now, or I will kick your ass before I move on to your friend here."

Aren moved as if in a trance, placing a kiss on Selina's sweaty forehead before handing her limp body over to Lyse. He watched as Lyse scurried away, Selina cradled in her arms. He had little to do with the gods, but he found himself mumbling a prayer for Selina's life. *Take me instead. Let her live.*

The creature lifted its blade again, and its entire body was surrounded in red light. *How did you know?* it demanded, taking a step towards them.

"Get up, brother," Gryf ordered.

Aren didn't have time to move. The monster attacked, the red blade slicing through the air so fast that he was surprised Gryf was able to counter each blow. The creature moved with an inhuman speed. Aren's mind raced. What did it say about its name? The jarring sound of metal hitting stone broke into his thoughts, and he looked over to where Gryf stood weaponless in a defensive stance, ready to fend off whatever else the creature would throw at him until the last blow. Too many lives had been lost or broken. Aren wasn't about to let Gryf fall too. These were good people who accepted him despite his doomed future, despite his flawed persona. He wouldn't let them die for him. He changed the spell, knowing what it could cost him if it worked. He changed it for the greater good of Tiede. What was the loss of one Unblessed compared to the last of the Tiede bloodline? Compared to his brothers?

He picked up his knife and staggered to his feet, the fury building.

Unleash the Terror... Aren recalled the message. The word "terror" in Old Magic...

"*Tsalmit!*" Aren roared.

The creature snapped its head to look at him. They stared at each other for a moment, then it stretched out its hand to level a blast of magic at Gryf, who turned, catching the blow with his upper back and shoulder. Gryf dropped to the floor, unable to lift himself, shards of magic littering his skin.

Aren's fury tore like fire through his veins at the sight of his strong, protective brother falling helpless. "I will have your death in return for what you've done here," Aren said, his voice cold and sharp.

Now I see you, Aren, son of no man. The creature laughed, speaking in Old Magic. *This is the energy you've been hiding, and yet only an inkling of it. It's magnificent; your power will feed me for years if I keep you alive, pet.*

The monster swung its blade, and Aren deflected it as he sidestepped, grabbing its forearm before it could complete the arc of the attack. The arm felt of bone and old, dry leather. Passing through the smoke felt like the stale breath of the dead on his skin. He twisted the arm back, pulled the monster close, and pressed the knife into one of the pulsing symbols, causing the creature to cringe.

"Who gave you your name, *Tsalmit?*" Aren asked in Old Tiede. The language was a bastardization of Old Magic and Ancient, and it was easier for him to speak. He pressed the knife harder and the red blade vaporized. "Who gave you life? I own your name and its power bends to my will. Answer me."

The mages, Tsalmit rasped. *Mages in Rose. I don't know more than that. How did you learn my name?*

Aren could feel the magic passing through him, and he redirected it into the knife. The symbol beneath it began to flicker and smoke. "Your magic is an abomination. Even the Wood wants you eliminated. The winds learned of your name, and the voices carried it back to me. You wanted me to become...this."

They'll never see you the same again, Tsalmit spat. *They'll fear you, question what you really are.*

Aren muttered a word, then sliced through the symbol. Fire without heat tore through the creature's arm. It shrieked and twisted in his grasp. He pressed the tip of the knife into another symbol, switching from Old Tiede to the Ancient tongue. "This is the *akaras.*"

Tsalmit shook his head and tried to pull away from his grasp. *The mages never foresaw you.*

Aren grinned, then pushed his knife straight into the symbol as the Ancient word escaped his lips and seemed to become something tangible in the dusky light. *"Jir,"* he whispered. The monster cried out once more before its body began to disintegrate into a fine black powder.

Tsalmit growled his final argument. *You're nothing. You're a boy who came from nothing, and you'll die as nothing.*

Aren nodded, his eyes seeming to lose its cloudiness. "I know," he said in Common. Then, he thrust his blade into the symbol for life, fading just under its collarbone. The Ancient symbol slipped out of his mouth before he could even register speaking it. *"Mirtin."*

Then, *Tsalmit* was gone.

The knife slipped out of Aren's hand as he dropped to his hands and knees, overcome with exhaustion. He could recall nothing except the comforting darkness that enveloped him.

Remedy

ONE

Tanghi watched as Taia shook her head in disbelief. She was tracing lines against a large map-like document she had rolled out over Alaric's desk, checking them against the myriad of lines that glittered in the air around her. He wasn't sure what the point was. Taia could trace all those fate lines from now until the end times, but she had no hold on the lines of the Unblessed. This had mattered little in the past, but after what he had witnessed in Tiede, the laws he had once known to be true on this world were breaking down little by little.

"Where is she now?" Alaric asked, referring to Kaila. He hadn't turned demon, but his black wings were out, restless and anxious.

"I left her at the springs to sleep," Tanghi answered, standing by the open window. "The blessing, the connection, took its toll on her. She's in her elemental state."

Alaric stopped pacing and turned to look at Taia. "Is there any way for us to break the blessing?"

"Why would you want to break it?" Tanghi asked before she could answer. "That link saved Vir, saved all of Tiede. If she didn't see what the child Priestess saw, she couldn't have warned them about the *istoq*. If she hadn't been able to communicate to the boy through the Priestess, then he might not have figured out how to kill the creature."

"You are talking about one incident that played in our favor," Alaric said as he approached him. "There are millions of outcomes for a million other situations where this connection could harm her."

"We only need to keep it secret from Aalae," Tanghi countered.

Tanghi had considered telling Alaric about how the child Priestess closed the *istoq*. At first, he thought Kaila was sending her powers through the link to the child. They knew of no other way to close an *istoq*, except with their powers or with magic. The strange thing was, Tanghi didn't feel Kaila's powers leave her, so it wasn't Kaila who closed the *istoq*. The little girl had called on Tiede, the powers that lay within the land itself.

He wondered if it had been Geir who had sent his powers. Geir held dominion over Tiede Wood and all its resources. Had he answered the child's calfl? Even if he had, that begged the question: What power did the child have to call on a spirit as powerful as Geir? Tanghi had no explanation for Alaric, other than that the *istoq* had been small and closed on its own once the creature was killed.

"Aalae must not know of this," Alaric affirmed. He met Tanghi's gaze, then Taia's. Her look was one of defiance, but at last she gave a curt nod before returning to her lines. "I will see what I can find to undo the blessing. Perhaps there's a curse to counter it."

Tanghi didn't care for the sound of that but was in no mood to argue. His mind was too preoccupied with the boy, Aren. He was Unblessed and not a mage, yet he said and did things to destroy the creature that Tanghi could not explain. Kaila, too, had been speechless as they watched the battle play out through the looking glass. A few times, Tanghi was tempted to break the boy's neck for his blaspheming tongue, but Kaila stilled him, reminding him that Aren was Unblessed and didn't know any better.

"Return to Trum when we're done here," Alaric said, interrupting Tanghi's thoughts. "There's only one tunnel left, and Geir and Sabana are going to smuggle the Priestesses out that way. There's fighting on the other end, so I want you to cover their escape."

Tanghi nodded, eager to return to a fight that made sense.

"How long before the mages finish off Trum and reach the edge of Thell?" Alaric asked.

"A month, maybe less," Taia said.

"The House Lady?"

"She won't leave her people, but she's sending her youngest daughters away with her eldest son and one of the Priestesses. Their chances are slim." Taia picked through books and papers on Alaric's bookcases. "Their best options are Tennar and Rose for shelter, and those are Light."

"I want Kaila on that caravan with the House blood while Tanghi, Sabana, and Geir protect the House as best they can. She can get the bloodline safely to Rose." Alaric folded his wings back.

"Kaila will be pleased to know that you trust her enough to send her on this assignment," Tanghi said.

Alaric straightened up and met his gaze. "I want to keep her far from the child Priestess. I don't want Aalae drawing any conclusions by their proximity. Also, having her in disguise with a caravan is relatively safe. Kaila wants to prove herself. Let's see if she can get a handful of refugee children to Rose."

TWO

Aren approached Vir's study and peered inside. Vir was sitting at his favorite leather seat by the cold fireplace reading pages from a stack of papers and occasionally lifting his pen to sign one. Aren knocked on the doorframe and dropped to a knee, his fist over his heart.

"Apprentice," Vir said by way of greeting. "How's Selina?" He indicated the chair across from him with his pen.

Aren took a seat and leaned forward with his elbows propped on his knees, rubbing the fingernails of one hand against the nails of the other. "She's doing well, my Lord. No lasting damage, nothing a little rest won't heal."

Vir set his pen and papers down on the small table next to his chair. "Tiede has always revered her Priestesses, and she will be remembered in our history as possibly the most blessed of all." He studied Aren for a moment. "What do you need, Apprentice?"

"I just wanted to apologize for"—Aren looked up at the ornate ceiling and took a deep breath before dropping his head—"the mess."

The House had been in complete chaos the past two days. There were dead who needed to be honored, marked who needed to be freed, mages who needed to be executed. The House was also swarming with engineers and craftsmen, rebuilding what had been broken, updating whatever needed to be renewed. The former nursery-turned-storage-room was being redone, and Vir had consented to a few electrical and bioluminescent updates in rooms that had depended solely on fire, like his study.

"What's done is done and we are stronger for it. We have awoken from a long slumber," Vir said.

"But all those things I said…" Aren was flustered, still not feeling completely like himself. He was embarrassed that everyone had seen whatever it was he had become. Who was he? He didn't know before, and he was even more confused now.

"I don't think anyone aside from Elder understood a thing you said." Vir leaned back in his chair, closed his eyes as if to rest them. "He thinks you've come a long way in your language studies."

"And the message I read?"

"The one which you swore yourself to secrecy?"

"Yes."

"You are impossible, Apprentice." Vir sat up, straightened his papers, and leafed through another batch. He sighed, changing the topic. "Counselor Darc and his daughter are preparing to leave for Illithe after the Priestess's initiation ceremony. I'm also sending you to Rose."

Aren sat up. "Rose? Why, my Lord?"

"Counselor Helmun is dead, and I had intended to send him." He paused, then said, "I don't want Rose to think I'm suspicious. Sending the Historian's Apprentice on a scholarly mission won't raise eyebrows. I just want you to observe and report if anything seems peculiar to you."

"I understand," Aren said, the shock paralyzing him from saying anything further.

Vir folded his arms. "I thought about sending Master Gryf with you, but to look at him Rose would know it was a show of force. Did you know he declined joining my elite Hunters? He said I'd benefit more from his training of future Hunters in the Guild than I would from adding him to my retinue. He's right, of course. All that aside, I'm sending the younger Gerrit with you to Rose."

"Dane?" Aren perked up.

"He's not intimidating, and he's a solid fighter in the event you end up in trouble. There will also be a Guard detail for Geyle." Aren's brows furrowed and he was about to speak, but Vir cut him off. "She's been wanting to visit home for a while, and it sends a very comforting message."

"But the detainment—"

"I'm hoping she can speak to her father and their Councils to end it," Vir explained. "She's going as Lady Tiede. They know that imprisoning her would be an act of war, daughter of Rose or not."

Aren wasn't thrilled at the prospect of going on a trip with Geyle. He wondered if there was anything he could say to change Vir's mind. "Is everything back to normal with you and the Lady? I don't mean to be rude, but I'd rather avoid a predicament similar to the one that got me thrown in the dungeons."

Vir sounded tired. "It turns out that the liquid in the vial, while it was intended for a specific purpose which I won't share with you, served another more important purpose. It counteracted the poison of the fumes I'd been breathing. Doctor Pember says that if it hadn't been for her slipping the concoction in my drinks, I'd be dead."

THREE

Aalae felt as though her entire world was falling apart. Tiede didn't fall as she hoped it would, and after Alaric had found out about the counter spell that Rafi had placed on Tiede, he had been in a less than pleasant mood. She wished she knew how he had discovered it. She drifted through her luscious green gardens, crushing full blooms, thorns piercing her delicate hands.

"I bring news," Rafi said as he approached, his voice hesitant. When she didn't say anything, he continued, making sure he didn't trip on her trailing white gown, and sidestepping the blood that dripped from her fingers and would seed new plants. "Tanghi has rejoined the fight in Trum. Our Priestesses will make it out soon, I'm sure of it." Still, she said nothing, keeping several steps in front of him. "The salves continue to work on Geir, and he doesn't know it," Rafi said, and she could hear his eager smile. "And the information he gave us on Kaila being in love—I think our opportunity to use it has come."

Aalae paused. "Tell me."

"Taia has just shared with me the most intriguing story…"

FOUR

Mercer waited for the Lady at the far western corner of the Wedge. He had spent days in hiding, nights cursing Aren's name, Aren's very existence. Everyone in Tiede or leaving Tiede was questioned on Mercer's whereabouts. He was wanted on numerous counts, including attempting to kill the girl Trista, attacking Aren, and conspiring to bring about the downfall of Tiede. He had no way out of the city, and with the price on his head being so high, it was only a matter of time before someone decided to turn him in. So, when he received the note from the Lady, he breathed a heavy sigh of relief.

She had detailed how she had slipped Copen the drug that killed him so he couldn't give anything away; how Aren had discovered the man named Tun, the *Catar*; how Aren had destroyed the monster. Mercer wanted nothing more than to slit Aren's throat himself, consequences be damned. If he could just kill Aren, it wouldn't matter what happened afterward. The Lady must have anticipated his feelings, and she set up a time and place to meet him, to help him leave Tiede and keep him focused on the overall mission: to overthrow the gods.

The sun was high, and two long shadows were cast down the street, alerting him to the presence of company.

"Mercer," the Lady's voice called out. "It's me. I've brought help."

He relaxed a little and stepped away from the building's shadow. He watched the Lady approach, her features hidden within the hood of the Apprentice robes she wore for the occasion. Walking arm in arm with her was a tall, disheveled man of indiscriminate age. His scraggly hair—blond, copper, silver; it was hard to tell in the light—hung to his shoulders, and stubble littered his thin face, his high cheekbones. In his free hand was a cane of ghostwood that he tapped about the cobblestones. His eyes were covered with a linen cloth.

"I can get you out of Tiede," the blind man said in a soft voice that Mercer strained to hear, "but I need something from you in return."

FIVE

Kaila sat facing west at the foot of one of the spires atop the House of Tiede. She was taking a risk by leaving Mytanth, but Tanghi and the others thought she was asleep, recovering. She had been supposedly recovering for several nights now, but it wasn't from any amount of energy she had expended communicating with Selina during the battle in Tiede. She just wanted to be alone, to feel the relief of Aren surviving, to try to understand the feelings she had for him, to start finding closure.

Right now, she just wanted to be in his presence, to know that he was truly alive.

Aren and Selina sat on the other side of the large spire facing east, staring out over the city towards the dark expanse of Tiede Wood. The sun was setting behind them, and tiny sparkles of stars winked in the darker parts of the sky. They had talked about the outcome of the battle in generalities, haunted by the deaths of so many of Tiede's elite Hunters, trying to regain some sense of normalcy. The sea winds raced over the rooftop, shaking them from their reverie.

"At least the voices are still," he said after the winds calmed down. It was nice to have the silence in his head, but it made him wary as well. "Maybe when I go to Rose, I won't hear them at all."

"Will you be safe?" she asked.

He nudged her but she didn't smile. Something in her eyes made her seem ten times her age. "I'll be with Dane, and Lord Vir is sending the Guard with us to protect Lady Geyle. I'm more worried about you."

"You said Syrn is the safest place in all Cordelacht."

"So I did, and so it is."

"You're okay with me being a Priestess?" she asked, turning her violet eyes on him.

He scratched at a healing cut on the back of his hand. "People will give you the respect you deserve," he said at last. "It's hard for people like us to make it in this world." He met her gaze. "It doesn't matter to me what you are. Just because I don't get along with Priestesses doesn't change anything between us. I wouldn't even care if you were a mage. You and I are the same. Do you understand?"

"I'm going to miss you."

He laughed, giving her shoulder a squeeze. "Maybe you'll be so busy in Syrn, you'll learn to stop worrying."

The smile on her face didn't quite reach her eyes. "The goddess said she'd do her best to watch over both of us."

Aren nodded, then stood up, lifting her off her feet. They looked up at the darkening skies, and he said, "Let's go realign the stars."

ABOUT THE AUTHOR

Emily Peraro English has spent most of her career as a systems analyst, writing and editing technical documentation and requirements for enterprise-wide systems. If that wasn't thrilling enough, in her spare time (aka the wee hours of the night) and over the course of five years she completed her first novel *Uniting the Heavens*, a story that had taken root in her skull almost 20 years ago.

Emily is heavily influenced by (and obsessed with) anime and the *Final Fantasy* video game series. She lives with her husband, two daughters, and a high-anxiety dorgi in the Washington, DC metropolitan area. You can keep up with her adventures at englishscribbles.com.

Emily is currently working on Book 2 of the *Uniting the Heavens* series.